THORN

Summary: Betrothed to a powerful foreign prince, Alyrra leaves home for her
new land. A shocking betrayal offers Alyrra the first choice she's every really
had: to start a new life or fight for a man she's never met.

Cover and Interior Graphics by Jenny Zemanek
www.seedlingsonline.com

ISBN-10: 1470181339
ISBN-13: 978-1470181338

AUTHOR'S NOTE

A portion of the proceeds from the sale of *Thorn* will be donated to Heifer International. Through gifts of geese, sheep, and other livestock, and by training families in sustainable agriculture, Heifer helps build self-reliant communities. As recipients around the world give one or more of their animals' offspring to others in need, the original gift multiplies. Find out more at www.heifer.org.

1

"Try not to embarrass us," my brother says. "If you can."

We stand at the center of a semicircle of nobles, Mother two steps ahead of us. I sidle back, wishing I could leave. Lord Daerilin, standing to my left, raises a hand to hide his smirk but that only calls more attention to it. I clench my teeth and glare at the gates, waiting.

My patience is rewarded when a sentry calls down to us, trumpeting the arrival of our guests. The party trots through the open gates, tack jingling, the first riders pulling to the side to let those behind through. And through. How many are there? I count a score of men, all in light armor, before I realize there must be at least double that. At their center ride five men, all similarly dressed. But where is the king?

"The carriage," my brother says to himself, watching it roll in behind the last of the guards. But that makes no sense. What king would leave himself unprotected from behind? Especially when traveling with near fifty fighting men?

With perfect discipline and no audible command, the whole crowd of horses and men resolve into formation, the guards mounted and lined up two deep to form an aisle between us and the five men that had been at their center. The men dismount in fluid leaps, as if they have no use for hands or stirrups. I catch a glimpse of our master hostler waiting by the stables to arrange for the horses, his brows shooting up, the look in his eyes one of admiration. But of course: Menaiyans are born horsemen. The king would ride.

"His Majesty, the King of Menaiya," one of his men announces as the king steps forward. I ignore the rest of the introduction: long lists of titles and genealogy. Instead, I study the king. He wears the traditional summer cloak of his people: a flowing, unhooded affair with arms and an open front, silver embroidery cascading along the edges and accenting the midnight blue cloth. Beneath he wears a knee-length tunic lightly embroidered with silver and stones, and the curious, loose pants of his people. His hair falls free to his shoulders, black laced with silver, setting off the warm bronze of his face and softening an otherwise hawk-like countenance. A fine tracery of wrinkles gathers at the corners of his eyes, lining his brow and accenting his mouth. He glances over our gathering of nobles and smiles, and there is nothing, absolutely nothing, in that smile. I cannot tell whether he despises us, or finds us no more impressive than Lord Daerilin might a mob of villagers; I cannot tell anything at all.

"Her Majesty, Queen Dowager and Regent of the Kingdom of Adania," Steward Jerash announces in turn, and though Mother wears her finest brocade dress—still too warm for this early in the fall—she has barely half the majesty the king projects. But then, our kingdom is nothing compared to theirs, a patch of forest fortuitously protected by encircling mountains. Menaiya is a land of sweeping plains, southern farms and northern forests. And soldiers. I swallow hard, training my eyes on the ground. We only *have* fifty men in our Hall. The king has brought enough seasoned warriors to take our Hall and add our kingdom to his like a spare coin to his purse.

Mother offers a curtsy to the king, who bows in return. At least she does not seem unduly concerned by the number of warriors in our courtyard. Jerash introduces my brother next, who bows a little lower than the king did. And then it is my turn. I curtsy, aware of the king's scrutiny, the way the whole of his entourage has turned their gaze on me. In just a moment, Mother will speak, inviting the king in. In just a moment—

"Princess Alyrra," the king says. My eyes flick up to his, my legs frozen in their curtsy. He studies me as if I were a prize goat, his gaze sliding over me before returning to my face, as cold and calculating as a butcher. "We have heard tell of you before."

"My lord?" My voice sounds unnaturally high even to me.

"It is said you are honest. An unusual trait, it would seem."

I open my mouth, close it, force some semblance of a smile to my lips. My brother has gone rigid, his hands pressed flat against his thighs.

"You are most kind," my mother says, stepping forward. The king watches me a moment longer, leaving my mother waiting. I cannot say what he thinks, why he would mention something sure to raise old grievances, why he would care. Or is he only toying with us?

He turns to my mother, offering her a courtly smile, and at her words he accompanies her up the three stairs and through the great wooden doors of our Hall. My brother and I trail behind him, a mix of our nobles and the king's entourage on our heels.

"Honest Alyrra," my brother mocks, his voice loud enough for those nearest us to hear. "What a very clever, sophisticated princess you must be."

I bite my lip. It is going to be a long week, watching my back and hiding down corridors. And with so many guests, the wine and ale will flow freely, which will make things even worse. *Just leave*, I think at the king's back. *Just go home and leave us alone.*

I manage to slip away when the king retires to his rooms to refresh himself. He will meet with my mother, brother and their Council of Lords before dinner. Even though it's unlikely my brother will come after me at once, I take no chances, seeking out one of the few places he would never stoop to check.

The kitchen is caught firmly in the throes of preparation for tonight's feast. Cook shouts orders as she spices a pot. Dara, Ketsy and three other serving girls hustle to keep up with the chopping, slicing and gutting. In addition, a soldier attempts to knead dough by squishing it between his fingers, and poor little Ano who only gets pulled into the kitchen in dire emergencies struggles valiantly to tie the roast to a spit.

"Give me that," I tell the soldier, rescuing the dough from him. "You help Ano with the goat."

He throws me a grateful glance and joins Ano by the fire. They have the roast spitted and turning over the fire and he is about to make a timely escape when Cook spots him.

"Where do you think you're going? And what about that dough?"

"But the lady," he stumbles, gesturing towards me.

"I've got it," I assure Cook.

"You most certainly don't," she snaps. "Dara, you take the dough. I hope," she glares at the soldier, "you have at least learned how to chop things?"

Before the man can stammer his reply, I put in my own argument, "Cook, I'm not needed anywhere else. At least let me finish this."

"I'll not have the king think we are in such dire straits that our own princess must help in the kitchens. You go sit in the gardens or do whatever it is that great ladies do in their sort of court."

"I've no idea what great ladies do," I say, pulling my bowl away from Dara. "I'm only a middling sort of lady. And our gardens are all herbs; they're hardly worth sitting in."

"Give it here," Dara says, making a swipe for the bowl.

"You'll give Dara that bowl or you'll not have breakfast tomorrow," Cook says with a glint in her eye. I hesitate, but she has made good on such threats before.

"Oh, fine," I cry, surrendering the bowl to the laughter of all.

"Go on, now," Cook admonishes me. "I'll let you help again when he's gone."

"Maybe I won't want to then," I suggest.

3

"Maybe you'll still be wanting your breakfast," she replies with a smug smile.

I leave to a chorus of laughter. I make a wide berth of the meeting rooms, unsure whether the meeting has begun yet or not. I expect Mother and her Council will harp on about the deplorable condition of the road through the high passes, and how it is beginning to crumble here and there and ought to be better shored up. I can't conceive of anything else to discuss: while we rely on our trade with Menaiya, they have much more significant trading partners than ourselves. I can't imagine the king worrying overmuch about the one road through the mountains to a tin-cup kingdom. He certainly won't obsess over it with the single-minded zeal of my mother and her Council.

I have discussed the state of the roads with my mother only once before. "If they are improved," I had pointed out earnestly, "we may get more slavers coming in."

Mother had raised her brows. "And then we might have more slaves."

"They take slaves too," I had said, shocked.

"What are a few peasants from our borders to us?" Her voice was cold, bored. "Really, Alyrra, you say such absurd things."

I never mentioned the roads again.

Now I pace the confines of my chamber, my door bolted, waiting for dinner. I would much rather go for a ride, but it is too close to evening, and I don't dare arrive late to the feast. I dig out my best dresses, brush them off, and inspect them for signs of wear. I have three I keep for special occasions, and I've already worn the best for the king's arrival. After all, it's not as if that many foreign kings come visiting. Three dresses are enough for the yearly assemblies, the feasts when my mother's vassals visit, though I suspect the king and his court would expect more. I shrug and settle down to mend a fraying hem.

Jilna checks on me as the day fades. "Cook is making an awful ruckus down there," she says as she runs her hands over the repaired hem. "Did you fix this?"

"Just now. What's she upset about?"

"The dough didn't rise so she had to start another batch, and the roast isn't cooked through yet, and any number of other things." Jilna straightens, her worn face easing into a smile. "I'm not sure if she just likes grumbling, or if it's her way of assuring she gets complimented when everything turns out."

"A bit of both," I say.

"Ha!" Jilna laughs and steps back to inspect me. "You need jewelry."

"What for?

"So you look more like a princess and less like a well-dressed scullery maid."

For all Jilna's efforts, as I join my family waiting to enter the Hall, I realize how shabby I must look in my old dress with my string of pearls and my

4

three gold rings. Mother still wears her brocade dress, a massive gold brooch pinned to her breast. My brother wears the long gold chains that were once our father's, his arms crossed over his broad chest, his boots planted firmly against the floor. And the king will wear his wealth not in gold but in the muted richness of the fabric of his clothes, the perfect finish of his boots. It is a much more subtle and certain majesty.

"He's coming," Mother says, cutting off their quiet conversation. "Smile."

They do, bright and cheery and falsely welcoming. The king, entering with the two other men we have learned are his vassals, glances at them with an answering curl of his lips. Then his gaze turns to me. I look back, wondering what he expects, what he is looking for. Why would he look at me so, but not them? His dark eyes, unsmiling, hard as onyx, give me no answer.

When he speaks, it is to Mother. I follow our party into the Hall for dinner, taking my usual seat as the rest of our party settles.

"Trying to look your part?" The voice, filled with contempt, could hardly be mistaken for any other. Not that I could, having sat beside him for ten years of which the last three have been torture.

"Lord Daerilin," I say, risking a glance at him. "I see you are wearing your velvet doublet."

Daerilin turns a mottled pink but keeps going. He must have a special barb saved up for me today. "It's a pity you can't manage to put on something finer for such a guest as this. Especially when he's come all this distance for you."

I nearly drop my goblet. "What?"

Daerilin leans back in his chair, his expansive stomach pressed against the table. "Surely you know why the king has come."

"I understood it was an affair of state." I set down the goblet with shaking fingers.

"How you are related to your mother is beyond me." Daerilin grimaces, reaching for his knife. A servant steps forward and serves him, carving three slices of roast goat and placing them on his plate before serving me. I can only hope the king's soldiers haven't noticed; Daerilin long ago bribed the man into serving him first as a slight to me. I never really cared, until tonight.

I glance towards the soldiers' tables surreptitiously. The foreign soldiers stand out like hawks among sparrows, their light armor glinting in the firelight, their ebony hair pulled up into tight knots. Our own warriors and women look pale and washed out beside them, our skin and hair so much lighter. And while our men wear their swords and daggers as well, with friendship bands binding hilt to scabbard, they have none of the practiced grace of the Menaiyans when they walk.

As I study them, I catch the eye of the foreign captain. Like the other soldiers, he wears his long hair in a smooth knot. Without a fall of hair to soften his features, he looks weathered and hard, his eyes flat, ungiving. I look away quickly, turning back to Daerilin.

"Why has the king come to visit us, then?" I ask, now that my fingers have stopped trembling.

Daerilin tosses back the last of his wine and waves his goblet in the air. "To find a bride for his son, little princess. How would you like to marry the Menaiyan prince?"

My chest feels hollow. I force myself to breathe, to keep my expression still. From the corner of my eye, I can see the king's long-fingered hand lifting his goblet. He speaks with my mother quietly; I can only just catch the faint lilt of his voice, the resonating strangeness of his accent.

"We are hardly a strong ally for them," I whisper.

"Perhaps they're just looking for a mouse to snap up," Daerilin replies as the servant fills his goblet. "Their women do seem to die young. They wouldn't want to upset their closer allies by accidentally killing off the bride." Daerilin smirks. "I daresay no one would raise an outcry if something were to happen. To you."

I stare down at my plate, the roast still untouched. I have lost my appetite. Perhaps Daerilin is only baiting me; God knows he has enjoyed his taunts these last years. But surely he would not make this up? Surely the king had not come for me?

"I hear," Daerilin observes momentarily, "that Prince Kestrin is not one to be crossed. Quite a temper he has when he is displeased."

I wish that I could come up with a snide rejoinder, but my wits fail me. If Daerilin is right, then the Menaiyan prince is no better than my brother. He may be infinitely worse, used as he is to commanding a much greater court than ours.

I spend the rest of my meal in silence. When I make no further response, Daerilin turns to discuss a territorial dispute in the south with the lady to his left. My eyes are drawn often to the foreign warriors. Their captain eats sparingly, one hand resting on the hilt of his dagger as if by habit. He watches me continually, unapologetically, as if he intends to take his full measure of me this night. No matter how long I look away, when I glance back I find his eyes on me. Eventually I lay down my knife and give up all pretense of eating, turning my gaze instead to the motion of the servants through the Hall.

The following morning I wait on my mother as she dresses for a second day of meetings with the king. She waves her maids away at last, peering into the oval mirror that hangs on her wall. It is one of her prize possessions, framed in silver and polished to a shine, just large enough to show her face. She smoothes her hair, checking for stray hairs.

"To what do I owe the honor of your presence?" she asks with cool amusement.

I gather my courage. "I wish to enquire as to the king's purpose in visiting us."

"Oh?" Mother flicks a glance at me, her hazel eyes hooded. "Has it finally occurred to you to ask?"

I clasp my hands together and stare at the ground, waiting. She sighs.

"Prince Kestrin is of an age to marry. His father has come to assess your worth as a bride."

"My worth?" I echo, my throat dry. Daerilin had not lied. "What is that?"

"Not much," Mother says brutally. "It is the only issue that gives me pause. We cannot be sure why he would settle for you." She purses her lips. She has discussed this in detail with her Council of Lords, I realize, and they can find no reason for the king's interest. The thought raises the hair at the back of my neck. Perhaps Daerilin is right: they seek a bride no one will miss should she die unexpectedly.

"I hope we will reach an agreement by tomorrow," she continues. She is beautiful in the sunlight falling through the windows, her hair glowing deep brown, her features smooth, emotionless. I can find nothing to say, looking at her and trying to understand. Tomorrow? Betrothed?

"Stay out of the way for now," she says, turning back to her mirror. When I do not move, she gestures sharply to the door. "Go on, then. I've more than enough to worry about with you underfoot. And do not speak to the king if you can avoid him. I do not want him realizing what a simpleton you are."

I ride out on Fleet Wind, taking the path that cuts away from the village to the woods. The trees stand spaced apart, the leaf-littered floor dappled with late summer sunlight. I guide Fleet Wind to a dell we have often visited. I have brought nothing with me to do, nor do I seek any of the herbs that grow among the trees and in the clearings for our wise woman's use. Instead, I sit on a sun-warmed stone, listening to the soft buzz of insects and the swish of Fleet Wind's tail as he grazes. As morning ebbs to noontime, a light breeze starts up.

"Old friend," I say, turning my head towards it. "Is that you?"

The Wind answers me with a puff of summer, *Here*.

I smile. "The King of Menaiya has come to visit."

The Wind ruffles my skirts. From my perch on a rock, I watch the few blades of grass bend over beneath its gentle influence.

"Mother hopes he will betroth me to his son. Prince Kestrin." I think of Menaiya with its sweeping plains and tongue-twisting language—a language of which I have only a rudimentary knowledge. I cannot imagine living there, with no forests to wander, no one to speak with, no one but a prince I do not know. When I lift my hand to pat down a stray lock of hair, I realize my fingers are trembling. I clench my hands together tightly, pressing them into my lap.

The Wind lifts up and brushes my hair back. *Do not fear.* I cock my head, considering. It is rare for the Wind to string words together, which means it must find this situation of grave importance. I smile: what could the Wind know of marriage?

"I've always expected that I'd have to marry eventually, to someone I didn't really know. But I thought it would be someone from hereabouts, not a prince from a great court in a faraway kingdom. Not," I add, "someone who may not even speak my language."

I think of the captain's cold assessment, and the distant court, and find it suddenly difficult to breathe. "I am afraid," I finally admit to the Wind, "of what will happen to me there." If I can survive, I add silently. As the other women of their royal family have not.

The Wind falls still. I wonder if it can understand, or if it too is lost for words.

I return to the Hall for lunch, the Wind whispering through the woods with me, leaving me only as the path reaches the main road. Redna greets me with a nod as I enter the gates, deftly reaching for Fleet Wind's bridle to help me dismount.

"They're still in the meeting rooms," she tells me. "But word is your brother's been looking for you."

This time, Cook does not send me away. Instead, she gestures to a stool beside one of the tables, informs me I'm not to work, and leaves me there. I stay, listening to the other girls gossiping and occasionally teasing Cook. No one here will mention my presence outside of the kitchen, not with the king here and my brother on the prowl.

I go to my rooms only just in time to change for dinner and hurry down to the Hall, meeting my mother and brother only bare moments before the king joins us. Mother looks at me only once, a measuring look that fades to contempt before she turns away. What does she expect me to do? To ask? If she has nothing to tell me now, then they haven't reached an agreement yet. She would not bother to take any of my own wishes into account, even if I did ask. The only wish I do have is not to marry the foreign prince, and for that she would laugh in my face.

This time, when the king enters, I do not meet his gaze. It would tell me nothing if I did. Instead, I watch his boots, following silently after my family as we go in to dinner.

The following morning I make a mistake. I had assumed the meetings would continue, that I could pass down the hall without concern, but just as I reach the entrance to the meeting room, the door swings open. I step back, my stomach lurching as I meet my brother's eyes. He smiles.

"Alyrra, what a surprise." He crosses the hall, his hand closing tightly around my forearm. "Why don't we walk a little?"

I nod woodenly, aware that I don't dare pull away before the curious gazes of the other men leaving the meeting room. My brother leads me down the hall, the pressure of his grip a warning of what is to come.

"Princess Alyrra," a voice says from behind us. My brother and I turn together, for the accent is Menaiyan. The king strides towards us. "I see you wish to converse with your brother. I hope you will not mind my taking a few minutes of your time?"

"Of course not," my brother says for me, releasing my arm. "We can always speak later, my lord."

The king nods towards my brother, but the expression in his eyes makes me suddenly wish that it was still my brother I was walking with. I fall into step with the king, and we quickly leave behind the others.

"Do you have gardens here?" he asks. "Somewhere quiet to speak?"

"Only herb gardens, my lord."

"Good enough," he says, his teeth flashing between his lips. I lead him down to the back entrance to the gardens, and we walk along between plots of oregano, rosemary and mint.

"How much does your mother confide in you?"

I slide a look at him from the corner of my eye. "Enough. My lord."

His lips quirk, the first true smile I have seen from him. "Is that honest?"

I pause beside a bed of thyme. "How much do I need to know, my lord? You are here seeking a wife for your son."

"I am," he agrees. "How often do you normally participate in the discussions between your mother and her Council?"

"I don't, my lord. You should know I am not …" I hesitate, aware that I have no place telling this king what he should or should not know. Or jeopardizing such an alliance for my land.

"Not what?"

I struggle to find an appropriate way to finish. "Not—it is not thought my place to attend."

"You would never inherit?"

I pause, at a loss. I could inherit, it is true, but I doubt the Council would allow it. They would pass over me in favor of our nearest cousin. "It is unlikely," I say.

"I doubt that," the king says. "It has been my experience that even young men die. What you mean to say is your Council would not accept you. Why?"

If he knows all the answers, why is he asking? I look him in the eye and quip, "Perhaps I am too honest, my lord."

He laughs. "And too straightforward. You will have to learn to play with your words more." He reaches out, his fingertips brushing my arm where my brother had held me. I flinch back reflexively, as if the bruises have already darkened. As if he could see them through my sleeve. He watches me, his eyes glinting in the sunlight. I have no words for him. "Once you are Menaiya's," he says, "your brother will never hurt you again."

He dips his head in a bow and leaves me standing among the herbs.

I wait in my chamber all the following day. I do not know how long such negotiations take, how much my mother will hope to gain from this marriage and what she will have to give up. When the knock I have been dreading sounds, it is late afternoon. I remain still for a moment, thinking, *perhaps it is only Jilna,* but she only knocks when I have locked the door.

Steward Jerash waits patiently in the corridor. "Highness, the queen requests your presence in the meeting rooms."

"Of course," I say, and follow after him.

Jerash announces my entrance to the room, bowing low. I feel at once the sharpness of my mother's gaze, the hooded coldness of my brother's. They sit together with the king at a great table at the head of the room. Before them, seated in chairs or standing respectfully, are arrayed my mother's closest vassals as well as the king's own retainers. I curtsy. When I rise I meet my mother's gaze, she smiles at me, the smile of a merchant having sold her wares.

"Alyrra, the King of Menaiya has offered a match for you with his son. Will you accept?"

At least I have had the morning to find the words for my answer. "I will do only as you wish, Mother."

My brother, sitting beside her, frowns. The corner of the king's lips curl slightly upward, as if he were faintly amused.

"It is a good alliance, daughter," she replies smoothly.

"Then I accept." The words rustle through the room, carried by the shifting of nobles, the soft exhalations of satisfaction, for none expected a different answer. I wonder, for a single fluttering moment, what might have happened had I refused—but I would have been made to accept in the end, and would have the king's anger to contend with as well.

A court scribe lays a sheaf of papers on the table before me, placing beside it a quill and inkpot. I turn through the sheets quickly, noticing only that my mother has settled some border estates on me. The last page has but a few lines of writing, leaving space for our signatures. I sign carefully, vaguely pleased at how smoothly I write, at the way my hand does not tremble as I put down the quill and straighten.

The scribe places the papers before the king. As he reaches for the quill, he meets my gaze. I see neither satisfaction nor sorrow in his eyes, in the set of his features. There is nothing to tell me his emotions; his composure is complete. He leans forward to sign his name in lieu of his son's, and then Lord Daerilin and another lord step forward to sign as witnesses, followed by the two lords accompanying the king. As the scribe collects the papers and steps back, the betrothal is complete.

The king turns to me once more and smiles, though I cannot tell whether it is a true smile or only a courtly one. "I am pleased to have gained a daughter," he says, his words clear and carrying.

"I am honored to be welcomed to your family, my lord." It is strange to me that I answer so easily, so well. My mother speaks then, about the honor such an alliance brings to our land, and a moment later she has dismissed me. I leave, barely aware of Jerash opening the door for me though my eyesight is clear. While I see everything—the way the soldiers at the door straighten as I pass, how Jerash steps out with me as if he wishes to speak and then thinks better of it—yet somehow I do not see it at all. I simply remember it afterwards, as if I watched from a distance.

The rest of the evening blurs together. Jilna dresses me for dinner, bringing with her jewels from the treasury for my neck and hair. My mother announces the betrothal to the Hall as soldiers and servants alike cheer. There are toasts made to the new couple's good health, so many so that I am grateful for the juice that fills my goblet, watching as the men below grow more and more drunk. Even Lord Daerilin makes a speech on the long-standing friendship of our two kingdoms, yet I do not quite hear him, cannot quite recall the sound of his words a moment later, as if I live a long-ago memory.

I leave the Hall at the end of the meal, my head ringing with the din of so many people, my eyes tearing from exhaustion and smoke. I grow aware in a strange, detached way that there have been footsteps behind me for some time. It occurs to me to wonder who follows me, and then a hand closes on my arm and spins me around, shoving me against the wall.

"Think you're something special now, don't you?" My brother towers over me, his shoulders blocking out the light, his breath stinking of ale. His eyes are red-rimmed, narrowed with drink and anger.

"Brother," I say. I do not immediately understand him. My fingers tingle with fear. His hands tighten on my arms, pressing me against the wall, his face hovering just above mine.

"Going to be queen, are you? You think you're better than us now?" His fingers dig into my flesh, nails pressing through the thin fabric of my sleeves to gouge my skin with bruising intensity.

"No," I waver.

"Of course not." His hair falls over his forehead as he leans even closer, speaking into my ear. "You're only doing what you're told, aren't you?"

I turn my face away; try to pull out of his grip. He laughs. "Oh no, I don't think you're going anywhere quite yet."

"Brother—"

"Do you know what a prince does when he marries a little witch like you?" I squirm in his grip but he tightens his hold. "There are stories, lovely stories. The poor little princess is found floating in the well one morning, tripped and fell in quite by accident. Or they find her body beneath the castle walls: cast herself off in a fit of despair. These things happen, you see. Terribly sad. But the alliance stands strong, and the family mourns, and the prince remarries." He laughs, winding his hand into the hair at the base of my neck, forcing my head back so that I must meet his gaze.

"I expect he'll have his fun with you. Perhaps he'll throw you to his soldiers and let you choose your future: a brothel or a knife for your throat. You'd like that, wouldn't you? Kestrin's a good man for having some fun with a girl."

"He's not like that," I whisper.

"Are you calling me a liar?"

I swallow a sob, shaking my head. His fingers yank at my hair.

"Do you think your betrothal will protect you from me, little sister? Do you dare to insult me?" His voice rises as he speaks, spittle spraying my cheek.

"Is the princess unwell?"

My brother starts, twisting to look over his shoulder. I sag against the wall as he drops his hand, my braid swinging free. "This doesn't concern you."

"If the princess requires an escort to her room, I would be pleased to provide it."

I sidle sideways, past my brother, and find myself facing the Menaiyan captain. His face is all planes and hard angles in the dimness of the hall. I gaze at him wordlessly. Is he actually challenging my brother?

"Do you require an escort?" he asks with a slight dip of his head, as if he were my dancing partner. He has the same lilting accent as his king.

It takes me two tries to get my words out. "N-no. Thank you." I take one step back, then another, the captain watching me impassively, and then I turn and begin walking, my feet uncertain beneath me. It is only a temporary escape; when my brother finds me again he will be doubly angry. Ruthless.

Behind me, I can hear the captain speaking, his voice too low to pick out the words. I can barely keep from breaking into a run as I turn the corner to my room. What if my brother has gotten away from him already? And then I do run, pelting down the hall to my room. I slam the door shut, shooting the bolt home. My breath rattles in my chest. I lean my forehead against the door, half-listening for the approach of booted feet.

When Jilna comes a half hour later, she knocks thrice, calling her name that I might know it is not my brother. I sit hunched on my bed, listening, but I do not let her in. She is used to me, used to these things, and when I do not answer she leaves. I undress slowly, awkwardly, running my fingers over the bruises on my arms, brushing out my hair, careful of the tender spots where my scalp still aches. But I cannot wipe my brother's words from my memory, cannot escape the echoes of his voice.

It is long and long before I sleep.

3

Four Menaiyan soldiers snap to attention as I leave my room the following morning. I stop, staring at them. They flank my door and the opposite wall, making a perfectly balanced quad. All of the Menaiyan forces are broken down into quads: four men with a balance of skills between them. I had known this, but I had not thought of it when the king arrived with so many men. Yet here is a quad waiting outside my door. They neither look at me nor speak, and after an uncertain breath I continue on. They fall into step behind me.

No matter where I go, they stay with me. At first I wonder whether they mean to accost me or merely monitor my every action. By noon I know they are there to protect me: when I pass my brother in the hallway, the glance he gives me is filled with cold fury. The soldiers do not bother to bow to him, their step behind me steady. Only when I enter the Hall for lunch do they leave me, joining their table while I sit on the dais. Still, I can feel their eyes on me and I know that they will follow me out when I finish. Now I am theirs, as the king had said, and so they guard me from my brother.

After lunch, my mother calls me to her rooms to select fabric for my new wardrobe. She bides her time, waiting until the servants have been sent off on errands: one to find a matching trim, another to fetch ribbons, the third to call the cobbler to commission slippers.

"An interesting fact has come to my attention." She taps her finger against a length of rose linen, frowns, and changes the subject. "Linen may be too common a cloth to wear at court; we'll only have two traveling outfits made of it. Fetch a darker rose to match with this."

"Yes, Mother." She hands me the cloth, waving from her chair to where the remaining linens are piled.

"Not cream; the darker rose." I let go of the cream with a twinge of regret, straightening as she says, "A quad of Menaiyan soldiers has been shadowing you."

I lift up the next batch of cloth: precious cotton brought up from the south. "They were outside my door this morning."

"Are they outside now?"

"They followed me here."

"Do they think I will attack you? Or that we cannot keep you safe ourselves?" Mother rises and reaches for the cottons, eyes flashing.

I let her take them, feeling anger blossom in my breast. Mother has never kept me safe from my brother. The only time I can remember not fearing him was before my father's death. "I expect so."

She stiffens, drops the cloth, and slaps me. The blow is not hard—at least it does not have half the force of my brother's blows. It jerks my face to the side, bringing tears to my eyes. But inwardly I am laughing. The sound bubbles up, bursting from my lips to fill the room.

My mother stands before me, her face flushed and blotchy, nostrils flared in anger. She does not look beautiful at all. I raise my hand to my mouth and press my lips closed, my shoulders shaking. Now I know my mother as I never have before. She is no different from my brother: no better and no worse. The same thoughts run through her, the same wishes propel her forward, the same passions guide her actions.

"Mother," I tell her. "You are not as wise as my brother. He is careful not to leave marks that others might see."

"I will not be treated thus by my own kin."

"It is you who have struck me," I point out insolently, "not the other way around."

"You understand me perfectly."

"I do." I meet her gaze, aware that I have never fought her so before. I feel the same sweet rush as I did the first time I rode Fleet Wind through the forests alone.

She smiles suddenly, her mask settling into place. "I see there is more to you than I had thought. Very good, Alyrra. You will need your wits about you to survive in Menaiya.

"Pick up the cottons." She returns to her seat, waiting as I bend to retrieve the cloth. Already the heady sense of success begins to fade. As I turn back to her it is Menaiya that fills my thoughts.

The rest of the day passes in the first flurry of preparations—after ordering my new wardrobe, which will be made in the Menaiyan fashion of a tunic and sash over a long skirt, there is my jewelry to see to, the commissioning of trunks, my trousseau—the list goes on and on. By evening, I am exhausted with it all. Jilna ignores my grumblings, hurrying me into one of my good gowns. I cannot even remember if I have worn this one before or not.

Jilna gives my cheeks a hard pinch to bring back their color.

"You look terrible," she admonishes me. "Like yesterday's porridge left out all night. You don't want the king to think you're unhappy with this, do you?"

I wince. "No."

"Good then. Keep your chin up, smile, and get to the Hall at once. They're holding the feast for you."

I follow her injunctions, taking my seat at the high table with a smile that hurts my cheeks. Tonight is the official betrothal celebration; the food and drink will last till the darkest hours of night. A troupe of performers makes a grand entrance, somersaulting and leaping down the Hall to stand before the dais. They juggle apples and daggers in dizzying patterns, telling bawdy jokes and engaging in mock fights that show off their tumbling skills.

The Menaiyan warriors observe the performance with raised eyebrows, glancing at each other occasionally. Their faces when they laugh are not kind. I watch them, wondering what amusements they are used to, and wish that our old troubadour had made the night's entertainment. Though his voice has begun to waver, his ballads are yet things of beauty.

By night's end, the watching and wondering has drained me, leaving me brittle, empty. My quad slips away from their table as I leave the dais, following me back to my room. I dare not turn to look at them, and so I am not sure if they are the same soldiers who accompanied me through the day.

A bulky package waits for me in my room, wrapped in velvet, resting innocently on my bed. I stand before it warily, not wanting to know what it is. Or who sent it.

"What's that?" Jilna asks when she sees it.

I shake my head.

"Open it, then," she says impatiently.

I unwrap the cloth to find a winter cloak. It is woven of wool softer than any I have felt before, embroidered in the same shadow-dark hue as the cloak itself: a blue so deep it might be made of night. The wool is lined with the dark fur of a creature I have no name for. It is no ordinary cloak but a work of art and time, something that would have taken months to complete. I run my fingers over the cloth, the fur. I have never received such a gift before.

"That'll be from the king," Jilna says with evident satisfaction. "And high time he gave you a gift. It ought to be jewelry, but no doubt there'll be plenty of that later."

I drop the cloth and turn to Jilna. "The king speaks our language."

She regards me curiously. "Aye."

"What of his soldiers?"

"A few of them do, so I hear. And their captain. Sarkor's his name." I nod; he had spoken clearly enough last night.

"And the prince?"

"I haven't heard," she admits. "But don't fret; Dara helps serve the Menaiyans' tables. If she can't find out, no one can."

I let Jilna pack up the cloak and hustle me into my nightdress. She blows out the lamp as she leaves, the room settling into darkness. Exhaustion tugs me down into sleep almost at once.

I wake suddenly, yanked back from a land of vague and unformed dreams by a sound that has no place in my room. I sit up with the shock of it, my breath quick and loud in my ears.

Silence.

I lie back down. Perhaps it was only a dream-sound.

A man clears his throat.

I sit up again, half-paralyzed with fear, as sluggish as if I move underwater. Once more silence fills the room, laps at the window. But this time I know I am not alone and my first, terrified thought is that my brother has come for his vengeance. I hold the covers up to my chest as if they might protect me.

"Who's there?" Someone shifts with a faint whisper of cloth, but my eyes can make out nothing. "Show yourself," I say, my voice high, pleading.

Another soft whisper—I turn my head sharply toward the sound—and a flame leaps to life behind a cupped hand. It catches on the wick of a candle set on the mantle. The intruder steps back and with a rush of relief I realize it is not my brother at all, for this man has dark hair and sand-gold skin. He dresses in the Menaiyan fashion: a long dark tunic belted at the waist and loose pants tucked into riding boots. The light glints off metal at his side—a sword—and gleams in his eyes. He meets my gaze, and I have the uncanny feeling that he can see me perfectly well despite the dark.

"What do you want here?" Fear has left me with the thought of my brother. I feel now only a quiet curiosity.

"To speak with you." His voice has the same telltale lilt as the king's.

"Why?"

"You have changed your allegiances."

"I have gained new allegiances," I agree carefully.

He studies me a moment before asking, "What do you know of Menaiya?"

"Very little: there are the king, his son, and a third person—a nephew, I think. The queen died one year ago." I stop, unwilling to tell this stranger anything he would not already know. He waits, brooding in the shadows thrown by the single flame.

"You have come a long way to test my knowledge." He tilts his head, inviting me to continue. "You were not among the king's soldiers. Indeed, you dress more carefully than any of them, except perhaps their captain. So you must have traveled here alone, and it is a long way for a man to come by himself."

He makes no response. I swallow and try another tact. "Will you not tell me your name? You know who I am."

"We will meet soon enough."

"In Menaiya," I hazard. He nods. "And you have given your allegiance to the king?"

"Yes." He smiles, one corner of his mouth rising higher than the other. A foolish question then; he must be sworn to the king, here because of his oath.

"What do you seek now that cannot wait till my arrival?"

"I wished to see you myself," he explains. "To warn you." He crosses the room to the shuttered window, facing it silently before turning back to me. I smooth the sheets with my hands, surprised I am not more afraid. But he has not moved toward me.

"Menaiya has many enemies, my lady. Now that you belong to Menaiya, those enemies are yours. You will need to be careful these next weeks. The king can offer you only so much protection until you reach his walls."

I swallow to ease the sudden dryness of my throat. "Menaiya is feared by its neighbors."

"And rightfully so," he agrees, and again I hear amusement lighten his words. "I do not speak of the surrounding kingdoms."

"Then whom do you mean?"

He hesitates. "I cannot say—not here. Not now."

A shiver runs under my skin. "How can I protect myself from a phantom?"

He steps towards me, his voice grim. "You must beware. Do not put yourself in a vulnerable situation; do not walk alone; do not remain with anyone you do not trust."

I swallow a nervous laugh. "I don't even know who I will travel with. How can I avoid them?"

"Be vigilant," he presses. I wonder if he even heard me. "Do you understand, my lady? You are in danger until you reach Tarinon. Even there, you may not truly be safe."

No, I think. There is the prince to worry about, and a court more powerful and sophisticated than ours, and no one who speaks my language but the king and a sorcerer with veiled warnings.

Behind him, the shutters crash open with the shrieking of wood, splinters and panels flying into the room. He cries out, spinning towards the window. Light explodes, outlining his profile in blazing white, momentarily blinding me.

I squeeze my eyes shut, huddling beneath the covers. When I open them again the light has diminished to bright moonlight. Amid its pale, cruel rays stands a woman. She is ancient, older than the very land. Her skin is smooth and pale as milk, her hair shining and dark. But her eyes—they are cavities in her face: deep, bottomless pits. They hold me tightly in their grasp and I cannot move to look away. Then she turns her gaze from me, dismissing me.

I find myself gasping for breath. I realize dimly that I am still crouched in my bed, the man having backed up to the foot of it. They watch each other steadily. I sidle to the edge of the bed, glancing sideways at the man, seeing him clearly for the first time. He seems almost familiar now in the cold wash of moonlight, for he at least is human. Long night-dark hair tied back, high cheekbones, defined jaw—his profile imprints itself on my mind in the moment that I see him—and then my eyes fly back to the woman as she raises her hand and snaps it through the air. The man staggers sideways, towards me. I scrabble to my feet, shocked by the line of blood that appears on his cheek. His eyes pass mine, intense, turning back to the woman.

"Leave," the lady says. Her voice is the murmur of water on rocks, of snow falling on oaks. The man shakes his head, braced against another attack. "The girl is mine, as are you."

"No," he says, but the word is that of a little boy's plea. He falters under the woman's gaze. *Her eyes,* I think. And then, *he is not my enemy.* It seems crystal clear to me with the moon shining in, lighting up the room with its strange whiteness.

"No," I agree, my voice strong and resonant in the stillness. "You are not welcome here. Leave us."

When I look into her eyes I see my death looking back.

"I will teach you your place, girl," she says tightly. Her hand comes up and I see the glint of a gem on her finger. Beside me the man shifts, bracing himself as if expecting a blow—or perhaps expecting to catch me as I fall.

"No," I reply, my voice trembling. "You cannot own me." And then, as if the man has thrown the words to me like a lifeline, as if he has whispered them in the back of my mind, "You have no power over me."

For a moment that lasts a lifetime she stands unmoving, hand raised, and then she smiles: a terrible, terrible thing that turns my blood to ice in my veins. "No," she agrees, "over you I have no power. But do not think you are safe; you are mine as surely as if your mother swore you to me before your birth.

"Tonight it is not you I am concerned with." She turns back to the man and her hand reaches out, gesturing elegantly towards him. "It is you."

He cries out, throwing his arm up to ward off her casual attack. Light envelopes him: bright, blinding light that sears my vision, scorches my mind—a light that floods the room and takes all detail with it. The lady, my room, all disappear, and I am falling through the shadows of my life further and further away from the moon.

4

My last day at home passes in a whirl of errands—packing last items; reviewing my trousseau and jewelry with my mother a final time; receiving farewell visits from whichever court nobles wish to curry favor with my mother. It is late afternoon when I manage to slip off on my own. Only my quad notices, but then not much escapes them.

When the king departed, he left me two quads as well as his captain. I have gotten to know the faces of the eight men of my quads, but they do not speak before me and rarely look at me directly. Most, I realize, do not speak our language. I have learned only two of their names: Matsin son of Körto and Finnar son of Hakin. These two are most often with me, and I wonder if they are captains in their own right, reassigned to their king's escort and then to me, or just more able to understand my language and report what they hear.

I stop through the kitchens and Cook gives me a teary-eyed smile, promising to send up my favorite meat pies as a treat in the morning. Dara and Ketsy catch my hands and dance me around the kitchen, the scullery maids giggling and the kitchen boys clapping. I finally break away from them, laughing. As I move to the door to the courtyard, my quad steps in from the hall, following me across the room. The kitchen falls unnaturally quiet, the only sound that of their boots. It is all I can do to cheerfully call my last good-byes.

I find my old tutor, Bol, sitting in the herb gardens, much as Cook had advised me to do. Rather than looking like a lord at his ease, Bol looks like a bent old gardener kicking up his heels and enjoying the sun. He smiles as he sees me, holding out a hand.

"Bol," I say, going to him. "It's good to see you out and about."

"I like the gardens, my lady. And the gardens don't mind me."

I smile. I will miss Bol dearly.

"You've come to say good-bye," he says, drawing me down to sit beside him. I look out across the gardens to where my quad lounges. Here, where there is no cover for them, they look terribly conspicuous; the sight of them guarding the entryway, armed and watchful, would have been laughable had they not looked quite so dangerous.

"I've a question for you."

"Aye?"

"Has Menaiya any enemies?"

Bol rubs his chin. "None that would openly attack. Why do you ask?"

"I just wondered," I say, my eyes on the soldiers. "Who would have cause to hate the royal family?"

"More than a few people, I suspect," Bol says with amusement. "But they haven't had a war in over a hundred years. This king's grandsire, I believe it was, took it into his head to cross the Winter Seas and loot the Far Steppes. Foolish of him."

"Why?"

"The war followed him home and killed off most of the royal Family. The Family's dwindled since then. Strength gone out of the bloodline, I suppose, though some call it a curse."

"Hmm," I say, no closer to the answer I am looking for. After all, the sorceress I remember could hardly be so old, could she?

After I leave Bol, I head for the stables, casting an anxious glance at the long shadows. It is getting late, but I cannot leave without this last farewell.

Redna takes my hand and gives me a quick peck on the cheek, smelling of horse and leather. "I'm glad you came down here. Your brother's got you a horse." She glances to where my quad waits at the entrance.

"A horse?"

"Great white stallion, handsome as can be, but don't you ride him. He won't take a rider."

I grimace. "I see."

"We're going to miss you something awful what with your brother's idea of kindness."

"You'll be fine," I say lamely. "Just stay away from him."

"And when he's king?"

"Maybe he'll fall off his horse and Cousin Derin will get the crown."

Redna snorts. "I'll wish the queen long life, and hope I'm married and gone when the crown passes." I nod. "There's two hostlers will be going with your escort; I gave Westrin an earful and he'll listen to you and keep that horse from causing trouble."

"And the other?"

"He's your brother's man."

"Thank you, Redna."

"We'll all be praying for you." She squeezes my hand. "Them Menaiyans as came here seemed to be good men; they didn't flirt with the girls and they didn't kick the dogs. They've put a guard on you, but that's kept your brother off, hasn't it? I think your prince will be a good man as well."

I nod, and Redna hugs me tightly. I carry her words with me as I leave, but I cannot take much heart from them. Most of our guards are kinder men than my brother.

Jilna is waiting to dress me for dinner: one final banquet in honor of the betrothal and my departure. She helps me into my gown, shaking her head at the state of my hair. When I am ready, she turns to me almost hesitantly. "I've something for you—just a little thing to remember me by. I know you're going to a great court, and you won't have much use for the likes of this, but—"

"Jilna," I interrupt. "What is it?"

She presses a pouch into my palm, then clasps her hands together tightly, watching me. I pour its contents into my palm. A small, worn silver pendant on a thin chain tumbles out, shining in the lamplight. At the center of the oval pendant is an engraved many-petaled rose. I swallow, my throat constricting. This is a family heirloom; a bit of wealth passed from mother to daughter through the generations. But Jilna has no daughter of her own to give it to.

"It's beautiful." I close my hand around the gift. "Thank you."

Jilna looks back at me, her face alight, and then takes a quick step forward to wrap her arms around me. "Don't cry, dear heart."

I take a few watery breaths, leaning into her, and then step back. She lets me go gently, watching as I fasten the chain around my neck. "I'll treasure it always."

"Aye, well, if you lose it, I'll send my spirit to haunt you the rest of your days," Jilna warns. "That was my mother's fore it was mine."

"Bring her with you then," I say, grinning. "I'd like to meet her someday."

Jilna gives me a little shove. "Get on with you. You'll be late for dinner."

I doubt anyone would notice or care, but I hurry out the door regardless. Afterwards, in the later hours of the night, I stand in my mother's apartment, watching the flame-thrown shadows flicker across her face. She sits in a brocade armchair, a goblet of wine held loosely in her fingers. She looks to me like some dark predator—perhaps the fabled black cats of the Western Forests, as large as our wolfhounds. When she smiles, her teeth bared, I feel a chill run down my back.

"I will ask you one last time," my mother says without preamble. "What are you hiding from me? Why did the king have a guard set on you before anything happened?"

To keep my brother off? But she would never believe that. "I don't know. Perhaps he has enemies."

"Who would they be?"

I shrug. "He wasn't worried until after the betrothal." It had been my Menaiyan quad that raised the alarm that night. In their story, a soldier had been passing down the hall when he heard a strange sound, as of wood shattering. Immediately, he knocked on my door to make sure all was well. When his hammering received no response, he tried the handle. By then his shouts had roused other guards (the rest of his quad who were standing beside him, I suspect) as well as those who slumbered in the rooms near mine; so it was a number of people who saw the broken shutters and the princess lying senseless by her bed.

"You don't know what happened that night?"

I shake my head. Some believe an owl hit my shutters, but Jilna tells me that most believe the Fair Folk had come for me; the soldier's knock and sudden entrance saved me from being carried off. The truth seems far less comprehensible to me than either of these possibilities.

"Surely you remember something."

As I watch her, I think perhaps I should tell her, perhaps she would know something about the man and his unknown enemy ... but surely she would have spoken had she any idea. Or would she? I lick my lips. "A woman came to my room and spoke to me, but I don't remember her words. It could have been a dream."

"A woman?"

"Yes. She was—I thought she was a sorceress, but ..."

"You don't remember what she said?" Mother leans forward in her chair, intent.

"No," I say firmly, hating the lie. "But she ... didn't seem quite human. I can't imagine how she got there. It seemed like a piece of a dream."

Mother sits back, thoughtful. "Perhaps. Or perhaps Menaiya has enemies we don't know of. If she is real, and is what you say, then no soldier could have protected you. This is a riddle indeed."

I look down at the carpet. The soldiers were assigned to protect me from my brother; it was only by chance that they heard the shutters break—or was it? And why had it taken so long for the soldier to enter? I remember clearly how long I stood facing the Lady, how she had spoken to both the man and myself; it had been much longer than the time it takes for a soldier to raise an alarm and open a door.

"If she is real, what will I do?"

"You will have to be careful. If this sorceress is an enemy of Menaiya, then she will want you to betray the royal Family to her somehow. Beware of her. This alliance hinges on you, Alyrra. If you betray it, you betray our land and put us at risk of war. If Menaiya attacks," Mother shrugs elegantly, "we have no hope of victory. You know that."

I nod.

"Do you remember nothing else?"

I shake my head. Having said this much, I cannot tell her about the man, a sorcerer himself and from Menaiya. It would tell her nothing more than that, indeed, the Lady is an enemy; but it would bring to light my own dishonesty. It isn't dishonesty, I tell myself tightly. It is that I do not trust Mother. How can I tell her everything?

Mother sighs. "Jerash tells me you've ordered new tack for your horse; you won't need it. Your brother has brought you a new horse."

"I know, but I'm taking Fleet Wind as well."

"No, you're not," she replies placidly. "If you want to push the matter, I'll send the horse to the knacker to make meat for the dogs. Do you understand?"

I nod, my hands curling into fists, buried within the folds of my skirts.

"Good. As for your companion on the journey there, I have spoken with my Council of Lords. We have settled on Valka."

"Mother! Not Valka—"

"Enough. She will be your companion until you reach Tarinon, at which point you may do what you wish with her. You are not to send her back."

"But what would I do with her? You know what lies between us. How could Daerilin agree?" Even I can hear the desperation in my voice.

My mother closes her eyes in long-suffering frustration, her voice laden with disgust. "Find her a husband, Alyrra. She must marry among peers and you destroyed such hopes here. It is up to you to get rid of her."

"Can no one else come?"

"No." Mother frowns. "As for the woman you dreamed of, come to me tomorrow morning. I may have some help for you."

She nods towards the door, dismissing me.

I make my way to my room quickly, the steady tread of boots behind me no longer any comfort. I try to imagine what help she could give me as I undress, Jilna muttering about the late hour and my early departure tomorrow. What could my mother possibly offer against the Lady with her empty eyes and finger-flicked light? I lie down on my side, staring at the shuttered window. Sleep eludes me. I am unused to the new room Mother assigned me, the size befitting a princess who will one day be queen, the barred window assuring my safety. This, in addition to my quads and a speedy departure for Menaiya, are all compromises to appease the king's concerns: I will winter in Tarinon, and in spring be wed.

I do not remember falling asleep, but when I open my eyes the shutters are open. An owl, pearly white in the darkness, perches between the bars, its great eyes watching me. I return its gaze, feeling the slow rise and fall of my breast. Eventually it turns and flies away, dropping into the darkness. I sit up and light the lamp next to me. I remain watching for a long time, long after I have ascertained I am alone. Jilna finds me asleep, leaning against my pillows with the lamp still burning, when she comes to wake me.

I dress quickly, aware of how well Jilna knows me, how she holds out the sleeves of my dress just so and brushes and braids my hair. She brings me the cloak the king gave me, that our nobles might see me wearing it. I take her hand as she pins the cloak closed and for a moment I am still the child she reared, the girl to whom she told stories every night and comforted when my brother was cruel. I hold her tightly to me and she in turn embraces me, and it is a strange good-bye, without words.

My mother has prepared a different farewell for me in her apartments. The curtains are still drawn across her shuttered windows. She sits next to a carven desk, illuminated by a single lamp.

"Well, Alyrra, you are off. Are you worried?" I incline my head in assent. "With good cause," she agrees, her voice relaxed, sleepy. "I have devised some help for you against the sorceress, if she is truly a danger. It is a simple but potent spell."

I nearly choke—magic? Since when has my mother dabbled in magic? And how abysmally little I know her if I do not know this! She unfolds a square of white silk no larger than a kerchief.

"Wh-what spell is that?" I manage to stammer.

She smiles a slow cat smile. "Watch."

She picks up a needle that glints gold in the lamplight and pricks her finger. As the first drop wells up and falls to spread on the silk she begins to chant:

"Heart's blood, ruby drop
Bind my love to you;
Mind's blood, dark drop,
Bind my knowledge to you;
Soul's blood, last drop,
Bind all strength to you."

A wave of dizziness passes over me. I stagger sideways, bumping into the edge of the desk. When I raise a hand to my face it comes away damp with sweat.

"What have you done?"

She folds the cloth and slips it into a pouch. "I should think it abundantly clear: I have bound my knowledge and love of you to the blood. When you meet the prince, find a way to dip this in a drink of his—a goblet of wine should work well. I expect you will have to wait a few weeks. Make sure no one sees you, especially not him."

"What will it do?"

"Naught but make him aware of all that I know and what little I love of you." I shake my head. Mothers frowns but elaborates further. "It will make him more your ally than anything else I can do. He will know who his enemies are; if he loves you even a little, he will try to protect you. Keep the

25

pouch safely." She hands it to me. "I shall meet you in the courtyard in a few minutes."

"Mother," I say hesitantly.

"Leave be, child."

"What did the last line mean—about strength?"

"I have bound your strength to it. What did you think? That's why you mustn't lose it. Now go; your escort is waiting."

5

I wait with Jerash and my brother at the Hall door. My brother does not speak, his eyes slitted against the bright morning light, his face a little too pale. For once, I am thankful for his penchant for drinking. When Mother arrives, we walk out together, pausing at the top of the steps. Mother smiles and wishes me health and happiness in a voice that carries to the farthest servant in the crowd. I curtsy to her, and my brother leads me down the stairs to the carriage, pausing as a hostler brings forth a white stallion.

"My gift to you on your betrothal," he says, his voice hoarse and grating. The horse stands tall, bright eyes turned towards me.

"A noble creature," I say, "and a beautiful gift. I thank you."

We continue on, my brother muttering a few words about how well trained the horse is. I try not to care. We pause again to greet our escort: Lieutenant Balin from our own guard will accompany us to the Border along with an armed escort. The Menaiyan quads, with their own captain—Sarkor—will ride with us as well. Sarkor bows to us but does not speak. Indeed, he has not spoken to me since the night he intercepted my brother and me in the hallway.

My brother hands me into the carriage and steps back, smiling. Even now, when I am finally out of his reach, the veiled malice of his smile makes me stiffen. I sit down gratefully, noting that Valka is already seated opposite me, her face turned to the windows. My greeting dies on my lips as I note her stiff posture, her hands clenched tight. Beside her sits the maid we are to share for the journey. I do not recognize her, but by her cold expression as she bows from the neck, and her comfortable seat beside Valka, I guess that Valka was wiser than I in seeing to her journey companions.

The carriage starts forward with a jerk. Mother raises her hand in farewell, the gesture empty, a mere show for the watching nobles. We turn out of the courtyard, the carriage rattling over the gravel, and as easily as that, my old life is gone.

I settle back in my seat, glancing covertly at Valka. It might not be possible to be friends, but perhaps we might be courteous with one another. I should at least make the attempt.

"How are you, Valka?"

She ignores me, not a flicker of her eyes suggesting she might have heard my words. I sigh, looking out the windows to the passing trees. I wonder what I will miss from home. I am surprised to think I will miss Mother. Mostly, I will miss Jilna and Bol. I will miss Cook and Redna and the other servants, their smiles and small kindnesses. I will miss my rides in the forest, and the little dell where the Wind visits me.

The Wind. I press my lips together. I have not spoken to it since my betrothal. When I tried two days ago it did not answer. Its silence is just another good-bye, another friend I know I must leave behind. Yet I had expected a clearer farewell; I expected to be the one to leave.

We pass the better part of the morning in silence. I take off my cloak and set it aside. It is still too warm for these late summer days and far too fancy for traveling. The carriage rattles along the road, and slowly the forest changes from birch and elm in the morning to the occasional stand of pine or aspen as the day draws on. Sometimes the forest falls back from the road, giving way to grassy meadows and little herds of goats driven by village children, or small villages that turn out to watch us pass.

We break at midday, stopping at a clearing by the roadside. A brook burbles at its edge, separating it from the surrounding forest. The soldiers spread a rug on the grass for Valka and me, bringing out platters of food brought from home. I watch them without enthusiasm; sharing my meals with Valka for the entire journey makes me want to fast.

"Come get some water with me," Valka says, appearing beside me with a goblet in her hand. If it weren't an invitation, it would have been a command.

"Oh," I say, so surprised that I accept the goblet. I follow her to the stream, but she does not speak again. I think better of addressing her, unsure if her words were a token of peace or only a momentary lapse.

At least the stream is too shallow for her to drown me in. As I kneel to fill my goblet I measure its width: I might easily have leapt across it. I lift up the goblet, the forest water sweet on my tongue. Behind us, I can hear the Menaiyan soldiers speaking, their words mingling with the water's voice. Valka stands further downstream, holding her own goblet. She looks at me strangely, anger and confusion playing over her features. When she meets my gaze she whirls and stalks back to our meal, never having tasted the water herself.

I carry the strangeness of her actions with me through the day, wondering if I might ever make peace with her. We stop for the night at a small inn nestled at a crossroad. I am grateful for the tiny room I am given, separate from Valka, but tranquility eludes me. Strange visions haunt my sleep, and twice I wake expecting the Lady to have returned with her death-still eyes. Each time I find nothing but the darkness of my room, no sound but the creaking of old wood. I lie still and think of my nighttime visitor: surely he was a Menaiyan sorcerer? That would explain his appearance. Then again the Menaiyan soldiers watching my door may just as easily have allowed him to pass. But why had he kept his name secret when he expected I would meet him in Tarinon? And just how many sorcerers does the Menaiyan court boast?

At length I rise and dress myself, splashing water on my face from the basin. The cold of it makes my skin prickle. The pouch my mother gave me I hang around my neck, tucked under my gown. The cord looks odd next to Jilna's thin silver chain and pendant; neither, I think, should be worn by a princess traveling to her wedding. One speaks of sorcery and deception, the other of friendship and love. I stand for a moment holding the cord and chain together in my fist, and then let them go.

A quad made up of a combination of our own guards and the Menaiyan soldiers trails me to the stables. Despite the early hour, the hostlers we brought with us are already awake and tending to the horses. The white stallion stands at the center of his stall, tail swishing, head turned towards me. One of the hostlers approaches me deferentially.

"Is this horse in your charge?" I ask.

"Yes, Your Highness." The man is small but sturdy, his face broad and weatherworn; there is gentleness written in the lines by his eyes. I have seen him before in the stables, but rarely spoken to him.

"What is your name?"

"Westrin."

Good then; this is Redna's friend. I turn back to the stall. "What breed is he?"

"He's from the Southeast—a special breed from the Fethering Plains. They've a fancy name, Highness, but I don't know it. They're known for their strength." The man hesitates, glancing over his shoulder to where the guards wait at the door, and then whispers, "You won't want to ride him, Highness."

"Redna told me." I watch the horse, aware that the man has gone as still as a wild creature scenting danger. "Can he be broken?" The white is in the prime of life, with a high crest and proud bearing. He tilts his head slightly, his ears swiveling to catch our conversation, his dark eyes shining in the faint light.

Westrin licks his lips. "He went wild when we tried to saddle him, and he isn't young. Even so, it might be possible."

I can hear the sound of people crossing the yard to the stables, and am mildly gratified when my guards step out to stop whoever approaches. "Can you free him?"

Westrin stares. "Free him?"

29

"He's a wild creature—he deserves to go free."

"I don't know." He wrings his hands.

"Try," I suggest.

"We are too closely guarded," he murmurs. My guards step back through the doorway, followed by two of the inn stable hands.

I keep my eyes on Westrin, but he will not meet my gaze. He is right; there is hardly a moment when the soldiers do not watch their charges. "Very well," I say sadly, glancing back at the white.

Just past dawn we ride forth once more, Valka grumbling about the early hour. The maid, Tarina, makes commiserating sounds. As becomes Valka's habit over the following days, she falls asleep soon after the carriage begins its slow, steady rumble. The road stretches out before us, cutting through the forest. The wind blows steadily, sifting through the horses' manes, and cooling the hot riders, but it is not the Wind I have known all my life and that only aids in worrying me until I realize that my Wind may be as much of a homebody as I was, spending its wind-sprite life in the same dells and shaded glens where it was born. At night, my brother's words echo through my dreams; his smile flashes before me, eyes hooded, and I see the way his mouth shapes the name "Kestrin," and I hear his laughter. I wake in fear of seeing him, or the Lady.

Valka and I reach an unspoken agreement: we do not care for each other's company, but we will endure it as well as we might. She makes no attempt at conversation, and after a few awkward efforts, I let her be. But sometimes, as we sit with the trees rolling gently past, I find her gazing at me with a look I have seen in the eyes of village children: hunger. Every day I trust her less, for wherever I turn she follows. She watches me continually, silently, coldly. It comes to me that I feel as a small bird might before the gaze of a viper. And yet I cannot imagine what Valka can do to me. She is not one of Menaiya's secret enemies, but my own trouble.

On our last day with our guard from home, we break for lunch at a high mountain meadow. As I step down from the carriage, Lieutenant Balin approaches me. "Your Highness, there is a river running through the woods there, if you wish to refresh yourself before eating."

On a whim, I turn to Valka and ask, "Are you going?"

"Yes," she tells me. "Here is your goblet next to mine." I take it with a half-smile, knowing better than to read friendship into her words, and start through the tall grasses towards the trees. Valka follows, and when I glance back she smiles at me. It is a strange, nervous smile, making me think of a girl going to her first ball.

As we pass the soldiers, I notice Westrin at the back of our little caravan. He watches the men nervously, and then lifts his hand to the white's halter and slips the buckle open. The white drops his head and steps back, pulling at the suddenly loose halter. I look away as Westrin walks off to help with the soldiers' horses. I hope the white makes his bid for freedom as softly as he can.

I reach the river, kneeling to fill my goblet, my thoughts still with the white. The water is sweet and pure. Setting the goblet aside, I scoop up water to wash my face, the crisp coolness driving away the heat of the day. Valka remains where she emerged along the bank; I can feel her eyes on my back and resolutely ignore her.

I reach to scoop up more water and then pause, staring. There is something odd about my reflection but I cannot make out what, for the water does not run smoothly but in ripples and eddies. I dip my fingers into the river, breaking the image. But it does not break.

A hand reaches up and closes around my wrist. I choke on a cry of terror, jerking away, but it pulls down—hard—and I lose my footing on the muddy bank, falling headfirst into the rushing waters. The world is strange, blunted, beneath water. I twist, striking out, but cannot quite find my attacker. The hand still holds my wrist in an iron grip. I kick, desperately trying to tear myself away, push my way to the surface. The air burns in my lungs, spots dancing before my eyes. Something touches my throat—a knife? I flail away from it, feel a slicing pain, and abruptly I am released. I find myself on my hands and knees, coughing up water, gentle waves lapping around my chest.

I look up in terror, my hair sending an arc of droplets flying over the quiet waters. The river runs clear. But the birds are silent. I struggle to my feet. On the bank, I see Valka smiling. For one sodden moment I think she smiles at me, but she is looking past me. A terrible fear settles in my stomach, as heavy and dark as lead.

The Lady stands in the water a few paces away. Her hair falls white as snow over her shoulders, framing pale skin, high cheekbones. Her dress seems made of water, her body beneath as indistinguishable as the sea's bottom from a ship's deck. It is her eyes I recognize, dark holes in her skull, fathomless, empty. She holds out her hand, a small, cruel smile flitting across her lips: a pouch swings over the water from the cord she holds. I stare at it entranced.

When I finally raise my eyes to meet the Lady's, I recognize the look in her eyes. But when she speaks it is to Valka. "You have served me well." Her voice has the whisper of daggers through night air. I raise my chin, refusing to look away from her.

"My Lady, I have," Valka answers from the bank. "And you have promised me a reward."

"You shall have your reward." The Lady's gaze remains on me. "You shall be princess."

"No," I say thickly, as if half-drunk and slow of wits.

"Be quiet," Valka snaps. "You've no say in this. The Lady has promised: I shall be princess in your stead and none will know the truth."

The Lady lets her hand fall to her side, the pouch melting into her dress. When she raises a hand again, it is the one from which a gem gleams. She makes a quick sweeping motion, her fingers flicking out exactly as I remember, and power washes over me. I stumble back, falling against the low bank. I hear a faint cry behind me—Valka—and then my bones twist within their sockets, my muscles shrieking, my eyes filling with flames. I open my mouth to scream and my tongue shrivels at the touch of air. And then the pain vanishes, departing as swiftly as it came. For a moment longer, I remain unmoving, huddled against the bank, the current tugging at my legs, and then I force myself to straighten, looking up to see Valka above me.

But it is not Valka. On the bank I see myself, straight brown hair braided back, small features pinched and tired, yet happy—happy because Valka is happy. As if in a dream, I catch hold of my braid and pull it around: red and curly. My breath rasps loud in my lungs as I stare at my hair, and then at my fingers, long and slender and soft.

"What have you done?" I cry, my voice high and wavering, staring at Valka-become-myself. Her lips turn back in a sneer. I feel a strange emotion coming to life within me; I wheel to face the Lady, my face tight. "You cannot do this!" I cry, as if I might prohibit the action, undo it with my outrage.

The Lady smiles. "Indeed I can, and I have, little princess. What will you do?"

"She will be found out as a fraud. I have only to tell ..." my words die in Valka's throat.

The Lady laughs: a fearful sound, pure and clear and cold. "You will never speak of this." A second time her hand moves, sunlight glancing off the gem. A gold chain forms in the air and flies towards me, but I cannot move, rooted to the spot, frozen in an unfamiliar body. The chain wraps itself around my throat, tightening as if clasped.

"What?" I manage to gasp, and then it constricts, choking me. I fall against the bank, clawing at the thing, my vision filled with the dazzle of sunlight reflecting off water. Dimly, I hear my own laughter falling from Valka's mouth. I stiffen, my anger cooling, hardening into a lump beneath my breast. The chain loosens but I can still feel it, hugging my skin, halfway up my neck.

"If ever you feel the urge to speak of this to another person," the Lady murmurs, "the choker shall convince you otherwise. Farewell, dear princess."

When I look up, one hand at my throat, the Lady is gone.

"Girl," Valka says. I find I cannot meet her gaze, cannot bear to see her face, and so my eyes drop to her neck. A red mark shows bright against the paleness of her throat: it is where the Lady's knife cut the pouch from my neck. "You will call me 'Your Highness' and treat me with all due respect from now on. If you try anything, I shall have you executed for treason."

I do not really hear Valka, have no words for her. She turns to rejoin our escort, leaving me alone. A shudder runs through me. I look around at the river, the sand showing clear through the water. My eyes come to rest on a silver glint. Dimly, I realize my teeth are chattering. I clench my jaw to stop them, staring down at the sparkle in the riverbed. Slowly, I bend and reach into the water, closing my fist over the glinting sand. When I open my palm, I find Jilna's silver necklace, the chain snapped but the rose pendant still there, caught in a loop. I close my fingers over it and pull myself up the riverbank.

As I stand, the water drains from the dress I wear—Valka's dress— running in rivulets past my feet and back down into the river, leaving me bone dry. I shudder once, and close my eyes. Not my eyes, I think, and jerk them back open. Not my eyes. Not my sight or hearing or feeling. Not me.

I am shaking again. I wrap Valka's arms around me and breathe slowly, staring at the ground, thinking only of the path before me leading between the trees and out through the tall grasses. With each step, a part of the clarity of what has happened slips away. I succumb to the enfolding grayness, letting myself drift up the path. It is a dream, a dream, naught but a nightmare.

The soldiers treat me as they had Valka, calling me "my lady" when they speak, but mostly they are distant and cold. They dislike me, I think, and it is a foggy moment before I realize it is Valka they dislike and not me. I do not know how the meal passes; I am stepping into the carriage almost before I realize I have eaten. Valka remains outside, watching the men pack up.

Tarina, the maid, enters the carriage, seating herself beside me. "My lady, are you feeling quite well?"

I nod, the motion jerky.

"Can I fetch you anything? A glass of wine, perhaps?" She has shown more concern for me in these few moments than in all our trip. But then, she thinks me Valka, not myself.

"No," I force myself to say. "Thank you. It will pass." Even though I know it will not. The sorceress is hardly one to let her plans go awry. Tarina, however, accepts my answer, asking nothing further.

The princess returns to the carriage when the soldiers are ready to move. Valka glances nonchalantly at me as she enters, but something in her stiffens. As she settles herself gingerly on the cushioned seat, I begin to understand: she too has lost her body. She feels the same revulsion, the same instinctual terror at the change of her hands, her hair. The cold anger I had felt growing in my breast when I faced the Lady reawakens, and I find myself swearing not to show my fear, my discomfort. So, looking at her, I smile. She flinches, and I laugh: a high-pitched, quick sound that is not my laugh at all, that comes from some distant place I cannot name, but her face pales.

"Stop it!" My own voice raised in anger against myself wrenches me to a halt. She raises her hand to her mouth, eyes bright and angry.

"Whatever happened to your voice?" My voice sounds smoother and sweeter to me than ever before, for it has now her honeyed tones. Tarina glances between us warily.

"Be silent! Or I shall—"

"What? What will you do?" I begin to feel a pressure around my neck, the golden chain—invisible, untouchable, yet there—pressing gently against my windpipe. I must not openly challenge her, I realize.

"I shall make you pay when we arrive in Tarinon." I see myself angry, eyes flashing, face pale. But the expression is strange—it is molded to Valka and not myself.

"Perhaps," I say, not really hearing her anymore, for another thought has occurred to me: in Tarinon I might finally meet the mage, the Lady's enemy. He surely would be able to help me. I lean back against the seat, thinking of how I might find him. With Valka present, it may be impossible to reach the king, but surely she will not notice or care if I seek out one of his men?

We reach the Border house at sunset. Built at a rocky pass, it stands in mute testimony of the friendship (or simple indifference) of our two lands—rarely have we gone to war, never have we needed more than a stopping house here for Border patrols from either kingdom. Menaiya has had little interest in us until now, for the gem mines lie north of us, the fruited valleys south. Indeed, the Border house often stands empty through the winters, open for any who need it.

Now, the house overflows with light and men. They pour out of the building, filling the road. As the carriage pulls to a halt, two men stride forward. I cannot see them past Valka, who moves at once to the door, waiting impatiently to alight.

As she descends, Captain Sarkor addresses the princess with a bow. "Your Highness, may I present Lord Melkior, High Marshall of Menaiya, and Lord Filadon of Barinol." The two men bow deeply to her; she inclines her head in return.

The men could not be more different. One has the sense of great height when looking at Melkior, though not all of it physical. He bears himself proudly and his eyes hold definite authority; he is used to his power, I think. So I understand at once why Filadon is mentioned second: he is slim and unassuming, his eyes gentle though shrewd and his lips used to smiling. He pauses to look past his new lady to where Tarina and I still sit in the carriage, and nods to us while Melkior addresses the princess.

"It is our great honor and privilege to welcome Your Highness to the Kingdom of Menaiya," Melkior begins, and drones on at length, finishing with, "The prince himself wished to accompany us, but he has been taken ill of late and could not join us."

"I pray he recovers his spirits," Valka murmurs while I wonder what illness would so debilitate a young man in his prime.

Melkior smiles, revealing two lines of pearly white teeth. "By all reports, he is recovering well. We have prepared a meal for you and your escort, Your Highness; we pray it will be to your liking."

"That was most thoughtful of you, Lord Melkior," Valka purrs. She starts forward and the two lords fall into step with her, accompanying her into the house. It is a strange thing to watch; she has not found the smooth pace of my mother, yet in these few hours she has developed her own walk. She moves with a certain confidence, her chin raised just high enough to require her to glance down as she reaches the threshold.

Tarina clears her throat, and I realize I am still standing in the carriage door. I jump down, hastily following them inside, Tarina right behind me. A rough table runs the width of the room, laden with silver platters of food and pitchers of both water and wine. I hesitate in the doorway, my eyes adjusting to the lamplight. The princess sits at the head of the table, a lord on each side. I must take my place now, I think with a sudden urgency, or I shall lose even that. I hurriedly seat myself next to Filadon, remembering his quiet smile.

Valka glares at me. I understand now more clearly than ever why neither my mother nor any of the courtiers took me seriously: my body does not lend itself to grandness. Valka, trying to look proud and above me, looks only petty and cross, a mere child of fifteen years. Still, she must introduce me before she can snub me, else her companions may not know whether they dare join her. Her words are laden with contempt. "My lords, allow me to introduce my companion, Lady—Valka." Melkior and Filadon bow from the neck.

I dip my head in return. "My lords."

"And my maid," Valka finishes, nodding to where Tarina has taken up a station along the wall. So Valka has made me merely a lady-in-waiting, without known title or parentage, hardly worth mentioning before a maid. Neither lord addresses me more than to offer food or drink. Valka pointedly ignores me. By the end of the meal it is clear I will make no friends here.

The soldiers have prepared a back room for our use and Valka happily retires there after the meal, escorted as always by four soldiers, Matsin and Finnar among them. Tomorrow they will form a true quad, for our soldiers from home will leave. Tarina follows after her, as she used to with me, to help her change in her usual brusque manner. This time, though, she will remain and wait for me to enter, fluttering over me and granting me all the courtesies she showers on Valka. I do not want her mistaken kindnesses, or Valka's sneers. I do not want to watch Valka change, or fumble with the new shape of my body. I rise and make my way outside, following the road to a stand of trees overlooking the pass. I find a seat on a stone, wrap my arms around my knees, and breathe in the clear mountain air.

The soldiers at the house quiet, the horses picketed outside lowering their heads to sleep. The night spreads its mantle over the world. I look up through the branches at the canopy of stars. It is cool, with a slight breeze blowing, and I left my cloak in the carriage when I hurried after Valka to the Border House.

Valka. I close my eyes. The fragile peace the night has constructed around me begins to fray at the edges. That is my name now. And I must think of her as—what? Alyrra? No, but neither traitor nor princess seem right. She is Valka, whatever body she may wear, just as I am still the girl who was princess this morning. While I cannot claim the name Alyrra, I will not be Valka either.

I am not the princess. The unspoken words whisper through me, raising the hair at the back of my neck. They mean more than just that I have lost my body, lost the story of my life written upon it. I am not the princess. I will not be queen. I will not marry a foreign prince, nor live in a court where my language is barely spoken. I will not have to learn to politic, to question my friendships, to trust no one. I need fear my brother no more, nor the cold contempt of my mother, nor the prince who awaits me. I have before me now a new life, if I choose to take it.

I feel a ripple of something sweet and wonderful wash through me. I am done with that, I think. I wonder if it is joy I feel.

7

I leave our room before Valka wakes, stepping out for a quick walk. Tarina, yawning and eyeing me askance, had helped me dress, no doubt expecting me to grump as Valka does. She seemed taken aback when I refused her company for my walk. I wonder how close she and Valka are: clearly she does not suspect our switch, yet Valka had expected more of her and used her more than I ever had.

Melkior and Filadon stand together by the carriage, deep in discussion with Captain Sarkor, while the soldiers make ready to leave. They do not notice me and I do not disturb them. As I reach the end of our little party, I stop in dismay. There, already tethered to the supply wagon, stands the white.

I go to him, reaching out to offer him my hand. "I'm sorry," I murmur. "I thought you had escaped. I didn't even remember you till now—but you must never have gotten away." He blows into my hand, one ear swiveled towards to the men loading the wagon. They hardly spare me a glance. "I'm sorry," I say again before turning to take my little walk, but the pleasure of the morning has left me.

By the time I return, all that remains within the Border house is a tray with breakfast foods. I sit down and help myself to the cold meats and bread laid out. Eventually, Valka emerges. I had not truly seen her when I returned to the room last night, and so it is a shock to see myself, lips pursed, reaching for a piece of bread. I watch her eat, intrigued by the way she chews, by the play of light on forehead and cheeks. My own body lacks the softness of Valka's, the shapely form and unscarred flesh. As Valka reaches for more food I touch the scar that curves across her knuckles, my own fingers pale against her skin. She jerks away from me.

"Do you know how you got that?"

"I don't know what you mean." Her voice is sharp.

"I was gathering rosehip to make a tisane for Jilna. I slipped at the top of a ravine and slid all the way down. There were brambles at the bottom and I sliced my knuckles open on them. Mother was furious." I rub my own knuckles, remembering the pain. Valka stares at me silently; I cannot tell if she is frightened by my friendliness or merely disgusted. I rise and leave her, making my way out.

Lieutenant Balin and his soldiers have gathered before the door, ready to take their leave of the princess. They do not give me more than a passing glance as I walk to the carriage.

Valka emerges soon after, smiling radiantly as she addresses our escort from home. "Lieutenant Balin, I thank you and your men for the service you have done me on this journey." She glances towards where I wait in the carriage. "I pray you will tell my mother you left me well."

"Your Highness," Balin bows deeply. "It has been the greatest honor to serve as your escort. I shall deliver your message to the Queen myself." Within a few minutes the whole of our escort from home has mounted up and left, the horses' hooves raising a fine cloud of dust that drifts across the road.

Valka enters our carriage, followed by Melkior and Filadon.

"Where is Tarina?" I ask in surprise as the carriage starts forward.

Valka flicks her fingers with disgust. "I sent her home. She has been rude and not particularly helpful. I saw no need to keep her."

Of course. I look out the window, making no further comment. Tarina might have eventually realized something was amiss. Now Valka will be safe.

Valka and her two lords keep up a lively discussion through the morning. Their conversation is fraught with allusions to politics, to Tarinon and Menaiya. While there are the usual remarks on the weather and the view, they return always to matters of court.

"The prince took ill unexpectedly about a month ago," Filadon says.

"He went hunting one day and the next—" Melkior begins.

"The king's best healers have been attending him," Filadon continues, as if Melkior had not spoken. Strange that he should override Melkior so. "They assure us he will recover."

Melkior smiles amiably, but the press of his lips tells me that he is well aware of Filadon's slight. As if to spite his younger, and lesser, peer, he goes on. "Prince Kestrin's illness was not unlike what took the Queen. We were worried at first that we would lose him as well."

"Then the Queen died quite suddenly?"

Melkior nods somberly, a brilliant act. "Took ill one day, and the next day she'd gone, dear lady. She was as good a queen as we've ever had."

Filadon dips his head in agreement, but the tightness of his eyes betrays his contempt. I wonder what Filadon's standing is in the court: he might snub Melkior in passing, but Melkior, rather than returning the snub, instead blathers on in concealed fury. As High Marshall, surely Melkior holds the most powerful position among all his peers. Who, then, is Filadon, and why was he chosen to meet us?

At midday we break for lunch. The rocky pass has given way to sparsely forested mountains once more. Now more and more we see open slopes with lush grasses and the last wildflowers of the season stretching between the thinning stands of pines and aspens. As the soldiers set out our meal at a makeshift table along the roadside, Filadon turns to me. "Lady Valka, you have been very quiet. I hope you are feeling quite well."

I have a malicious wish to tell him I would have been more talkative had he spoken to me, but refrain in favor of a different statement. "Oh, quite well. But please, my lords, I beg you will not call me Lady Valka. It is too strange. My mother's name is also Valka—I have always been called Lady Thoreena instead."

"Why of course," Filadon says, with a slight bow. Valka glares at me, her cheeks paling in anger.

"Thank you, my lords." I smile at Valka, for I will be able to let her identity go while she must ever live with mine.

The rest of the day passes much as the morning did: the men and Valka conversing while I sit in my corner. We reach our night's destination in good time, the sun still a handbreadth above the horizon. After washing up, I make my way around to the corral that holds the bulk of our horses. The hostlers have gone in for dinner, leaving the horses unattended, though visible from the kitchen door. At the far end of the corral I spot the white stallion. He watches me, head raised, bright eyes alert.

"I don't know how I'm going to free you," I tell him, resting my hand on the wooden rail. "Valka's the sort that will send you to the knacker when she realizes she can't ride you. I wish you'd gotten away when you could."

"I chose to stay, Princess," he replies, his voice deep and gentle. My mouth drops open. What? A talking horse?

"Your brother, by the by, is quite the fool," he continues conversationally. "I'd lost almost all hope for humanity until you came along."

At this I burst into laughter. I can hear a slight hysterical note and know I should stop, but it is all I can do to wipe the tears from my eyes: my brother called a fool by a talking horse, and I the hope for humanity!

The horse waits until my laughter dies away and I am left gasping for breath, leaning against the fence between us. "I stayed because I like you. You have something of justice and mercy in you."

"That's not a good reason," I tell him, my voice rasping. "Whatever I may or may not have in me, I haven't much power to protect you. And the princess will surely want you for her own..." I trail off.

"I know what happened to you, Princess. I had left your party and was in the woods further down the river when your life was taken from you and

40

given to her. I had not the power to intervene, but I could act as witness and help you as I may."

"And so you stayed with us," I finish softly. "But tell me, what are you? Where do you come from truly?"

"I am a Horse as all horses once were. Your hostler was not too far off when he claimed I came from the Fethering Plains, for I was born not much farther south than that. That was long and long ago, even as humans measure time."

He shakes his mane, glancing towards the kitchen door. "Have you thought on how to undo the spell?"

"Undo it."

"Of course! You wish to undo it, don't you?"

"I did initially, but—but I have had time to think about it, and I don't want to anymore."

"You don't want to anymore." He says the words carefully, as if they might change their meaning as he speaks them.

"No."

"Why?" If a horse could look flabbergasted, I imagine it would look much like the white before me.

"I don't have to be a princess. Don't you see? I never was much of one, and I hate the court, and this is my chance to leave it all. I can choose my life!"

The white studies me, and when he speaks next it is with certain accents of disappointment. "You feel no duty towards your people?"

I feel a slight flush warm my cheeks. "My people I have left behind; even if I were a princess, I couldn't help them from Menaiya."

"The Menaiyans *are* your people. They have chosen you. Would you send them a viper in your place?"

I pause, thinking about Valka, about court life. "She could only do as much harm as the royal family permits; if they allow her anything, then they are probably just as bad. I wouldn't know how to counter them. Besides, Valka will make a much better princess than I; she understands politics."

"It is rare that someone who wants power truly deserves it. She will bring unhappiness to this land; you would do your best not to." He is trying to be patient with me, I realize.

I shake my head. "Valka is not innately evil. She is simply unfeeling and petty. She will care more for her dresses and jewels than anything. As princess, she will have everything at her disposal. There are much worse things in a ruler than love of trinkets."

"Do you care nothing for your own name and position?"

"There is more to life than names and positions," I tell him angrily. "I have never truly been a princess."

"Yes," he agrees after a short pause. "You have never wanted your power; that only makes you a better princess than most."

A contrary talking horse—who would have thought it possible? "Why do you care what position I hold?"

"I thought you would care. I think you still might, given time. And it seems that you will have as much as you wish." He turns away, stepping past the other horses. "Come visit me again, Princess."

I watch him, watch the way other horses take no notice of him at all: a talking horse with a sense of honor. I do not know what to make of that. I return to the inn, and spend dinner mulling over our conversation. If I barely notice Valka and her lords, I doubt they realize it. Even lying in bed I cannot quite fathom why the white would care when he had his own freedom at hand. Or hoof, as the case may be.

Eventually, I fall into an uneasy sleep and dream that I walk the plains. It is a moonless night, the land brightened only by starlight. The grasses seem deceptively short at first, but as I walk they rise up to stand shoulder to shoulder with me. It is hard walking and, while I travel a straight and purposeful path, I do not know where I go.

I come to the break so suddenly that I fall, sliding down its steep sides in a shower of shale. It is but a few paces wide, the rocky sides so sheer they tower like stone walls above me. I pick myself up, rubbing the grit from my hands, and look around. My eyes are drawn to a faint light glowing farther along the rift; when I reach it I find the opening of a tunnel.

The tunnel continues straight for a few paces with the light remaining steady, growing neither stronger nor weaker. I reach the end, turning the corner to step into bright lamplight. A spacious circular room has been hollowed out of the rock. Nothing adorns its walls; no furniture clutters the room. Only at the center stands a great, carved stone pedestal. Above it hangs the lamp. I approach cautiously, glancing around, but I am alone, the entrance I came through the only one.

I find a shallow pan filled with sparkling water set upon the stone. I peer into the water uncertainly, remembering the last time I looked for my reflection. But I see nothing strange, nothing but myself.

Myself. The face looking back is the face I have always worn. My breath escapes me with a grunt, as if I have been struck. My face! But as I watch, the water ripples from the touch of my breath and the image—shifts.

I see myself now, dressed in Menaiyan clothes, smiling a smile that is not mine. I walk through a stone courtyard towards a man. With a sickening lurch I realize it is the mage from my chamber; he smiles as he sees me, holding out a hand, but when the vision of myself reaches him, it is not my hand I give him. No, it is the blade of a dagger I place in his hand, wrapping his fingers around the sharp metal so that his blood flows down to stain the stones underfoot.

And then he is looking at me, dark eyes intent, and behind him I see the self-same walls that surround me now. His brow creases, shadows flickering across his face, and his lips move, shaping my name: Alyrra.

I shake my head, my fingers curled tight around the edge of the pedestal. The vision in the water fades and the face that looks back at me now is Valka's. I stumble away from the pedestal, tripping over my own feet, falling towards the stone floor.

I wake with a start, my sheets tangled around my legs, my breath panting in my chest. I do not sleep again that night.

We descend from the mountains the following day. The Golden Plains stretch out as far as the eye can see, vast, waving, the grasses golden with the late summer heat. I note with relief that these grasses barely reach the horses' knees, unlike those of my dream.

The villages we pass are spread out, the land surrounding them planted with crops: wheat and corn, as well as lower-growing vegetables, small orchards of fruit-bearing trees. Sometimes we pass great areas fenced all around, within which horses roam. These, Melkior tells the princess, are the ranches upon which some of Menaiya's finest horses are bred.

After dinner, I make my way to the inn stables. The hostlers have yet to return from their meal, though a soldier stands guard outside the building. As I reach the white's stall door, he turns towards me, head high and eyes bright. He wastes no times on courtesies. "Have you reconsidered your choice?"

I shrug noncommittally. "You're very intent on—that," I finish raggedly, the chain tightening around my neck. "What makes you think you can do anything?"

"I can't," he answers with complete frankness. "Only you can undo the spell."

"Me?"

"You must either cast a counter spell of equal strength or you must convince her to lift it."

"I am no sorceress," I point out.

"Then you must find out what she meant to gain by attacking you."

My thoughts fly to the dark-haired mage in my chamber. "Perhaps she has already gained it." It was revenge she wanted against me, and that she has. The question has more to do with what the man thought to gain by talking to me: he had warned me, but why would it have mattered to him whether I lived to reach Menaiya or not? I am hardly a prize to be protected; there are five more princesses from stronger kingdoms than my own who would happily agree to such a match should I die. Though, as Daerilin had said, they will be missed where I will not.

"You have met her before."

"Yes."

A lone hostler enters the stable, pausing to bow when he sees me. "My lady, can I help you?"

I smile, happy to hear him speak my language. "No, thank you." I leave the hostler to his work, returning to the inn for the night.

The next morning begins as any other. I do not suspect trouble until I catch Valka's smirk as she steps out of the carriage to stretch her legs at mid-morning.

"Would you have my horse saddled?" she asks Captain Sarkor sweetly. "I am tired of the carriage."

"Your Highness," Sarkor replies, his usual curt if courteous self. He walks down the road to the end of our party, where the white is tied to the supply wagon. I watch after him surreptitiously.

"You will join me, my lords?" Valka turns a sunny smile on our companions.

"With pleasure," Melkior says. Immediately a second soldier is dispatched for the lords' mounts. I feel Filadon's quick glance, but there is no fourth horse for me; had there been, I would have opted to ride long before this to escape Valka's company. I wander away from their little group, watching as the hostlers unload the requisite saddles from the wagon. Daerilin had not given his daughter a horse to take with her; I wonder if she had asked for one, if it had occurred to either of them, or if he had simply refused her one.

A thin hostler with a crooked nose approaches the white, placing a saddle blanket across his back. The white snorts and steps away, his head snaking around, teeth bared. The hostler jumps back with a shout. The white rears in response, the blanket flying off his back like chaff, the whole wagon jerking as his lead snaps tight.

"Easy," I cry, running towards them. The soldiers form a ring around the white at once, as if he had gone mad, their hands going to the hilts of their swords. He snorts and pulls at his lead, the muscles of his neck bulging. The wagon rolls back a foot, the horses at its front prancing nervously, the whites of their eyes showing.

"Easy," I say again, darting between two soldiers to get to the white.

"Lady—get back," Sarkor orders.

I hold out my hand to the white, willing him to listen to me. "Easy," I repeat. He drops down to look at me. "Gently now." The white stands perfectly still. "No one's going to ride you," I tell him. His ears flick towards Sarkor, who has begun to walk towards me. With two quick steps the white reaches me, dropping his nose into my hand.

"There," I say, patting his cheek with my other hand. Sarkor's hand closes on my elbow, pulling me back. "He just spooked," I say, trying to pull out of the tight grip.

"Indeed," Sarkor replies. "That is why I ordered you back."

"They shouldn't try to saddle him." I let Sarkor guide me out of the ring, for his grip is like my brother's and will brook no argument. Surely he will not strike me?

"They won't," he replies, and fires off a string of commands to his men in Menay. I glance over my shoulder: the men keep their distance from the horse, moving off to go about their duties.

Sarkor walks me away from the road, across the grass until we are no longer within earshot of the escort. They are still easily visible, but I am not sure enough of Sarkor to take comfort from that. His grip is tight, unyielding, but not painful. Yet.

"You fool," he says, swinging me around to face him. He releases my elbow, his hands settling in fists at his waist. "What were you doing?"

"He wouldn't hurt me."

"You've seen less of that horse than the princess has," Sarkor snaps. "He went wild and you *approached* him. Against my orders."

"I didn't mean—"

"Don't lie to me," he growls. I stand completely still, my eyes on his chest barely two hand spans before me. I wish he would step back; I dare not move. "You heard me and you did as you wished. Had you been harmed, I would have been called to account."

"I'm sorry," I whisper.

"As long as you ride with me, you ride under my command. Do you understand?"

"Yes."

"I have sworn to deliver your princess, along with her companions, to Tarinon in safety. If you endanger your lady or any of my men again, I will see that the king deals with you. He will not be pleased."

"I'm sorry," I repeat, my voice wavering. "I didn't mean to endanger anyone."

Sarkor hardly looks appeased. "Do not draw my attention again."

"I won't," I promise with all my heart.

He turns and strides back to the road, leaving me alone in the grass. I wait until my hands stop trembling before I follow.

Three days later our caravan reaches Tarinon, our destination. The days have passed quietly, with no further incident. Valka has not tried to ride again, though both Filadon and Melkior have offered her their mounts.

Filadon has surprised me. Whenever he and I find ourselves alone together for a few moments—waiting in the inn yard before a departure or arriving at breakfast before the others—he has spoken to me kindly. He has not asked about Valka, or our relationship, or given any indication that he has a motive in befriending me. Nor does he dismiss me as Melkior has; even in company with the princess, he has a smile for me, and will offer me food or drink before I think to ask. Valka has had to bite her lip more than once, for how can she be angry with Filadon for such small attentions when he has tendered her no insult? I wonder if this was why Filadon was chosen to meet me: because, at heart, he is a kind man.

So the rest of our journey passes pleasantly enough. We reach the city in late afternoon, having watched the great walls rise before us for nearly an hour. The whole of the city lies crowded within these stone walls, built up into many floored buildings of yellow brick. Today, people fill the streets, overflowing into alleys, hanging off of stairwells. Children perch on lower rooftops, barefoot and laughing. I watch them from where I sit across from Valka. She, smiling and laughing, waves to the people as we drive through the streets. Melkior and Filadon both ride before the carriage and the soldiers flank us, their horses keeping the crowds back.

The crowds end abruptly at the palace gates. We clatter into a gleaming courtyard, the horses' hooves ringing on the cobblestones. Valka rises as we roll to a stop, stepping to the door even as the footman moves forward to open it. She descends at once, eagerness written in every move.

"Your Majesty, the Princess Alyrra ka Rosen," Melkior intones, having dismounted bare moments before, and Valka drops into a curtsy.

I stare past her, my breath stilled in my lungs. Standing beside the king is his son. They are equally tall, with the same dark hair as all their people, but where the king has curved, hawk-like features, his son has the more feminine high cheekbones. Still, they share the same defined jaw, the same air of natural authority. The prince stands stiffly, as if he still battles illness and fears to let any sign of weakness slip him. His shadowdark eyes flicker once to the carriage and then back to Valka.

"Alyrra, may I introduce my son, Prince Kestrin," the king says, and the sorcerer from my chamber bows to Valka's curtsy. When she meets his gaze she smiles and looks away coyly. He watches her, his emotions so well hidden I cannot say whether her behavior strikes him as strange.

I want desperately to step forward, to tell him: do not trust her. I understand; it is you the Lady wants, and she will use Valka to betray you. She meant only to get me out of the way. But even as the words form in my mind, the chain tightens around my neck. My fingers scrabble at it uselessly, finding only skin.

The prince leads his lady across the courtyard towards a set of doors, huge, intricately carved and elaborately inlaid with brass. I stare at them numbly, thinking of the big double doors to our Hall at home that I had once thought so great with their iron bands and blue and white paint. They would look like a piece from a child's play house here, small and ridiculously simple.

At the king's nod the doors are thrown open in welcome. But instead of entering he pauses on the threshold, turns around. Melkior and Filadon step back so as not to crowd their king, as do the other nobles around them. I see his eyes come to rest on me, and he speaks to Valka where she stands with the prince. I step down from the carriage carefully, my legs creaking, as if I had turned old in the time since we arrived. I am too late, I know, though I do not know what for. I cannot hear their words, but Valka glances at me once and then they continue into the Hall.

I am lost in a sea of sound and movement. Our horses are led away, hooves clattering over stone; the soldiers call greetings across the courtyard; servants bustle past; and the remaining nobles retreat to the Hall. Everywhere there is the sound of talking: laughing, shouting, swearing. All, all in Menay. And the one ally I thought I had, the one man whose enemy I share, is no ally at all but my betrothed. I feel as if at any moment parts of me might start breaking away, my soul splintering beneath the sudden onslaught of knowledge.

"Lady?" A short, severe-looking man stands at my elbow. I turn to him as one drowning reaches for aid. "Follow me." His voice is deep, his accent so thick it nearly obscures his words. I latch onto his face: well shaven but dark with bushy eyebrows and sharp brown eyes. His hair, unlike the soldiers', is cropped short. I follow him across the courtyard to a side door, and then down hallway after hallway. I follow blindly, not caring where I walk. Finally, the man stops and opens a door, gesturing for me to enter.

"Thank you." I step into a small bed chamber. Behind me the door click shuts, the man's tread fading into silence. After a time, I walk to the small chair set beside the window and sit down. I smooth the fabric of my skirts over my lap, arrange my hands carefully. I know the white stallion will be well cared for, that my trunks will not be lost, that the only thing, truly, that may be lost is the prince, and of him I will not think.

9

Evening gathers in the corners of the courtyard below, soft blue shadows spreading their wings over the mosaic tiled floor. The floor looks like a tapestry of flowers and circles interwoven and spread across the ground, too exquisite to set foot on. This courtyard alone, set away and barely used, makes me wonder why the king had done more than glance within the roughly cobbled yard of our Hall before moving on.

I do not know how long I sit. Eventually, a knock comes on my door: a confident tap-tap-tap. I turn towards it, gazing through the half-remembered scape of my darkened room. I rise and move to the door, opening it hesitantly, squinting against the sudden wash of lamplight.

Captain Sarkor stands in the hall, accompanied by a soldier. I think it must be Matsin son of Körto, but he keeps his chin down. Sarkor sketches a slight bow. He looks ancient to me, his eyes grim, his lips straight. His is a face of strength and intellect; I wish suddenly that I had not angered him the day Valka wished to ride the white. Had I not, I might be able to speak to him now.

"Lady, the king requests your presence."

I slip out to follow them. The hallways are lit by sconces set in the wall, evenly spaced. At first the halls strike me as rich, with wood floors and a band of mosaic tile towards the ceiling, but as we walk the corridors grow richer, more exquisite, with woodwork and carving on the walls, meeting with mosaics at shoulder level that rise to the carved ceiling, the doors ornately worked. I can hear the quiet rumble of many people, distant laughter, music drifting through the halls.

We stop before a door of carved and inlaid wood. Sarkor knocks. Where I had crept to the door, here a voice answers: a short, distinct command.

Sarkor opens the door, stepping in to bow. "Your Majesty, may I present the Lady Valka, called Thoreena, companion of the Princess Alyrra."

I enter and curtsy, my eyes resting on the carpet. Despite the light of numerous lamps, the colors of the weaving seem dark to me, and what might be reds and blues and greens present themselves as black. Sarkor steps back and I hear the door click shut.

"Lady Thoreena," the king says, and I rise from my curtsy. He is dressed in a cream tunic trimmed with beige and gold; his sword belt replaced by a gold sash. He does not need a weapon at hand here, I think. At least, not one of metal. In one hand he holds a goblet, fingers curling gently around the delicate gold stem. I drop my gaze to his feet and see that he wears slender leather slippers, embroidered, with a long curled toe. I stare at his shoes, mortified. He had thought our Hall filthy. Obviously—from cobbled yard to scuffed floors to the rushes and dogs in the Hall itself. He must have. He had never worn anything but boots during his visit.

"I hope you have been made comfortable here."

"Quite," I say, and then catch myself. "Y-your Majesty."

The liquid in his goblet twirls as he considers me. I have not changed or washed since my arrival, and feel a slight blush warm my cheeks. He lets my words pass. "You are aware that you have displeased the Princess."

"Your Majesty," I agree, unsurprised.

"She has asked me to find you some work, to make use of you." He pauses, but I make no reply as I watch his fingers on the goblet. The cup cradled by the gold stem is glass: that fragile, glorious stuff. "Can you tell me what has so displeased her?"

"She has said nothing?" I ask, half-caught between the detached swirling of wine and the shame of seeing his shoes. Valka is not the type to pass up a chance to express displeasure.

"She has said very little," the king replies. "I would hear more." I consider him. In the half-lit room, my thoughts are more lucid to me than the dream of this conversation. I think: he is trying to bluff me into speaking the truth, believing that Valka has already spoken half of it. But he has no idea of the truth, any more than Sarkor who watched the Princess's every move but one.

"I would not say more than the Princess herself wishes to tell."

He smiles a lovely though empty smile. "I have spoken to Steward Helántor in the hopes of finding some employ for you. All we have to offer is the job of goose girl. I assume you will accept it." He lifts the goblet to his mouth, takes a sip. I think of Redna and her horses, and of Dara and Ketsy—now I will be among their number. I could almost smile.

"Unless you are able to provide an escort for yourself," the king adds casually.

"An escort?" I echo.

"You cannot make the journey alone. While I might offer you one, I would want to know more before I did."

"Your Majesty." There is nothing for me at home: that much I know. Daerilin would easily find me out as an impostor, but would never believe me to be myself. The king waits, watching me. I am aware of the hardness of his gaze, and I think faintly that he is not unlike my mother. I wonder what he sees in me, what it was that Valka said.

He turns away, sets his goblet down on a small table. "Helántor will come for you in the morning." His words are cold, half-bored. I curtsy and turn to leave. His voice stops my hand on the handle. "If you decide you would like to speak with me again, he will arrange it."

I dip my head in acknowledgement and slip out the door. Sarkor and Matsin guide me back to my room in silence. I feel ill with the words I have heard tonight, with the coldness of the king and the ruby red of the wine in the goblet. At least I know now what I had feared: that the king is like my mother, and so his son must be as well.

Helántor turns out to be the same man who showed me to my room. I follow him down to a courtyard where a carriage awaits us early the following morning. We drive down one of the main roads, though I cannot be sure if it is the same one I traveled yesterday. Within sight of the city gates the carriage turns and rumbles past a large stable before coming to a stop before a second stable. I have to bite my lip to keep from gaping. *Two* royal stables, of such size?

Inside, we climb a dim stairwell by the door. Two doors face the stairs; Helántor opens one of these to reveal a small, bare room. "This is your room," he explains. "Your trunks we will bring here. This is the key." He hands me a small key; I curl my fingers around the cold iron. "Come."

I take one last look around the room. In the dim light from the tiny, shuttered window I can make out only a rolled mat and a stool.

Outside once more, we walk to the next building. It is smaller than the stables, and while the doors are open a second low gate closes off the inside. A milling, honking flock of geese fill the barn.

"Corbé!" calls Helántor from the gate. A figure makes its way towards us from the depths of the building, shooing geese out of his way with a staff.

"Ayah?" The word is abrupt, harsh. Helántor replies in Menay. They talk for a few minutes, but my coming is clearly no surprise to Corbé. He looks at me once, a long measured, measuring look, and I think that I do not like his eyes but I am not sure why. He is well built, with stocky shoulders and big hands; he must be a few years older than me and a head taller to boot.

Helántor turns to me. "First, you and Corbé take these geese outside. Then you return and clean this barn. Corbé will show you. Then you will go back to the geese. At night, you help bring the geese in." He turns once more to Corbé. A few more words and, without a backward glance, Helántor leaves.

Corbé opens the gate for me. I step in, following him across the enclosure. The floor is covered with straw and feathers and goose droppings. I grimace, my slippers squelching in filth hidden beneath the straw. The barn itself smells so strongly of both goose and droppings I have to hold my breath to keep my stomach settled.

On the back wall hang shovels, rakes, a pitchfork and a variety of staffs. Corbé mimes raking the ground to collect droppings, points to the shovel to lift them, and then shows me a barrel by the door to dump them in. A ladder against the wall leads to the loft, and Corbé points to a trapdoor towards the center of the loft and mimes throwing down more straw. Finally, he points to the staffs and then myself, holding up his own so that I understand him.

With a shout he rouses the geese, driving them towards the gate. I grab a staff and hurry ahead, opening the door at his nod. The geese pour past me into the open yard. With another shout and a few pebbles expertly thrown, Corbé herds them around the corner of the stable opposite, towards the city gates, gesturing for me to follow behind. I do, hesitantly using my staff to hurry along the stragglers. A few of the geese try to nip me, turning and honking at me when my staff comes too close to them; I have to push them with it harder than I like in order to get them to follow after their brethren.

It seems like a long walk around the stables, through the city gates, and on down the road to their pasture. The land here lies untilled, kept as meadowland for the king's geese and other livestock, sheep or goats. The same low stone walls run along the road, occasionally dividing one pasture from the other. We come to a crossroad and I pause, looking up and down, but I cannot tell where it runs. By the time we finally leave the road for a narrow path between two short stone walls, and from there turn through a break to a pasture, I am heartily sick of the geese, having received several hard pecks.

Back in the barn I rake up the goose droppings. The work is tiring and dirty, and by the time I am done and ready to shovel the mess into the barrel, I am drenched with sweat. It is noon before I have thrown down more straw and raked it out evenly. My arms and back ache with the unaccustomed lifting. I push a tendril of red hair behind my ear, the feeling of wrongness so slight now that my hand hardly wavers before completing the movement.

Before I leave for the pasture, I return to the stables hoping to find a common room like the one I remember from home. I see two of the hostler men in the hall, talking together as they look in at a horse. They glance curiously at me as I pass, and a moment later the elder of the two—perhaps ten years my senior and built like a bear—sticks his head into the common room to check on me. I freeze as if caught stealing, but he takes a glance at the small piece of flatbread I have found, and nods with understanding. He produces a burlap shoulder sack from a cabinet, as well as some cheese wrapped in a cloth and two apples. He adds a tin cup, and hands the sack to me with a smile.

"Shurminan," I say belatedly, as he steps through the door.

"Ifnaal," he replies. *You are welcome.*

I reach the goose pasture after only one or two false turns onto likely looking paths from the main road. Corbé does not even glance at me. I cross to the geese wondering if I have inadvertently offended him. I can't think of a thing.

The geese have congregated around a small stream running through the pasture, resting and splashing by the water. A goose opens her clipped wings and flaps them in vain, beating at the air, straining with all her might and managing only to ripple the water around her. My fingers graze a bruise on my thigh from a peck this morning, but still, watching the geese now, I pity them.

The afternoon passes quietly. I eat my lunch, sitting in the shade of a tree that has grown up alongside the wall. I must doze off at some point, for I rouse to the sound of Corbé shouting to bring the geese together.

Our return is slow going; Corbé ignores wherever I am and so I must constantly turn aside for wandering geese. It is only when we reach the city gates that Corbé takes full control of the flock, gesturing once for me to go ahead to the barn and then turning them into the yard. I hurry past the stables to open the gate and let the feathery crowds in. Corbé considers my morning's work while I put away my staff. He nods once, almost sullenly, and turns his back on me.

I open my mouth to speak and then close it. None of my language tuitions ever included the words to ask a goose boy why he dislikes me; or whether I had not done a good job cleaning a barn. I return to the second stable, my feet dragging. The sounds of voices raised in conversation carry down the hall from the common room. I peek in from the doorway. A group of hostlers sit together over their dinner. They laugh as they converse, their manner easy and assured.

One of the women glances up as I waver on the threshold. Her eyes are a gentle brown, laughter lines softening them just as age has softened the skin of her cheeks, left her fingers gnarled and callused. She raises her hand in greeting, and at once the attention of the room flits to me.

I rub a fold of my skirt with my thumb, gripping it tightly in my hand. They bob their heads and then wait, watching me. I feel as out of place among them as one of my charges might among theirs. They are all of them certain in themselves, strong and purposeful, their movements sure.

53

The gentle-eyed woman stands up and pulls a stool to the table, speaking words that shuffle across the distance between us and slip out the door behind me. How useless are the courtly words and phrases I have learned! She gestures to the stool, then places her hand on her breast and speaks one word: "Darilaya."

I smile hesitantly, point to myself. "My name is Al—" The choker snaps tight around my neck, and I break off, shocked at the pain, at the way the walls spin, that I should so easily have given this woman my name.

A hand closes over my elbow, and as I begin to cough, regaining my breath, I find that I have been hustled to the stool. The woman pushes a cup of water into my hands. I smile gratefully, sip the water as I recover myself. The hostlers eye me cautiously, as if I might fall over before them.

I set the cup down on the table and point to myself again. "Thoreena."

Reassured by my ability to speak, the hostlers introduce themselves in a quick round of pattering, sing-song names I cannot catch. They ladle out a bowl of stew for me, hand me a flatbread, and wait patiently as I eat, only occasionally murmuring a comment to each other. I leave as soon as I am done, smiling and nodding to them, as glad to escape, no doubt, as they are to have their common room returned to them.

The same woman hands me a bowl of cinnamon-spiced porridge in the morning, gesturing to the table. Other than her, the common room lies empty. The porridge has been kept warm in a ceramic bowl wrapped in a blanket, and is more delicious than most breakfasts I can remember. We never had cinnamon for our porridge at home. The woman looks up from the pieces of a harness set out before her, smiling at my look of rapture, and pours me a cup of spiced milk. I want to ask her name again but she returns to her work at once, deft fingers piecing the harness together.

My day passes much like yesterday. Corbé gives me no greeting, his broad face hard, black hair pulled back in a tight tail. He opens the gate and drives the geese out without a glance at me. I return from the pasture, a different one from the day before, and spend the morning cleaning out the barn. That is the worst part of the day; the best is my afternoon in the pasture. There is a particular peace to the land, a quiet that the honking of geese and flapping of wings only enhances. There is only the slowly creeping shadows of the rocks by the stream, the waking and napping of our charges.

When it is time to return, driving the geese back to the road and up through the city gates, I find myself coming awake as if from a dream. I hurry ahead, throwing the barn gate open just as the first geese get to it. I close it behind Corbé, but still he does not speak to me. I wish he did not dislike me so.

I eat dinner with the stable hands again, and today they speak more among themselves, welcoming me and then hesitantly forgetting me except to make sure I have what food and drink I wish. I watch them covertly, studying the three men, who are all within a few years of each other, and whose features carry a certain resemblance mirrored by the younger woman at the table. I wonder if they are all siblings, and if so, if the older, gentle-eyed woman is any relation of theirs as well. I listen to the patter of their conversation; their words are quick and their meanings, I guess from the frequent laughs and lasting smiles, varied. It is enough to make me want to shout—what use was my studying courtly phrases? Why couldn't have Bol taught me the language of living and laughing? I will have to learn, I think wearily. Somehow, I will have to teach myself.

Before I leave, I touch the older woman's sleeve and show her a small wild rose I had found beside the goose pasture. "Thoreena."

She looks at it. "Thorn." She points to the thorny stem, nodding, and turns to her companions before I can stop her, speaking quickly.

"Thorn," they say, pointing from the rose to me.

"No, no," I say quickly. I have to resort my own tongue, explaining uselessly, "Rose and thorns together: the whole plant–thoreena."

But they do not understand, and when I leave a few minutes later I am only "Thorn."

I venture forth from the stables, twirling the rose between my fingers, unsure whether I should laugh at myself or shout with frustration. Outside, the night air is chill. I leave the rose by one of the drinking troughs and cross the empty yard to the first stables. Curiosity carries me through the still open doors to walk past the stalls in the hopes that, perhaps … yes, there.

The white turns his head to watch my approach, ears pricked forward, his face faintly luminescent in the half-light.

"Well, it's about time," he murmurs as I reach him. "What do you find so amusing?"

"Did you miss me?"

"No," he replies immediately. If he were human he might have blushed. "Do you realize I've been locked in this stall since we arrived?"

"They didn't take you out to the practice ring?"

He snorts in disgust. "They tried to saddle me. Can you imagine? A hostler riding a true Horse? Unheard of!"

"I suppose you didn't let them, then?"

"Of course not," he snaps. "Would you?"

I blink, try to imagine myself being taken as a beast of burden. "I don't know," I say, wondering if I have always been that, if I have only just now escaped it. He glares at me, and I say quickly, "I hope not."

"Well then." He looks at me expectantly. I look back. "Let me out!"

"I'll have to put a halter on you, for form's sake."

He acquiesces and with a minimum amount of fumbling with tack on my part we walk out to the ring together. As I unbuckle the halter, the ring's gate closed and latched behind us, I ask, "What's your name?"

He shakes his head free and then pauses, dark eyes meeting mine, "Falada." He takes off, running at breakneck speed around the edge of the ring. I climb up to the top of the fence and sit there to wait.

It is not even a quarter of an hour before a hostler comes sprinting out of the stable. He glances around, spots the halter hanging over the gate, and the next moment has climbed into the ring with it in hand. I sigh and jump down again, watching as the hostler tries to corner the white. Falada will have none of it, prancing away, then breaking into a canter and swerving around the poor man.

"Falada!" He comes to me at once, the hostler watching grimly. I turn to him with a forced smile and hold out my hand for the halter. He crosses the sand with a few long strides, studying me carefully as he hands it to me. He is as old as the hostler woman in my stable, tall and sinewy. He watches me as I reach towards Falada with the halter, and I hope I have not angered him as I did Sarkor. Falada cooperatively lowers his head to me, and a moment later I hand the hostler the lead. Falada promptly plants his feet apart and refuses to move.

"Falada," I say again, gently, and with one hand on his crest I reach out and touch the hostler's shoulder. The man makes no move. "For God's sake, don't be an ass; go with this man." Falada snorts and glares at me, but when the hostler tries to lead him out of the ring again, he follows.

In the stables, the hostler ties the lead to a ring and leaves, returning with a box of brushes and hoof picks. Recognizing disaster when I see it, I take the box from the man, gesturing to Falada and then myself: I will care for him. The hostler looks at me again and I wonder what he has heard about me, what the rumors say of the princess's cast-off companion. His gaze is measuring, knowing. He steps back, tilting his head. He will watch me work.

Only after I have vigorously brushed out clouds of white hair and picked out all of Falada's hooves does the hostler seem satisfied that I know what I'm doing. I am grateful to Redna for humoring me many an afternoon, teaching me how to help her with Fleet Wind, and I murmur a soft prayer for her as I work. Still, the hostler relaxes only once Falada is back inside his stall, the halter hanging from the hook by his door.

I turn to him before he can leave, pointing to myself. "Thoreena."

"Thorné," he echoes, the last part blending away so that it sounds to me almost as if he too has said, 'thorn.' He introduces himself as Joa, and with a nod departs.

"A fine fellow, that Joa," Falada mutters darkly.

Chuckling, I turn back to him. "I'll try to take you with me to watch the geese tomorrow. Would you like that?"

"It will be good to be out on the plains again."

"All right." I turn to leave.

"Before you go, princess, there's something you might want to consider."

I glance at him quizzically. "What's that?"

"Won't your mother notice if you don't write to her, or if, when you do, your script had changed?"

"She might," I concede, the quiet of my day quickly slipping away. My mother's voice, directing me to write often, echoes in my ears.

"You'd better figure out what to do then, hadn't you?" The white watches me intently. I shrug. "Hadn't you?"

"Yes," I sigh. "I will."

"When?"

"Tonight ... I'll go up to the palace and talk to—her."

"You'll tell me about it in the morning."

"Yes," I agree without enthusiasm and turn to the door.

The walk to the palace takes me half an hour. I see no one but a few drunkards; I hurry past, head bent, and though one or two call out, no one follows after me. Here and there an inn door stands open, light pouring out with the sound of voices.

The palace guards give me only a passing glance before waving me on through the gates. The Hall's doors stand open, and as I ascend the steps I see that the palace still feasts. Great tables are set out across the Hall, stretching down the corridors created by the rows of pillars. The floor shines, for there are neither rushes nor dogs here. Instead, tiled mosaics spread across the floor: flowers and circles and vines, much more intricate than the courtyard I had seen. Far away, across the Hall, I can make out a dais at which the royal family and highest nobles sit. The lofty ceiling is lost in dim shadows.

A doorman steps forward and clears his throat as I stand gaping the in doorway. I drag my eyes away from the Hall. He speaks, but the words are in Menay and I can only shake my head in frustration.

"I am Lady Thoreena," I say carefully in Menay. At least I have this much. "I must see the Princess Alyrra." His brow creases as he deciphers what must, no doubt, be an atrocious accent, but then he nods, waving over a page. I follow the boy out of the Hall, through hallway after hallway, coming finally to a sweeping marble staircase that takes us up to a carpeted hallway of deep red, lit by small lamps set in carved niches along the wall. The woodwork rising from the floor, the mosaic walls, the carved ceilings here are like nothing I have seen before.

The sitting room the page shows me into is lavishly decorated. The floor is spread with a silk carpet depicting more flowers and vines as well as songbirds hiding in the greenery. A chandelier hangs from the ceiling, fully lit, light shimmering through the hanging crystals. Low couches line the wall, and a series of ornate tables no higher than the couches are arranged at intervals, no doubt to bring refreshments easily to hand. There are two latticed windows in the far wall, the shutters drawn closed, and a fireplace to one side, empty and shielded from sight by a three-paneled painting of storks in flight. A large, many-sided table with an inset silver tray, exquisitely engraved, draws the eye to the center of the room and the crystal vase with its bouquet of flowers set upon it.

I stand gazing at the room as the page calls a greeting, wondering if I should feel regret. I feel a twinge of envy—how different is this room from my own in the stable! But I would not want to be princess.

A woman answers his call, entering from a connecting room. She looks like a lady of some import herself, but she is holding a folded tunic in her hand. A lady-in-waiting or attendant of some sort, I wonder? The page tells her who I am as well as, I believe, that I seek an audience with the princess. She considers me shrewdly, dismisses the page, and leads me across the room towards the window. A small chair has been set in the far corner, half-hidden behind a folding silk screen of mountains and snow. I thank her, sinking into the chair. She shrugs one shoulder and leaves, her expression a mix of contempt and amusement, and returns to her duties. I lean back, grateful. At least this way I have the chance to organize my thoughts without Valka present.

Some time later, I hear voices from the hallway, muffled by the door but vaguely recognizable. Then the door opens and closes, and Valka snaps, "Mina! Zaria! Where are you both?"

My mouth drops open in surprise. Surely her attendants are higher born than common maids. I would have expected some semblance of respect for them from Valka. They hurry into the room murmuring apologies, the words foreign but the sound familiar. Valka snaps at them again, her voice growing weaker as she moves into the other room. Still, I can hear her railing against the uselessness of attendants who hardly know her language.

Time passes gently, marred only by Valka's grumping at her attendants. I close my eyes and think of the forests, the dell, my old friend the Wind. Eventually, the attendants emerge once more, closing the door softly behind them. I listen to their fluid voices, the whisper of their skirts as they walk. I wonder if they have forgotten me, but then the woman who had shown me my chair appears before me. She smiles as she gestures for me to go through to the next room. It is a cool, mocking smile, and the other woman hides a laugh behind her hand. They must not like Valka.

I thank them both, taking the lamp they offer me. They leave without another word, but I hear their muffled laughter as the door closes. The second room is another sitting room, this one smaller, simpler, and yet even more elegant. The third is Valka's bedchamber.

I set the lamp down on a carved stand beside the low divan that serves as a bed. She snores softly. It is strange to see myself lying there among the pillows and silken sheets; in sleep, the emotions of the day have fallen from my features so that I look not so much arrogant or petulant as young.

"Princess," I whisper to myself, and Valka opens her eyes.

She well near flies out of bed, face white. She faces me across the divan, one hand clutching her neck, her chest heaving. Brown hair, straight as always, falls over thin arms poking out of the sleeveless nightgown. My face is filling out, I note dispassionately.

"I'll scream! Don't you come near me!" she cries.

I almost laugh at that. "I've only come to talk to you. After all, I've no interest in being hung for a traitor."

Her eyes flash. "I shall have you thrown out of the city. You forget that if it weren't for me you would have nothing now."

Does she think I have a great deal with my sleeping mat and stool? I meet her glare, trying not to rise to her bait. "Only a fool would send me away."

"You insolent witch!"

"You need me for my knowledge," I snap, my patience at an end.

She looks momentarily taken aback. "Oh?"

"I promised to write to my mother upon my arrival. She will wonder if she receives no word."

"If that's all, I'll write her in the morning. I don't need *you* for that."

"You may have my body but you do not have my script," I point out, seething.

Valka absorbs this without a hitch. "Then you shall write what I tell you, or I shall have you thrown out."

"I shall write what I wish, or not write at all."

We glare at each other over the divan. Valka is the first to look away. "How do I know you won't betray me?" she asks sullenly.

"You'll have the reading of every letter I write," I say, as if offering a compromise.

"Every letter?"

"I will have to write regularly. My mother is concerned with the alliance this marriage is to make."

"What is your price?" Valka asks tightly. I smile: like my brother, she gives little of her own and so expects avarice of others. It never occurred to her that I might not demand a payment.

"Only this: that you will leave me alone; and if I should ever need anything, you will provide me with it."

A smile lights Valka's face—it is frightening to me to see those features burning with greed and happiness. Her words are laughably conservative in comparison. "I suppose I can do that."

She walks to a writing table and gathers up a sheaf of papers for me. "You are content to be a servant, then? You are more the fool than I thought."

I ignore her words. "How will I get the letter to you?"

"I will send a page."

"It will be ready in the morning." I pause in the doorway. "And Valka? If you betray the prince to the Lady, I will kill you, cost me what it may."

11

In the morning, I take a few minutes to go through my—or rather, Valka's—trunks. They had been delivered the day before while I was out with the flock, but I hadn't wanted to look at them after meeting Valka. The first trunk contains the clothes and belongings Valka brought with her, including a small box of jewelry; the second contains her trousseau. I sit back on my heels, my single-candle lantern throwing a dim light on the contents. Daerilin truly did not wish to see Valka again. She had been sent here, to Menaiya, to marry where she might and be forgotten. I remember my mother's words and a sadness wells up inside of me for the future Valka had been faced with. I almost pity her.

I look through her belongings hesitantly for I do not want to take anything of hers, but my old slippers, caked in goose dung and sagging at the seams, will hardly last another day. And gloves for my hands, rubbed raw by the shoveling and raking, would be wonderful. Thankfully, I find a pair of riding boots that fit perfectly. The gloves are all silk and utterly useless.

As promised, a page knocks at my door a few moments later. He is dressed in a different version of the hostlers' outfit: where they sport olive tunics and tan trousers, with a dark green sash at the waist, he is all blues and white. When I open the door, he bobs his head and says, "Letter." I have folded the letter into an empty sheet of paper and closed it with a few drops of wax; Valka will be able to read it before sealing it with the royal crest. The page departs with a quick bow.

Once the goose barn is done, I seek out Joa. It takes a few broken phrases and plenty of gesturing before he understands me, for I have no wish to be mistaken for a thief. Eventually, he assents and I lead Falada away by his halter. Once through the city gates, I unbuckle the thing and he takes off, racing down the road and then trotting sedately back to walk with me.

"Feeling a little cooped up, were you?"

"Of all human inventions, stalls are by far the worst," Falada informs me, humor tingeing his words. I grin and shrug noncommittally.

"Did you meet with that Valka woman?"

"We came to an agreement." I am suddenly loathe to tell him more.

"Yes?" he prods.

"I'll write letters home for her. In return, she'll leave me alone."

Falada jerks to a stop. "That's all?"

"I did tell her I'd kill her if she betrayed the prince," I admit, continuing down the road. After a moment, Falada follows.

"Would you?"

"No. I don't know that I could kill anyone. But I thought the threat would make her think twice."

He makes a slight sound of consideration—a hmm of horsely sorts—but lets my words pass. "Do you think this sorceress is after the prince as well?" he asks instead. I nod, feeling a tightness begin around my neck.

"Shouldn't you warn him?"

"I'm sure he knows."

"Are you? How?"

"I think she wanted me to betray him," I reply slowly, one hand massaging my throat. "She saw that I wouldn't, so she—" My breath stops in my throat with a jerk. I grab a handful of Falada's mane as pain slices through my neck. The world sways around me. I close my eyes, clinging desperately to Falada. And then the chain loosens. I take a long, faltering breath, then another. Falada stands stone still beside me. I force myself to step away from him, smoothing down his mane with shaking fingers.

"My apologies," I rasp.

"Let's keep walking," he murmurs. "If you are able." I shuffle along beside him. I see the reason for Falada's concern a moment later: a wagon approaches. The driver—a farmer with a load of ripe melons—watches us intently as we pass. We must make an odd picture: a small, foreign woman carrying a halter, accompanied by a white stallion wearing not a single piece of tack. The crunch of gravel beneath wagon wheels steadily dies away, to be replaced by the honking of the geese.

"You will have to tell me how the prince is involved," Falada murmurs as we draw near the pasture. "Perhaps tonight."

"We'll see," I say. I doubt he will think much of me once he knows.

The day passes in the same quiet rhythm of the day before. Falada grazes nearby. Corbé watches us darkly. I can almost feel his anger in the air. Even Falada, as he pauses next to me in the early afternoon, softly asks, "Your fellow goose boy doesn't always look that black, does he?"

"No." I reach up to scratch Falada behind his ears. "I don't quite understand him."

"Jealousy," Falada says and steps away, leaving me to worry at that one word for the rest of the day.

Falada helps drive the geese back to the barn, prancing along near me, chasing feathery rebels back to the flock. He seems to take a sheepish pleasure in enjoying such work—as if he would have thought it beneath him to drive geese and is somewhat embarrassed to find that he enjoys it.

I rub him down and brush out the grasses caught in his tail when we reach the stable. Falada waits patiently, eyeing the serving of oats and grains awaiting him in his stall.

"You can't possibly be hungry; you've been eating all day!" I say as he goes straight to his food.

He throws me an amused glance. "Think of it as dessert," he suggests.

In the common room, I tear into my own dinner in a way that would have made Mother purse her lips and glare icily at me. My meal is a steaming bowl of vegetable stew seasoned with spices I have no name for, served up with flatbread. I doubt any meal has ever tasted half so delicious as this. The other hostlers glance at me, grinning, and bend over their bowls as well.

When I am finished, I push my bowl back, ready to leave. The older hostler woman reaches out and sets a twig with leaves before me. I glance from it to her; she points to herself, saying her name slowly. I pick up the twig, study the leaves, and feel a smile break across my face: her name is Laurel. When I look up, the second woman presents me with a dried violet, perhaps got from an apothecary's shop. She is young and pretty, a few years older than me, her eyes bright and merry. Her brothers grin and hold up their names—the youngest a rowan branch, the second the leaves of an ash tree, and the eldest two oak leaves. They teach me their names in Menay, and I laughingly repeat them, committing them to memory: Laurel, Violet, Rowan, Ash and Oak. I carry the warmth of their kindness with me to bed and wake in the morning still smiling.

Falada asks me about the prince again on the way to the pasture. It isn't until he asks if I am afraid to tell him that I finally do give him the gist of what happened during Kestrin's visit to my room. With a harrumph, Falada tells me I am a fool.

"You should have told me before," he says, stopping to glare at me.

"What difference does it make?" I ask, pretending nonchalance.

Falada sputters. "Your prince is a sorcerer! Has that occurred to you? Your prince, and no doubt the king as well. There is no other way Kestrin could have reached you." He shakes his head. "They must have fallen out with this sorceress and she is looking for revenge."

I flush. Of course I'd known that. "I did say that it was the prince she wanted, not me."

"Excellent thinking," Falada says with derision.

I flinch but forge on. "Since the prince is a sorcerer, and knows quite well who is after him, I'm sure he can take care of himself. As long as I can keep—the princess in check." I come to an abrupt end, remembering how the prince had faced the Lady.

Falada merely looks at me.

"Alyrra, why do you think the king and his son chose you?"

I shrug. I had intervened to help him against the Lady, certainly, but the prince could not have foreseen that; that encounter had come after the betrothal was announced.

"What makes you a better choice than a princess from a richer nation, a princess raised to be a queen? One who could never learn to be a goose girl?"

"Thank you," I say, glaring at him. "No, I don't know why they wanted a clumsy, incoherent princess from a tin-cup kingdom like ours. Even Mother couldn't figure it out."

"Then how did you convince them you were the right person?"

"They were already convinced when they came."

"In that case, they could have sealed the betrothal by letter. They wanted to meet you. Or at least, the king did, and I have no doubt that he told the prince what he thought of you."

"Just because the prince dabbles in magic doesn't mean his father does too." I wipe my palms on my skirts; they are sweaty despite the cool day. "Does it?"

"You don't have any sense of magic, do you?" Falada asks. "Transporting oneself to another kingdom—which is to say across a mountain range as well as over plains and forests—is no easy task. To do it with enough precision to arrive in a particular person's bedroom, when you have neither met the person nor seen the room, requires mastery."

"And he could not have become a master without the king's knowledge," I finish.

"The king's knowledge, yes," Falada agrees, "but also his help: in training, in finding tutors, in keeping it secret. Mastery at such a young age as his is unusual. He would have had to devote much time and energy to it."

"Why do you think it's a secret? Wouldn't the court know—and the—the Council of Mages?" I stumble, trying to dredge up what memories I have of the regulation of magic in Menaiya. "And certainly then everyone would know." Then again, I had never guessed at my own mother's witchery.

"I have never heard magic mentioned in relation to the royal family, not before we arrived and certainly not since. Why they would want it secret is easy enough to guess: the Council of Mages can't control what they don't know about. It's a question of power."

"You understand Menay?" I ask in surprise.

"Of course," Falada says, not to be deterred. "But consider this, Alyrra: you have a family of sorcerers with a great and potent enemy; they must have seen something in you to make them choose you. What did you do?"

"I exchanged less than ten sentences with the king up until the betrothal. I was put under guard for my own protection in my own home. And I generally stayed out of the way."

Falada considers this for a moment. "You showed yourself to be without pretensions, requiring protection ..."

"And vulnerable and biddable," I finish. We are nearing the flock now, having already left the road.

"Perhaps," Falada muses. "Perhaps they were looking for someone whom they could trust, someone who would accept their authority and be grateful for their continued protection."

"Maybe they wanted a princess whom no one would miss if she were to get killed," I say bitterly.

Falada does not respond immediately. When he does, it is to ask, "What would you have given to be valued and protected?"

I pause, staring at the ground. I wish that I could lie to him. "A lot," I say roughly.

"Your loyalty?" I don't look up, but I know he is right. Perhaps Falada can see the truth of it written on my face, for he says gently, "Then there's only one question left, isn't there?"

"What's that?"

"Can they trust you?"

12

A quick, hard knock sounds on my chamber door. I open it to find the soldiers Matsin and Finnar standing in the shadowy hall. Matsin makes a cursory bow and says, "Lady Thorné will come with me."

A small carriage awaits us next to the practice ring; a single hostler passes us as we walk to it, for with nightfall the stables have quieted. Matsin hands me in and shuts the door, and he and Finnar climb up behind the carriage box. The other two soldiers in their quad sit up with the driver. With the crack of a whip, the carriage turns out, rattling up West Road towards the palace. I wonder if the king intends to question me again, and if so, why he did not send a page to fetch me that I might feel more at his mercy. Perhaps the carriage is meant to remind me of what I have lost, or perhaps the soldiers are meant to intimidate me.

It is not the king that the quad takes me to, however, conducting me down quiet hallways. When Matsin opens the door to a small evening room, nodding for me to enter, I find it is the prince instead.

I curtsy at once, keeping my head bent to hide my confusion. What would Kestrin want with me, thinking me nothing more than Valka's cast-off companion? Behind me, Matsin closes the door, leaving us alone. The room is well lit, showing two low arm chairs tilted towards each other before a small fire, the floor spread with a plush, knotted carpet, and a writing table and chair standing against the wall.

"Rise," the prince says, his voice already familiar to me. I straighten, raising my gaze to meet his. He is exactly as I remember him, dark eyes glinting in the lamplight. Only his face, as serious as it was that night in my room, seems more drawn and weary than before. His expression as he considers me is guarded.

"I apologize for bringing you here in such an abrupt fashion. I am afraid there are few here who speak your language. I hope you have taken no offense." His voice is gentle, even sweet, and utterly lacking real emotion.

"No, Your Highness," I reply on cue. Yet I remember hearing Matsin speak my language to my own escort on our journey to the border. He had spoken well enough; he might have offered an explanation tonight had he been told to.

"I am glad," Kestrin says, stepping toward me. "I have a small favor to ask: I need a letter written to your queen. While I pride myself on speaking your language, I have not yet mastered its written form. You will help me?" Though the words are phrased as a question, the authority in his voice will not be belied.

"Of course, Your Highness." My heart beats painfully loud in my ears. What could he possibly want from my mother that Valka couldn't ask for herself?

He gestures to the writing table. "I will dictate the words," he explains as I sit down. He takes up a station at the corner of the table, watching as I ready myself for the task.

Kestrin dictates a simple formal letter, beginning with the usual "To Her Majesty the Queen," proceeding through to "the delivery of a particular cloak, gift from His Majesty the King of Menaiya, which Her Highness left behind," and ending with, "sincere gratitude." By the time I am done my palms are sweaty, my stomach knotted. And all the while he has watched me as I wrote.

I lay down the quill and hand the letter to the prince. He takes it from me and then, to my surprise, he moves to the small table between the two chairs and picks up another paper. He stands, his back towards me, studying the papers. I rise and wipe my palms on my skirts. I cannot see what the other paper is, nor can I imagine what it might be.

"Your Highness," I finally venture, throat dry. He turns to look at me. "May I return to my room?"

He lowers the papers. "Your letter has raised some interesting questions for me."

"Your Highness?" I pray he does not hear the slight wavering of my voice. His story is beginning to unravel in my mind—there must surely be court scribes, scribes that accompanied the king and helped to prepare the betrothal papers, scribes that could easily have written such a note to my mother. Why did he not ask them?

"Come sit with me." He takes one of the chairs, the papers still in his hand. I move with leaden feet to the other.

"You seem to have displeased the Princess Alyrra during your journey," the Prince observes. I dip my head in assent: it certainly seems so. "Tell me then, how did you send Alyrra a letter for her mother—or rather, how did you write a letter from her to her mother?"

"Your Highness?" My words are hardly more than a whisper, and as I meet his gaze he smiles, but there is nothing good in that smile.

"Perhaps you have forgotten. I traced a copy to be sure you would not. Listen:

"'Dear Mother:

It has been two full days since we arrived in Tarinon. I hope you will forgive my tardiness in beginning this letter, but I have been kept very busy. As I am sure Lieutenant Balin gave you a favorable report of my well-being at the time that he left, I hope you have not worried.

We were met at the Border by two of the king's lords, Filadon and Melkior by name—'

"Shall I go on? Or is it starting to sound more familiar now?" the prince asks amiably.

"It is familiar," I say hoarsely.

"Why is that?"

I shake my head; I can think of no explanation but the truth, and that I cannot tell him even if I wished to.

He drops the letter on the table between us. "I do not believe Alyrra cares for you enough, or trusts you sufficiently, to have you write a letter for her. Certainly she would not request a letter of such an intimate nature. How then did you come to write this?"

I sit silently, my gaze now trained on my hands. They are clasped just so on my lap, the fingers of one hand cradling the other.

"And how came you to sign it for her?" His voice is rich and low, and laden with distrust. "You have the exact same signature as the princess; I compared yours to her signature on the betrothal papers and could hardly note a difference."

Still, I cannot look at him. I study the way shadows gather in the hollow of my palms, the contours of my hands. I have no answer for him.

"Look at me." My eyes snap to his, for his voice is that of my brother's. But he does not raise his hand, does not lean forward to reach me. Instead he speaks, his voice as cold and hard as iron. "How do you write her script and sign her name?"

I study his features—the high cheekbones, the sable hair, the tightness around his eyes, his lips. Whatever small trickeries he may use now, I still owe him something for the trust I have betrayed in accepting the life of a goose girl. By allowing Valka to take my place, I have offered him the blade of a dagger.

But when I open my mouth, different words slip out. "Let me go."

Kestrin arches an eyebrow, but I see something in his eyes shift. *Pity?* "My father offered you a chance to return to your home," he says, willfully misunderstanding me.

68

I shake my head, making myself answer. "There is nothing for me there. My—family would be upset if I returned." At least my voice is stronger now.

"Lord Daerilin doted upon his daughter."

For a moment I am at a loss, and then I almost laugh. "At court. Every person is different alone with their family." It is a truth I have long known; Valka's trousseau stands witness to Daerilin's rejection of her. "He has wished to be rid of me for years, since I was sent home from the Hall in disgrace."

Kestrin leans back in his chair, thinking, his arms crossed over his chest. In the lamplight he cuts a dark and imposing figure.

"Tell me how you wrote that letter," Kestrin says again. The words settle around me. I know he will not let me leave until he is satisfied with my answer. Yet I would not lie to him. There is a way, I think, to explain the letter without telling the full truth. He meets my gaze, waiting, and into the silence I begin to speak.

"There was a time, Your Highness, when you might have considered the princess and I inseparable. We grew up together, took our lessons together. We learned to write similarly, and I often wrote letters for Her Highness, only bothering to show them to her before sending them. I learned her signature to simplify matters.

"Despite our disagreements before and during the journey, I still owed her a favor. I agreed to write the letter for her, since she felt unable to write it herself." For the space of a breath, I think he believes me.

"You are lying." My heart jumps a beat. He continues, "The princess had few friends growing up. She never had a long-time friend as you claim to be."

His words are accurate—but they do not sound like Valka's. She was never lonely. Friends and family had always surrounded her—both at the Hall and her own home. No doubt that is the truth she would have spoken of.

"Did she tell you that?" I ask.

"No," he admits.

"Then how do you know?"

"I have my sources," he responds enigmatically. The words make me want to laugh, for they remind me of children keeping secrets from each other: I know something you don't.

"Perhaps your sources erred," I suggest, half-amused.

He looks at me sharply. "They could not have."

"Your Highness, you have seen enough of the world to know that there is never only one truth, one side of a story. Perhaps your sources are true; I do not doubt they faithfully reported what they understood. But perhaps I am also telling you some part of the truth. To say that your sources lied, or that I do now, is to claim knowledge of the unknown.

"The princess and I spent our childhood together at the Hall. Your sources can verify that. We shared our tutor. How your sources have interpreted our friendship beyond that I cannot guess, but you must remember it is only their interpretation. That we had a disagreement no one will deny; perhaps you will understand that we have now made a certain peace between ourselves."

"After she banished you to a life of hard labor."

I wince and then catch myself. Kestrin gives me a sad smile. "There is another thing I do not understand," he says.

I wait.

"Why did you use her script just now?"

For a long moment I can only stare, like a hare watching the falcon's descent. Then I stammer, "I did not think."

He turns his gaze away, quiet. "Be more careful in the future, lady," he finally warns me. "I doubt the princess will like how lightly you use her script."

I feel myself hunch down, afraid suddenly that he might tell Valka himself. Afraid that he will ask other questions of me, keep asking until I have tied my story in knots.

"Go," he says with a wave of his hand. "My quad will see you home."

I leave before he changes his mind.

The following morning, I tell Falada about my interview with Kestrin. His response is just what I expect.

"You told him you were her closest friend? Are you mad?"

"It was the closest I could get to the truth." I pause to brush a piece of straw from my skirts, glancing down West Road.

"The truth! You call that truth?"

"Until the journey, the princess and I were inseparable," I point out. "I certainly wrote everything for her and signed her name. And Valka and I shared our tutors, though she was more my brother's friend than mine."

"Sometimes," Falada tells me, "half a truth does more damage than any lie."

"I didn't want to lie, Falada, and I had to say something. What else could I tell him?"

"That you could not speak of it—that if he wanted an answer he should ask that woman."

"He wouldn't have let me be. I had to tell him something." I hesitate, then admit, "And I owe it to him to make him suspicious of the two of us. If he doubts my story even a little, he will doubt her too."

Falada shakes his head. "If you want to help him, then regain your position."

"Enough," I say, throwing up my hands.

"What good will it do him to learn that you and Valka were hardly friends—which he will, once he looks into the matter. He'll think less of you, not her."

Kestrin hadn't believed all my story, but I'm not sure that he held that against me. He had let me go. "He will question both of us," I say. "So long as he questions her, I don't mind what he thinks of me. Please, Falada, let it be."

Falada's hooves kick up puffs of dust that hang in the still morning air. Finally, as we near the flock, he asks, "What will you do about the cloak?"

"Hide it. I put it at the bottom of Valka's trunk last night. I'll find somewhere safer for it later. Mother will write back saying she doesn't have it, that I wore it when I left. Valka will have to say she lost it and that will be that."

"It would be better if you got it to her somehow," Falada says worriedly.

"How? She'll never admit that she overlooked it or accidentally misplaced it. The only other way is to send it to her, and I can't replicate a courier from my mother."

"Then get rid of it. Don't keep it," Falada urges me. "If anyone finds it, you'll have a much harder time explaining yourself than you did yesterday."

"I know." I chew my lip. "I can't sell it; people will remember me too well. I can't return it to her. I'll have to figure out something else."

"Yes," Falada agrees, and then we are too close to Corbé to speak.

With each passing day, I learn a little more of Menaiya: that the quads stationed at the city gates never grow lax, continuously drilling and practicing; that the bakers' boys bring their goods out into the street, crying their wares as they walk beneath buildings; that the children are often playing, but their clothes are ragged and they seldom wear shoes. From Laurel and Violet, I learn the words of our meals: bread, porridge, nutmeg, water. From Joa, who sometimes meets me when I bring Falada in, I learn to speak of the stables: harness, lead rope, saddle. I practice them during the day as I watch the geese, Falada murmuring corrections and helping me with phrases I do not know how to ask for.

The hostlers listen to me patiently when I do ask, pointing to different objects, and they speak carefully that I might hear each inflection, each accent. I am surprised at the time they take, even Ash and Oak, listening to me, making me repeat a word until I have it right. How can it benefit them to help me, to offer in their own carefully distant way some form of friendship and comfort? For I know that my story must have been publicly canvassed, passed around the dinner table until it grew stale with the telling.

"They like you," Falada notes one evening after Joa has stopped by.

I pause, currycomb in hand. "Why would they?"

"Same reason I do." I have begun to recognize certain expressions in his eyes, the way they settle around his mouth—now I see humor twinkling from his eye.

"They see me as the last hope for humanity?" I quip, sliding the comb through his coat.

He gives a soft huff, a horse laugh, and returns, "Perhaps not that. But you are quiet and easy to get along with, and you do not shirk your duties."

"Being a goose girl is not all that rigorous."

"You carry it off with great aplomb. Not every high-born lady would sing ballads while raking goose dung."

"Hmm." I return the currycomb to the bucket of brushes, bending to hide my blush. It had not occurred to me that anyone would hear my singing, or that it might be discussed to the point that Falada should hear of it in the stables. It had seemed only natural, after a few days, to sing as I worked. I would never make a minstrel—Valka's voice is too uncertain for that—but I still enjoy a short ballad by myself. My own voice, which I remember now as faintly as an echo, was too husky for most songs. So, either way, it is a good thing I was not born to a musical profession.

After a moment or two of rooting around in the bucket, I come up with a hoof pick. Falada cooperatively lifts a hoof, and I start working the day's rocks and muck out.

"I want to walk around the city," I tell him. "At home there was only the village below the Hall. I can't imagine what such a number of people would find to do in one place. Would you like to come with me?" I set his hoof down and straighten, stretching my back. "I'm not sure I want to go alone."

"Certainly," Falada says.

I kneel, reaching for the next hoof. "Tomorrow?"

"I don't believe I have any other pressing engagements," he says wryly. I rest my head against his leg and laugh.

We start up West Road towards the palace, but I haven't much interest in walking the same—the only—road I know, and strike off on a side road almost at once. To my surprise, the streets are full of life despite the nearing dusk: children shout and chase each other, women meet in doorways and on corners, men shoulder their way into taverns. The alleys we follow break off the main road to twist and turn between ancient stone and brick buildings. Wide doorways glowing with lantern light invite customers into shops selling everything from baskets to knives to cloth.

"It's so strange," I murmur to Falada as the alley we follow takes a sharp left turn, proceeds down a set of wide, cobbled stairs, and then turns right before intersecting with another alley. "I always thought of roads as straight. Or curved. But not," I wave my hand as the alley appears to take another turn leading us back in the direction we came, "not like this."

Thankfully, between Falada's memory and mine, we find our way back out again before darkness descends. Just off West Road, tucked behind a building and facing into a narrow alley, I find what I had not realized I was seeking: a temple. It is a quaint thing, no larger than my room in the stables. A simple arch in the wall acts as a doorway, with a mat beside it for worshippers to leave their shoes. Best of all, it is barely a five minute walk from the stables. I follow Falada home, my steps light.

That evening, tired from the long walk, I linger in the stable common room after dinner, and discover that my fellow hostlers spend the evenings together as well. They pull out the boys' sleeping mats—normally rolled and stored in a cabinet—throw out a few cushions, and settle on the floor. Violet calls me over to sit beside her as I hesitate by the table, putting a saddle blanket with an unraveling hem in my hands for repair. The others all settle with their own small tasks, and take up their conversation once more.

So, over the polishing and repairing of tack, I listen to the discussion of each day's events, the newest rumors, the happenings in the city and the court. Every night as I lie in my room, I think through what I have heard, and day by day, night by night, I begin to understand more, begin to piece together Menay. The words I do not understand I commit to memory and ask Falada about as we walk to and from the pasture; he translates most of them easily, teaching me their use and helping me to understand the basic rules of Menaiyan grammar.

In addition to language, I learn what kind of people I live with. Oak, of all of the hostlers, is the shyest, sitting in the furthest corner of the room bent over his work and only offering occasional tidbits to the conversation, his deep voice booming up from the darkness. Ash, tall and lithe to his elder brother's barrel-chest, does everything with quick, sure strokes; his laughter flashes through the room, his words, in all matters, are given at once and affirmed continually thereafter. Rowan is the youngest of the brothers, still in his final growth, his elbows sharp and likely to knock against things, his crow's nest hair throwing a tangle of shadows over his earnest face.

In comparison, Violet shines as a jewel in their care, her gentle brown eyes clear and untroubled, glowing with a light that softens her features and is reflected in the way her hands flicker across her skirt when she is upset, in the way a gentle touch and soft word to a troubled mare will soothe away anxiety. Laurel, I learn, is also a relation of sorts: their aunt by a degree or two of separation. She watches over them as a mother eagle over her nestlings. She rarely flexes her wings, a sharp look enough to quell Ash's protestations, or Oak's hesitant suggestion of an idea she disapproves.

They are good people, I think, as I listen to them night after night. Not unlike Redna and Jilna, and nothing at all like my family, nor anyone I have met in the palace here. As the days pass, I find myself more and more grateful for their welcome, for a place safe from the court.

Valka sends for me when my mother's response arrives. I am impressed by the change she has wrought: her hair shines in the lamplight, a deeper, more lustrous brown than I remember, her skin cream and rose in contrast.

Her figure has begun to fill out, developing curves I never had the appetite to sustain. She has begun to look the part of princess.

"Here," she says, thrusting the letter at me once her attendants have retreated to the outer room. I read it over with interest. It is short but surprisingly kind in tone:

'Alyrra,

I am pleased to hear you are settling in. You must establish yourself well. Your behavior now will decide how your family will treat you in the future. I always considered you rather weak and stupid in politics, but perhaps you will prove me wrong.

I will expect another letter from you shortly. Describe your acquaintances as well as you can; I shall advise you as I am able. For now, keep your relations with Melkior and Filadon; do not offend but do not strive to please.

'Mother'

When I look up from the letter, Valka rests her hands on her hips as if I were a naughty child. "When will you have the reply ready?"

I raise my eyebrows in exaggerated surprise. "How can I? I have no idea what you've been doing. You'll have to tell me yourself."

Valka purses her lips, eyes narrowed. "All right."

I seat myself at her writing table, straightening the papers there. "We'll start with Filadon and Melkior," I tell her as I dip the quill. "What have you seen of them this past month?"

It seems that both the lords have distanced themselves, Filadon receding to a bowing acquaintance while Melkior might pause to greet her before moving on. Their replacements I do not like the sound of: younger men and women who dance attendance upon her. The ladies join her most mornings to embroider (the princess is making a tunic for her betrothed), but from Valka's description they are all gossipmongers vying with each other for her favor. She has accordingly used them to gather information on each person she meets, though most of it I distrust. How can one trust informants who care only for their own good graces? Surely they would not hesitate to blacken a rival's reputation. But Valka seems oblivious to such possibilities, happily describing each of her companions as I listen and then laboriously write out the letter in my own words but without my perspective. It is a strange thing. I feel slightly ill by the end of her tale.

I make Valka seal the papers, her crest pressed into the wax. I pray the prince cannot replicate the seal and so will not read the letter. It has not occurred to Valka to fear for its security; she leaves it on the table and retires to her room without a second glance. She makes no provision for the possibility that her attendants may report on her to others, or that her belongings may not be inviolate. For the insidious politician she is showing herself to be, she is surprisingly naïve when it comes to this. Perhaps my mother's letter to her was more applicable than might at first appear.

The following morning I find a thin carpet of ice over the ground. The trees at home would be nearly bare now, and the frost would have traced out the fine veins of the leaves, coating the pine needles with fairy dust. I know these things and yet I cannot quite remember the sight of the forest from the road, the trees of my little dell.

As I leave the goose barn, my cleaning done, I hear voices from the far side of the barn. I turn towards them, confused, for a wall runs between the king's buildings and rest of the city. Only a narrow disused alley lies between the barn and the wall. I creep closer, listening curiously to the quick patter of conversation—I can hear a man's voice clearly, and a second voice, quieter, responding, but they are low enough that I cannot make out the words. I hesitate at the corner, peek around uncertainly.

Violet stands deep in conversation with a young man. A single lock has escaped her braid and she plays with it absently as she speaks. The man listens to her intently, his head tilted and his eyes trained on the ground. Like the other hostlers, his hair is cut short, falling in a fringe by his chin, setting off the sharpness of his jaw, the fine line of his nose. He does not wear the hostlers' uniform though, but his own clothes. When he answers her his words are measured, as steady and sure as a farm horse.

Violet makes a quick retort, the corner of her mouth dipping down in a mock frown. The man laughs, glancing at her sideways, and his whole being lightens. She looks up at him, eyes shining, her voice a question. I can see the answer in his eyes as he looks at her. I pull back, leaning against the wall, my eyes pressed shut. I can still hear the tone of their conversation: it is sweet and full, skipping ahead when Violet speaks, and dipping down to rest when the man does.

I walk away from them, my feet heavy, my boots scuffing the earth. I wish that I could watch them longer, could listen to the wonder that is their conversation—but it is not right. They sought the passage behind the goose barn for privacy, not to share their time with me. I swing open Falada's door, mutely falling into step with him. What would it be like to speak to a man like that? To have him look at me so? I had never hoped for it before, knowing that my marriage would be a political match. I am not sure I dare hope for more now.

I am still thinking of Violet and her friend as we pass the guard house. I start with surprise at the sound of a familiar voice, looking up to see Captain Sarkor at the gates. His eyes flick to Falada, walking without halter or lead, and then back to me. He speaks a question, and the guards who stand with him turn towards us. I train my eyes on the ground, counting the steps it takes me to pass through the gates: eleven. I cannot make out the guards' replies.

Falada walks beside me, eyes far away. I cannot tell if he noticed Sarkor at the gate. I wonder if Violet will marry the man she spoke to, or if he is only a good friend. I wonder if I will ever know more of Falada than he has already told me, for he shies away from questions about his race, rarely answering me directly.

"Do you miss your home?" I ask Falada finally, not wanting to be alone with my thoughts.

It takes him a moment to come back to me. "My home?"

"Is that what you're thinking of?"

"My home," he murmurs softly. "No, I wasn't thinking of that. We Horses do not have a particular home: every open space is ours. But I was missing certain places," he glances at me. "Certain other Horses."

"You have a family," I say disbelievingly.

"Of course, is that not how most creatures come into the world?"

"I don't mean parents."

"No," he agrees. "I have two children, both grown."

"And a wife?"

"Yes."

"What is she like?"

"Selarina is always laughing. She is wise and gentle and more stubborn than anyone I have ever met." His eyes twinkle. "Even you."

"You should go back to her."

"I choose to stay with you, Alyrra."

"Won't she worry?"

"No."

I nod, careful not to press him with more questions. We all need our quiet, I think. We all have our unspoken wishes, hopes we cannot mention, choices we may yet regret.

Today the geese are pastured at the nearest meadow. I have learned by now that there are four different pastures for the geese, each with its own little stream or pond. We cycle through them, allowing each to grow back for a few days before returning. Most of the pastures lie within sight of the road, though the one we visit today sits in a slight dip of land, more like a shallow bowl than a valley in these flat plains. This pasture I like the least, for it is hard to see past the walls of the pasture; I am always most grateful for Falada's presence here.

I sit perched upon a rock, brushing out my hair as I watch the geese, running through the words I have most recently learned from the hostlers. Violet, with a mischievous smile I can only now appreciate, has taught me "handsome" and "strong," while Rowan took me through the painstaking process of counting to ten. Falada stands beside me, occasionally murmuring a correction.

I take my time brushing my hair. Every week I fetch a bucket of water to my room to bathe with, rubbing myself clean with a rag and then washing my hair. With the colder days and nights, Valka's thick curls have little chance to dry out—either when braided or when tossed over my pillow at night. So I have taken to brushing my hair out while watching the geese. Falada does not like it, but I prefer this to developing a chill. We have agreed only that he will stand between myself and Corbé, blocking his view.

Corbé has improved not at all. Though we have kept each other's company these past weeks, we have grown no friendlier than his dark looks and grunted greetings will allow. Falada has counseled me to refrain from more than my daily greeting, delivered with a progressively more strained smile. That I have taken his advice is no source of pride to myself.

I braid my hair up again quickly today, then sit with my knees drawn up, watching the flock. The geese ignore me, waddling across the ground digging for insects or pulling up grass with their beaks, or dipping into the stream. They are strange birds, I think. They care nothing for the humans among them. Or perhaps it is us who are strange, thinking so much of ourselves.

I am still thinking of the geese as I brush Falada down that night. He turns his head to watch me, and I wonder what he has thought of all day out in the pasture.

"What is it?" I whisper, though there are no hostlers in sight.

"Only this: if I should die—"

"Why would you die?"

He watches me calmly. "If I should die," he repeats, "then keep a part of me near you."

"Why?" I ask, coming to stand at his head.

"Because I ask it of you."

"You'll see your wife again," I tell him. "I know it."

He does not answer me.

Two nights later, when I enter my room on our return from the pastures, I find it empty, my belongings gone. All that remains is the small stool and the rolled sleeping mat. When I turn back to the door, I find Matsin and Finnar waiting for me.

·14·

"Come sit with me." The prince lazes in his chair at the table, before him a silver platter heaped with fruit. As I sit down he picks out a peach and begins to cut it with a small, jeweled knife, setting each curving, golden slice down on a plate before him.

"Are you hungry?"

"I am well, Your Highness." I drop my eyes from the peach to the tabletop. My stomach tightens as I think of Laurel and the others hostlers sharing their dinner, then of the peach. It must have come from afar, for winter draws near already.

He sets the last slice down on the plate before him, glances at me inquiringly. "Surely you miss such treats now?"

"I am grateful for what I have, Your Highness."

"Hmm." He spears a peach slice with the tip of his knife and lifts it up, meeting my gaze as he bites into it. I blink—when did I shift my gaze to him? I turn my face back to the table, waiting as he watches me.

"Yet you seem to have taken more than your share."

"Your Highness." It is not so much a question as an acknowledgement.

With studied casualness he says, "Explain how you neglected to mention you had the princess's cloak in your keeping when last we spoke."

I consider the angles. There are not many. With a small smile I reply, "Your Highness did not ask."

"A clear failing on my part." My eyes dart to him, catch the faint curl of amusement at the corners of his mouth.

"It is not the cloak that concerns you," I hazard.

"It is not *only* the cloak the concerns me," he corrects me. "I have taken the liberty of looking through your trunks." I flush, embarrassed that he should have seen my clothes, or Valka's. It is an unsettlingly intimate violation.

"Are you upset?" His voice is almost teasing, as if this were all a good joke among friends. But I do not count him a friend. Like my brother, he will either laugh at my anger or hold my impudence against me. I dare not answer him.

"Come now, lady. I thought we had gotten past the part where you sit still as stone and refuse to speak. Or have you turned to stone?"

"Your Highness?" I ask, unsure what he might ask next if I don't answer.

"Ah, good; you have found your voice." He taps the butt of his knife against the table. He is growing irritated with me, I think, a bitter taste on my tongue. "I was surprised to find you have a trousseau."

"Yes."

"Lord Daerilin expected you to marry?"

"Yes." Whether he thought me Alyrra or Valka, he expected us both to marry.

"Yet he knew your prospects were not good. Your strained relationship with the princess would not have placed you well. Even we have heard of your reputation here. "

"Of course," I manage, mortified. Poor Valka. Even Mother had said how slim Valka's chances were. I watch his fingers turn the jeweled hilt, his thumb rubbing against the precious stones.

He sets the knife down on the table. "Why did you not return the cloak?"

"I would have been charged with stealing it," I admit, looking up.

"And now that you have been found with it?" His eyes are dark, intent and ungiving. I try not to think about what exactly the punishment for stealing from a princess might be.

"I didn't steal it," I say, my voice growing whispery with fear. I clear my throat, press my lips together to keep from speaking.

He doesn't believe me. Or maybe he does. "How did it come into your keeping?"

"It was given to me," I say vaguely.

"By whom?"

I don't want to lie to him. It surprises me, actually, to find that I don't. I would have lied to my brother without thinking if it would have bought me an escape. Now, instead of answering directly, I ask, "Who do you think would give me it, Your Highness?"

Kestrin watches me shrewdly. "Alyrra had no cause to give you a gift meant for her."

I shrug.

"Lady, I cannot help you out of this if you will not help me. Tell me how you came to have the cloak."

"It was given to me," I repeat.

"When you were yet called Lady Valka."

Why is it that everything I say must be a lie? "As you wish," I murmur.

"It is not as I wish. You puzzle me exceedingly, Lady."

"I do not mean to cause trouble," I tell him.

"I almost believe you," he says so quietly I wonder if he speaks to himself. "Here are the puzzles I will unravel: the cloak, which passed from the princess to you without her remembering. Your name, for you told Lords Filadon and Melkior that you preferred Thoreena to Valka, that being your mother's name. Yet your mother died many years ago, and was named Temira. Then there are your trunks, trunks containing marriage gifts that a father you claim has no love for you would not have given you. Your character is also an enigma. Spoiled, pampered child that you were, you now work uncomplainingly, one might even say happily." He laces his fingers together. "Your conversion mirrors that of the princess; she has turned from a shadow into a spoilt brat in a matter of days."

I flinch—torn between pleasure that he sees Valka for what she is and humiliation that he had meant to marry a *shadow*. Is that what people had thought of me? Kestrin, watching me, allows the briefest of smiles to touch his lips. I cannot say what he thinks he has seen in my face.

"Will you explain these things?" he asks.

I force myself to answer him, starting with the easiest mystery first. "It is true I changed my name. I saw that in coming here I would begin a new life; I wished to leave behind my past. Start anew."

"A simple explanation," Kestrin agrees readily, and when he smiles it is the bared teeth of a predator scenting blood. "Believable, even. And yet it does not seem likely."

I shouldn't have tried to explain, I realize. "It is what it is," I say, striving to sound slightly irritated.

He leans back in his chair. "The matter of the cloak yet remains." His words are heavy with warning.

"I leave it to your discretion." I let my eyes drop back to the tabletop. It is a golden wood, the surface as smooth as water. I wonder what he will do to me.

"You are too trusting, lady." I incline my head. Falada would likely call me a fool. Kestrin looks at me thoughtfully. "What does your new name mean—Thoreena?"

"It is—thoreena," I stutter to hide my initial confusion. "A small rose that grows wild in the mountains, it has only a few flowers; mostly it is leaves and thorns."

"Why did you choose such a name?"

"I have always loved the plant." Even as I say the words, I realize my mistake. Once more, I have painted for myself a history that is not Valka's. With each detail, I convince him further that I am not the person I claim to be.

"Your Highness must understand, I have spent the last few years in the south, on my father's lands. I have changed much since I left our queen's Hall. Your reports will have told you only of the girl I was—not of who I am now." I speak a little too fast, even to my own ears. Yet truth bleeds into fiction, and fiction into fact, and I am beginning to lose hold of the threads of my own reality.

"You care for thorn bushes where you once cared for jewels?" he asks lightly.

"Your Highness mocks me."

"Admit it is a strange thing to claim, Lady."

I hesitate, searching for an argument. "I could not name myself Ruby or Diamond, could I?"

He smiles, and I know that the silence between his demand and my answer has told him what I wished to hide. "No," he agrees. "But let us consider your story: the pampered aristocrat, having turned into a rather charming goose girl in the course of a month or two, shows herself to have that which does not belong to her, coupled with riches enough to buy her a station well above that of a goose girl."

I feel my jaw loosen in shock.

"Well?"

"I had not thought to sell anything."

I think he is truly amazed by the simplicity of such a statement. "You had not thought?"

I spread my hands before me. "I can hardly speak Menay, Your Highness. Who would I go to? How would I explain myself to avoid suspicion of thievery?"

"You are already under suspicion of thievery," he observes.

"Precisely."

"Why did you not seek help?"

I laugh. I do not mean to, but the sound comes bubbling up before I can help myself, as it did long ago when I spoke with my mother. I press my hand to my mouth, but I cannot quite stifle my mirth. "Forgive me, Your Highness," I say, "but who should I have asked? Should I have asked your father's help when he has made me a servant? Should I have asked your help?"

His face has grown hard as I spoke. Abruptly he stands up, his chair scraping back against the stone floor. "How dare you speak so to me?" he growls. I flinch back, the hand covering my mouth tightening into a claw so that I gouge my own cheeks with my nails.

He leans over the table, palms pressed flat against the wood, eyes boring into me. "Do you disdain our kindness in keeping you when the princess wished you cast off? Dare you suggest that we would not have helped you in so simple a matter as this?"

"Yes." My voice is hoarse with fear, and even as the word leaves my tongue I brace myself for the blow that is sure to come. But it does not.

He straightens and turns, stalking to the window. I consider his back, the rigid line of his shoulders. I think that I am already lost, for he will neither forgive this incident nor forget the matter of the cloak. So I speak.

"Your father offered me passage home if I informed him of certain matters concerning the princess. When I refused, he sent me to my new duties assuring me that, should I wish to betray her, there would always be a willing ear.

"As for Your Highness, you care for me only for the knowledge you believe I have. Each time we speak, it is only that you may try to pull some fact from me you are convinced I know. You would not help me to better my situation any more than your father, for you need me to feel that I need you, that I will be in your debt for your help. Is this not the game you play, or have I—have I mistaken you?" I end uncertainly, wishing desperately that my diatribe is wholly undeserved. But the prince makes no sound, and the silence grows between us.

When he turns back to me his face is closed, expressionless. I cannot read the look in his eyes. I think that he will beat me for the satisfaction of hearing me scream.

Kestrin crosses the room slowly, deliberately. I stand up as he nears. I know that I am trembling, but I cannot hide it anymore than I can hide the fact that I draw breath. He stops a handbreadth away. His eyes are sharpened onyx, glinting in the lamplight. I think Kestrin is enraged and the force of his wrath will put my brother to shame. But even now he stands still, gazing down at me.

"You fear me." It is a statement requiring no agreement. I look away, turning my head to stare at the wall. Will he play another game, then? Is he worse than my brother, or only his equal?

"Sit," he says, surprising me, one hand waving toward the chair by my side. I slide back down into the chair, my hands curling around the edge of the seat as he takes his own seat. I focus on the table, trying not to think.

"That white stallion you take out to the fields with you every day—what breed is he?" Kestrin asks, as if he had just met me outside the stables. It takes me a moment to reply.

"I do not know, Your Highness. I was told ... he comes from the Fethering Plains."

"A beautiful specimen. The Master of Horses is considering breeding him."

"Breeding him," I repeat idiotically, unable to follow this new thread of conversation.

"The horse has a good build. He is strong and fast," he explains, the epitome of a casual conversationalist.

"I expect—I expect that is true. I just don't know that—Falada will breed. He hasn't yet." After all, Falada's having a wife is rather different from the stable idea of breeding.

"You seem to know more of the horse than the princess does," Kestrin notes.

Damn his word games. I dare not remain silent, and yet I dare not speak. I do not understand Kestrin: had he been my brother or like him, by now he would have finished his games. I do not know why he drags it out, why, having drawn me into the open, he does not attack.

"Tell me, Thoreena, your father's southern estate that you have lived on these past few years, what is it like?"

"Your Highness?"

"Has Daerilin a hall or a manor house? What are the grounds like? I have heard much of them, but would know your opinion."

I stare blankly at the table. I do not know. I have never listened to what little talk there was of it for such talk invariably involved Valka.

"I think you have never been there, little thorn," he says, his voice almost gentle in the silence. I do not think it strange that he no longer calls me lady. I bite my lip, then take a breath to answer but he cuts me off.

"Remember that it is a crime to lie to one of the royal family: a crime punishable by death, for it is considered a betrayal."

"Your Highness, tell me what you want of me," I plead.

"The truth. Who are you?"

"I am the goose girl. There is nothing more I can tell you, Your Highness." The chain presses gently against my throat.

"If you were not the Lady Valka before you reached the Border, then what happened to Lady Valka?"

"I cannot say, Your Highness." His face has lost its frozen aspect, his eyes glinting in the lamplight. I think he is closing in on the kill.

"Then you admit to having lived a lie among us?" He raises an eyebrow, half grinning, and though he has just warned me of the dangers of lying, his demeanor now invites confession. I find myself hating him for it—for the ability to play with people so easily.

"I admit only to wishing to live in peace," I say bitterly.

He considers me. "Tell me why you fear me, lady."

I try not to flinch, but his damned eyes see everything.

"At least twice I have seen you look at me with such fear as I have seen only in the eyes of hunted deer."

I let my gaze wander across the table, pause over the plate of fruit, and finally come to rest on the small, jeweled knife. "I have only ever known one other prince, Your Highness."

He nods. "Do you judge me by his standard?"

"I am not in a position to judge princes."

84

"Yet you expect the same from me, don't you? He would hurt a woman for the sake of inflicting pain. He has hurt you before."

I swallow, refusing to meet his gaze.

"Your fear is a strange thing. You fear brutality from me more than you fear punishment within the law—and yet you are guilty of breaking the law. Why?"

I cannot imagine that he does not know. How can he be so quick to grasp what I wish to hide and yet not see this? Or perhaps he only wishes to make me speak.

"Lady?"

I glance up at him. "You and your father *are* the law. Shouldn't I fear you before I fear it?"

"Perhaps." We sit in silence. He reaches out to play with the jeweled knife absent-mindedly, then sets it down, raising his gaze to me. "This has been a most educational evening, Thorn. I thank you for it."

I stand, one hand gripping the table edge.

"Tell me one more thing before you go: shall I trust you?"

I remember how he had urged vigilance on my journey. How could he ask me this now? Unless it is a trap of words—for how can I say no and not meet a punishment, or say yes and not be called to account for failing to answer him earlier? But then his words echo back to me from our conversation. "Your Highness has long known of my reputation for dishonesty," I say, my voice small with shame. "I cannot counsel you on this."

He does not answer me.

I seek out the temple again the following night. Falada waits patiently while I linger inside, listening to the sounds of the city going to sleep. I sit cross-legged on a woven straw mat, the stone floor hard and cold beneath it. Closing my eyes, I sink into the quiet.

What is it I truly wish for? I see Corbé, his lips curling back as he meets my glance every morning at the barn door, and I want safety from that look and its attendant meanings. I think of the books I used to read, and while I miss them I now have the time to think back over them, consider their arguments and opinions as I watch the flock; this I would not change. My life has the necessary comforts—food daily, work to keep me busy, time to reflect, and some small company to share it all with. While a hot bath might be nice, it is too small and irrelevant a thing to pray for.

Then of course come the larger wishes: I wish safety for Kestrin, as little as I understand him—safety for him and from him. I wish Valka might be kept in check, her interests bound to the court and affecting the people not at all. I wish the Lady might find some peace within herself.

I am roused from my meditative prayers by the distant echo of shouts, and then Falada's voice, sharp with apprehension. "Alyrra! Quickly."

"What is it?"

"Trouble," comes the succinct reply as I reach the doorway. "We need to leave."

"My boots." I struggle to pull them on, leaning against the doorframe for balance. "Ready." I stamp my boot against the ground to get my foot the rest of the way in, and then the chase is upon us.

A tall boy hurtles around the corner from the street, his cloak flapping behind him. The alley here is so narrow that he slams into Falada's bulk before he can stop. He falls back, cursing. Shouts echo from the street, closing in. The boy stumbles to his feet awkwardly, cradling his arm in the folds of his cloak. Falada snorts, pressing towards me to give the boy space to pass. But the boy will never make it now.

"Let him into the temple," I order, side-stepping Falada before he can hem me into the doorway. The shouting is nearly upon us. The boy whips his head to the side to look at me, the motion making him stagger as if drunk. "There," I snap, pointing to the shadowed interior. "Quickly. *Rah!" Go!*

He bolts through the darkened doorway. "Falada, stand here beside me," I hiss. Falada does, blocking the doorway with his flank. When I lift my hand to his neck, the muscles there are rock hard.

A quad barrels around the corner. In the faint light of the alley I can see the glint of swords at the ready. They skid to a halt, the gleam of question and doubt in their eyes.

"There," I say in Menay, pointing to the where the alley opens out into another street. "There!" For a moment longer they pause, and I know that they will remember me. I only hope they will not blame me for having lost their prey.

"Niroh," the first soldier shouts and they are off once more, boots pounding the hard-packed earth.

The moment they round the corner I duck my head into the temple. "Niroh," I say, echoing the soldier. *Let's go.*

The boy approaches the door warily, turning his head first towards me, then Falada. Though I doubt he can see my expression, I smile as I unfasten my cloak.

"Wear this." I hand him the cloak. He understands at once, clumsily slinging it around his shoulder, its somber color masking the brightness of his own cloak. "What's wrong with your hand?" I say sharply, reaching out to catch his arm. He pulls back, his breath hissing between his teeth. My hand comes away slick with blood.

"Falada, he's hurt!"

Falada watches me mutely. Belligerently. He must be furious. I sigh. I have gotten myself into this, and I must get myself out—but not without helping this boy. And Falada will help me, despite himself.

"We need somewhere quiet so I can see to his wound," I say, careful not to look towards Falada. He snorts and starts towards the street. I hustle the boy along beside me as fast as possible. If the soldiers return they will certainly recognize Falada and I. To be caught helping their fugitive escape would be no small offense.

Falada leads us from the street down another tight passageway and into a back alley behind a row of derelict buildings.

"Show me your arm," I say in Menay when we come to a stop. The boy stands unmoving, the cloak wrapped around him and his hood pulled up. He is taller than me, and I realize as I look at the shadowy place where his face should be that I have no idea as to his actual age, thought him a boy only because he was slim and quick.

"Your arm," I repeat, pointing in case I have the words wrong. He complies, holding out his arm, letting the cloak fall back. His sleeve is soaked in blood. I push it up to reveal the cut. The boy inhales sharply, and I hear Falada shift, his breath warming the back of my neck, but the boy makes no other move. With the sleeve pushed up, the wound is terribly clear—a deep gash almost the length of his forearm, from wrist to elbow, traveling along the outside of his arm. It bleeds freely, and I think he must have great restraint not to pull his arm away from me.

I release his arm, my thoughts racing. I must staunch the bleeding. The boy squats down, his back against the wall, head bent. I yank at my sash, my fingers sticky with blood. The boy looks up, nodding when I mime my intent. He makes no sound as I wind it around his wound in a makeshift bandage. Immediately, the blood flow lessens.

He cradles his arm against his chest as I move away. "Shurminan," he murmurs, and I cannot make out the age of his voice either.

"Ifnaal." I lean against the wall, my legs weak beneath me.

The boy stands and then staggers sideways, unbalanced. It is only Falada's quick step up to him that prevents his falling. He hangs on to Falada, one hand thrown over his neck, gasping for breath. He will not be able to make his way to safety alone, nor can he walk hanging onto Falada, for Falada's back is too high for comfort.

So, when the boy raises his head to get his bearings once more, I take his arm from Falada's neck and hang it over my shoulders.

"Where?" I ask, wrapping my arm around his waist. He nods his head towards the end of the alley, and we begin to walk. It is a slow and awkward passage, with Falada following us like a phantom. I lose track of our path before long, for in the dark the buildings are hard to see, and the weight of the boy bears me down so that I look up only when he does, pausing at cross streets and the mouths of alleys. Occasionally someone passes us; always they hurry, eyes averted, keeping as far from us as possible. It is not a side of the city I have seen before.

Twice I stop, depositing the boy on the ground beside me before sinking down to rest. My legs and back ache fiercely with the strain of supporting him, as do my fingers when I uncurl them from their grip about his clothing.

Finally, we come to a small wooden staircase running up to the second floor of a building. We shuffle to a halt, and a moment later my legs give out. I fall forward with the weight of the boy, slamming into the stairs. My head bounces off the wooden stairs, my arms too numb, too slow to break our fall. I blink my eyes to clear my vision and lever myself up painfully. The boy lies perfectly still.

My heart fails me. What if he—what if I have—

"Alyrra," Falada murmurs behind me. I turn my head. A white pain streaks past my vision, splitting my skull. I whimper, then bite my tongue in shame. It is nothing compared to the boy's wound.

"I'm fine," I whisper. "But he's…"

"Check."

I roll the boy onto his back, clumsily trying to shield his wounded arm. At least he doesn't suffer the pain of it. I lay my hand uncertainly against his chest and feel it rise gently and fall back.

"Unconscious."

"Get your cloak." I pull the edges of my cloak out from under the boy, unwrapping it. "Come," Falada says as I swing the cloak around my own shoulders. The edge of it flaps against my arm, soaked with blood. He turns back up the alley.

"We can't leave him here." I hang onto the wooden rail; standing, the pain in my head leaves me slightly off balance.

"He'll be fine. In a few hours it will be dawn, and whoever lives up there will find him. Come."

"No."

"Alyrra, this is no safe place for you."

My breath comes in short gasps as I stare at Falada. I pivot, gritting my teeth as the world swings with me, and start up the stairs.

"Child," Falada hisses after me. I ignore him, concentrating on making my legs move forward and up. The staircase ends at a small wooden platform. From the crack beneath the door comes the shine of lamplight. I rap twice on the door and step back. There is the muffled sound of movement on the other side of the door, and a voice calls out sharply with words I do not know.

I glance down to where Falada stands beside the boy. Again, the voice orders an answer from me. The speaker has come up to the door.

"I don't know," I say in Menay, hearing the high-pitched waver to my voice.

The door crashes open. A hand flashes out, and in that hand is a sword. I stand perfectly still, listening to my blood thunder through my veins, echoing in my ears. The blade wavers in the air a bare hand's breadth from my throat. I follow the shining length of metal down to the gloved hand that wraps around its hilt and up that arm with its long pale sleeve to the man's face; it is a strange thing, all hard angles with a straight scar running from one corner of his mouth down his chin. His hair is cut short, lying gently against a high forehead.

"Your friend," I rasp in Menay, and move one hand to point down the stairs.

"Yendro," the man says. I blink at him. Another man steps up beside him to look at where I point. This second man says something I do not quite catch, the white of his teeth glinting in the lamplight. The sword wavers before me. I watch it, half hypnotized by the play of light upon it. Then it is lowered and the second man descends the stairs.

The scar-faced man watches me while we wait, his gaze keen. My foreign clothes and scruffy appearance will not be lost on him, I realize unhappily. The second man calls out, his voice concerned. The scar-faced man sheathes his sword, starting down. I back into the corner made by the railings as he passes me.

I can see into the room now; three more men stand around a table, their chairs hastily pushed back, hoods pulled up to hide their faces. They too wear swords. I wonder uneasily exactly who the boy is to have such friends.

The two men lift my nighttime companion and maneuver him up the stairs. Their faces are grim as they pass me. As soon as they step past, I hurry down. One of the men calls after me. I glance back to see one of the hooded men, sword in hand. I pound down the stairs.

"Stop!" he shouts.

Falada stands at the bottom, waiting tensely. I throw myself at his back, scrabbling for a hold on his mane as I heave one leg over. He springs into a trot, then a canter, nearly knocking me off. I hang on determinedly. With each pounding step, pain jolts through my skull, bringing tears to my eyes. Behind me, I hear the man cursing, his voice disappearing beneath the beat of Falada's hooves.

We fall into a walk within a few blocks. I breathe a prayer of thanks and turn to slither from Falada's back. He side steps up against a wall, stopping me. "Stay," he says simply. "You are tired, and we will make better time this way."

"But…"

"Quiet," Falada says, and starts off once more, his gait gentle, smooth. Long before we reach the stables I fall into a doze, waking only to open the doors and let us in to Falada's stall.

"What's wrong with your head?"

"Nothing." I cup my hand over the bump on my forehead, impressed despite myself that I understood the question.

"Nothing?" Violet grabs my hand, breakfast forgotten. "By the One— what did you do? What happened?"

"I fell." I push her hands away. She mutters something in Menay and yanks my hand from my forehead.

"What is it?" Ash asks from the door as Violet gasps. He sets down a bucket of water. "Something wrong?"

Violet launches into a tirade of unknown words, and a few known but strung together so quickly that I cannot quite catch them, gesturing angrily at my head. Ash walks over, his eyes on the long lump at my hairline.

"Who did it?" he asks me so quietly that at first Violet doesn't realize he's spoken.

I shake my head. "I fell."

"That's what she says," Violet says. "Does that look—" she launches into another whirl of unknown words, turning to glare at Ash.

"On stairs," I explain, wishing for the umpteenth time I had greater dexterity with Menay. Ash reaches out and touches the tender skin around the hard central lump. I stiffen, but Violet stands next to me. She pats my shoulder comfortingly.

"Okay," Ash concedes. "Who pushed you?"

"No one." He looks skeptical. "I fell," I repeat. I would swear it if I had the words.

"Well." He fetches the bucket and takes it to the counter.

"Ash." Violet stands with hands on her hips. He shrugs, speaking quickly, and she replies on the heels of his words, their sentences overlapping and cutting through each other. I slip out unnoticed, hurrying to the goose barn.

"You're happy this morning," Falada observes as we walk down West Road soon after.

I break off humming to grin at him. "I—well, yes, I am." Deep inside, I hear Ash ask *Who pushed you?* I am amazed the sun does not shine.

"I wouldn't have thought a bump on the head would improve you so. The next time you walk around looking like a rainy day, I'm taking you to find another youth to save."

I laugh, and immediately regret it as pain laces across my forehead. "Was I that bad?"

"Worse," Falada tells me, stepping sideways to avoid my shove. "What happened?"

I take a breath, let it out. "The hostlers are thinking to breed you."

"Are they? I shall be sorry to disappoint them. And how did you, with your limited vocabulary, learn of this new plan?"

"The prince told me."

"Kestrin? Indeed." And then, gently, "What else did he tell you?"

"Only that he knows I am a fraud. He considers me a puzzle of sorts, not particularly important, perhaps entertaining enough to keep for a winter evening's amusement to unravel." Falada's breath makes dragon smoke before us. "He had my belongings brought to him, and he found the cloak, as well as Valka's trousseau. He knows I was never Valka."

"You do not wish him to find you out."

"No," I agree quietly.

"What do you think he will do when he does?"

91

"I can't say. Perhaps if he hasn't guessed yet he won't."

Falada eyes me askance. "He knows you have the princess's signature."

I swallow a curse, furious with myself. Of course he knows I have her script. My own script. What maid could do that? If I'm not Valka, and I'm not a maid, that leaves only one other person: the princess herself. I shake my head in denial. I wish I had thought through my words to Kestrin. I wish I had been able to think at all.

"Will you not be princess?"

I hesitate. But Kestrin is both sorcerer and prince. He frightens me more than my own brother; at least I had understood my brother. "How could I marry him?" I ask Falada, leaving my fears unspoken. "What would I do as princess? I listen to Valka's account of the court—I would no more fit there than a goose girl born and bred. I do this post more honor than I ever could that of princess."

"Every post is what you make of it. Valka may adorn the title of princess better, but you will put it to better use."

"How?" I ask plaintively.

"You care for more than yourself," Falada says. "That is an excellent start. You have grown much these past few months, since the king first came for you. You are certainly capable."

"I'm afraid of Kestrin," I admit finally, keeping my head bent. "I'm afraid of what he might do to me."

"He won't harm you," Falada says confidently. "I've heard the talk of the court, and what is said about him; he is not a violent man."

"What a man does behind closed doors," I say with a shrug.

"He will never harm his wife," Falada says patiently, "because if anyone learned of it, it would weaken his position as well. The king offered you his protection in your own home. They will grant you the same now."

I do not quite believe him, remembering Kestrin's restrained anger. He had been close to violence. And fists aren't Kestrin's only weapon. "There are more ways than one to hurt. His wit is sharp as a blade. And ... I am no princess." I don't know how to play at politics, or protect myself from him.

Falada makes a sound of frustration.

I take another tack. "Kestrin may not wish me harm, but he cannot even protect himself from the Lady. She would never forgive me if—"

"If you fought back against her?" Falada interrupts.

"Well, yes."

"Not very long ago you felt you owed the prince for having betrayed him to the Lady through Valka. What we discuss now is an alliance with him. Don't you owe him that?"

"I told him to beware; that's enough. I *owe* him nothing."

"Don't you?"

"Why should I give more?" I ask angrily. It was all Kestrin gave me—useless warnings.

"At some point you must take responsibility for your life, Alyrra. No one, you least of all, has the right to betray a person who has implicitly trusted you."

"There is no trust between us. He would be a fool to trust me or the stranger that is his bride ..." I trail off. I had stood beside him against the Lady that night, an excellent reason for him to trust Valka now. Or to trust whoever he suspects to be princess.

Falada does not notice my uncertainty. "When he knows who you are, he will expect you to act with honor, to keep the trust you agreed to when you signed your betrothal papers."

"He can have Valka instead. He'll know her for a fraud and can do what he likes from there. It isn't my concern," I argue, though I am not sure I believe myself.

"Can you in clear conscience name Valka your successor?"

If only Valka weren't who she is. But then, if she had been a better person, she would not have betrayed me to the Lady. Having betrayed me, I don't doubt she will betray Kestrin. Unless he discovers her first. I rub the back of my neck, my muscles tight. At least he does not trust her.

"Think on it then, if you will," Falada tells me. "You still have a little time."

"And then the choice will be made for me," I say. I have a fleeting thought to run away, but I don't know where I would go or how I would survive.

Falada touches my shoulder with his nose, a gentle tap. "You will always have a choice."

I don't answer. We continue on towards the goose pasture in silence. As we near the boundary wall, I ask hesitantly, "Will you stay with me?"

"Only so long as you need me, and then I will leave."

"Where will you go?"

"South of the Fethering Plains."

"To your family," I murmur.

"Yes." He throws me a sharp look. "You are stronger than you think. I could leave today, and I expect in the end it would be the same with you."

"No!" I say fiercely. "Don't leave me now."

"I won't."

16

The following days dawn in shades of gray, layers of clouds obscuring the sun from sight. A cold wind blows from the mountains, rustling across the plains and whistling through the walls of the city. For a week or perhaps longer they withhold their promise of rain or snow, I know not which. I miss the crisp coldness of the forest winters I have known. I daydream of warm bread and mittens and the weight of snow on pine trees. The winter here is a different creature all together, lying heavily over my shoulders and stealing into my bones.

Today a hunting party rides out. A line of horses wait, tethered to the practice ring fence; they are outfitted with sleek hunting saddles, or else richly caparisoned in gold and silver for the ladies who will accompany the hunt. Young men in palace uniforms rush in and out of the stables, pestering the hostlers and checking the horses' gear.

Done with my cleaning, I slip into Falada's stall, going to stand by his head. "It's too busy to take you out, isn't it?" I whisper.

"You do not want to attract undue attention from Valka's quarter," Falada concurs. "The hunt might pass the pasture."

Unsaddled, unbridled, and in the company of a servant, Falada would attract as much attention from the palace folk as the appearance of a gryphon strolling through the city gates. "We'll go for a walk together tonight," I promise.

The flock is settled into the hidden pasture, set back from West Road. I cast a quick glance at our charges to ascertain none are in danger of casually wandering off, select a stone seat some distance from Corbé, and unbraid my hair. It is still wet from last night's washing, and the curls have tangled abominably despite the braid, or perhaps because of it. Even as cold as the day is, my hair could do with a good airing out. I open up the first short span and spread each lock over my knees to work the comb through it a handbreadth at a time.

I think of a hundred things as I brush: that the hem of my skirt will require mending; that I would have liked to ride through the plains and see more of them; that I do not yet know the plants of this land; that I no longer like to sleep in my room though my trunks have reappeared as quietly as they vanished, only the cloak gone.

It takes a moment for the crunch of pebbles beneath booted feet to make its way to my ears. I turn to see Corbé advancing towards me. I stumble to my feet, my hand clenched tightly around my staff as he closes the distance between us. He smiles, and it is a smile that turns my stomach to ice. I glance around in panic for Falada, for anyone, but there is no one here.

"You're a pretty thing," he says, his voice low and gravelly. "I've been wanting to get a hold of that hair."

"No." I back away. I do not know the right words, can't think of how to tell him to stay back. He darts forward to catch hold of my braid, hauling me towards him. For a moment it is not him I see but my brother, eyes glittering, lips drawn back in sneering enjoyment. I feel the whistle of my staff through the air and then the satisfying jolt of wood in my hand, hard against my palms.

Corbé roars, his face twisting in pain. I raise the staff and bring it back again, watch the way the dark pole meets his cheek. Blood spurts from his nose, droplets spattering my face as his head jerks back. He shouts words I have not yet learned, loosing my braid to clutch his face.

It is only when I feel the shape of my mouth as I gaze at him that I realize what I have done. I gain the crest ringing the meadow in moments, throwing all my mind and energy into one thing: to run. If all that I am and have been and can be is focused into this one reality of running, perhaps I can escape all that I may be. It is the only thought I will allow myself.

I run until the plains are strange to my eyes. Though I cast my gaze back, I cannot see how far I have come for there are no landmarks but the city itself, a dark blot on the plains. I have left the farms behind, stumbling now through the plains themselves. Still I think that should I run so far that I reach the sea I should not have run far enough, for the thing I run from rides on my back and in my blood and will not be shaken.

Finally, exhaustion takes over my limbs and I drop into a shuffling walk. Once more I feel the grain of the wooden staff in my hands, the way it swings so easily—as if I had practiced such a move in so close quarters more often than I have drawn breath. Blood lifts in the air, arcing away, taking my breath with it. My lips twist in a vicious smile. Again and again. So it is that, though the world is still bright with light, I do not see the ridge until I set my foot upon the air where the ground should have continued.

I swallow my cry as I fall, rolling and skidding to the bottom of the rocky ravine. A shower of pebbles comes loose, pelting me like so many memories. I huddle there, pressing myself into a ball and concentrating on the pain of my hands rubbed raw by the fall, my scraped knees and the cut across my shins. These things are real, their pain deserved. I realize dimly that someone is sobbing: the sound comes from far away, echoing through my mind as if down dark stone corridors.

I lie there long enough for the ragged weeping to still, long enough for my blood to close up the scratch on my shin. I sit up slowly, propping myself on my hands, using my tattered cloak as a cushion for my bloodied palms. The rift walls rise around me, twice as tall as a man. The sides are a mixture of dirt and rock, sheer enough that few grasses grow here. The first drops of rain from the clouds overhead spot the ground. I doubt I will be able to claw my way back up now, certainly not if the rocks grow slippery.

I will walk then, until I find a way back up. The going is slow. I dropped my staff in the first frantic moments of flight and even now when it might have helped me I am no longer sure I want it. The rain falls steadily, weighing down my cloak and skirt, wet folds sticking to my legs. Cracks in the stone begin to appear, shallow fissures barely an arm length deep. A breeze whips through the rift, cutting through my clothes. When I look at my fingers, they are white with cold. My teeth chatter uncontrollably. Yet I do not think it can really be that cold. There is no sleet, no ice.

I pause finally at a fissure tucked between two slabs of rock. It has the vague comfort of a half-remembered haunt, and seems deep enough to offer some shelter. When I stoop to enter, I realize that the fissure has been hollowed out, the tunnel behind it cutting up through the rock so that I can move without bending over. I stand for a moment in the twilight of the tunnel, listening to the moan of the wind, the patter of raindrops on stone. The air lies still here. I rub my hands over my face as if I could wake myself from yet another nightmare. But the tunnel remains, neutral in its reality, and behind me the rift.

I make myself follow the tunnel, one hand trailing along the rock wall. It makes a single turn and ends at a slab of rock as smooth as a baby's cheek. I rest my forehead against it, wrapping my arms across my chest. Darkness surrounds me, leaching away detail, leaving only the slightest trace of reality. I know already what I will find. Closing my eyes, I press my palms against the rock.

The stone door swings back, moving smoothly on hidden hinges. I put one hand on the doorframe, peering in. I can make out nothing of the room before me. What dim light illumined the stone door fails at this point, but my dream-memory serves me well enough: it will be a round room, the circular walls smooth and unmarked. At the center stands a stone pedestal, hanging from the ceiling above it an ornate lamp.

I scrabble to pull the stone door shut once more. The dream had been from Kestrin. I swallow down a wave of nausea. He had called me here, meaning to call the princess—I remember the confusion in his eyes when he had looked up at me from the basin of water. I clasp my hands together to still their trembling, take a deep breath, and then let them wander over the stone door until they encounter what they must: a well-disguised handle that has pulled the door shut countless times before.

I shuffle towards the mouth of the tunnel. I am but a pace away when I hear voices—men's voices, the words unintelligible, thrown about by the wind. Instinctively I back away. Where to hide? I dare not return to the room. The tunnel itself offers perilous little cover. Still, there is a slight outcropping of stone between the mouth of the fissure and the turning point in the tunnel. I seat myself in the fold created by the stone, pushing myself back as far as I will go, knees to my chest, and spread the dark folds of my cloak over my skirt and boots. It is not much of a hiding place.

The voices echo into the tunnel. I tuck my hands behind my knees. A few more words, the sound of boots on the stone floor, and then a cloaked figure passes me. He walks confidently, looking neither to the right nor the left. Moments after he disappears around the corner, lamplight flowers, filtering out into the tunnel, then narrowing to a sliver as he shuts the door. I venture only one look towards the tunnel mouth—a figure sits on guard, blocking the entry.

The cold of the stone climbs up through my legs from the ground and wraps around my chest, sliding like a knife between my ribs. I think my blood must freeze in my veins. I cross my arms over my knees and rest my head on them, partly for the comfort of moving my back away from the stone, and partly to muffle the sound of my teeth chattering. Eventually, though, they stop of their own accord. I think that I have been waiting a hundred years; almost I cannot remember what for or why. I let my eyelids fall shut, listening to the half-heard sound of my heart.

"Lady."

The word makes its persistent way through the foggy tunnels of my mind.

"Lady, wake up. Wake up."

I have the distinct feeling of being shaken—a disjointed, unreal sensation, for I cannot quite remember the way of my body.

"Thorn."

I force my eyes open, focusing on a pair of dark eyes. They are the gentle brown of a forest stream-bed, dappled with sunlight. I wonder if I am home again; if the darkness I have surfaced from has carried me to another time and place so that, when I step forth fully from the depths, I will find myself in woods once more.

"Here now, drink this." A liquid pours into my mouth. I swallow reflexively. Water, deliciously warm, flows through my chest, cascading over my ribs to settle in a warm pool in my belly. When I look up again, I do not see his eyes anymore—I see him.

"More?" Kestrin asks. I nod wordlessly; it was the lamplight in his eyes that glittered gold. He moves away, going to a small brazier of coals with a pot over it. Kneeling by it is a second man, dressed in hunting clothes much like the prince. He looks vaguely familiar but I cannot place his name, staring blearily at his fine features, the dark hair curling around his collar.

I don't know how long I remain there sipping water. The prince wraps my hands around the warmth of the mug and helps me to drink at intervals. I realize gradually that I am nearly dry, that I am wrapped in various layers—blankets as well as cloaks. I have begun to shake again.

"She is too weak to leave on her own." The prince kneels beside his companion, though I do not recall him leaving me.

"It is not cold enough for her to have frozen," the man says, his voice stirring echoes. Where do I know him from?

"No," Kestrin agrees. "It is not the weather she fights."

The man looks towards me. His face is too bright to focus on, the lamplight falling directly on him. "She has had a shock."

Kestrin nods, dropping his voice as he answers.

I look around, observe bleakly that I have seen this room with its smooth walls and stone pedestal before, though the tables pushed against the walls, the candles and bookshelves and sheaves of scrolls seem strangely out of place. The room looks used now, has the feel of a study rather than an ancient, forgotten sorcerer's room.

Sorcerer.

The word echoes in my mind, as if I had spoken it out loud. I close my eyes against it.

"Thorn." Kestrin touches my hand. I start. How did I not notice him approaching? "We must get you to the city. Can you stand?"

I nod uncertainly, and Kestrin holds my arm to help me up. The other I use to push off the stone wall. It is an awkward process, but finally I gain my feet. The room twists around me, light streaked with darkness. I gasp, stumbling sideways against the wall. Kestrin has done with courtesies at that. He picks me up as one might a child: one arm beneath my knees, the other behind my shoulders.

Somehow Kestrin and his companion carry me to the top of the rift. I do not realize that the rain has touched me until I feel a cloth dabbing my face dry. I look up to find that I sit sideways, and that the man that holds me before him is not the prince at all.

"Where?" I gasp.

"Easy," his friend says soothingly. I look around dazedly. "The prince returned to the hunt," he explains. "I am taking you to the palace."

"But I live—in the stables."

"There are no fires in the stable to warm you. Softly now."

I close my eyes, too tired to argue, and sink into oblivion.

17

"Awake?" A gray-haired woman leans toward me, meeting my bewildered gaze. She sits on a mat in a well-kept room with mosaics on the wall. I lie on a low divan, swathed in blankets.

"Good," she says, though I have not answered. "The prince wants to see you. Let's get you dressed."

I sit up with the shock of my memories returning, but the woman gives me no chance to worry about them. She whisks me into my clothes with alarming efficiency. They have all been washed, fraying hems darned, and smell delightfully of lemon. There is a new sash as well, replacing the one I used to bind the wounded boy's arm. Even my boots have been repaired and polished.

"How long did I sleep?" I ask as she surveys me critically. It has taken me that long to remember my Menay.

"A day or so," she says, absently. "You'll do. Come along."

She sets a brisk pace from the room. My body aches, and I feel more tired than I would have thought possible. Have I really slept a full day? What must Falada think?

The woman ushers me through a narrow door at the end of the hall, down a servants' corridor, and into a private library through the servants' entrance. Kestrin sits alone at a table, intent on the book before him, three more piled beside him.

He looks up at the sound of my entrance and smiles. There is neither mockery nor flattery nor cruelty in it. It is the quick, instinctive smile of a man whose gaze alights on something he likes. It shocks me to my core.

"Thorn," he says, rising. "You are feeling better?"

I nod mutely, still unnerved by that look.

"Will you return to the stables?"

"Yes, Your Highness." What else would I do?

He hesitates. "I thought you might consider a position here, in the palace."

He knows. I feel the blood drain from my face and it is all I can do not to flee. No no *no.* Panic churns in my stomach. I won't. I won't.

"Lady?"

"No." I clench my jaw to keep the other words in: *Please. I don't want this. Leave me alone.*

A silence draws out between us. I train my gaze on the table, afraid of what he might see if he looks in my eyes. Perhaps I am wrong. Perhaps he means only to offer a distressed servant a change in employment.

"What were you running from?" he asks, surprising me. "On the plains?"

I open my mouth and then close it again, unsure what to tell him. Would he punish Corbé, or bring the blame back to me? I cannot let myself trust his smiles or the tenor of his voice. I know that he can play games.

"Or were you running *to* something?"

"No," I say quickly. "Away."

"You might be safer in the palace," Kestrin suggests.

"I doubt it," I say. And then, belatedly, "Your Highness."

I risk a glance at him. He watches me, dark eyes shrewd. If he knows, wouldn't he force the question?

"As you wish," he says. "If you need anything, you will let me know."

I bob my head and retreat to the servants' door, grateful to escape him.

The woman tries to usher me back to my room. When I tell her haltingly that I wish to return to the stables she raises her eyebrows and then acquiesces, as if I had requested a great favor. She leaves me at a servants' exit onto the side road skirting the palace, nodding towards the gates before striding off to other duties.

The walk to the stables is longer than I remember. I stop at intervals to rest against the buildings, my legs weak beneath me. By the time I reach the temple, I have neither breath nor balance to take me farther. I stagger through the door and sink down on the mats, my cheek pressed against the coarse straw. I'll let myself rest a little and then go on.

Something scuffles against the straw. I open my eyes to see a young boy looking down at me, hesitating just within the temple door. He is a slight, bony creature with great brown eyes and stringy hair. I close my eyes; when I open them again he is gone.

Voices wake me, echoing into the little temple from the street. The temple is shadowed now, filled with evening gloom. Gradually, I become aware of a second presence: a man sits against the opposite wall, wrapped in a cloak, unmoving. I watch him, and some part of me tells me I should run, that this might be Corbé or another like him, but I have not the strength to fight this.

"Are you awake?" the man's voice rumbles from the depths. I consider not answering, but if he meant me ill he would have acted by now. I lever myself up. The temple tilts as I move. I take a gasping breath, my eyes trained on the straw mat. I do not want to be ill here.

He stands up, a fluid rippling of cloak and shadow, and crosses the temple to me. "I will escort you home," he tells me, putting a hand under my elbow. I stumble to my feet with his help.

Outside, the men whose voices I heard straighten from where they lean against the opposite wall. Two head for the street, the other two watch us leave: a quad that has nothing to do with the king's guards. I lean heavily on my companion, keeping my gaze on the cobblestones. As we near the stables, the two men who had left before us pause to speak with a cobbler, allowing us to pass. I wonder if I could spot the other two if I looked back.

My companion stops at the edge of the road. "Can you go the rest of the way on your own?"

I consider the distance: I will have to walk the length of two practice rings and the first stable between them to reach my room. Falada's stall is much closer. I look up at the hooded face of my helper and realize I know him, know the scar that runs from lip to chin. He would not want to set foot in the king's stables.

"I will be fine," I assure him. "Thank you."

"You are welcome."

I start forward, striving to walk steadily. By the time I reach Falada I have only the strength to pull the stall door closed before I sink into the straw in the corner.

"Alyrra, are you well?" A great brown eye regards me from barely two hand spans away. I reach up to run a hand along his cheek.

"Fine, Falada. Just tired."

"Where have you been?" His voice is gruff with worry.

"Is it safe to talk?"

"You may speak with impunity," he replies. "Only I must beware."

"Yes." I lean my head against the wooden wall, breathing in the smell of horse and sweat and sun-sweetened hay. "I went out to watch the geese as usual," I tell him. "Corbé had taken them to the lower pasture. When I got there he came over to me and—I spooked as a colt might, I suppose. I hit him with my staff. And then I ran and lost myself and part of the hunting party found me and brought me back." I gasp as I finish, as if I have not breath enough left in my life for this short story with its shadow truths.

Falada sighs, and in that simple exhalation I hear the rest of my story. "Child," he says softly, and that is all.

I wake with a jerk from murky dreams to a grim realization: *Filadon*. It had been Filadon who had kept Kestrin's watch, and returned me to the city. I scrub my face wearily. So. He must know Kestrin's secrets, or at least the prince's study of sorcery. Does he know about the Lady as well? Regardless, now I know why Filadon was chosen to meet us at the border: he may not have great holdings or a fine title, but he has the confidence and trust of the Family.

I force myself up, for it is near dawn. My chest aches and my throat is raw; thrice during the night I woke coughing. Still, I feel more rested than I was. I had better not miss any more work.

Laurel smiles when she sees me standing in the common room doorway and hurries to bring me a bowl of porridge. I sit at the table, watching her pretend not to watch me eat. Her brow is furrowed, and her eyes when they meet mine are anxious. She puts my lunch in a new cloth bag and sits opposite me.

"Where were you?" Her voice is quiet, gentle.

"I—" I stop, not sure how much to tell her, if I even have the words to tell her.

"Corbé came back alone with the geese. We *ilakina*." I shake my head, and she tries again. "We waited and waited. Ash and Rowan went to the pasture to look for you. Then we heard from the palace that you were ill and would return later."

I nod. "I was ill."

"Corbé would not tell us anything."

"He does not like me," I say haltingly, aware of how terrible an understatement this is, that it does not begin to catch the darkness that lies between us. I try again. "I am afraid."

Laurel reaches across the table and closes her hand over mine, squeezing gently. "Corbé is not bad. He is very angry and hurt." She hesitates, searching for a simple way to speak to me, that I might understand her words. "His father is a lord. His mother is a *gierana*—like you and me. We work. He hates his father because his father left him here. Perhaps he does not like you because you are a lady; you had what he could not."

"His father is a lord?" I repeat, shocked.

"Yes."

I look down at Laurel's strong, callused hand holding my own newly work-roughened hands. "But I work too. I am a *gierana*."

"Hate is a strange thing, Thorn. We do not always understand it. You are here, but you are still a lady, and the people of the palace still ask about you." I look at her sharply. "They ask and different people tell. We here," she tips her head to indicate the common room, "we do not talk about you. We say only that you do good work, and that you are learning Menay. But others watch you and report what you do. You should know that."

"Thank you." My words are so quiet I think that they could hardly have reached her, but she gives my hands one last squeeze and stands up.

"Corbé will be waiting for you."

I nod, feeling sick to my stomach. All the way down the hall and out the doors I can feel her eyes on me. I take Falada with me to the goose barn, standing by his side while Corbé drives the geese out. Corbé seems no different to me than before, but for a scabbed cut and a fading bruise below his eye. It is only when he looks at me that I see my brother in his eyes; it is a look that takes the breath from my lungs and leaves my throat so dry I cannot find my voice.

I think of Laurel's revelation but I find that my fear overpowers my pity. I do not want to care about Corbé's past, his half-noble lineage. I do not want him near me. Falada watches me covertly, staying by my side. He steps away only a few times to usher back geese to the flock that have slipped my notice. I nod to him gratefully but do not call out; my throat aches fiercely, and I wonder if I will yet catch my death of cold.

On the way back from the field, Falada says, "Have I told you the history of my people?"

I glance at him curiously. He has never mentioned anything of the sort. "No."

"I want you to hear it." Falada lifts his head, looking out over the plains, and when he speaks again his voice is deep and fluid. "There was a time when all the thinking creatures lived in harmony. Men and Horses shared an equal space as companions and caretakers of the earth, for neither race yet called themselves rulers, nor cared for power."

Falada's words spin a path into a history so long past no human has recorded it. I sink into the comfort of his knowledge, the depth of his voice. "Then Men began to take a different course from Horses, using our lesser cousins, the unspeaking horses, as beasts of burden and breeding. Where the Horses had once taught humans how to venerate God and eulogize the world about them, the humans now used those songs to glorify themselves. Corrupted by greed and wishing for glory, the humans grew power-hungry. They thirsted to be remembered by future generations, to gain a measure of immortality. They became warlords and princes, calling others to fight for them, continually killing for a piece of land over which they might have absolute control for a little time. The Horses these humans drove from their lands, wanting neither their honor nor their peaceful example.

"It was the Horses that pushed humans to develop writing, for writing allowed humans to politic and communicate without our knowledge. Here humans could exemplify their superiority without question, proving once and for all their right to master the earth.

"In the end," Falada tells me ruefully, "it came down to our hooves versus your fingers. Not to mention your opposable thumbs."

I look down at my hands.

"If one of my brothers were found, whether Horse or horse, so long as they were caught in the wild, they were put to death. We became hunted, a danger to society, for we created an imbalance in a world where only Men were to rule. We were the seed of revolt, the possibility of another option. That is why you had never heard of us; we have learnt to keep away, to stay out on the empty plains or wander only those lands left untouched by Men."

"I am sorry," I whisper.

"It is no fault of your own."

Isn't it, I wonder. But I ask only, "Why did you stay with me when I am part of what has exiled your people?"

"Did I not tell you that in you I saw some hope for humanity?"

I grin. "Right."

"It is because you did not want your power, nor treat those around you as chattel."

My eyebrows shoot up. "How could you have seen all that in just a few days of traveling?"

"You wished to free me, and you treated the soldiers with respect."

It sounds like very little to put his trust in to me, but then Valka had done neither. Still, "Weren't you worried about trusting me?"

"I did not ask a hostler to call you the first time I spoke with you, did I?" Falada's eyes gleam with humor.

"Well, no, but…"

"But nothing."

"Hmm," I say, and stamp my feet against the cold. We have come to a stop some distance from the city gates. I look up at them, still far enough away that I cannot make out the separate figures of the guards, then turn and sit on the stone wall running alongside the road.

"That," Falada says, as if I had posed him a question, "is why I cannot teach you how to read Menay. We Horses are illiterate."

"Fingers," I muse.

"And thumbs."

"Do you think I should learn to read Menay?"

"Perhaps. You will need to eventually. For now, since I cannot offer you that help, you must focus on learning to speak instead. Language is a weapon, Alyrra. You must learn to defend yourself with what you can."

I wrap my arms around myself, cocooning myself in my cloak. "I don't think any words would have helped me—with Corbé."

"Perhaps not just then, but before, and now after, there are chances."

I think of Laurel, and how differently our conversation might have gone had I told her of Corbé's attack. I wonder what she would have done, if anything might have changed. I wonder if I could have trusted Kestrin with what happened. With a sigh, I look up at Falada. He is beautiful in the dim morning light, his coat shining white, his eyes dark and kind.

"How is it that you are magical?" I ask. "Why would you be created differently from humans?"

Falada smiles. "Perhaps to offset the lack of thumbs."

"Falada!"

"We believe in the same God as you, but where you are told that God created you from earth, we are told that He created us from both earth and fire. Each of our races has certain advantages over the other—these inborn abilities allow for mutual advancement, mutual rivalry, or mutually agreeable separation."

I consider this. "Then what of the Lady? How does she wield magic so easily if it isn't natural to her?"

"I did not say that Horses and humans were the only races, only that we two once lived together in peace."

"Then the Lady …" I stop, caught off-guard by a fit of coughing. I turn my head to the side and spit phlegm into the dirt by the wall. I have a momentary vision of Jilna's face, of how her eyes would have widened, her eyebrows shooting up, at the sight of such behavior and I have to bite back a smile.

"The Lady is not what you would call human," Falada tells me, jerking me back to the conversation.

"Then what is she?"

"You have heard of—how do humans term them—the Fair Folk?"

"Yes," I say, and I hear Jilna's voice once more in my chamber, discussing my nighttime mishap, recounting the rumors that the Fair Folk had come to steal me away.

"They were created from fire alone."

"I don't understand."

"The Fair Folk are created from a different element. They see the play of light and shadow around us in a way that we cannot begin to understand, and so they can touch the lifesong of everything about them to weave what you call magic."

"Which is why, even if the prince has studied magic all his life, he doesn't stand a chance against the Lady," I finish for him.

"Exactly."

I hold myself perfectly still as if our words might fade into the plains, their meaning gently borne away by the morning breeze. Falada watches me, his breath misting in front of him. Finally, he says, "We should keep going. It is cold out here, and you are not yet strong."

We walk back to the city in silence. It takes me longer to clean the barn, my back and legs aching. I set the rake in its wall bracket when I am done and wash my face and hands in a bucket in the back room. When I come back out to the main area, Falada nods towards the staffs that lean against the wall. I walk over to them. It seems to me that they are bars stolen from a prison, that I have seen their smaller brothers strung across my window at home.

"Take one," Falada tells me; it is not strange to me that his voice is both sad and stern. The wood grain is familiar to my hand, the roughness of it sliding easily against my callused palm. It is a familiarity that leaves me slightly nauseous.

Falada walks beside me all the long way down West Road in silence. I wonder if I should ask him again about Horses and the Fair Folk, but I know that he has told me what he wished. He has given me enough to turn over in my mind to distract me from what I am afraid to consider.

That night I take the blankets from my room and move them to Falada's stall. The trunks I leave closed where Kestrin's men have stacked them. As the days pass I use the room only for washing and changing. And every night Falada stands by the stall door, and raises his head to watch me when I cough.

18

My days pass in a haze of work and tiredness. I go to the palace only once, following the page Valka sends, and sit with her to compose another letter to my mother. Valka sneers at me but she cannot hide her discomfort with the contempt of my mother's words. I find myself agreeing with my mother, studying her response carefully, then listening to Valka's account of her life. Valka is indeed acting foolishly in choosing her companions and setting about her intrigues, yet I am not so sure of my mother's advice either. She believes Filadon of little importance, never questioning why he met us at the Border. Surely that simple fact deserves her consideration.

The letter is not ready until late, Valka cross with having to devote such time to it, but I am grateful to leave it signed and sealed on her desk. I meet no one else while at the palace—even Valka's attendants are absent—yet I know that that means nothing: the prince will know of my visit and I wonder what he will make of it. Or rather, I fear I know exactly what he will make of it.

I wake the next morning to find the world buried beneath drifts of snow, the usual sounds of the stables strangely muffled. Horses stand patiently outside, each with their own woolly horse blanket, their breath puffing forth like so much dragon smoke. When Falada and I reach the goose barn, I learn what I have occasionally wondered: that the geese will no longer be taken out. Instead, Corbé and I rake up around them, Falada watching silently from the gate. After we lay down fresh straw, we haul in buckets of grain to pour into the feeding troughs and then part ways, silent as always.

With the change in weather, I spend significantly more time in the common room with the hostlers. Often, in their conversations, they glance at me, inviting me to speak. Remembering Falada's advice, I join in, determinedly asking questions and making comments; while Rowan might sometimes duck his head to hide his amusement, or Violet discreetly rub the smile from her mouth when I say something particularly confused, mostly my friends listen thoughtfully and phrase their replies so that I may catch their meaning.

It is Laurel who brings me an herb to steep in hot water to soothe my cough. And it is Violet who makes it in the morning and leaves it out for me to drink before I leave for the goose barn. Yet both, when I thank them, shake their heads as if they have done nothing at all or as if it is silly of me to mention so small a thing.

After I have reviewed these conversations and kindnesses, lying on my patch of straw, Falada asleep nearby, after I have worried away at the importance of writing and the use of speech, the creation of Horses and Fair Folk, then the darkness begins to fill with shadows I cannot keep at bay any longer. I lie on my back, staring open-eyed at the stall, and I cannot calm the beating of my heart, cannot blot out the words and cruelties of my brother, the daily memories of Corbé, the feel of wood in my hands.

Eventually I venture back to the temple in the company of Falada. I scan the streets as we walk, wondering if I will see the large-eyed street urchin who had spied on me in the temple, or if he was only a figment of my illness. As we near the temple, I spy a trio of boys playing in the shadow of a building. One of them spots me and nudges his friend; he looks up and I see the same peak-faced child. He stares, and then scrabbles to his feet, sprinting down a narrow passage between buildings, his friends at his heels. I watch them, wondering if their departure will herald the arrival of the scar-faced man at the temple for a visit.

I have prayed often: through the long chill afternoons watching the geese, Falada always but a pace away; in the warm darkness of the stable at night when I wake from liquid dreams that shift and swirl and lose their form, but hold always within them the glint of eyes and the gleam of teeth in a smiling mouth. Now, in the temple, I remember how I had prayed the night the boy was chased by the soldiers. I wonder if he had been sent to me, if had been given chance to help him—or to choose between helping him or the soldiers. Had I made a mistake in helping him? For surely the soldiers would not have chased an innocent.

I rub my hands together to warm them, wrapping them in the ends of my cloak. The boy's friends had not been particularly peaceful, friendly citizens; but then there was the scar-faced man who had helped me to the stables when I lay resting in the temple. They had discovered me, known exactly where I lived, and had helped me in return. I have never mentioned the scar-faced man to Falada, just as he has not spoken again of the boy we saved. I wonder what he thinks of the incident; if my actions proved me more or less deserving of the title 'hope for humanity.' I grin to myself in the darkness of the temple, rest my chin upon my knees.

I let these thoughts fade away, listening to the sounds of the night around me. I shift, kneeling, and whisper my prayers again, praying for all the things I have known and learned and felt: for the look in Corbé's eyes and for his father's abandonment, for the prince and his hopeless struggle against the Lady, and for the Lady herself and the emptiness in her eyes, and again and again for myself, and for the feel of wood in my hands, and the stretch of a smile across my face as Corbé bled.

Outside, I hear Falada give a warning snort, one hoof scraping against the temple wall. I go to the doorway, knowing whom I will find: the scar-faced man watches Falada from a few paces away.

He inclines his head to me. "Peace, lady."

"Peace, sir." I stand by Falada's head. I doubt Falada recognizes him, for Falada only saw him in the darkness of the alley that night.

"A friend of ours has asked that you meet him. He waits for you at the Clever Fox." I glance at Falada. "There is a stable there for your horse."

"Where is it?"

He approaches, talking to me as he kneels to pull off his boots. He does not face me, speaking quietly to the temple doorway, describing the turns I must make. I pull my own boots on, listening. When he is done, he steps past me into the temple. "Will you remember the way?"

"Yes."

"He is waiting."

I follow the alley towards the backstreets, Falada at my side. Tension radiates from him like heat. "Remember the boy we helped?" I ask, stepping over a discolored puddle, my boots sliding in the mud. "That was his friend who opened the door that night."

Falada lets out his breath with a huff, unappeased. I pat his shoulder. "I'd be more worried meeting Kestrin than this man. Don't worry."

Falada tosses his head in disagreement.

The stable hands expect us, waving me over and pointing out the stall for Falada. "You'll want to take that back stairway up, miss. Old Timi said you'd be by and there's a room she kept for you up on the second floor," one of them tells me as I swing Falada's stall door shut.

Upstairs, a serving boy scrubs the floor. He backs out of the way, watching as I walk to the third door on the right and knock. A man opens the door, his beard and hooked nose visible even in the shadow of his hood. I step back in confusion, but he gives me a slight bow.

"Please come in, lady." He opens the door wider, gesturing for me to enter. I cross the threshold hesitantly, wondering if I've made a mistake. I wish desperately that Falada had been able to accompany me—but the man leaves, shutting the door behind him. I hear the faint snick of the lock turning.

On the far side of the room a pair of wooden benches flank a stone fireplace; towards the middle huddle a collection of mismatched seats facing each other. It is an odd attempt at a sitting room, and I wonder if it was cobbled together for the occasion or is actually used by the inn. It is a moment before I realize that a man sits motionless in one of the high-backed chairs. Like his friend, he wears his hood up. I look away from him, as if surveying the room further. He does not speak. I cross the room, coming to a stop before a chair, grateful to have something between us.

Before I lose my courage I say, "What do you wish of me?"

"Two things," the man replies. "First, I would settle my debt with you." He gestures to a pouch that sits on the little table beside my chair.

I glance down at it. "What debt?"

With his left hand the man draws up his right sleeve, letting his cloak fall away from his arm. A still-new scar runs the length of his forearm, the skin stretched pink and tight over the closed wound.

"Oh," I say stupidly, staring. The wound looks even more wicked in the light of day. I had suspected it was him, but the sight of the arcing gash not yet fully healed steals my presence of mind. And I had thought of him as a boy always before. But his bearing, his height, suggest he is more man than boy.

"I would thank you for your help," he reiterates, straightening his sleeve.

"I don't want money."

"I have nothing else to give you," he tells me. "And I would not be in your debt."

I peer at the hooded darkness of his face. "You have already repaid me. Your men helped me home when I was ill."

The man inclines his head. "That is the second matter I would speak with you about." He leans back, tilting his face to watch me. The light from the window outlines the barest details of his features: a smooth-shaved chin, slender nose, deep-set eyes. A young man, not yet in his prime but no longer a boy. "It is not wise for you to walk alone at night. Even during the day, you must be aware of where you are."

"I was ill," I explain, flushing.

"All the more reason to be careful," he observes. "Your horse is a peculiar protection to you; I have seen dogs trained to protect, but not horses. He has a mystery about him that keeps you safe when you are with him. Alone, it will only take one drunk, one lout, to destroy your honor."

I nod mutely.

"Good. Do you understand further you were a fool to come here today?"

Fear makes my palms damp. I rest them on the back of the armchair and say as easily as I can, "I recognized the man, and the boy in the street. I knew they were friends of yours."

"You have no reason to trust me."

"Your men helped me home."

"You are alone with me here," he points out coldly. "You are locked in, away from any who know you. I could easily overpower you." I shake my head, backing away from the chair. I glance towards the door: solid oak, thick and ungiving. The window is the only other route out, and the man might easily catch me before I reach it.

"You see the danger," he observes, satisfaction warming his voice. "You are safe here, but do not be so reckless in the future."

I dare not take my eyes from him.

"So you caught sight of Tarkit as well?"

When I do not answer he clarifies, "The boy you saw. I assume it was Tarkit."

I swallow to ease the dryness of my throat. "He came into the temple that day. He must have eight or nine years."

"He is eleven. Children who are not fed well do not grow well." I clasp my hands before me, aware that they are just barely trembling. The man gives no indication if he notices. He stretches out his legs, his eyes on my face. "Tarkit is useful but too honest for the streets. He also lacks the necessary discretion: he was not to let you see him. I will have to put him somewhere else."

I struggle with the implications. "You were having me watched?"

"I owe you a debt. I also considered it likely that you would need protection given the circumstances under which you helped me."

"You've repaid your debt," I say, grateful to shift the subject.

He laughs and I look at him in surprise. I had not expected this man to laugh much; he seemed too somber, too grim for that. "What you did for me that night can hardly be repaid by walking you home when you were not in danger."

"I was unwell."

"But not directly threatened."

"I don't want your money. I did not help you for a reward."

"Yes." He pauses. "Why did you help me?"

I walk around the grouping of chairs to sit next to the man so that we face the room together. I do not want him to see my face. More than that, I want to show him that I trust him. My eyes wander over the scuffed wood floor, the worn furniture. "I don't know," I tell him. "You were slowed by us; I couldn't let that mean your capture."

"Then you could have misdirected the soldiers and left me." I lean my head back against the chair, look up at the ceiling. Soot darkens the beams, wiping away detail. In the far corner a dusty spider web hangs abandoned.

"You needed help."

"I see," he says.

After a breath, I ask, "What will you do with Tarkit?"

"He should be apprenticed to an honest trade, but I cannot apprentice every boy who needs it. I will see about him."

"What does he want to do?"

"He wants to be a baker. I believe he thinks that then he'll never go hungry." I hear the amusement in the man's voice, and a hint of sadness.

"How do you know?"

"I take a personal interest in each of the young boys and girls who run my errands. He is the only son of a widow; she can use the extra coppers he earns from me."

I consider this, remember the boy's angular face. "How much does an apprenticeship cost?"

"Ten silvers a year; he will need two years before he will be offered wages."

I think of Valka's trunks, of the wealth within, and feel a curious sense of lightness as I say, "I will pay for it."

The man tilts his head as if in thought. "You are very idealistic for a servant. You will end up hungry and on the street if you are not careful."

"When I do, it will be my idealism that will send an escort to keep me from harm." The man laughs. I smile, turning toward the sound. He leans forward, elbows on his knees, eyes studying the ground. "And when I am cold and hungry, I will remember that I have helped a young man learn a trade that will keep him warm the rest of his life."

He turns his head to look at me. The very keenness of his regard frightens me. "You are not what any of us thought," he murmurs.

"What do you mean?"

"You are neither goose girl nor lady, but something better than them both."

"You are mistaken," I say, the words bitter on my tongue. "I am nothing."

He considers me, shakes his head. "I hope you do not believe that."

I study my hands, the dry and cracking skin, the ragged nails. Calluses have formed on my palms, replacing the first blisters that developed when I began to clean the barn. They are working hands now. He was right the first time around; I am nothing more than a naïve fool of a serving girl. I shake my head. "How will I get the payment to you?"

"I will send Tarkit to your temple; he'll tell you where to meet one of my men. I am afraid it would not be wise for me to meet with you again."

Elsewhere in the inn, the sound of men laughing drifts up to us. The man remains silent; I am not sure if he watches me or only sits forward, so I keep my eyes on my hands. I wonder what I have done in helping a man who has others he can order to guard or meet me, who is informed by a network of street children and beggars. Did I obstruct the path of the king's justice? But if he is a criminal, why would he not beware of me? Surely he knows of my visits to the palace?

"Why would you trust me enough to send Tarkit to me?" I ask abruptly.

"You have just offered to apprentice the boy."

"I could be trying to lure you into a trap."

"Even if you tortured him, Tarkit wouldn't know where to find me. Nor would you."

"You've spoken to him twice, and will speak to him again," I point out.

"You assume I speak to him directly, rather than through my men," he says, amused. "I am careful whom I meet and how often, especially when the boy is as indiscreet as young Tarkit."

"You have many enemies."

"Enough," he agrees.

I moisten my lips. "Will you tell me who you are?"

He does not answer at once. When he speaks, his voice is quiet, emotionless, "Go back to the stables and ask the hostlers there who Red Hawk is; they will tell you. As for the debt I owe you, I will clear it with you soon. I prefer not to owe debts."

I shake my head. "Your debt is repaid."

He chuckles. "It is *not* repaid, though if I had no sense of honor you would have long since convinced me that I have repaid it ten times over."

"You have trusted me with your name, guarded me when I was alone, and are helping me to do what I wish. Surely you are free of your imagined debt."

He eyes me with disbelief. "Imagined? Had those soldiers caught me, as they surely would have even if I had not stumbled into your horse, I would be dead by now. Instead I am alive and well. My sending men to walk you home when nothing threatens you, or helping you to apprentice one of my own street boys—for that is all you ask—hardly equates."

"Then I don't know how you will get yourself free," I tell him. "I can't think what else you can do."

"We will just have to wait and see."

Falada and I walk out to the snow-buried meadows together; there is something in that part of my day I do not want lost. The road has been traversed by both horses and wagons; their passing has churned the snow to mud. It is the Plains that steal my breath. Here is the reality of white plains running out till they blend with the gray horizon. The wind whistles in my ears, catching at the hood of my battered cloak and slicing through me to numb my bones. Only a few trees grow here, small copses at the corner of meadows or a straggling line along a pasture wall; they greet me like old friends, their branches laden with snowscapes and icicles. Strangely, I find my eyes growing blurry, tears running in icy tracks down my cheeks.

We return from our walk just past noon. I rub Falada down, the work bringing warmth back to me, needling my fingers and toes. Hooves picked and horse blanket draped, Falada follows me into his stall. I settle on the straw, watching him watch me, and can't think what to do.

"Bored?"

I throw a handful of straw at him. "It isn't funny. I've a whole winter ahead of me."

"Then you'd better find something to do."

"Yes, well," I grumble and trail off, having nothing else to say. Falada huffs softly and turns to put his head over the door, his ears swiveling to catch the sound of a conversation from the common room. I look at him, then at the opposite wall, then at my stained and ragged skirt. What was it I used to do every day for the first fifteen years of my life? I loved to go for walks or rides, but it is too cold for that. I used to read what books I could find, but here I have none. What else? Surely I did more than read and walk?

I close my eyes and breathe in the damp horse smell of the barn. I suppose I used to watch people—during receptions and hearings and meals, and in the laundry room and kitchen, and even in the village. Read and walk and watch. They are not even enough to count off on one hand.

But for all my watching, I had never dreamt that my mother dabbled in sorcery. Nor had the court, I expect, or I would have heard it mentioned among the servants.

"Falada?" He flicks an ear towards me. "When I left home my mother cast a spell on me. Have I told you that?"

Falada swings around. From the look in his eye, it is clear I have not; I had assumed he had seen the pouch—and understood what was in it—that day at the stream. So I'd never thought to mention it. Falada stamps his hoof, waiting.

"My mother called me into her room the morning of our departure. She … pricked her finger with a needle and recited a spell while the blood fell on a napkin. Three drops. One was for her love of me, one for her knowledge, and the last … it had to do with strength. I'm not sure if it was hers or mine that she bound to the blood."

"What happened to the cloth?"

"I lost it."

"Lost it?"

"At the river."

"The Lady has it," he murmurs.

I nod.

Falada lifts his head and pokes his nose out, looking about carefully, then turns back to me. "It is of no great concern, I expect."

I swallow a laugh. "That's a change of heart! I thought you were going to kick me."

"Your mother put all that she cared for you into that cloth. Had you let Valka write those letters in your stead, I doubt your mother would have noticed. She gave up her knowledge of you." He hesitates. "It was for the prince, wasn't it?"

"Yes," I say as his words sink in: if only I'd spoken to Falada sooner, I would never have had to write those letters for Valka. Then Kestrin would have had no reason to suspect me. Or at least, not as much—there would have still been the cloak. But he may never had had my belongings searched.

"Would you have used it?"

I shake my head, trying to focus on the conversation. "I hadn't really thought about it."

"It is the kind of magic that can easily backfire."

"I really hadn't thought about it." Falada nods and glances out the door once more. "What about the bit about strength? What did that mean?" I prod.

"What strength you gained from being your mother's daughter was bound into that blood. Had you used it on the prince, he would have held power over you, just as he would have known you better than you might have wished."

"Is that how," I pause, the cord about my neck pressing firmly down. It is a feeling I have not experienced in many weeks, and my hand goes to my throat. Falada understands at once.

"The Lady needed some hold over you: much of magic is a question of power and strength transferred. Whether you willed it or not, you had given her some part of yourself. That chain about your neck is likely your own creation."

"What?"

"Your strength was in silence. She bound you by it."

I consider this, my hand absently massaging my throat. "She only held it," I say, the last word clipped off as the choker tightens further. I clench my jaw shut, holding my breath until the pressure eases.

"She took it from you in the water, didn't she?"

I nod.

"Then she did more than hold it."

"How do you know?"

Falada's ears flick to the hallway and he turns away. I hear footsteps and then Joa steps up to the door, offering his hand, slightly cupped, to Falada. Joa, I have learned, is not just another hostler, but the head hostler of the first stables. He will be the next Master of Horses when the current Master retires. Falada considers Joa carefully before reaching out and blowing lightly into the cupped hand. From where I sit I can see the smile that touches Joa's lips.

"He likes you," I observe. Joa blinks once into the darkness of the stall before he sees me.

"He's a hard one to win," Joa replies, leaning against the door.

"You're winning him."

"I've a long way to go to get where you are. How are the geese?"

"Fine. We aren't taking them out anymore so it's just the cleaning in the morning and an extra feeding at night."

He nods, studying Falada who has moved to the back of the stall and is snuffling some hay, the picture of equine detachment. "Why don't you help out around here in the afternoons?" Joa suggests casually.

Why not? I shrug. "Okay."

"We're short a hostler," he explains, swinging the stall door open for me. I scramble to my feet. "It'll be good to have an extra set of hands in the afternoon, and of course I'll see you're paid for it." I follow after Joa as he explains to me what I have just gotten myself into. It is in some ways exactly what I have been doing since my first day of work: mucking out stalls. It is back-breaking, palm-blistering work, except that now, having been broken and blistered by the geese, I find I am only achy, callused, and inordinately proud of myself.

"One would think you'd discovered how to turn lead to gold, the way you strut around grinning," Falada comments a seven-day later as we take our daily walk. Joa and I have struck a bargain: between cleaning the goose barn and lunch I take my own time, which typically includes a walk out to the pastures or up to the temple. After lunch, I become a full time mucker.

"I have found my calling in life," I explain with mock seriousness. "I have finally discovered the one thing I excel at—"

"Shoveling horse dung?"

"Quite," I say loftily. "As a Horse, I cannot expect you to understand."

"Mmm."

"In the first place, horse dung is far superior to goose dung, being of larger size. In the second, it is of greater import, being of significantly magnified stench. In the third," I break off as Falada butts me with his head. "Hey!"

"Spare me, O Lady of the Shovel."

"Don't forget the pitchfork," I reply tartly.

Falada snorts, then shakes out his mane. "Really, though, I am amazed."

I kick a clump of snow. "My happiest moments at home were either with Jilna or out riding Fleet Wind." I think of the little dell where the Wind would visit, and then of Redna and the many afternoons I spent with her. "I used to envy his hostler for the time she had with him and the other horses. Now I'm in her place, doing the work I've always only watched."

We return to the city in silence, following the road up to the temple. As we turn into the now-familiar alley, I spot Tarkit. He huddles in the doorway, as sallow and scrawny as ever, dark hair hanging in rat tails over his eyes. He jumps to his feet now. "Lady!"

"Tarkit," I return, my voice warm.

The boy flushes slightly. "Did you really see me those times?"

"Yes, I did."

"Oh." He looks down glumly.

"But I had to look for you," I amend.

He brightens at this. "Really?" I nod. "Well, my mother wants to meet you. Could you visit tomorrow?"

"Your *mother*?" This cannot possibly be a code name for the young man I'd helped—Red Hawk.

"She can't walk much," Tarkit explains. "Or she would have come herself."

"I would be honored," I assure him, recovering myself.

Tarkit looks at me oddly.

"I'd like that," I clarify.

"Can you come earlier tomorrow? Without your horse?"

I agree and Tarkit departs with a wave, pelting down the alley. I smother a smile, ducking into the temple to pray. I do not stay long for the days are cold, making the stables a much more comfortable place to make my devotions. Falada agrees, and it has only been because of Red Hawk's promise to send Tarkit that we have come so often to the temple.

On our way back to the stables, a group of riders passes us, drawing the street's attention. Falada and I press ourselves against a building, turning to watch as the riders approach from behind us. I count two quads; in their midst rides the prince. The people recognize Kestrin as well, and many bow or curtsy to him. He rides silently, wrapped in a cloak, one gloved hand holding the reins, his eyes running over his subjects. I wait, standing straight against the wall, and just when I think that he will not see me, he glances to the side, his eyes meeting mine. I look back at him and he nods, a nearly imperceptible dip of his chin, and then they are past.

I am still thinking of the prince after mucking out stalls for Joa all afternoon. I stow my pitchfork in the tack room and pause, looking down at myself. My clothes are all stained and faded to a nondescript mixture of browns. I raise my arm and sniff hesitantly, grimacing at the smell. Even with a weekly wash, it is impossible to keep the stench of sweat and manure at bay.

I let myself into my room, a bucket of water in hand for a quick wash. On the threshold lies a small white square. With a sinking feeling, I set the bucket down, close the door, and retrieve the envelope. From the dust on it, I know it must have lain nearly a week—since my last wash. Inside I find a short message written in my language. It is an invitation to a private dinner to be held in two days' time. It takes a moment for the signature to sink in: Lord Melkior, High Marshall of Menaiya.

After my bath, my water-logged braid hanging heavy as a stone down my back, I take the invitation to Falada's stall and read it to him.

He considers me thoughtfully. "Will you go?"

"I don't know," I admit.

"Why?"

"Why what?"

"Why don't you know?"

I stare down at the bright envelope with its elegant script. Kestrin knows who I am. He must. And I don't want to see him if he does. I take a breath, but all I say is, "I'm not sure about the politics of the court. I'd rather not get Valka angry, and I'm not sure if this invitation is from Kestrin." I twist the end of my braid, thinking of Kestrin, of his discreet greeting as he rode by.

"Aren't you curious why you've been invited?"

"Curiosity doesn't seem like a good reason to court trouble."

"Melkior is one of the king's closest vassals," Falada observes, unperturbed.

"Yes."

"And he hasn't shown any particular interest in you till now."

"Filadon showed more, which is to say we had above two conversations while traveling," I respond wryly.

"Then the invitation is either from the king or Kestrin," Falada concludes. "The only question is why."

I sigh and run my finger over the dark ink, turn the envelope over, touch the broken wax seal. "I've still two days to decide. No need to hurry."

Violet's secret friend shows up to dinner come evening, his hair slicked back from a recent wash, his clothes carefully mended. From the way he embraces Ash and ruffles Rowan's hair it is clear they are old friends, his appearance no great surprise. Despite Violet's best efforts, Ash and Oak maneuver the young man to sit between them. I am introduced to him simply as 'Thorn,' and he, with a polite nod, turns his eyes to Violet and keeps them there. His name, I learn in turn, is Massenso.

Massenso brings more news of the city. He tells us that Lord Melkior, in his capacity of High Marshall, has ordered a crackdown on the thieves in the city, and I think with some guiltiness of Red Hawk.

"The king thinks they are a danger, but they're only thieves," Rowan observes. "Not snatchers."

"Snatchers?" I query when no one answers this.

"Slavers," Ash explains, his voice quickening with anger. "Melkior would do well to track them down instead."

"But surely you don't," I stumble. *Menaiya? Have trouble with slavers?* "You mean the slavers—"

"Snatch our young women and children," Rowan finishes for me. "From the street, from their beds, from wherever."

I glance around at my friends, aghast. Their faces are hard, but they do not speak.

"Thieves are also a danger," Oak rumbles. "Perhaps not as much as the snatchers, but the feuds between the thieving rings must be stopped or there will be blood on the streets."

"I would take Red Hawk any day over the snatchers," Violet says lightly. "They say he's not all bad."

I nearly choke on my bread.

"That's right," Ash agrees, pouring water into my cup. I drink it thankfully. "A good man with a thousand gold coins as bounty for his head."

"A thousand gold coins?" I echo, nearly spilling my water. In all the time I have worked, I have not yet earned a silver.

Violet nods. "He's the leader of the ring of thieves based in the South side."

"Not like Bardok Three-Fingers on the East side or the Black Scholar on the West. They've only got five hundred a piece." Rowan winks at me.

"It will be the death of him one of these days. One of his men will take it, hand him over, and retire into the country to live on their own private estate. Greed's a powerful thing," Laurel says.

"What has he done?" I am painfully certain that I do not want to know.

"He's stolen from half the nobles and our wealthiest merchants, not to mention the king himself. I expect his victims have pledged to pay the reward in return for his death," Massenso tells me.

"Why?"

"Because he stole from them," Ash repeats.

"No, I mean, why does he steal? Where does the money go?"

Massenso shrugs. "To hear the king's men, he's a power-hungry bully, buying his way into every dark business there is. Though no one believes he deals with the snatchers."

"He takes care of his own," Ash adds. "He hires poor folk who have nothing to live on and gives them enough to get by. There're probably a hundred street urchins who would give their lives for him, for the coppers he tosses their way to keep their eyes open for him. But he's playing his own games too, setting by a store for himself. If he's wise, he'll know that he can't keep on without getting caught."

"I've heard enough of Red Hawk to hope he doesn't get caught," Rowan says bluntly. "Better him than the Black Scholar."

The others shoot him warning glances but none contradict him, Laurel simply turning the conversation away altogether to the delegation from Chariksen, visiting from far across the Winter Seas.

·20·

"Finally!" Tarkit cries as I turn down the alley the next morning. Beside him, his two friends gather up their marbles. "We waited *forever*. Come on."

"Sorry." I have arrived a full hour earlier than usual, but clearly not early enough. We start down the alley together. "Who are your friends?"

"I'm Torto!" the first boy pipes up. "I'm ten, and my Papa's gonna apprentice me to a carpenter."

"That's nothing," Tarkit boasts. "I'm gonna be a baker. I start tomorrow!"

"Who is your master?" The question unleashes a flood of information, including the size of the shop, the number of apprentices, the new set of shoes he will be given, and how his first task will be to draw water for all the baking. When he pauses for breath, and perhaps to dredge up any additional details he has somehow left out, I turn to the third boy. "And what's your name?"

The boy, by far the youngest and the dirtiest of the three, shrugs his shoulders and looks to Torto.

"That's my brother," Torto explains. "His name is Fen but he doesn't speak to no one."

I nod knowingly. "He's shy."

"No, he stopped talking. He doesn't talk to no one now, not even our Mama."

"Why?"

"He got snatched," Tarkit whispers. "They found him and he was all hurt and beat up bad. He got better but he didn't ever talk again after that." Fen glances at Tarkit, then up at me, his small body tense.

"I'm sorry," I say without thinking.

"It's not your fault." Tarkit looks at me curiously.

"No," I respond, but I am not sure what I mean by it.

"Anyhow, he doesn't remember it."

"What?"

"Being snatched," Torto pipes in. "Whenever we get back one of the snatched, they have to be blessed. The snatchers put a curse on them, the Darkness, but the blessing makes it okay."

"What's the Darkness?"

The boys look at me in surprise. "It's just the Darkness," Tarkit says. "Their minds go dark. But the blessing saves them from that."

"By taking their memories?"

"Just of the snatching, sometimes a little more than that. And who would want to remember that anyway?"

I frown, fighting a niggling sense of wrongness over a 'blessing' that takes your memories whether you want to keep them or not. Clearly this is something the boys accept, though. They lead me through a wide cobbled square. A set of gallows have been erected here, and while they are empty, their solid, enduring presence brings a dark gloom to the square. A beggar sleeps curled up against the platform, shielded from the wind. "What is this place?" I ask, forcing myself to move onto another topic.

"Hanging Square," Tarkit says as indifferently as if we were passing through his kitchen.

Torto, noting my stare, expands on this. "It's where all the bad people are killed. Sometimes they chop off their heads instead of hanging them."

Torto proceeds to describe a particularly gruesome tale of an execution where a murderer made an ill-fated attempt to escape with his head intact, only to be mobbed and torn to pieces. I try not to listen, letting his story patter past me, and at the first opportunity ask more about his apprenticeship. So, between carpentry and baking, we arrive at Tarkit's home.

Tarkit lives in a rundown yellow-brick building. Refuse litters the street, though the stained halls have been swept clean. The slightly warmer air wafting out of the occasional opened door brings with it the stink of dirty bodies. I clench my teeth as we descend to the basement, ducking through a low door covered by a cloth into a dark room. I stumble to a halt.

"Is that Lady Thorn, Tarkit?" a woman asks, her voice gravelly.

"Yes, Mama. I brought her to see you like I said."

"Light us a candle and go play out front. Stay near, hear me? You'll walk her back."

"Yes, Mama," Tarkit lights a stubby candle, throwing a wavering yellow light over a woman lying huddled in blankets on her sleeping mat, a stool beside her. Tarkit leaves the candle on the stool and departs, Torto and Fen right behind him.

"Good evening," I say, dipping my head to the woman.

"Come closer, lady. I want to see your face."

I kneel beside the sleeping mat, meeting the woman's gaze. Her features, ravaged by illness and hard living, still shows traces of youth. While her eyes are old, her cheeks are yet smooth; while her brow is furrowed with wrinkles, her lips are still firm and pretty. Her hair has a sprinkling of gray. I would guess her to be barely more than a handful of years past my own.

"You're a pretty girl," she says, smiling. "Tarkit told me about you, and then I heard that he'd been given an apprenticeship. People don't do that, you know, pay for a whole apprenticeship just like that. I asked Artemian and he wouldn't say at first, but then he said it was you.

"I wanted to thank you, lady. You've given my Tarkit what I always wished for him. I'd given up hope of getting Tarkit a place once his father died." She reaches out and grasps my hand, her own hard and knobby, her fingers stiff as claws. I wonder if her feet are equally deformed, her legs bent by illness and cold, leaving her bedbound. "Thank you," she says.

"I didn't," I hesitate, clear my throat, start over. "Tarkit's a good boy. He helped me. I'm glad I could help him back."

"No," she says. "You weren't paying a debt. You know that. I just wanted to see your face and thank you myself. That's all."

I nod, at a loss for words. She pats my hand and asks me what I do, and we talk for a few minutes about the geese and the stables. Then I say goodbye and walk back outside.

Tarkit greets me with a shout, Torto and Fen racing up alongside him. "We'll show you the city now, okay?"

I hesitate, but I had told Joa that I might be late returning. "All right."

"We'll start with the well," Torto says imperiously. "The others will be there."

The well lies only a short walk away, a small stone circle at the center of a square, a bucket lying beside it attached to an iron ring by rope. A group of children play around the well. As we near them my escort breaks into a run, shouting names. They are swallowed immediately by the group, disappearing into a dizzying swarm of arms, legs and heads.

"Who's that?" one voice cries. The little figures turn to look at me as one.

"Yeah, Tarkit, who's that came with you?"

"Oh, that's Thorn."

"Yeah?" says one of the boys. He stands about a head taller than Tarkit, his face long and his ears protruding like the two handles of a jug. "Where'd she come from?"

"She works down in the king's stables," Tarkit explains. "But she used to live out in the country, and now she's the friend of a friend." The children look me over with interest.

"There aren't any country girls that work in the stables," says one of the girls.

"That's right," I agree. "I've been staying in the stables but I'm actually a goose girl."

"Goose girl!" cries one of the boys. "Honk! Honk!" He is joined at once by the rest of the group, who honk and scronk in a most un-goose-like manner, milling around me and yanking at my cloak and skirts.

I stare down at them, momentarily speechless, then burst into laughter. "You'd better be grateful I don't mistake you for my geese. I've got a staff I keep just for them." I catch hold of the nearest girl and give her a good tickle. She shrieks and breaks free at the same time two boys jump on me, holding on tight as leeches. I stagger to the side, tickling one while I try to wriggle free from the other. Just as I get free of him, two girls reach up to tickle me as well. With a cry, I go down in a mass of arms and legs, tickling as fiercely as I can amid shouts and howls of laughter.

"Okay!" I cry as three more children throw themselves on top of me. "Mercy! Mercy!" The children take a few more minutes to calm down, but as I offer no further resistance they eventually allow me to sit up.

"She's okay," says the jug-eared boy. I look around at them, their thin faces and sharp elbows, their ragged clothing and unkempt hair. Their breath makes puffs of smoke before them so it is as though I look through a mist at them, as if they are fading even as I watch.

"Yeah," Tarkit says as he picks himself up off the ground.

"And what's your name?" I say to the boy.

"I'm Lakmino," he says, raising his chin proudly.

I nod knowingly. "Of course. And what are the rest of your names?"

They introduce themselves in what amounts to a shouting match, jumping up and down and shoving each other. While I manage to catch at least three names, within a moment I have lost which little person each name belongs to.

I push myself to my feet. "Since I'm new to the city, why don't you tell me what I should know about it?"

The children glance at each other, then to Lakmino.

"Well," he says importantly, "We know everything that happens here." The other children nod in agreement. "Don't ever go out after dark. There are good thieves and bad thieves, and the bad ones go out at night, and sometimes they steal people."

I flinch, even though the common room conversation last night should have prepared me for this.

"It's true," says one of the boys from the back. "They snatched my sister last year, and we didn't never find her."

"Yeah," Tarkit says. "And they snatch children too, like Fen. So you better be careful."

"Tell her about the guards," whispers a girl.

Lakmino takes the cue. "Don't go to the guards if you need help. They'll only laugh at you unless you have money. You can come find us, and we'll get you help. My brother's big and strong, and so are Gira and Moté's brothers." The other children nod and mutter their agreement.

"Thank you," I say soberly. "I'll remember that."

"And there's an old witch that lives over there," another girl points down an alley. "She'll put a curse on anyone who bothers her; and she was trained in one of the mage schools so you can't even report her."

We spend the next hour or so together, the children showing me all their favorite spots, vying with each other to be the first to explain. In addition to the well, I see the doorway to the witch's house, walk past the healer's home, look down from the roof where the children normally pelt people with snowballs, see the back of the local butcher's shop where wormy meat can often be got, and spy on the guardhouse at the corner of a large square.

The city feels different here from the streets where I have walked with Falada. Here people move slowly, as if walking were marginally easier than standing still. Some carry sacks of coal or bundles of wood; others pass with the whiff of food; most merely wrap their clothes tightly about them. Many have upon them the look of hard work, their naturally tan faces pale and thin, their eyes shadowed. Occasionally, a man or woman huddles at a corner, bundled in ragged blankets and cloaks and scarves. They hold out empty tin cups and shake them at me, but I have left my purse at the stables and have nothing to give.

The only place I see that speaks of plenty lies on the very edge of the children's domain: they take me to see a great temple built on a cobbled plaza beside South Road. The building is magnificent, carvings flowing up the marble facade and decorating the arched doorways, the doors themselves left open to give a glimpse of a mosaic-spread inner courtyard and a splashing fountain. "That's Speakers' Hall," Lakmino says in a voice hushed with longing. "They have a free school, if you can pass the test for it, and everyone who studies there never goes hungry again." The other children are still for once, and in their eyes I see the reflection of unspoken, unattainable dreams. Despite the beauty of the building, I am glad when we turn back into the narrow alleys and they begin to jostle and laugh again.

By the time we head home, my stomach has begun to grumble, telling me lunch is long past. Tarkit's face is pale with cold, his shoulders hunched. We walk quickly, Tarkit's head darting back and forth.

"What are you looking for?" I ask, half teasing.

"You should always be careful," he says. "Torto's cousin got beat up by robbers last month in the middle of the day. It's okay when there's a bunch of us, but now there's only you and me. The snatchers don't always care what time of day it is. They just sneak up on you and—wham!—you're gone."

I keep watch after that, scanning the alleys and doorways for men or groups of boys. I follow Tarkit as he crosses streets or turns down a different alley to avoid others, his route no longer seeming quite so erratic or whimsical.

"This isn't the way to the stables," I say, recognizing the streets from my walks with Falada.

"No," he agrees quietly. "I'm taking you to meet Artemian."

"Who's that?" He puts his finger to his lips to hush me. I watch the streets carefully for landmarks. Finally, down a narrow back alley we enter a brick building. We climb a shadowy set of stairs to a landing with two doors, one of them boarded up. Tarkit knocks on the other, calling out his name.

I hear a step from the other side and the door swings open. "Come in."

I follow Tarkit into the lamplit room. My old friend, the scar-faced man, closes the door behind us. "Wait by the door, boy. I'll speak with the lady in the next room."

I follow him, studying his long stride, his broad shoulders and wiry build. A swordsman, I think. There is gray in his hair and I realize with shock that he must be more than twice my age. I wonder how Red Hawk won such a man's loyalty.

"Artemian," he says, closing the door behind us. I *had* guessed that.

"Thorn."

"Do you have the money for the boy's apprenticeship?"

I slide my fingers under the sash at my waist and pull out the pouch I had taken from Valka's trunk, handing it to the man. He opens it and tips its contents into his palm: a delicate gold pendant adorned with pearls. Wordlessly, he drops the pendant into the pouch, closing his fingers around it. I watch him, wondering if I have misjudged it.

"You haven't much experience with valuing jewelry, have you?"

I flush. "Is it too little?"

"This little trinket of yours will pay for ten boys, not one."

I let out my breath in relief. "Then use it for ten boys." He pockets the pouch but makes no move towards the door. I lick my lips and say, "Thank you for helping me that day."

Artemian shrugs. "Our friend asked that we keep an eye on you. I myself am grateful for the service you did him." His fingers flick to his pocket. "You've got this pendant here, enough to keep you for years, and you're willing to work at the stables for a pittance. Why? Why not use a portion for the boy, and keep the rest for yourself?"

"I don't need it," I say. "Not the way he does, or the other boys I see on the street." I am aware of the man's eyes on me, aware of my cracked and callused hands, my stained tunic and threadbare cloak, the sores at the corners of my mouth. But every day I have three meals, every night I have a place to sleep. *And it isn't mine to take.* I stare at the ground, wondering what I have become, if I have turned into a Red Hawk myself, stealing Valka's jewels.

"I see." He rubs his arm with his hand, as if his muscles ache. "I want you to remember this place. If you need something more from our friend, come find me. If I'm not here, leave a lock of your hair and I'll find you."

"My hair?"

"It's an uncommon color. I'll know it's yours."

"Oh."

He opens the door, waving me out. Tarkit smiles as he sees me. "Go in peace, lady."

Alone in my room later that night, I throw open my traveling trunk and go through my clothes, searching out something to wear to Melkior's dinner.

The carriage driver hands me into a plush interior of velvet cushions and gilded metalwork. I have brushed the straw from my hair and scrubbed the grime from my hands, unearthed an embroidered silk skirt and tunic I half-like from among Valka's trunks, and even dabbed a bit of lilac water on to hide the scent of the stables that yet lingers. Even so, I feel nothing more than a servant playing at dress-up, riding in a carriage meant for greater people.

We pass through the palace gates and follow the well-cobbled road that circles the palace, rolling to a stop in a private courtyard. Sitting in the darkness of the carriage looking out, I feel as I did that first time I came to the palace, Valka across from me and the tastes of familiarity and fear mingling on my tongue. I cannot remember much of Melkior: he is tall, with a wide smile and shrewd eyes. I search my memory for any other bits or images that might offer further insight, but come up empty-handed.

The driver clears his throat, standing at the door, and I realize he has been waiting more than a moment for me to alight. So it is with muffled laughter that I first set foot into Melkior's courtyard. I cross to the doors still smiling, unperturbed by the silent welcome. There is, after all, a single main door and two smaller ones: it would not take my brother to sort out which to use.

I enter a small foyer. It is richly adorned in mosaics, lit by candles in wrought bronze candleholders, the wooden floor gleaming. I pass through the far door and enter a plush sitting room. Here I detect the hand of a woman; no doubt Melkior is married, I think, and then am surprised his wife did not address the card to me herself. The room is carefully laid out, low gold and maroon couches lining the wall, interspersed with small gilt tables of various shapes and sizes that are set with silver trays filled with delicacies.

Kestrin rises from where he had been lounging on one of the couches, offering me an elegant court bow. "My lady, may I welcome you? Our hosts will join us shortly."

So it had been him—not that I am surprised. I curtsy. "Your Highness, I thank you. I hope I have not inconvenienced his lordship."

Kestrin is dressed elegantly in a dark green tunic and cream sash. They are lightly embroidered, with a touch of cream at the cuffs of his tunic, and green chasing its way along his sash. He wears calf-length boots, and I can just make out cream pants tucked into them. "Lord Melkior did not expect you quite so soon. We are notorious for starting our functions long after the appointed time."

"I see," I say, my voice sweet. He had planned this little tete-a-tete; I'm not about to take the blame for it. "It is not my habit to keep a carriage waiting. I suppose in future I should, that I not abuse my hosts' hospitality."

I startle a genuine laugh for him. He gestures to the sofas. "Won't you join me?" I take a seat as he moves to a side table. A decanter of wine and a set of crystal goblets wait on a silver tray. "May I offer you refreshment?"

"I thank you, but I do not drink wine." He arches an eyebrow, his hand pausing as it curves around the bottle. "Do not let me deter you," I stammer, catching the glint of recognition in his eyes. I have hated the stuff since my brother first made a habit of seeking me out after he'd had a bottle— something Kestrin might well have heard about. "I would not decrease your pleasure."

"There is no worry of that." His hand drops from the bottle. "I take more pleasure in good company than I do in wine."

Here is an opening then to find out what he wants of me, what he really knows. "You must be hard-pressed indeed, Your Highness, to count me as good company. Have you found the court so troublesome you would rather spend an evening with a servant?"

"The particular goose girl in question has more of the court in her, I believe, than she gives herself credit. Certainly it is in her blood."

I stiffen, but I cannot tell whether he means Valka's noble lineage, or my own royal heritage. I wave my hand dismissively, trying to keep the conversation to a lighter tone. "Your Highness must not expect any of the latest court gossip from me, whatever sort of blood I may have."

He stretches his legs out before him, his lips quirked in a smile. "I am tired of gossip. I expect we shall get on very well, the two of us."

My stomach flutters unexpectedly. I find myself smiling at him as he regards me warmly. "Who will make our party tonight?" I ask abruptly. "Will your lady join us?"

"The princess and her closest friends have traveled a day's journey north for the purpose of an outing."

"I am not much of a replacement, Your Highness, though I may speak the same language."

"Oh, I would not worry about that," he says. "As for the rest of the party: Lord and Lady Melkior are our hosts, their two daughters, Fesa and Tahima, will accompany us, as well as their son Jashi. My cousin, Lord Garrin, will also attend. He is usually as prompt as yourself."

I remember vaguely being told about him—the only other member of the royal family. It had not occurred to me until now to wonder what became of his parents. "I do not believe I have met him before."

"He was in his lands to the west when you arrived. While he has come here for the winter, there have been few opportunities for an introduction."

"No," I agree. "I tend to avoid the court unless I have an errand, and apparently he has a similar contempt for goose barns."

"Though your errands have proved most intriguing," Kestrin says, his eyes crinkling with amusement.

I manage a small smile. "My errands or my property, Your Highness?"

"Both, I must admit. Though you have left off your errands of late, and so I have had little indeed to occupy my idle hours."

"Is that why I have been invited here, that you may allay your boredom on a winter day?"

"I thought it might not be a bad thing for you to have friends among the court," he tells me, and though his tone remains light his eyes turn serious.

I consider him, but he is still too like my brother for me to accept these words from him. Certainly Melkior and every other member of this small party owe Kestrin what loyalties they have, and would easily betray any thoughtless word of mine to him. "I doubt I could command any true friendships among the court, considering my position."

"I think you underrate yourself, my lady."

"Am I a lady again, then?" I ask. If he thinks me foolish enough to forget the danger the court poses to a serving girl, I have no qualms with reminding him of what he himself has called me before. "Pray when was I restored to such a title from that of 'thorn'?"

He laughs a court laugh but his features grow still, his expression bland. I have turned his mood. "My lady by her own admission has always been a thorn."

"No, Your Highness, not always. Just upon my arrival here. It is a distinction of a sort, you know, to be a bother to a prince."

"I believe you have likewise always been a lady of high distinction."

I bite my lip. I had forgotten the barbed sting of the language of the court, and now my mind stumbles over its dusty store of half-meant responses and finds nothing fitting. "I did not think I was so very early," I finally say.

"Our hosts will be in momentarily. Lord Melkior is thought to be the essence of punctuality; I'm sure he will be sorry to have kept you waiting."

I meet his gaze steadily. There is one thing I did want to ask of Kestrin, and I had better ask it before anyone else arrives. "I would not want to abuse his hospitality. Much as you may wish me to have friends among the court, I do not want enemies."

Kestrin raises an eyebrow. "Are those lines not already drawn?"

"A personal disagreement can be pushed into something greater. My friends are in the stable, not here."

Kestrin studies me, dark eyes unreadable. "You will not be harmed for having answered this invitation."

I look away from him. I had not expected such a frank response, and for a moment I can think of nothing to say. My mouth is dry, and I almost wish I had accepted his offer of wine that I might wet my throat. But it would have loosened my tongue as well, a much worse fate. I swallow once. "We have discussed trust before, Your Highness. You wished to know how much you might trust me. I tell you now that I have little trust in those I know. There is more of honesty among the common folk than the court, and even there friendships are sometimes betrayed."

"I give you my word," he says, his voice hard. I wonder if he has ever had his honesty questioned before.

"Your Highness, why have you invited me here?"

"Melkior," the prince begins, but I interrupt him.

"—Invited me here on your bidding."

Kestrin nods his head once. "He too may be a friend to you."

"He too?" I echo. Kestrin's eyes flicker earth and gold in the lamplight. "Have I another friend in the court?"

"Are you so surprised?"

I look away. I do not want to play this game. Why would he want to present himself as an ally? *He knows.* Here it is, plain as day. He has offered me his protection in meeting Melkior. He plans to introduce me to his cousin, Lord Garrin. He referred to the court being in my blood—

"You are afraid again," Kestrin says softly.

I begin to turn towards him and then stop. I do not want him to see my fear any more clearly. I look down to my hands folded in my lap and curse him silently.

"I owe you an apology for how I have treated you. I put too much stock in my betrothed's words, and thought you were not to be trusted. I was wrong, and I am sorry for it." He pauses and then says simply, "I trust you."

I flinch, though he has made no move towards me. "You shouldn't," I tell him abruptly.

"Why?"

Because I have already betrayed you once. I shake my head, for even the thought of the words brings the familiar pressure to my throat.

"Why?" he says again, his voice gentle.

"I have told you, Your Highness, that you must not trust many people. I am not among those you should trust."

"Would you betray me?"

"I hold no allegiance to you," I say stiffly, knowing I must warn him away from trusting me, and so falling victim to the Lady.

"Would you betray me?" he repeats, his voice even and measured.

"I am—easily manipulated."

"Then I will not trust your enemies or mine."

I purse my lips. He intends to make himself out as my friend and ally now, whether I will it or not, but the greater danger is to him, not me. Before I can formulate a response, the prince shifts in his seat. I hear a faint step in the hallway.

"I expect the evening shall begin shortly. I hope you will enjoy it." The court has returned to his voice. I incline my head in acknowledgement and smooth my hands over my skirts.

A young man enters, dressed much like Kestrin, but where the prince tends towards darker clothes, his cousin prefers the light. His tunic shines a sky blue trimmed with silver and tan embroidery. Garrin shares Kestrin's sculpted features and shrewd eyes, though I think from his easy smile and casual bow that he may have more of a way with ladies than Kestrin has displayed.

I rise to curtsy to him.

"Garrin," Kestrin says quietly from his seat, "the Lady Thoreena. Lady, my cousin Lord Garrin of Cenatil."

"I am honored to make your acquaintance, my lady," Garrin says gallantly, and his smile has more intimacy and less truth than his cousin's.

"The honor is mine, my lord."

"Won't you sit with us, Garrin? Melkior should be in momentarily," Kestrin says smoothly. I sit down again, settling my skirts around me while Garrin finds a seat. Just as Garrin leans back and looks towards me, Lord and Lady Melkior make their entrance, inciting another round of bowing and scraping.

"My lord and lady," I say mechanically in response to the introductions.

Melkior's wife, Lady Dinari, is exquisite, her form petite, her fingers delicate, her hair smooth and lustrous. She wears jewels about her neck, delicate earrings, and gems hung on gold threads that settle over her hair. It is difficult to tell whether she is meant to adorn the jewels, or the jewels to adorn her. I think she must be twice my age at least; her face, while showing maturity in the fine touch of crows' feet by her eyes, yet displays the youth of her manners. Her voice when she speaks is light and feathery, her manners impeccable, and yet I cannot bring myself to trust her. When I meet her gaze as we discourse on the weather, I find them to be half-veiled; I wonder if Melkior knows what he has married, or if he treats her as she dresses: a fragile and invaluable doll.

Their daughters arrive upon their heels, and then the son: Fesa and Tahima resemble their mother in all but the color of their eyes, for Fesa's eyes are a golden brown and Tahima's a honeyed amber; as for Jashi, he is but a boy of thirteen, and while he is well-versed in the court and the titles of his father, he still has much to learn.

We proceed to a magnificent dining room, where we are served course upon course of curried meats, creamy soups, and spiced vegetables. I had forgotten what feasts these dinners are, and how much is wasted, left behind uneaten on our plates. The conversation is light, in keeping with the atmosphere, and when I am not pretending interest in the court-related discussion between Fesa and Tahima, who sit to my left, I struggle to make the same kind of conversation with Lord Garrin, who sits to my right.

I find this cousin of the prince delightful in word and manner. He is all that is animated and thoughtful and ... not shallow, I realize. He is quite probably as deep and shrewd as Kestrin. It is that I am not sure what lies beneath his friendly facade. Is he truly what he seems, or are the games he plays much more complex because he cannot be read at all? I can only hope that Kestrin has good reason to trust him now.

We withdraw to an evening room after dinner. The men sit to one side, discussing the politics of the day. The ladies pick up their embroidery, conversing amongst themselves. The discussion here is of a different tenor than that of the dining room, for with the men slightly removed there are less inhibitions among the women. Fesa, especially, seems more open and less pleasing, and I take it from her occasional contemptuous glance towards me that she has entered into the good graces of Valka and hopes now to gather some gossip. I do my best to offer her nothing at all, murmuring vague replies to questions about our court at home, my journey with the princess and everything in between.

At length, the men rise and Kestrin and Garrin make their adieu. I curtsy, and once Melkior has seen them out, he returns to escort me to my carriage.

As we leave the evening room, I realize that I have an unexpected opportunity in his escort. I turn to him, slowing my pace. "Do you spend the winter at court, my lord?"

"There is much to keep us busy this winter. We will stay on till spring."

"I understand that there has been some trouble in the city."

"My lady speaks of the thieves," he replies darkly. "They are a plague in the city this year."

"I mean specifically those thieves who snatch people as well."

Melkior glances at me from the corner of his eye. "Oh, I do not think that happens very much. The threat of slavers is much blown out of proportion. It is the thieving rings we are concerned with: the Black Scholar, Red Hawk, and their ilk. It is my work to track them down."

I have to bite my tongue to keep from arguing about the Snatchers. But I am unlikely to convince Melkior to act upon the Snatchers in the few moments of our walk to the carriage. I can at least learn more of Red Hawk. "What then?" I ask. "What is the punishment for thievery?"

"For simple thievery—very little. A flogging and a day in the stocks will do. But for such as these men are the king has decreed the punishment as death."

"Death, my lord?"

"A lady might not understand the gravity of the offense," Melkior says, all condescension. The door to the foyer has been closed, and he reaches to open it.

"Is it so grave a thing to steal when given no other choice?" I ask quickly.

"It is not simple thievery that we discuss, but organized rings. They make their own laws and demand their own allegiance, flaunting the king's authority. Judge for yourself, my lady." Melkior opens the door, standing back to allow me through.

"My lord argues well," I agree reluctantly; as a threat to order and society, the rings of thieves might appear dangerous. I do not yet know enough of the thieves to argue the point. I step through the door to find Kestrin waiting for me.

"Peace, my lady," Melkior says from behind me and shuts the door.

"Your Highness," I say to Kestrin, taken aback, "I did not expect to see you again tonight."

"I am glad I can occasionally surpass your expectations," he says, grinning, and offers me his arm. I take it hesitantly. He notes my reluctance, and his eyes darken, his tone is stiff, hurt, as he says, "I wish only to learn how you enjoyed your evening."

"It has been most interesting," I reply evasively. We enter the courtyard where the carriage waits.

"I thought as much. How did you like my cousin?"

"He is very different from Your Highness."

Kestrin hands me up into the waiting carriage, then pauses, retaining my hand in his. I take my seat, my hand still outstretched and caught in his, and wait.

He smiles crookedly. "You have a way of not answering questions I am coming to enjoy."

I feel myself flush, but it is not all embarrassment. "Thank you, Your Highness," I mutter.

"I hope you will join us again."

"I would not intrude more than I have already."

"It is no intrusion, lady, but a pleasure."

I look past him to Melkior's door. "While Your Highness may find me an interesting topic to fill your idle hours with, I pray you will pity a poor goose girl and let her be."

My words sink into the quiet. A horse shifts, his hooves scraping the cobblestones, and that is all. I meet Kestrin's gaze, waiting, hoping.

"There will be another dinner in three weeks' time. Will you not come?" He holds my gaze, and I cannot read the emotion written there.

"Your Highness," I look away, knowing how it must go. I am, after all, a servant now. He can use that easily enough, even knowing who I truly am. "I can only obey."

He releases my hand as if I had burnt him. "No. I would not rob you of your choice. But if you change your mind, I hope you will tell me."

I glance at him wonderingly. "Your Highness."

"I thank you for this evening, my lady." He swings the door shut, calling up to the driver. I fall back against the cushions and close my eyes, but the whole drive to the stables I see the prince as he stood in the courtyard, telling me of the next invitation, listening to my response: face drawn and serious, woodland eyes shadowed. The expression lingering about his mouth and lurking behind his eyes haunts me; it is only once I have changed and settled down once more in Falada's stall that the right word comes to me: despair.

Falada and I follow West Road to the plains, Falada's hooves crunching into the frozen gravel. The wind lies quiet, making the day seem almost warm, though the clouds hang low and foreboding as always.

"Falada," I start, and then stop. Only last night I shared dinner with Kestrin, and realized he knows who I am. Yet he has not forced me to return to the court. The only thing he has forced on me is his trust: it is the one thing I would not have.

"Yes, Alyrra."

I shake my head, and we walk on in silence, turning off the road to follow one of a myriad of ragged paths. The grass here is bent and broken, white with hoarfrost. I take a breath and say, "If the Fair Folk are so strong, why do you think I could help the Prince?"

"They are strong," Falada replies, "but they are not invincible."

"What is their weakness?"

Falada laughs. "You are still naïve, child. They have no one overbearing weakness, just as humans do not. They were simply created as limited beings, as were all creatures."

"Then how can anyone expect me to help Kestrin? I'm no sorceress, nor have I any interest in magic. I don't see what you or he could expect me to do."

"I hope you will answer your duty to your people and to Kestrin."

"What will that accomplish?"

"Only you can guess at that, Alyrra."

"It will do nothing," I respond savagely. "Kestrin will die one way or the other, and I will be used as a pawn again if I am not sent back home."

"And Valka?"

"Valka deserves whatever she gets."

"What will she do when the time comes?"

"What time?"

"The time for the Lady to kill Kestrin."

I stand completely still at that, listening to the whisper of his words fade away. It is easy for me to suggest that the prince might die, but to hear Falada so bluntly refer to Kestrin's eminent murder brings me back to myself.

"What will Valka do?" Falada prods.

"She will give him up," I reply, hating her, hating myself.

"When?"

"Once she is well settled. Married, perhaps with child."

"So she will not allow herself to be a pawn."

"No."

"Can you not find your own way and help Kestrin as well?"

"How? I'm a goose girl, Falada. I'm dispensable, a pawn by definition."

"That is your choice."

"You are impossible," I snap. Falada sighs and turns back towards the city. When we reach the road again I hold out my hand to him, touching a wisp of his mane. "I can't make the rules, Falada. This isn't my game."

"If you are in the game then you can make it yours."

"I can't learn magic. I don't want to."

Falada glances at me curiously. "No one has asked you to."

"No," I mutter. We walk the rest of the way to the city in silence, Falada throwing me the occasional unreadable glance. My mood follows me home, clinging like so much mud to my boots.

I dream of a brown forest, the sky overcast and gray. I find small corpses littering the ground, dried to husks, bones protruding: rabbits stretched full length behind skeletal bushes, foxes torn apart at the edges of clearings, little creatures—moles and squirrels—curled into death-still balls, cushioned on the fallen leaves.

I do not care. I am driven by thirst, my throat so parched it may bleed if I cannot find drink. Eventually, I stumble upon a flowing stream. When I bend to drink, my eyes encounter fish floating belly-up. I straighten, my gaze fastening on the stiff bodies of deer, half-submerged. When I open my mouth to scream, my throat tears and fills with blood, choking me.

I sit up gasping for breath, coming back by degrees to the stable and its smells, the soft whiffling of horses. Falada sleeps, undisturbed by my sudden waking. I watch the soft rise and fall of his chest, trace the clean curves of his body against the darkness of the far wall. It is a long time before I fall back to sleep.

Joa comes to the stall door at dawn. I had heard soldiers come through earlier, a strange occurrence, but they were far enough away that their muted conversation did not reach me. Now, from the look on Joa's face, I wish I had tried harder to listen.

"What is it?"

"Orders from the princess," Joa says, his face sallow in the half-light.

"I thought she was gone."

"She returned yesterday." He looks away. "She wants her horse put to death."

I stare at him blankly. He nods past me, to Falada.

"No." The word jerks from me as if a hand has yanked out my heart.

"I am sorry," Joa says quietly.

"No! Falada isn't hers. She can't kill him."

Joa shrugs, refusing to meet my gaze.

"When?" If there is enough time for Falada to get through the city gates—

He makes a helpless gesture. "They're waiting."

"Give me a moment," I tell him. He leaves without a word. "Falada," I whisper, turning to him. "If I ride you they won't dare hurt you. We can get away—the city gates are right here."

"No, child."

"No? What do you mean, *no*?"

"They will shoot me and arrest you. We would be hunted even if we escaped the gates."

"You cannot let them kill you."

"If I struggle, they will know I am a thinking creature and I will endanger my people. If you struggle for this, you will endanger all that hangs in the balance."

He is right. I feel perilously close to tears. "I will kill her."

"Don't be ridiculous. You will not attempt to avenge me. Do you understand?"

I cannot escape his gaze. "Yes."

"Have my head hung in the city gates that I might see you."

"What?" I stare at him, appalled.

"Do it."

"As you wish." I hear the sound of approaching boots. "Oh Falada," I whisper, and step forward. He lowers his head, his chin resting on my shoulder. I throw my arms around his neck, burying my face in his mane. The boots stop outside our stall, silence rolling out to smother every other sound.

Falada lifts his head, disengaging himself, but as he does he brings his mouth to my ear and breathes softly, "Stay." I nod, touching his cheek, then turn towards the men. I do not recognize the soldiers. I ignore them, addressing Joa instead.

"I want his head mounted and placed in the gates, that I might remember him."

"What you ask will cost money," Joa says uneasily.

"I will pay." One of the soldiers reaches out and unlatches the door, swinging it open. The other throws a harness to me. I catch it clumsily. "Joa, see that the blade is sharp, and it is done well. Gently."

"I will," he promises.

I turn back to Falada, holding the harness. He watches me, unmoving. I toss it into the back of the stall. "He has followed you once before and he will follow you now. He will not require a harness." Joa nods. I glare at the soldiers. "Nor will he require direction."

"Very well," Joa says. "Let's get this done." He starts towards the stable doors, the two soldiers holding back for us to pass. Falada walks in step with me. When we reach the doors I put a hand on his crest. He looks down at me and then steps out, following Joa around the practice ring and out of sight, towards the knacker and his death.

I stay in Falada's stall until I hear Joa return, the sound of hostlers calling greetings to him. He stops at the stall door, his face is grim; I do not think I have ever seen his eyes so hard. He studies my face in turn, though I cannot say what he sees. At length he says, "It was done well; he had an easy death. I am sorry for this, Thorn. He was a good horse."

"Yes," I say softly.

"His head will be hung as you ask. If you give me the money, I will see to it."

"Yes."

"Are you well?" His eyes flicker over my face uncertainly. I nod once, step out of the stall, and close the door.

In my room, I throw open the traveling trunk. Wrapped in a kerchief at the top are the paltry few copper coins I have earned working here. I push them to the side, knowing they are not enough, and search through the clothes. I know that I could take Valka's jewelry, that I have only to open her trunks and look and I will find what her father gave her for her wedding, but I do not want anything of hers to touch Falada's memory.

At the bottom of the trunk I find a pouch with the gift Jilna gave me many months ago. I tip the necklace into my hand, the silver chain and pendant shining in the dim light. I lift the chain, barely believing my eyes: it has been repaired, the chain mended, the pendant polished. Why? Why would he have gotten it fixed? For surely only Kestrin had had the opportunity to go through my trunks in his search for the cloak. Had he hoped I would find it soon after he returned the trunks? That I would take it as a sign of the kindness I had insisted he lacked? Or was it merely a token action, something to assuage a guilty conscience? I am grateful, suddenly and fiercely, that I did not find the necklace until now, did not have the chance to choose to wear it. I think of Jilna, with her tired face and her thin arms holding me tight, and I do not want that memory tainted. No, Jilna would have wanted this instead. I clench the necklace in my fist and go down to find Joa, hoping it will be enough.

Night enters the temple long before it settles upon the rest of the city. I would find the symbolic meaning amusing, I think, if it were not simply a practical reality: in a room with a single door for lighting, and that set off of an alley, sunlight rarely enters and shadows come early.

I sit hunched in the corner, my arms hugging my knees, and fill my mind with imagined meanings for the things around me: the faint sound of people on West Road, rustling in the stillness and then fading to nothing; the dirt that has accumulated on the mats so that, when I press my forehead to the floor in prayer, the grains stick to my skin; the way the wind whips into the little room at intervals, slapping my cheeks and snatching away what warmth I might have gained since it last entered. On occasion another worshipper enters, offering me a nod or smile before going about their devotions, departing in silence.

The hours have slipped away like this. Now, with night approaching, I cannot focus my thoughts on my surroundings. They fall away from me, sinking into darkness, and I am left holding tight to myself. I hear Falada's voice echo in my mind, prodding me to accept Melkior's dinner invitation. I thought I'd weighed all the risks. I had gained Kestrin's word that nothing would harm me. But I had forgotten to speak for Falada.

I had thought I would cry, that I would mourn my friend with a river of tears, but I cannot. My throat aches so that it is difficult to swallow, my chest is tight, and my eyes are dry as bone. My breath hangs in the air before dissipating, coiling gently before fading to nothing. I wonder what Falada would tell me now, if he were suddenly returned to me. As if he stood beside me, I hear his voice: *What will you do?*

What can I do? I bite my lip, holding it between my teeth and concentrating on the pin-prick of pain.

I can imagine Falada turning his head towards me, nostrils flaring in irritation, eyes sparking. *Will you leave her to practice her mercy on the prince and all Menaiya?*

I can't face the Lady now. I don't know what to do.

With a half-gasped laugh, I realize Falada's response: *I did not suggest you face the Lady.*

I stand up, my joints creaking and popping. Outside, I look up at the sky; there is still a hint of light above. West Road bustles with end-of-day business, lantern light pouring out of open shops, the scent of food on the air. With so much activity, at least I need not fear for my safety.

I pass through the palace gates without glancing at the soldiers. If they note my passage, they say nothing. The main doors are closed against the cold. I follow the wall until I come to a servants' entrance, the door propped open. I pass down strange corridors with quick steps, making my way in the general direction of the Receiving Hall. Once I reach familiar halls, I continue on to Valka's apartments. Twice I pause before turning a corner, waiting for those already there to move on, their voices fading. Once I retrace my steps, hurrying before whoever approaches reaches me.

I drift to a stop when I reach the sweeping staircase up to the royal suites. I have not decided what I will say, only that I must address her. Now, standing before the stairs, I try to order my thoughts.

"Lady." I jump, twisting to face the prince. It would be him of course. There is no one else I could possibly meet in this godforsaken place but him.

"Forgive me; I did not mean to startle you."

"No," I agree.

He looks at me sharply. What a contrast I must present to the last time we met: the tunic and skirt I wear are stained from work, threadbare at the seams. I cannot guess what he sees in my face.

"If you would accompany me, lady," he says. He holds out his hand and I place my own in it without thinking. He turns me, tucking my hand into the crook of his arm, and leads me up the stairs. We pass Valka's apartment without a word. He releases my hand only so that he may open a door, nodding for me to enter. I hesitate on the threshold. These are his rooms. I should not be here.

"Go in," he says from behind me. I do not know where to go, pausing in the middle of the sitting room before moving toward the fire.

Kestrin does not speak at once. I hear him walk to a side table, then cross to me. He holds a goblet out to me. I take it mechanically and bring it to my lips, then stop. The heady, fruity scent assaults my nose. I do not need to look down to see what I hold.

"Drink it," he says. I remain unmoving, the goblet nearly touching my lips, and I think of my brother, his breath sickly sweet as he towers over me. I step back, hurling the wine into the fire. It spits and smokes before flaring up brighter than before. Kestrin stands perfectly still. I hold the goblet out to him, my eyes trained on the fire. When he does not take it, I lift it up and set it on the mantle.

"You needed that," he tells me.

"No."

"Come sit down, my lady."

"I would rather go."

He laughs harshly. My eyes snap to him. "I am sure you would. I am always forcing you to speak with me." He shakes his head, and his words now are a command, "Sit down."

I meet his gaze just long enough for him to know that I choose to obey before moving to a chair. The prince takes a seat beside me, watching the flames. A silence grows between us, allowing his words to dig their poisoned talons into me, injecting a bitterness into my blood that I can well nigh taste on my tongue.

"You did not force me to accept Melkior's invitation," I tell him, my words so soft they seem to get lost even as they leave my lips. I wonder if they reach him, for he makes no sign of having heard. I turn back to the fire. "That was my own stupidity."

"Do you regret it?"

"Dearly."

"That is why you are here?"

I should not be here at all. Not in his rooms. But I say only, "I would speak with the princess."

"I suspected you were not seeking me."

"No."

"No," he echoes. "What do you need of her?"

I shake my head.

He tries again. "Will you tell me what has happened?"

I do not look at him. I do not want to tell him that Valka found a way to reach past the protection he promised me. I would not know how to explain what Falada was to me without letting slip his secret.

"Something has happened, I can see that. It has leached the color from your face." He purses his lips. "I gave you my word two nights ago that nothing would touch you. Now you appear in the palace like a ghost, with nothing to say but that you would see the princess. What did she do?" He half smiles. "Or has someone died?"

I start and turn away quickly. "Nothing. It's nothing."

"Who's dead?" His voice is hard, the question commanding an answer.

"No one—just a Horse—that is all." A log cracks on the fire, sending a small shower of sparks across the grate. My eyes sting when I close them, but still I have no tears.

"The white? Who used to go everywhere with you?"

I nod.

"When?"

I grip my hands together in my lap. "This morning."

"I see. You are sure the princess issued the orders?"

"Joa said so."

"He could not have been mistaken?"

"I don't know. I intend to speak with her."

He studies me. "What will you say?"

I shake my head. "I don't know."

"She is expecting you." I meet his gaze in surprise. "She has ordered her attendants to sleep in her antechamber tonight. You will not be able to pass through to see her in private."

I close my eyes, remembering my first visit to Valka, her terror at waking to find me beside her. Yes, she expected me tonight. For all her tricks and power, she fears what I might do in private. I feel a smile twist my lips, and then I press my hand to my mouth, forcing the smile away. I swallow, opening my eyes to stare ahead of me. This is why, I think. This is why Falada told me not to avenge his death.

I stand up. "I'm going now."

Kestrin raises his eyes to mine. "Are you sure it is wise?"

"I won't speak to her." I am so very tired of all this. "There is no justice to be had there. I am leaving."

Kestrin stands. "Did you walk here alone from the stables?"

"I—yes."

"I will arrange for a quad to escort you back down."

I close my eyes for the space of a few breaths. When I open them again, I say, "You cannot protect me or mine from your enemies, Kestrin." There is no protection to be had in this palace, I think, nor in all the land. I cross the room to the door.

"Thorn." I look back at him, my fingers curling around the door handle. He stands with his back to the fire, watching me. "It is not for fear of my enemies that you need an escort." He closes the distance between us. "It is because you are a woman alone in the city. Let me call my quad for you."

I think of Red Hawk, and of Corbé, and know Kestrin speaks truth. "I thank you," I say wearily.

Kestrin pulls an elegant, braided rope that hangs beside the door. I listen for the sound of a bell, but hear nothing. He reaches out, taking my hand and turning it to cradle in his own. He traces the calluses on my fingers, my palm. A shiver runs up my arm, curling in my belly, but I cannot move to pull my hand away. No one has touched me so before, as if I were precious. "I cannot protect you so far from the court," he says. "Will you not return?"

His words release me from the spell of his touch. I pull my hand free. "There is nothing for me here," I say, my voice shaking. The words hang in the air between us. I am not sure if I spoke them for him or for myself.

Kestrin does not answer. I hear the faint sound of boots. A knock at the door heralds my escort home.

·23·

I spend the night in my upstairs room, alternately pacing a tight circuit or stretching out wide-eyed and exhausted on my sleeping mat. Although the room is warm and should have felt more comfortable than a stall, the four walls bear down on me through the darkness. I doze fitfully, falling asleep near dawn.

When I go down to the common room for breakfast, Laurel has already set bread and cheese on a plate for me. Violet sits at the table, pressing her thumb against the crumbs on her plate and licking them off.

"You look terrible," she says without preamble.

"Violet!"

"Well, she does." Violet turns back to me, "You'd better start eating regular again. You didn't eat at all yesterday, and with this cold weather you'll be sick as—as Harefoot is, if you aren't careful."

"Harefoot's sick?" I ask, without much hope of distracting her.

"Like to die," Violet informs me. "And you look like death waking up. I thought it was just the dark last night when I saw you coming in, but it's actually you." She grins as she speaks, but the gravity of her words won't be undone.

"Thanks."

"Violet," Laurel explains, sitting down next to me at the table, "is worried about you."

"And Laurel," Violet responds, "sat up half the night listening to you stomp circles in your room not because she was worried about you but because she prefers to sleep sitting up with her eyes open."

"I didn't mean to wake you," I say guiltily. "I didn't realize I was that loud."

"You weren't; we just sleep next to you," Laurel tells me.

"And the floorboards creak." Violet points at my plate. "Eat your bread." I take a bite to humor her, glancing at Laurel for help.

"We both agreed it wouldn't do to speak to you in front of the boys," Laurel says.

"That's right."

"But we know you had a close bond with that horse, and that he was killed because you went up to that dinner." Laurel tips her head towards the palace. "If anything like that is like to happen again, you tell us and we'll keep you and yours safe."

I stare at her.

"Even," Violet adds, "if that means making someone up there cross."

"*Especially* if that means making someone up there cross."

"Eat your cheese," Violet finishes, smiling.

I obediently take a bite of cheese. With my mouth full, I stammer, "But that would be dangerous for you. And—"

"Dangerous? *Dangerous?* Did she say dangerous?" Violet cries. Laurel nods somberly, her eyes crinkled with amusement. "Thorn, let me tell you about dangerous. Dangerous is cutting your finger on a rusty nail and getting lockjaw. Dangerous is walking behind a skittish horse and getting kicked against a wall. Dangerous is walking anywhere in this city at night. Dangerous is *not* helping someone stay safe."

I shake my head, thinking of helping Red Hawk, then of Valka's vengeance. "If they're willing to kill a horse, they won't worry about hurting a servant as well."

Violet lets her breath out in a gust of frustration. "Thorn. Of all the dangerous ways I could die that I meet with every day, I would much rather choose to die from helping someone. Weigh it," she says, holding her hands up in an imaginary scale. "Die helping someone, get kicked against a wall. Hmm, what would you prefer?"

I rub my hands over my face. "I don't want any of you to get hurt."

"So you want Laurel to die of lockjaw."

I laugh despite myself. "You know I don't! I don't want you or Laurel or anyone else to get hurt because of me."

"Very noble," Laurel observes. "But we're family here—we are, and your name fits right in with ours, so don't doubt it for a minute. Family looks out for each other."

Her words warm me like the glow of a friendly fire—*family*. This is what I had missed all my life: Laurel's motherly touch, the boys' concern, Violet's love. They are everything I have ever wanted, and nothing like my own family. I can only grin foolishly in response.

"Well, I'm glad that's settled," Violet says, jumping up and heading for the door. "I've got to check on Harefoot again."

"But—"

"Don't even try," she calls from the hallway.

Laurel smiles. "No more putting yourself in harm's way, Thorn. You have trouble, you tell us." She reaches over and squeezes my hand. "We mean it."

Laurel shoos me off to the goose barn a few minutes later. Corbé has not yet arrived, so I open the doors and begin raking. I am grateful for his absence, working as fast as I can in hopes of missing him entirely, but just as I am shoveling the last of the dung into the barrel, he stumps through the gate.

I turn to him. "I did not come yesterday, so let me finish our work today. Then we will be even."

He stands at the gate with his back to the light, making it hard to read his expression. I think perhaps he is surprised, but the emotion is fleeting, his face closed and contemptuous as always. "I do not leave my duties undone."

I flush and shrug, turning away from him to stow the shovel. I hear him start towards me and instinctively I pivot back, holding the shovel ready. He pauses, then continues walking, passing me to climb up the ladder nailed to the back wall. He forks down straw from the loft while I replenish the food and water for the geese. Neither of us speaks again.

Joa comes by to check on me as I muck out stalls in the afternoon, but after a quiet hello and how-are-you there is nothing left to say. I feel his eyes on me a more than once as I move between stalls, but he does not approach me.

After work, I walk up to the city gates. There, within the great stone passage, hangs Falada's head. It has been mounted on a wooden board and nailed up, hanging an arm's length above my head if not more. I stare up at it, feeling my stomach tighten painfully. His eyes and mouth have been sewn shut with great, ghastly stitches. The silken fur of his face already shows gray with damp. I turn away, back towards the stables.

Princess.

I jerk to stop, eyes flying up to Falada's head. It hangs unmoving, the mane rimmed with ice, as dead as if it had been carved from stone. And yet— surely I had heard the echo of a voice?

"Falada," I whisper.

"What's the problem there?" One of the guards walks towards me, hand on his sword. I force a smile and lift my hand in acknowledgement, hurrying back to the stables. The soldiers on duty watch as I pass them, but they say no further word.

Two days later, Valka sends a page for me. He leaves me to wait in her empty apartments. I walk through the rooms, taking my time, observing the changes. The first sitting room has been rearranged to allow for larger parties, with fewer tables and more couches. Does Valka entertain here? Surely she would prefer rooms with private entrances for servants, though perhaps she admits the favored few into the intimacy of her own sitting room.

In the second room, there are new baubles on the side tables: priceless glass globes, little golden boxes, ornately painted vases. I walk to the desk and open the compartment. Inside I find letters from my mother, a new one topmost. I leave this aside, knowing that Valka will give it to me when she arrives. Below them lies an artist's sketch of Valka, poised for her portrait. I examine it, but the girl drawn there looks no more familiar to me than the face of any other court noble.

There are also two notes from Kestrin, hardly more than a line in length. I run my fingertips over his script. It is confident, smooth and well-practiced. The notes came attached to some gift, for they do little more than address the princess, suggest she might find pleasure in the contents of an unknown package, and end with his signature. I had not thought how Kestrin would handle his relationship with Valka, whether he would woo her or dismiss her. These two notes tell a tale I had not envisioned: Kestrin as the courtly lover, sending his betrothed trinkets. I imagine the occasional warm glance, the intimate smile, and feel my stomach clench.

I shove his notes back under the artist's sketch. Beneath them lie a few sheets of unused parchment. I lift these up, uncovering letters from home I have not seen before, letters from Daerilin. I pause, listening, but there is no sound yet of Valka. I open the first of these letters, and the next, and the third after that, skimming them quickly before returning them to the compartment. From Daerilin's words to his daughter, it is clear he believes her part of the court, enjoying her time in Menaiya. Each gives some news of her family and some token pieces of advice regarding her position, followed by a fatherly adieu. They are relatively kind letters, Daerilin's affection for his daughter apparent. But there is little of substance in them. He thinks his daughter well placed for marriage; that is the only news he wishes to hear from her.

Kestrin has read them as well, I am sure. I wonder what he thought of them, how far they helped him to unveil Valka's true identity. I smile thinly, thinking that my first statement to him—that my family expected my marriage and would not wish for my return home—might have been neatly corroborated by the letters. If only they were not in Valka's keeping. What a fool she has been for assuming the sanctity of her belongings.

I hear a step in the other room and drop into the nearest seat. I watch as Valka enters, tilting my head back and meeting her gaze.

"I see you have forgotten your court manners." Valka regards me contemptuously.

"Perhaps." Shouldn't she be the one to curtsy to me?

"How are the stables treating you? Still shoveling dung?"

"An honest living often involves dealing with others' filth."

She arches an eyebrow. "Indeed." She walks over to her writing desk and fishes out the newest letter from my mother. "This came a few days ago. We will write the response now. My attendants will be here shortly; I want you gone by then."

I take the letter from her and open it, perusing its contents. It runs long, containing strict admonishments for my foolish behavior in growing distant from Melkior and his ilk, recommendations on how to draw them back into my circle, a concise analysis of how my politicking may influence my future power, and suggestions on how to dress and act to keep Kestrin's interest alive. It ends with an injunction to send more news at once, and mentions the preparations being made for the queen and prince to attend the wedding in the spring. I weigh the letter in my hand, then drop it onto the desk.

"Where are you going?"

"Back to the stables."

"What of the response?"

"What of it?"

"We'll write it now." She gestures imperiously towards the desk.

"By all means, write a response."

Valka bristles. "You know full well that you must write it."

"We made an agreement: I would write for you and you would leave me alone. You broke that agreement. It is over." I start towards the door.

"You're angry about the horse, aren't you?" she calls after me, her voice light and mocking.

I squeeze my eyes shut, then turn to face her. "The horse?"

"The white. The Master of Horses said it couldn't be saddled. It was hardly fit for the dogs. I should have had it killed when we first arrived, considering how it went wild on the journey."

"It's a pity you didn't," I say coldly. "Then I might have excused you."

"Excused me? Since when do I answer to a servant for my actions?"

I shrug. "I might ask the same. But it doesn't matter, does it? The horse is dead, our agreement is finished, and I am going."

"You'll write these letters, or you'll be sorry," she snarls.

"You'll find a better reason for me to write them, or I'll disappear. There are other places I can work. What will you do then?"

She pales. "No one would take you."

"We'll just have to see."

"I don't need the letters that much."

"When my family comes for the wedding, do you think you'll be able to fool them? They'll want to know why you haven't written. They'll be watching very carefully because they'll know something is wrong. Only if you keep up the pretense now can you hope to slip past them then; they'll think your change due to living here, not something that has been done to you. Think hard on it, *princess*."

I watch the emotions slide through her eyes: anger, fear, hate. There will be no place for me in the stables and goose barn once she weds.

"What do you want?" Valka asks, her voice cold and haughty.

"I wanted you to keep your word."

"You dared to dine alone with my prince—with Melkior and his family—and you charge me with breaking my word? What of you? You filthy little witch! The horse was mine; I had every right to kill it. You are lucky I didn't have you whipped."

"You swore to leave me alone; you knew the horse was part of my life. I promised only to write your letters for you."

"You were to stay in your place! Instead you came traipsing up to the palace the moment I turn my back."

"Is that what you thought?" I ask, pressing my hands flat against my skirts. "A goose girl is invited to dinner by a lord: do you think it is a question or a command? Do you think I had the right to refuse? Go and ask Melkior's daughters if I maligned you! I kept my word. As for my place, what is that exactly? What am I?"

Valka glares at me, her face pale with anger. "You are nothing."

"Then you will not need me." I turn on my heel, striding through the outer sitting room. I hear the ink pot shatter against the wall as I close the door behind me.

Outside, the wind whips through the courtyard. I shrug deeper into my battered traveling cloak, wishing I had bundled up more. My cloak had been made for cool fall weather, not for these frigid winter winds. I keep my head down, trudging towards the gates. As I reach them, a riding party trots in. I step back against the stone wall, watching the front mounted guards swing past, followed by Kestrin and the king, and behind them the rest of the guard.

Kestrin catches sight of me at once; even with his face shadowed by his cloak's hood, I see the gleam of his eyes as they fasten on me. I shrug deeper in my cloak, dropping my head to stare at the cobblestones underfoot. I do not look up again until they are past. I hope Kestrin did not watch me all the way through, that his father did not take notice. Hurrying down West Road, I clench my jaw to keep my teeth from chattering and wish that I might never see Kestrin again.

"You're still not sleeping well, are you?" Violet asks me a handful of mornings later.

I shake my head. "But I'm trying not to stomp around as much now."

"Why don't you share our room?"

"What?" I say, not sure I have heard her right.

"You might sleep easier with other folk around you."

"I might." I have never shared a room before, other than my nights in Falada's stall.

"I can't imagine sleeping alone," Violet goes on. "I'm so used to the sound of other people, I think it would be too quiet. Laurel says I laugh in my sleep, but I'll tell you what I know for sure: Laurel snores." With a wink, Violet skips out of the room, her laughter drowning out Laurel's protestations of innocence.

I mull over her offer through the morning, wondering what it would be like to sleep in the same room as someone else. It must, I think, take a deep trust, an unshakeable certainty in the goodness of others.

As I enter the stables on my way to lunch, I find Rowan currying a horse by the door. He glances my way mischievously. "I hear there's a package for you in the common room."

"A package?"

"Ayah, a lad dropped it off this morning. Seems Violet isn't the only one with an admirer."

"It must be something else," I protest, flushing. "I haven't got an admirer."

He nods sagely. "Go see what it is, and then we'll argue."

"I will," I say, relieved.

I hurry straight to the common room, grateful to find it empty. The package sits on the table, a cloth-wrapped bundle tied with a bit of cord. I pull the cord to the side and squeeze the package out, then unwrap the rough burlap cloth. Inside, there is more cloth—a heavy, dark green wool. I lift it up, its folds falling open. It is a cloak.

"Isn't that pretty?" I look up to see Violet in the doorway. "Put it on, then. Let's see."

I unfasten my old cloak, dumping it over the bench, and swing the new cloak over my shoulders. Violet helps settle it on my shoulders, tugging the folds into place. "That green sets off your eyes. And it's a good warm cloak for this weather."

"There's a brooch, too," I say, spotting the feather-shaped bronze pin.

"Isn't that fitting," Violet says, grinning, and pins it on.

"Thorn has a lover!" Rowan shouts from the hallway.

I swing around, scrabbling to open the brooch. "I don't!"

Violet giggles. "She's turning redder than her hair. Let her be."

The next moment, Ash joins Rowan, jostling each other into the room. "What's this? Who's the man?"

"It isn't anyone!"

"Well then, who sent this for you?" Violet asks practically.

"I don't know," I admit.

"There's something still left in that package," she observes. "Take a look."

Violet is right: at the bottom of the cloth wrapping lie a pair of leather gloves and a small square envelope.

"Mighty suspicious looking," Ash says, peering over my shoulder.

"Can you read?" Violet asks. At my surprised nod, she says, "Well then, see who it's from."

I open the envelope slowly, wishing I was alone, and pull out a square of paper. In a script I recognize from the notes I saw in Valka's room are written the words: *Warm days, peaceful nights. K.*

"Not what you expected," Ash observes. I look up at him. "You went all still and serious," he elaborates, "so I'm guessing it isn't an admirer."

"And I was so hopeful." Rowan sighs.

"I don't think I should wear it," I say, putting the envelope down and making to take off the cloak.

"Don't, Thorn," Violet catches my hand. "You need that cloak. Whoever sent it to you knew your old cloak wasn't half as good as a threadbare horse blanket. And you could do with a pair of gloves to warm your hands. The One knows we could all use gloves."

"I'm not sure if I should."

"Can you return it?" Ash asks.

Without insulting him? "No."

"Would you be in his debt if you used it?"

I hesitate, considering the angles. Is it a peace offering? A token of friendship? Perhaps, but not a debt. "No."

"Then use it," Ash says simply, and the others nod their agreement.

Violet bundles up my old cloak in the wrapping cloth and hands it to me. "Keep this for the spring when you'll want something light."

In the evening, Violet walks into my room, rolls up my sleeping mat without a word, and carries it to her and Laurel's room.

"Good," Laurel says as Violet deposits it on the floor. "It'll be nice having you here."

"Not a word from you," Violet says, shaking a finger at me. I laugh, helping her straighten the sheets. "You'll sleep well," she promises. "You'll see."

She is wrong. I listen to my friends' even breathing, their faint shifts and—from Violet—the occasional endearing dream-induced giggle, and I find a strange peace stealing over me. I lie on my side, facing them, and think of their lives, of Tarkit and his mother, of all the people I have seen in the city, and while sleep does not come until late and late, in the morning I am not quite as exhausted as I have been.

My days begin to fall into an uneasy rhythm. In the mornings, Corbé and I clean out the goose barn. Afterwards, I walk out to the plains, or through the bigger streets of the city. As Tarkit taught me, I am careful of entering quiet streets or walking near groups of men, wary really of anything that might suggest the danger of being attacked or snatched. But I cannot help my interest in the city itself, in its inhabitants: the men and women and children, each with their own stories. So many lives, so much need and hope and laughter mixed in together. Only near the palace, where the wealthy merchants and the best artisans and guildworkers live, do I catch the scent of affluence in the air.

By late afternoon, I return to muck out my assigned stalls. "We'll make a hostler out of you yet," Joa tells me, stopping by to watch me work. I only nod and bend back to my work. At night I lie awake listening to Laurel and Violet, filling myself with the warmth of their nearness, their regard, before drifting off to sleep.

But as I work, or wander the streets, or sit with my friends in the common room, words echo in my ears, memories teasing the corners of my vision as if they are the future. I see the prince standing alone in Melkior's courtyard. I see him in his rooms offering what protection he can, feel his touch on my palm. Or, much worse, I remember him facing the Lady, fear in his eyes. I keep his note in my pocket, slipping my hand in to touch it, and wonder what he is doing, why I haven't seen him again. Everywhere I go, I carry him with me in the warmth of my cloak and the comfort of my gloves.

I think of Valka as well, of her smile on the river bank, of her foolish, self-gratifying politicking in court, and, inevitably, of a day long ago, before she left for Daerilin's lands in the south. I tell the story to Falada, leaning against the wall beneath his head, tell him because I have nearly forgotten, because the words spilling out in the dim passage of the city gates brings a new clarity to my shadowed thoughts.

"Valka and I were never friends. She kept me company because that was what she had to do. She liked my brother more; she would follow him around whenever she could. He was brilliant and handsome and so very, very much what she wanted to be, or have." I scuff the cobblestones. "They were always doing things together, causing trouble. I hated it, and she knew it. They drowned one of the kitchen cats once. They used to trick the servants, spread rumors about nobles, that sort of thing.

"My mother thought it was amusing. She would sit my brother down only to tell him how he might better avoid detection, or how to know which people might be laughed at and which ones he should respect. Because of her, he and Valka never paid a price for their actions.

"One day I saw Valka with a sapphire brooch. I didn't think much of it; I'd seen her with jewelry often enough. She was standing in the hallway looking at it, and when she saw me she stuffed it in her pocket.

"That afternoon, one of the ladies realized she was missing her brooch. She made a great scene of it, calling in all the servants. My brother, Valka and I, and half the nobles, all went to see about it." The memory has a bitter taste to it, as if it might yet make me sick. I take a breath and continue, "Valka said she had seen one of the servants with it that morning. It was a serving girl from the kitchen, a mouse of a girl who used to hide from the men. The guards caught hold of the girl and searched her. She started screaming that she'd never taken anything. They hit her, and asked her if she was calling Valka a liar, and Valka just smiled.

"The lady whose brooch it was said if the girl didn't return it, she'd have her hung. If she gave back the brooch, she'd only be flogged and thrown out of the Hall. The girl was weeping. She swore she was innocent but no one believed her.

"So I said they were wrong. I'd never been more frightened in my life. I said I'd seen Valka with the brooch that morning, and that she'd put it in her pocket. Valka laughed and asked who could believe such a thing, and I—I told the guards to check. They did; they caught her and emptied her pockets, because I was the princess and ordered it, and the brooch fell on the floor in front of everyone." I close my eyes thinking of that moment, of Valka's face blotched with rage, and of my brother's eyes, narrow and ugly, and the silence. The silence as the guards let the serving girl go, and as the guard who had emptied Valka's pocket picked up the brooch and handed it to the lady, and the silence as she just stared at it and nodded.

"Valka left the Hall that night. They would have hung the girl, and all they did to Valka was send her off in disgrace like a dog with its tail between its legs." The serving girl had left the Hall as well, fleeing before anyone remembered her.

The story spread like wildfire, borne on the tongues of servants and nobles alike. After that, the servants were always kind to me. With quick looks, flicks of their fingers, they warned me when my brother was nearby. I learned to value this, for it was the next day my brother first pushed me down a flight of stairs. His petty cruelties took on a sharper edge, and in my mother's cold smiles and studied ignorance of his actions I learned the cost of turning upon my peer, my mother's vassal.

I do not look up now as I start towards the stable, but it is as if I can feel Falada's gaze upon me. He had known Valka for what she was.

"Princess."

I whirl around. Falada gazes down at me, dark eyes bright as stars in the shadow.

"Falada," I whisper.

"Princess, what will you do?" he asks, as he always has.

I close my eyes. A tear spills over my cheek. "Oh Falada, I don't—"

"You, girl!" a soldiers calls.

I open my eyes. Above me, Falada's head hangs as it has these many days, cold and stiff and so very dead.

"What are you doing?" the soldier asks roughly. "I thought I heard voices."

"There's no one," I say, walking past him. "Only me and the dead horse's head."

Matsin son of Körto pauses beside me on his way through the stable, purportedly inspecting the horse I am currying.

"Come to the palace tonight as you are dressed," he says. "I will meet you at the gates at sundown."

"Who—" I begin, but he has already moved on. It will be Kestrin anyway.

At the temple, I sit against the wall, wrapped loosely in my cloak. The weather has begun to warm up, water trickling off of roofs, running in rivulets down the roads, churning the alleys to mud beneath the daily onslaught of wagon wheels, horses' hooves and boots. If the weather holds, within a week Corbé and I will take the geese out to pasture again.

I shift, listening for voices from the street. I have not seen Tarkit since the day I spent with him. I wonder if he has started his apprenticeship, and how his mother fares. I wonder what Kestrin intends, why he would send for me, specifying that I not dress up. At least he does not wish to attract attention to my arrival. I pick at the dirt beneath my fingernails. Does he intend for me to dress up when I arrive there? Or does he only wish for a private audience with me? I turn Matsin's words over in my mind, trying to ferret out what Kestrin has in mind. I am still worrying at it as I make my way back to the stables. As I reach a cross street a few blocks from the stables, I run into Torto with Fen and a handful of other youngsters.

"Thorn! Thorn!" cries Torto. "Lakmino says that you aren't really from the country. Is it true?"

I look at him, blink once to clear my mind. "In a way. I lived over the mountains in—"

"Then you *are* the new princess's serving girl!" Torto crows.

"No," I say sharply. "I was never her servant." The children stare at me. "I only traveled with her," I clarify.

"You speak Menay really well," says one of the other children. "The princess is terrible. I know because my aunt works in the palace and she's seen her."

"I live out here. I had to learn Menay. There's no one to translate for me here, is there?"

"No," Torto agrees. "But if you aren't her servant, what are you?"

"I told you that on the first day," I say, trying not to sound overly peeved. "I'm the goose girl. I serve the king, just like the rest of you."

"But shouldn't you serve the princess first?" asks one of the girls, Kiri by name. "After all, he's our king, not yours."

"He gave me a job and a place to stay when I didn't have either. I think I'll stick with him."

Torto nods. "I'd do that too."

"Did you used to live at court?" pipes up one of the other children.

"Yes."

"What's it like?"

"Yeah, what'd you eat there?"

"Did you have a lot of dresses?" Kiri asks, wide-eyed.

"Did you have a horse?" Torto asks.

"One question at a time," I say, laughing. "Walk with me and I'll answer what I can before we get to the stables."

"Did you have a horse?" Torto asks again, grabbing my hand and pulling me past the other children.

"I did. His name was *Fleet Wind*." I translate the name for the children, then repeat it in my language. I describe what he looked like, and how often I rode him, and where I went, and also—at Kiri's request—what I wore while riding him, which leads directly to the question of how many dresses I had.

I leave the children at the edge of the road, promising to tell them more another day, and make my way up to my old room to rummage through my trunk and find something half-presentable to wear. Most of my simpler outfits are work-stained by now, the formal clothes far too fancy to be worn walking up to the palace. In the end, it is just a question of choosing the least-worn of my work clothes, brushing the straw out of my hair, and scrubbing my hands and face with water.

As promised, Matsin meets me at the palace gates. He leads me through a side entrance, passing inner courtyards I do not recognize, then circling back through wood-paneled hallways. Finally, Matsin opens a small door set into a corner of a hallway. We enter an unused storage room at the back of which stands a second door. Matsin ushers me through this door into a narrow corridor lit only by a lamp hanging from the wall. He holds a finger up to his lips, then lifts down the lamp. His eyes are dark in the lamplight, his features still, uncompromising. Only the set of his jaw tells me that he is not as easy as he acts. We pass four doors before we reach one that Matsin opens. Again, he touches his finger to his lips before gesturing for me to enter.

Light falls through the top half of the far wall, creating an eerie twilight in the room. I walk over to it curiously, looking down through the back of an elaborate wooden carving into a formal dining room. As I peer out from behind the carving, I realize that it circles the room. I wonder if there are more secret rooms hidden behind the carving at other points in the wall, or if this is the only one.

My room acts as a balcony, the carving providing spaces just wide enough to view the dining room clearly. The table below is set for dinner. A single servant makes a last adjustment to the central candelabra and departs, his footsteps echoing up to me.

I hear a faint snick and look up to find Matsin gone, the door closed. I wait, my eyes adjusting to the half-light left in the absence of the lamp. When I no longer hear Matsin's boots, I walk back to the door and gently try the handle. The door does not give.

I may as well enjoy the meal that has been provided me, I decide. At the center of my room, a table laden with platters waits. Only one chair sits at the table. A carpet rolled out beneath the table mutes the scrape of the chair, just as a tablecloth silences the dishes. I serve myself slowly, aware that there is more food here than I have seen in a week of dinners. I wish that I had a basket or bag that I might take some of the food back with me, share this bounty with my friends.

It does not take me long to finish, my stomach bulging for all that I have eaten only a fraction of the food. I am not used to such heavy meals. I push myself up and go to sit in the chair overlooking the lower room, loosening my sash. Before long, I hear the faint voices of people approaching. A brace of servants step into the room through a set of double doors, standing at attention.

Kestrin leads Valka in on his arm, escorting her to the top of the table. He seats her on the right side of the table, facing me, and then walks around to take the seat opposite her. Behind them follow a set of young couples, lords and ladies, walking sedately to their own places in a carefully orchestrated play of hierarchy. Last to enter are two pairs of young men and women who take up stations along the wall by the head of the table. I squint, studying them. At least one of the women I have met before: she is one of Valka's attendants, who let me into her bedchamber while she slept.

As the servants enter with the first course the conversation starts up, Valka commanding the table's attention. Her grasp of Menay is limited, but a translator stands behind her chair, his clear, carrying voice cutting through the room as easily as Valka's own more strident, authoritative tones. I frown, listening to the sound of it; I cannot imagine this voice having been mine. It is as foreign to me as the language of Menay once was.

The conversation very nearly puts me to sleep. I lean forward, propping my chin on my fist, and try to focus. Between a long day's work, a full belly, and the pointlessness of the conversation below, I must struggle to stay awake. Valka gives a snide critique of her afternoon spent with a lady not present, the other ladies tittering in response, then discusses the plans for a ball the following week, the dreariness of winter, the coming of spring, and oh! What plans for the wedding! All present agree it will be a truly festive event, the palace swept up in banquet after banquet, ball after ball.

"And even the street children shall have something," Valka says, with a glance at Kestrin.

"You are so great-hearted, Your Highness," one of the ladies coos.

"With such a joyous event, even the common people should have the chance to join in the festivities," Valka affirms, her interpreter translating.

"And what does Your Highness intend to give the street children?" asks the man seated beside Valka. With a jolt I recognize Kestrin's cousin, Lord Garrin.

"Oh, some treats for them—what is it we've said, my lord?"

"Apple cakes," Kestrin says. I cannot quite place his tone.

"How perfectly wonderful," cries another lady. "They'll love you for the rest of your life!"

"It's the least we can do," Valka demurs. I stare at her. They are both right, of course. I have already seen Tarkit and Torto's excitement over food, and can only imagine their ecstasy at having such a precious, unexpected treat as an apple cake. It would be something they would remember well. And, considering the opulence of what must be a normal dinner here before me, apple cakes are indeed the very smallest thing that might be given. They would hardly make a dent in the royal treasury, providing only a temporary relief to the pinched, perpetually hungry faces of the street children, and yet would guarantee their love.

I stand up, my boots scraping soundlessly on the carpet as I go to the door. The handle turns in my hand, but the door remains locked. I lean against it, feeling a knot growing in my chest. I want to get out, get away, stop my ears from hearing anymore. My own words echo back to me, spoken earlier today: *He gave me a job and a place to stay when I didn't have either. I think I'll stick with him.* And Torto's words, *I'd do that too.*

I slide down against the door, crouched on the floor, my cheek pressed against the rough carpet. I think of Falada's words in one of our first conversations, his surmise that I had been chosen to marry the prince because they could trust me, because I would grant them my unswerving loyalty in return for their kindness. Truly I would have been speechless with gratitude to find protection, a shelter at long last, however easy it might have been for the royal family to grant it. And for what a small price might the loyalties of the poor also be commanded—the price, I think, of providing just enough. I do not know where the tears come from, why they burn my cheeks or why my sobs seem stuck in my throat. I pull my cloak up, bunching it in front of my face to muffle the sound, and weep.

Eventually, I sit back against the wall, listening to the ragged whisper of my breath slowly calm. The voices of the diners float up to me, but if I do not concentrate I cannot quite make them out. I heave myself to my feet and pour myself a cup of water at the table, drinking it slowly. I wet my hands and scrub my face, wipe away the traces of my tears. I slide into the waiting chair, staring at the cold remains of my dinner.

I cannot tell how long I sit, how many minutes or hours creep by. At some point the diners rise and make their exit, and in their wake come servants, dishes clinking as they are piled and carried away. It is as if I listen to a ghost, a memory of people and actions, from my dark chamber.

The sound of the servants clearing off below has nearly died away when I hear another faint noise: boots in the outer hallway. The lock clicks and Matsin pushes open the door, his face half-lit by the lamp he carries. I rise and follow him back down the secret hall.

"Why do you think the prince asked you to bring me here?" I ask Matsin as we leave the storage room.

He pauses, his gaze on the corridor ahead, and then he turns his head slowly to study me. "He asked me once what Lady Valka was like, if she could ever make a goose girl. I told him it would take a lady who dances through the kitchen with the scullery maids and hugs her hostler in farewell to accept such a fall with dignity and grace. Lady Valka was not such a woman."

"You," I begin to say and cut myself off before the chain around my neck tightens. I should not be shocked. Hadn't the Menaiyan quads attached to me had a fortnight to know my character before we ever started traveling? Of course they would have seen a difference. I had only assumed that they would not consider what it meant.

"Yes," Matsin says, his voice quiet. "So I beg you will speak with our prince, and meet with him."

"I come as he bids me."

Matsin's lips form a grim line. "I wish it were more than that."

I shrug, glancing down the hall. "Perhaps it is best this way."

Matsin begins to walk again, taking my hint, but as we reach our destination, yet another carved door in a hall that looks only vaguely familiar, he says. "I do not believe that, my lady. Neither must you."

Kestrin rises from his seat as we enter, a fire crackling cheerfully in the grate. It is the same small sitting room where I wrote a letter to my mother, dictated by the prince. I drop into a curtsy, sense Matsin's quick bow. With a quiet step he departs.

Kestrin sketches me a bow. "My lady."

"Your Highness."

"I hope you have enjoyed your evening."

"It has been most interesting."

"As always," he says, smiling. "Will you join me?"

"As always," I echo, taking the seat opposite him. He sits, his eyes lingering on my face. I watch the fire and find myself wondering wryly what I will do when the weather is too warm for fires: what will I have to look at then?

I turn towards Kestrin. "Tell me, Your Highness, what you hope to gain from this little game of yours."

He meets my gaze. "I wish you to know my betrothed as I do."

"I do not believe you."

"Would I lie to you?"

I shrug. "It is not treason for a prince to lie to his vassals."

"Do you consider yourself my vassal then?" he asks, his tone ironic.

"A step below, Your Highness; I have made no oath of allegiance."

"None at all?"

I tilt my head, evading the question. "I do not believe you, Your Highness, because I already know the princess, and you know that I do."

"Perhaps I thought to remind you."

"To what end?"

He shrugs, opening his palms towards me. "Lady," he says, then stops. "Lady, what can I offer you?"

I look directly into his forest-shadow eyes. "Apple cakes."

He stares. I stand up and cross to the door.

"Lady, wait," he calls after me, rising.

"Good evening, Your Highness."

"*Wait.*" His voice reverberates with authority. I turn back to him, aware that I am a servant again, that I must obey his orders, even that my clothes are appallingly shabby next to his.

His features stiffen and he looks away. "Do what you will."

I hesitate, watching the fall of shadows on his face.

"Get out then," he snarls, starting towards me. "Flee back to your geese and forget I called you here."

I watch as he advances on me, watch the familiar mask slide into place over his features, the way his eyes seem almost black. He stops a bare hand span before me. "That's what you want, isn't it? To get away from the court? Then run away, Thorn. I won't stop you anymore."

"If I truly wanted that, Your Highness, I should have left Tarinon by now."

He takes a heavy breath and lets it out slowly. "You told me once that you could not find a way to leave, nor a place to go."

"I have found a way since," I tell him, thinking of Red Hawk. He waits. I smile tiredly. "I still do not have a place to go. I suppose it could be arranged, but you understand as well as I that I cannot leave quite yet."

"You are waiting."

"Aren't we all?"

He shakes his head in frustration. "What did you mean by 'apple cakes'?"

"Her Highness intends to win the love of the common folk with apple cakes; you would offer me similar items of little worth to yourself in order to win my loyalty, wouldn't you?" He regards me silently and I flush, realizing that I wear the cloak he gave me.

"It is your friendship I seek," he says.

"You do not seek it as a friend; you seek it as a prince seeks the loyalty of a subject. The trouble is this: I will not sell my loyalty or my friendship."

"I see." He steps back, his eyes holding mine. "Then how is your friendship to be won?"

"I can hardly explain it to you, Your Highness. Suffice it to say that, while I might find experiences like tonight's highly educational, I neither respect nor admire anyone the more for it." I unclasp the cloak's brooch, swinging it off my shoulders.

"You have now seen two very different dinners. Surely, in comparing them, you see how—company matters."

"I never doubted it. I appreciate the illustration, but it was hardly necessary."

"Then what is necessary, lady? What do you suggest I do?"

I wince. "I don't know, Your Highness."

"I offer you my protection," he begins.

"Your protection has failed me once already."

His eyes flash, and for a moment I fear that his anger will ride him as it did when I challenged his motives one time before. Instead, the flash sparks into humor and he laughs. "I believe I have failed you more than once, lady. I am grateful for your kind accounting."

I walk back to the armchair, aware of his gaze following me. I fold my cloak over its back, then lean against it, staring at my hands.

"Suppose I returned, Your Highness. What would that accomplish?"

"There would be the small matter of justice to be carried out," he says softly, as if afraid his voice might banish my words. Justice. Against Valka, of course. But that isn't really what I want.

"I have seen enough here already to think little of my case for justice. There are other greater injustices that deserve your attention first. Is there no other reason?"

"You cannot be serious. We discuss treason—"

"Is that all?" I repeat sharply. He crosses the distance to the armchairs, leaning against the other one so that he can watch my face. I meet his gaze.

"A traitor once is a traitor always, lady."

"And a man warned is a man prepared, Your Highness."

"You have not considered the implications."

"I have. I believe you have greater concerns than the woman you are to marry. Tell me what would be accomplished by my return, beyond a traitor's punishment."

"You would be well placed to see to more than apple cakes if that is your interest. You may address whatever injustices concern you." I think that Kestrin's smile is that of a predator, of a hound scenting blood. How quickly he has understood me.

"An interesting proposition, Your Highness, but I doubt such a future."

"Why?"

"Because I doubt the surety of your future, and that of your family's." He lowers his face, turning away slightly, his features icing over. "Also, you are offering me apple cakes once more. You would tempt me with an offer of justice for your people rather than striving to such ends yourself."

"You speak well, lady. I perceive quite clearly why you prefer your work to the court."

"Then help me to understand why I should return. I see only lies, artifice and ultimate failure here."

"There is very little else to speak of." Kestrin leans against the back of the armchair, resting his elbows on its back. A few strands of hair have slipped free of their tie, falling like a tracery of shadows over his brow. He looks weary, tired past bearing. The firelight casts a waning warmth on his features that makes me think of the last flush of life on the face of a dying man.

"Isn't there?" I ask, almost pleading.

"If you are not tempted by power, wealth, rank or an offer of flawed protection, or by a personal concern for justice to be carried out for yourself," he looks up and catches my gaze, "then what else is there?"

I open my mouth and close it again. I can hear Falada's voice, see his dark eyes somber and penetrating, *At some point you must take responsibility for your life.* I know the answer, looking at Kestrin, but I cannot speak the words. As Falada once demanded of me, I know I cannot leave Valka as my successor; that, having been born to power, it is my responsibility to see it handled well by myself, by those who come after me.

"What is it?" Kestrin murmurs, his gaze razor sharp.

I shake my head. "You are right; such things do not tempt me."

He smiles wryly. "I will never look at apple cakes the same again, my lady."

I push my face into a semblance of a smile. "See that you don't. And if you can think of winning loyalty without the use of apple cakes …"

"I do not think I know how. I have been too long at court."

"Perhaps you should come to work with the geese," I suggest flippantly. "They may be temporarily won by treats, but their regard is as easily lost. It is a good lesson for us all."

"Perhaps I will visit you."

"I will look forward to watching their reception of you," I reply. "It is late now, Your Highness, and I must get to work at dawn. If I have your leave?" I walk to do the door.

"Your cloak, Lady." Kestrin gestures to where it hangs over the chair back.

I shake my head. "It is not mine; I should not have accepted it in the first place."

He grimaces. "It is not an apple cake, if that is what you mean."

"Isn't it?"

"You were cold; I saw you twice while out riding, and I could see the way the wind cut you." He lifts the cloak from the chair and brings it to me. "Take this, lady. If you do not want it for yourself, then do what you will with it. Only do not return it to me."

I accept the cloak hesitantly, holding it awkwardly, unsure whether I should put it on again or not. "As you wish," I say.

"Hardly." He steps past me and opens the door, "Go in peace, my lady."

"And you, Your Highness."

26

The next morning dawns with a soft exhalation of warmth. The air outside brings heady whiffs of green with it, and around the corners of the goose barn tiny purple flowers poke their heads above the earth. The geese honk excitedly, scrambling over each other in the rush to leave their winter prison, the ganders barely bothering to peck at me in their excitement.

I am amazed at how quickly my morning's work goes: even without Corbé's help, I am done within the hour. Without the geese underfoot, scronking and obstinately standing their ground, I suppose it should not have surprised me at all. Finished, I start for the goose pasture, pausing under Falada's head at the gates. I call up to him softly. As faintly as a leaf dropping from a tree I hear the word *Princess*. But that is all.

Once settled in the pasture, I think of opening up my hair to air it out, but a glance towards Corbé stills the impulse. I can just make out his form, his legs stretched out before him, staff leaning against the tree. His face is turned towards me, but I cannot distinguish his expression. I keep my staff with me through the day.

Upon our return, I find a page waiting for me. He shifts from foot to foot, arms crossed and nose raised away from the stench of livestock. "Her Highness wishes to see you this evening," he tells me as I shut the gate behind Corbé. "I'm to escort you up."

The streets are still busy with end-of-day traffic, and it takes us some time to thread our way up the road. I am grateful for the solid *thunk* of my staff against the cobblestones. I doubt I will be able to command an escort home tonight. I sigh, glancing at the page. He walks with a little bounce, his hair brushing his shoulders with every step. He isn't quite as uppity as he first tried to appear at the stables, I suspect.

"Have you been working at the palace very long?" I ask.

He looks at me in surprise, then smiles smugly. "Three months."

"You must know your way around very well by now."

"The palace's very big, you know. It takes a while to get to know it as well as I. But there are still a few places even I don't know. Haku says he's been working there a year and just last week went down a hall he'd never seen before."

I wonder just how much I might learn from my escort. "It must be interesting. Do you know all the nobles by sight?"

"Oh well, I know a few of them," he says with false casualness, and with only a little prodding launches into a description of the lords and ladies he has run errands for, the intrigues he has heard about, and any other rumor that has been breathed in the palace. I am amazed at the breadth of his knowledge, and at Valka's foolishness in sending such a talker to fetch me. No doubt the whole palace will know of my visit before I finish greeting her.

By the time we reach the palace, I've also received a full description of the ball planned for the evening, the intrigues expected to occur, and just how many lambs have been roasted in preparation. He breaks off only when we reach the royal wing, walking the last few paces in silence and rapping on Valka's door. A voice calls sharply for us to enter. He opens the door with a flourish, gestures for me to enter, bows and departs, leaving me alone in the room with Valka. At least he gives the appearance of discretion.

Valka sits in a chair in the outer room. She is dressed and groomed beautifully, her hair braided and coiled in a crown, her jade tunic and gold skirts stiff with embroidery.

"A ball tonight?"

Her nostrils flare, but then she smiles. "Jealous?"

"Hardly. What do you want?"

"One final letter from you."

"You know my answer."

"Every person has a price."

"Do you think you know mine?" I think for only a moment of Kestrin and of apple cakes.

"For all your apparent zeal for servitude, you must prefer a better position. I will grant you a place on one of my mountain estates. You will have a yearly stipend and may live the life of a lady. But you must write the letter tonight."

"My mother has written again, hasn't she? You're hoping to send a letter to catch her on the road here, to allay her concerns."

"She has written," Valka agrees. Her face is cold now, and I do not trust the very stillness of it. "The response must be written tonight."

"I do not believe your offer."

"You will have to trust me."

I laugh softly. "Have you forgotten why you were exiled? Because you cared nothing for the life of a servant. I do not think that has changed."

Her mouth twists, her eyes glittering with hatred. "Me? You blame me for what you did? What is a servant? That little rat is probably dead by now anyhow: they die like flies. And you—you betrayed me, made me the laughing stock of the Hall so that I had to leave." She snaps her jaw shut, glaring at me.

"It's still all about that, isn't it? You wanted your revenge. Is that what you like about sending me to live on a mountain estate you stole from me? That I will have gone into exile as you did? But that won't be enough for you. You want more, you've always wanted more. You wanted my brother, didn't you?"

"I would have been Queen," she hisses. "And now I will be. It's your own fault you've been turned into a servant."

"And servants die like flies, don't they? You won't be happy until I'm dead."

She takes a deep breath. "I would not mourn your death, traitor. But I will grant you this one chance to have a better life than you deserve."

"You are the one with a better life than you deserve."

"I would have married your brother but for you and your traitorous tongue! If you cared so much for that servant, you could have gotten her free later—but you had to betray me before everyone. In front of the servants!"

"I've regretted that, Valka, much as I have regretted that you blamed that servant that day. If you hadn't made a public show of her supposed guilt, I wouldn't have had to make a show of yours."

"Damn her! She was a servant. A nothing."

"Just as I am."

Valka bites her lip, her chest heaving. "What is your answer?"

"I will not write the letter for the price you named."

"Oh? And is there a price at which you will write it?"

"Certainly. Take up your own terms. I will be princess, and you will live out your life a nameless lady on a mountain estate."

My words sink into the room. She sits silently, vibrating with fury, and then she nods her head. "So be it. You've made your choice. I hope you are willing to abide by it."

"I am certainly willing to live by it." I do not know where the smile comes from that lifts up my lips.

"You know you have chosen to betray me."

"Hardly."

"I am princess now and you—"

"You will never really be princess, Valka. You will always and only be an impostor. Whether I die a servant or queen, I will always be my mother's daughter, and so princess."

"I hope you will take comfort in your royalty when I am done with you."

I shrug. "I cannot imagine we have anything left to say to each other. Good night." I turn and let myself out, and it is only as I reach the stairs that I realize I have begun to tremble. I cling to my staff, swaying slightly, and close my eyes, breathing deeply. Then I straighten my back and take the stairs down.

The geese raise their heads, quieting even the friendly chuckling and mumbling that is their talk. I glance around, but see nothing amiss: Corbé sits further down the field, nothing else moves. The geese, while alert, do not seem frightened. I stand up, casting my gaze around the pasture, past the low stone walls.

And then I feel it: a faint brush against my face, a rippling of the grasses around me, circling out, the sudden lone whisper of the newly-leafed branches above me while the other trees remain silent.

"Wind?" I whisper, hardly daring to believe.

The Wind whips a circle around me, flapping my skirts against my legs and scaring off the sparrows in the tree above me.

"Wind! You've found me!"

The Wind slows, breathing gently. *Alyrra.*

I close my eyes, listen to the familiar touch of its voice.

"How did you recognize me?"

The Wind does not answer, instead settling down to ruffle the grasses. I sit down, my back against the tree.

"Old friend," I say quietly. "I thought I lost you. I went to say farewell to you before I left, but you didn't come to the dell that day. I never imagined you'd find your way here. It's a long journey and I—am not the same."

Different, the Wind agrees.

I feel tears spill down my cheeks and laugh, wiping them away. "I don't know why I'm crying; I'm happy you're here."

Here, the Wind echoes, and I rest my head against the tree, smiling so hard my face hurts.

"Yes," I say, as fiercely as if the Wind's presence might transport me back to a time before I'd ever thought of Menaiya. "You're here."

I carry the coming of the Wind with me all day, for though it does not stay long the very fact of its presence, its recognition of me, has brought both a desperate homesickness and a feverish excitement to me. For the first time in months, I can remember clearly the dell where I used to meet the Wind, the forest paths. I think of Jilna's laugh, the warmth of the kitchen, the cool sanctuary of the Hall's little temple. Again and again I come back to this simple fact: the Wind saw through the enchantments and found me.

"You're happy today," Laurel says as she ladles out my portion of curried vegetables.

"I am," I agree. I know I cannot tell them of the Wind, so I say instead, "Joa has me working two of the younger mares before I go out to the pasture nowadays."

"Does he?" Rowan looks up from his plate. "He must have plans for you."

"He keeps saying he'll make me into a hostler," I say, amused.

"I wouldn't go telling anyone else; there're some boys as will be jealous," Laurel warns me. "Corbé's been hoping for that himself for a year or two now."

I hesitate. "But I don't know that much about working with horses. Wouldn't it be better to take someone like Corbé?" After all, my friendship with Falada may have impressed Joa, but it has nothing to do with being able to handle horses.

"Corbé has a mean streak in him. I wouldn't trust him with a horse," Oak says.

Ash nods his agreement. "Geese will fight back and no one cares if their roasted goose had a mean temper. Horses will get cold-backed if their hostler's rough. You can lose a good horse to a bad hostler, and that's not something Joa would want to explain up at the palace."

Rowan smiles encouragingly at me. "We'll teach you whatever you need to know; you've already got the basics."

I pause, thinking of how it would be to work with Laurel and Oak from now on, to never have to see Corbé again, or worry over what he might do. Imagine exchanging Corbé's black looks for Violet's laughter. I glance around the table. "Where's Violet?"

"She's running an errand in the city," Rowan tells me.

"Aye, but she should be back by now," Oak says, and in his deep voice I hear the beginnings of concern.

"Was she alone?"

"Yes," Laurel says tightly. "One of us should have gone with her, or for her. It's still getting dark early, and she's a pretty girl."

"She'll be back soon," Ash says, but his glance at Oak betrays his worry.

By the time we've finished dinner, Violet still hasn't returned. Oak goes to the common room door to look out, then looks back in at us. "I'm going to look for her."

Rowan and Ash are up and next to him in a flash. "We're coming too."

Oak nods. "She'll be between here and the smith; I'll go by way of West Road through Beggars' Square; Ash, you check the way there past the Dancing Goat; and Rowan, you search the side streets between the two."

"What about us?" I ask, standing beside Laurel.

"Stay here and wait," Oak says. "We don't want either of you hurt, and someone has to watch the stable. If Violet gets home without us, you'll be here to greet her."

"Why don't we ask the guards to help us?"

Oak stares at me, and it is Ash who answers. "The guards care nothing for missing girls. But we'll get the hostlers from the first stable; they'll help." He turns to Laurel, "If she comes back on her own, just keep her here. We'll come back to check." Laurel nods, and then the men are gone.

Laurel sits back down, smoothes out her skirts with her hands. I gather up the plates and stack them on the counter, cover the pot with a square of cloth, and then stand uncertainly in the middle of the room.

"What do you think happened?"

Laurel shakes her head. I go to the door to look out. Snatched or attacked? Enslaved or assaulted? My skin crawls. I cannot imagine one being better than the other. Perhaps she just twisted her ankle and has stopped along the way. Perhaps. I whisper a prayer and cross the room to the pile of tack requiring repair, pick out a bridle and a halter, and bring them back to the table, handing one to Laurel. We work silently, listening for the sound of boots, but the hall remains quiet. We finish our mending, and still there is no sign of the men. Laurel rubs her thumb back and forth over the grain of the wood.

"Surely the guards will help us," I say, breaking the silence.

"No. They don't bother with missing girls. Thieves they'll chase, on the king's orders, but this—they'll just laugh at us. They'll say she's found herself a man somewhere. They won't help; they never do. They say the children have run away and the girls have found lovers." Laurel grimaces, then covers her face with her hands. She makes no sound, and it takes me a moment to realize she is crying.

"Laurel," I say, wrapping an arm around her. I don't know what else to say.

"Something's happened," she whispers. "I know it, and all I can do is sit here."

I hold her tightly. She rests her head against my shoulder. Then, abruptly, I pull back and get up.

"Come on."

"What?" She looks up at me in confusion.

"There's someone we can ask for help, but I don't want to go alone so late."

"Who?"

I hesitate, and Tarkit's words come back to me: "A friend of a friend." She stares. "Please, Laurel, I know they'll help, but I have to get there."

"If they'll help," she says, and then she is up and we are well-nigh running down the hall. I make only one wrong turn, catching myself within a block.

We hold tightly to each other's hands, glancing continually over our shoulders, down alleys. Twice men call out to us from doorways or the corners of streets, but we hurry past, and they do not follow. Inside the building, the staircase is dark, and we have to feel our way up to the door. I rap hard on it, then step back waiting. We listen as footsteps approach the door.

"Who knocks?" The voice is sharp, hard.

"Thorn," I say. "I need help."

The door opens, a flood of lamplight brightening the hallway. Artemian holds his sword at the ready, and I am reminded of the night I first met Red Hawk, but then he lowers it and steps back.

"Come in, lady."

Laurel and I step into the room. I do not wait for him to close the door before I speak, "Violet—one of the hostlers from our stable—she didn't come home tonight. We think something's happened. The men have been out looking for her for hours, and haven't returned yet."

Artemian nods. "Where was she going?"

"To the smith," Laurel says, and describes the location, and the different roads Violet might have taken to get there. "Her brothers are searching them all, but they haven't come back yet."

"Not good," he says succinctly. "We'll look for her."

Artemian insists on escorting us back to the stables. We describe what Violet looks like, what she was wearing when she left, Artemian nodding and asking the occasional terse question. At the stable, Laurel checks the common room while I run up to our rooms to make sure neither Violet nor the boys have returned, but there is no one there. Artemian leaves at once, telling us he will send us a message within an hour.

Laurel and I return to the common room. It is late now. I think of the night Falada and I met Red Hawk, and I think that it is almost as late as that night. I pick out two more pieces of tack to mend, a saddle whose stitching is coming out for Laurel to repair, and an old horse blanket with an unraveling hem for me. We work silently, every stitch we sew a half-breathed prayer.

Laurel drops her work and runs to the door before I even register the sound of boots in the hallway.

"Rowan? What is it? Have you found her?"

"No," he calls back. And then, "she isn't here." It isn't a question, though from his voice I know he had half-hoped for it.

"No," Laurel says, sagging against the doorpost. I pour a cup of water and hand it to Rowan as he reaches us.

"We met some other men. Friends of yours," he nods to me. "They've been going through the taverns and inns, and have helped us search the alleys. One of them told me to come back and tell you how things were. We're still looking. I'm going back out to keep on."

He downs the water and turns to the door.

"You bring her back, you hear?" Laurel's voice is hard. "Don't any of you come back without her."

"We'll find her," Rowan promises. He strides down the hall, his shoulders bowed with exhaustion but his pace still fast, still hurried by hope and fear.

They return near dawn. We hear the tread of boots first, and then Oak's voice calling to us as we burst from the common room. Behind him trail his brothers as well as hostlers from the first stable.

"Quickly," he cries. "We need a place to lay her down!"

Laurel and I run back into the common room, drag the table and bench to the side, shove away the stray stools. I pull out one of the boys' sleeping mats, and then the men are there, Oak kneeling to lay Violet down. Beside me, Laurel makes a faint sound, as of a small animal crying, and stumbles into me. I stagger under her weight, crashing against the table as I wrap my arms around her, and then Ash is there, his face pale, taking Laurel from me and carrying her out of the room to lay her down in the hall where the other hostlers wait.

"Your friends are sending a healer," Oak says, his voice trembling. He has not stood up, has not moved from Violet's side. I clench my teeth and kneel next to him, forcing myself to look.

They have wrapped Violet in a dark cloak so that only her face, one hand, and her bare feet are visible. Her face is swollen past recognition, dark with blood and bruises, her lips split and bleeding. Her hand, settled on top of the cloak, is swollen as well, bruised, her fingers not quite jointed right, and there are marks near her wrist that I know to be bruises from a tight hold, or perhaps ropes. Blood has clotted on her feet, but I cannot tell if she is wounded there or if the blood has only run and dried there from another wound.

I cannot breathe, cannot find the air to fill my lungs. I turn my face away and see Rowan standing beside Oak, and behind him, returned from the hall, Ash, their faces white, their eyes dead with shock and horror.

"She must be washed." It takes me a moment to recognize the voice that spoke as my own. Oak turns towards me, waiting. I stumble on, "The healer will need to look at her wounds. We should wash her."

"What do you need?" Oak asks.

I swallow hard. Must it be me? "Water—and strips of cloth." Oak and Ash are gone at once, half running to fetch water, find cloth that can be used, grateful to have something to do. But Rowan still stands, swaying, staring at his sister.

171

"Rowan," I call, "Rowan." He looks up slowly. "Laurel needs you. When she wakes up, she'll need you. Go stay with her. Go on. She's in the hall." He leaves, his shoulder knocking against the doorframe.

Ash brings me the cloth, and Oak the water, and I send them out to calm Laurel. Her sobs echo into the room, and the horses in their stalls snort and whinny to each other in concern. I do not want to touch Violet, do not want to hurt her, or wake her, or see what else has been done to her. I dip the cloth into the water and work slowly, wiping away the blood from her face, then her hand and feet, not wanting to push back the cloak. I cannot see clearly and I have to pause often to rub my sleeve across my face. I wonder where the healer is, why he is taking so long. I grit my teeth and move the cloak back to reveal the rest of her arm, and after wiping this clean, I move on. When I am done, the water is dark red. I pull the cloak back over Violet, my teeth chattering, and stand up. The room sways around me, darkness chasing the edge of my vision. I back up until I hit the table behind me. I breathe slowly, staring straight ahead, but it will not matter where I look, I will still see her.

"Here!" Ash cries from the hall.

"The healer is here," Oak calls in to me, and then a man hurries into the room, Oak and his brothers and Laurel beside him. "Thorn was washing her—she hasn't woken yet."

"I see," the healer says.

"Oh Violet," Laurel gasps, leaning into Ash. He holds her as gently as if she were his mother.

The healer sets down his bag of supplies. "Go out all of you, except the girl who washed her." Oak hesitates, and the man looks up at him sharply. "Go on. I'll take care of your sister."

"I'm staying here," Laurel says.

The healer looks at her, then shakes his head. "No. Stay outside till I call you in."

Laurel opens her mouth to argue but Oak touches her shoulder. "Do what he says. He'll help her." Laurel closes her jaw with a click, turns, and stumbles from the room, the others following in her wake.

"What did you do then?" the healer asks, peeling back her cloak.

I avert my eyes, though I have already seen everything. "I washed her. That's all. I tried not to move her."

He nods and continues his inspection. I sit down on a nearby stool. I look down at my hands, but there is blood dried beneath my fingernails and in the ridges of my palm. I look up quickly, then away to the lamp, my chest aching.

"She's cold," the healer observes as he rummages in his bag. "Was she left out all night?"

"I don't know."

"Get her some blankets. I'm going to stitch up her cuts. That's about all I can do. You'll need to keep her warm, feed her broth, and give her some time to heal."

"Her fingers are broken."

"And a few of her ribs," he agrees. "I'll do what I can."

I go to the door. "She needs blankets." Oak barrels down the hall to the staircase, followed by Ash. They pound up to our rooms, returning within moments with all the blankets we have, piling them into my hands. I wait for them to step back before I turn back into the common room, using my body to shield their view. I fold the blankets over Violet, keeping only that portion folded back where the healer works. Then I sit down opposite him, one hand resting gently against Violet's arm, and watch him. It is easier now that she is covered, now that the healer is doing something for her. He works systematically, lifting the blanket to check each part of her before moving on.

He bandages her hand and then tells me, "I'm going to roll her on her side to check her back. It will hurt her, and she might wake. I want you to stay in front of her and help her to balance. I don't want her to roll onto her stomach." He slides his hands beneath her and lifts. I join him, helping to turn her as gently as I can. She moans once, a long, low sound that fades to nothing. The healer works quickly, wiping her back clean and inspecting her carefully.

"She'll be fine. Roll her back." I ease her down, grateful that I did not have to look, grateful that there was nothing requiring the healer's stitching.

"She's still cold," the healer says. "I want you to sleep next to her, under the same blanket. Don't touch her much or you'll hurt her, just try to keep her warm. If you have to go out, warm stones by a fire and wrap them in the blankets."

He stands up, resting his hands on his waist and stretching out his back. "I've seen worse, but not much. The cold isn't good for her. You'll have to be careful."

"Healer?" Oak asks tentatively from the doorway.

"Aye. I was telling the girl here what to do," the healer takes his bag and joins the hostlers in the hall. I can hear them speaking, but the words are far away, garbled. I lie down next to Violet, lifting the blankets and edging as close to her as I dare. I tuck them around the two of us and stare up at the ceiling. There is light now from the doorway, and I think it must be full day, but I cannot quite imagine that the sun was rising while I sat here with Violet. I listen to her breath: it is so faint and slow that I begin to worry, between breaths, that she will stop.

Boots enter the room. I tilt my head to see Laurel, and behind her Oak, Ash and Rowan.

"Lie down," I say to Laurel. She slides under the blankets on the other side of Violet. The men glance at each other uncertainly.

"Go rest," Laurel tells them. "We'll call you when she wakes up." They nod, but it is still a time before they turn away and trudge out into the hall. They do not go up to their rooms; instead, they lie down in the hall and wait silently for their sister to wake.

Violet does not wake. By noon, her skin burns, her breath rasping in her throat. She moans when Laurel wipes her forehead with a damp cloth, but eyelids remain still. We take shifts sitting with her so that we can each see to our work. By the time I reach the barn, Corbé has already taken the geese out. I clean quickly, throwing myself into my work that I might return that much sooner to the common room. I leave only to help Corbé drive the geese back in. Joa and the other hostlers come and go, helping with the horses in our stable so that Laurel and the boys may sit by her side.

Laurel and I take turns feeding Violet, spooning a thin broth Joa had sent down from the kitchen. We prop her head up gently, afraid to move her, emptying a single spoon at a time in her mouth and praying she will swallow. We cannot tell, at the end, whether she has drunk any at all, or whether it has all run back out the corners of her mouth.

The healer returns at sunset, sending the men into the hall while he checks Violet. Laurel and I remain, watching. It is the first time that Laurel sees the full extent of the damage done to Violet, and when I glance at her, I think she has aged ten years. She sits with her jaw clenched, lips pressed together, her eyes dry.

"The fever's bad, and these cuts don't look good," the healer says, pointing to the stitches he had put in the night before. "Make an infusion of these herbs." He hands Laurel a pouch. "Give it to her every few hours, mixed with the broth."

"Is there anything else?" Laurel asks.

"Rub ash into her cuts to prevent rot. Beyond that, there's nothing we can do."

At night, Laurel and I lie silently beside Violet. The men have gone up to their room at Laurel's urging.

"I can't sleep," Laurel says.

"I know."

"I don't even know what to pray for."

I press my eyes shut and a vision of the common room flashes before me: our hands all busy with small repairs, Laurel laughing at some joke of Rowan's, and Violet, her head bent over her work, the lamplight shining against her sable hair, a slight frown creasing her brow as she tugs her needle through the tough leather. I don't know what to pray for either.

"Will you sing one of your songs?" Laurel asks. "That you sing when you work?"

I open my eyes to look towards her, past Violet's unmoving form.

"I don't know any in Menay."

"I know. Sing them in your language. Violet always liked the sound of them." And so I sing quietly into the night, picking an old love ballad from home, sing until my voice is hoarse and I can hear Laurel's deep, even breathing, just past Violet's harsh, rasping breaths.

The following afternoon, Oak and Ash go to the palace to petition for justice. They return in the evening, coming to sit beside Violet, silent and grim-faced.

"Well, what did you expect?" Laurel asks, her voice hard.

"We don't know who did it," Rowan says.

"It won't be that hard to find out," Ash snaps. "And we will, and God have mercy on those—" he clicks his jaw shut, glancing towards me. "We know where Thorn's friends found her; and the types of men who do this like to boast. The king's men could find out if they cared to."

"They don't," Laurel says with finality. "But they will care if we take justice into our own hands."

"We're not going to let those men go on," Oak says, his deep voice hoarse and gravelly. "Let them think they can do this to other girls."

"Justice is not men beating each other up," Laurel says quietly. "Justice is teaching men that there is a law and, if they don't abide by it, there is an established punishment."

"If the king won't uphold the law—" Ash snarls.

"Did you ask him?" Laurel cuts in. "Or was it some idiot captain?"

Oak grimaces. "It was a captain. We couldn't hope to see the king himself; you know that."

"I'll try," I say suddenly. They look at me uncertainly. "Someone might listen to me."

"Aye," Laurel says after a moment. "If the king doesn't, perhaps your other friends will."

"Justice?" Oak asks, raising an eyebrow.

"Thieves' justice or King's justice, so long as it's a known law, I don't care." Laurel reaches out to smooth the blanket over Violet.

Walking up to the palace with Rowan and Ash, I try to figure out how I will find Kestrin. Always before, it was a chance meeting or an arrangement through one of his men. I realize now that I don't know how to contact him. Rowan and Ash leave me just below the gates, promising to wait until I return. I continue on, entering and turning right on instinct to follow the wall. I find a side door, and from there wend my way to the royal wing. Hopefully, Kestrin will be in his apartments when I knock. Not likely in early evening. More likely he is dining somewhere. A prince does not sit alone in his apartments of an evening.

At my knock, a man I have never seen opens Kestrin's door. He looks me over with growing disdain. "Yes?"

"I wish to speak with the prince," I say. Instead of sounding commanding, my voice has the weakness of a plea.

"Ah. The prince ... does not take petitioners in his apartments. How did you get here?"

"I think he will see me, if you would ask him."

"Indeed." The man's voice is laden with contempt. "But he is not here now."

I bite my lip. I don't want to demand entrance, nor do I want to go back and tell Rowan and Ash that I hadn't even managed to see Kestrin.

"Who is it?" a second voice calls.

"A serving girl," the man before me replies. "Wants to see His Highness."

"The foreigner?" The second man peers around the door, and his face lights with comprehension.

"She seems to think the prince will see her."

"He will. Come in, my lady. The prince is at dinner, but we'll let him know you're waiting."

I smile as graciously as I can, stepping in as the first man gapes at me. The second man introduces himself as Ferin and seats me in the inner sitting room. I can hear him softly berating his companion once they close the door.

A full hour slips by, the men—Kestrin's attendants, I surmise—discreetly passing through the room once or twice. Finally, I hear the door open in the outer room, followed by lowered voices. A moment later, Kestrin enters, pulling the door shut behind him.

"Lady," he says, bowing to my curtsy.

I forge ahead before he can ask. "I'm sorry to come like this, Your Highness, but I didn't know how else to find you. I have something to speak to you about."

"I should have made an arrangement." He grins, gesturing for me to sit. "I never imagined you would want to speak to me of your own accord."

I smile wanly. "Your Highness has heard that the hostler Violet was attacked two nights ago."

He sobers at once. "I have. A very unfortunate incident."

Incident? I make myself ignore the word and go on. "Her brothers came here today to ask for justice; they believe the men who attacked her can be found. They were turned away."

Kestrin frowns. "Who did they speak to?"

"Second Captain Elann."

"On what grounds were they turned away?"

"That the attackers could not be found. We know where she was left, Your Highness. It would only be a matter of looking for witnesses, listening to the men in the taverns."

Kestrin runs his hands through his hair. "I don't know Elann, but my expectation is he knows what he is doing. I will look into the matter myself and see if anything further can be done. I can't make any promise though, Thorn. It's a terrible situation."

"Yes," I agree. A cold anger has begun to grow in me, so that I think my bones have turned to steel, or that my voice will flash silver when I speak. It is all I can do to hold my anger in check.

"How is the girl doing?"

I meet his gaze. "She's dying." He stares, and I know in that moment that what I have said is true: that Violet is slipping away with each breath, and I am no longer sure she will be able to come back to us.

I move to the door, "I thank you, Your Highness."

"I will try," Kestrin repeats as I leave. I make my way out without mishap, meeting Rowan and Ash in the shadow of the first building past the palace gates. We walk down to the stables in silence, the men throwing me the occasional unreadable glance, but I have nothing to tell them.

The next day brings no improvement. After cleaning the goose barn, I sit by Violet while Laurel and the men ready horses to be sent up to the palace; with the weather warming up, the palace folk have begun afternoon excursions. I sing to Violet, wiping her face with a cool cloth. The bruises have begun to fade, but her fever rages on. Now she moans often, turning her head, shifting her body. Her stomach is bloated, tender to the touch. Her cuts have festered beneath the stitching, despite the ash we have rubbed into them. They weep drops of pus, discolored a murky gray by the ash, the skin around them streaked red.

When Laurel comes in, I stand up. "I'm going to the temple."

Laurel nods. "Be back before dark."

"I won't be long," I promise.

At the temple, I pray for Violet. Eventually, I lie down on my side, exhausted, half-numb with the worry and horror of the last days. I wonder if Kestrin will really do anything, if the attackers will be caught. I remember the cold anger I had felt when I spoke to him, and it sparks within me once more.

I push myself up and begin the walk to Artemian's. I knock three times on his door before accepting that he is not there. Crouching in the darkened hallway, my nose filled with the stench of urine and sweat, I open up my braid and use my teeth to snap enough hairs to make the thinnest of braids. I loop this around the doorknob and make my way back to the stables, wondering how much Red Hawk will do in payment of his debt, and whether he will accept payment from me for what goes beyond that.

I wake in the middle of the night. Something is wrong, something is missing: the room is too quiet. I sit up with a jerk, throwing off my blanket, and Laurel wakes with a gasp.

"Violet," I say, reaching out. Her skin is cold.

"No," Laurel whispers. "Oh no."

Violet is dead.

Oak and Ash leave at dawn, shovels over their shoulders. Laurel and I bathe Violet one last time, wiping away the ash and pus from her cuts with damp cloths. We bring down her spare dress from our room and gently dress her, then wrap her in a single sheet, tying it closed with cord. Joa pulls up a wagon, the bed softened with a layer of straw, and he and Rowan carry Violet out. The hostlers from the first stables join us, as well as a few people I don't recognize, and with them also the pale face of Massenso. We ride beside Violet, Joa directing the horse out of the city gates and down West Road, turning north at the crossroads I have never taken before.

Ash and Oak are still digging when we arrive. They switch off with Rowan and Massenso, taking turns until the grave is deep enough. When the men are done, her brothers lower Violet into the grave. We stand next to it while Oak, in a hoarse and broken voice, recites the Final Prayers, and then we each toss a handful of earth down into the grave. The dirt patters down on the white shroud, hardly audible among the rustling of so many people, and yet it echoes in my mind so that, even after the men have filled the grave, I can still hear those first small handfuls of earth falling down upon Violet.

Violet's brothers walk across the road to the field there, Laurel with them. They return, each bearing a single rock and set this at the head of the grave. The whole of the graveyard is filled with these graves: small piles of rock, grave after grave, men, women and children, all the same in death.

Joa drives us back to the stables, the wagon wheels rattling over the uneven road. It hardly seems possible that we are back by midmorning; the hostlers move away in small groups, their steps and voices slow. My body feels heavy now, my limbs weighing me down so that it is an effort to climb down from the wagon, to take one step and then another. I walk away from the stables, away from Laurel and the men, and habit carries me to the goose barn. I stop at the inner gate and stare in at the empty space, the trampled straw and scattering of droppings.

I let myself in, fetch a rake and set to work. Once I am done, I return to the stables, but I cannot bring myself to enter it. I cannot yet look at Oak or Laurel and see their grief written on their faces, for it is too fresh.

"Thorn?" a small voice calls. I turn towards it. Torto peeks around the corner of the stable. "Thorn? Come here!"

I trudge over to him. Behind him, Fen stands with arms crossed over his chest, staring at the ground.

"We're not supposed to be here," Torto explains in a whisper. "Children aren't allowed. But I'm supposed to find you and tell you to spend the afternoon in the temple."

"Thank you." My voice sounds strange to me, as if it comes from someone who stands just behind me.

"Are you okay?"

As I look down at Torto, and at Fen standing silent beside him, the tears finally come to my eyes. "My friend—was attacked," I explain. "We found her, but she died this morning."

Torto stares up at me, and it is Fen who pushes past him to hug me tightly, skinny arms wrapping around my waist. I kneel down and hold him back, and then Torto is hugging us as well, patting me on the back as my sobs break free. I wish that I could protect them, protect myself, from harm.

Torto and Fen walk me up to the temple, each holding one of my hands.

"We have to go," Torto says when we reach the temple.

"How is Tarkit?" I ask, holding on to Torto a moment longer.

"He's good. He's apprenticed to that baker now, and when there's burnt bread all the boys at the bakery split it. Once he even had some extra he gave us."

"Say hello to him from me."

"Okay," Torto says. "You're sure you're all right?"

"I'm fine." I smooth his hair with my hand, offer him a final smile, and step into the temple, listening as Torto and Fen scuff their way down the alley.

Time passes slowly. A young woman enters the temple, prays quietly at the front of it, and, with a nod to me, leaves. I hear children running by, their voices high with excitement. Finally, though, a boy enters; he is a few years older than Torto, and somewhat better dressed.

"What's your name?" His voice is as sharp and hard as his face.

"Thorn."

He nods. "Go to the Curious Cat—that's the big inn with the stable two alleys south of Hanging Square. Use the side door next to the kitchen—not through the kitchen, hear?—and go up the stairs there. Knock on the second door on the left. Got it?"

I repeat his instructions back to his satisfaction and he leaves without a second glance.

The Curious Cat, unlike the inn where I met Red Hawk, is a large establishment, the hallway and stairs wide and well lit by windows open to the spring air. I knock on the second door upstairs, and at once a voice calls for me to enter. The room holds just a bed and two chairs set by the window. I squint, looking towards the window, and make out a figure seated in one of the chairs. The man nods to me, so I walk over and sit in the companion chair, watching him. It is Red Hawk himself.

"I did not expect to meet you again," I say.

He tilts his head as if equally surprised. "I am sorry about your friend. I heard this morning that she died."

"Yes." I look away from him, back towards the door.

"Is that why you are here?"

"That's why," I admit and stop again. The silence stretches between us.

"Lady, I would not have come to meet you myself if I did not believe there is more here than this. Tell me what you came to ask." I look at him, taken aback at the gentleness in his voice. I cannot tell from the shadows touching his face whether it is a true kindness or a calculated one, but I find I do not particularly care.

"I want to understand justice in this land. The men who hurt—who killed Violet can be found. Ash and Oak both believe it; they say that the men will talk, will boast, and that there will be witnesses. Yet when Ash and Oak went to petition the king for justice against Violet's attackers, they were turned back. And no one even bothered to ask the guards to help search."

Red Hawk smiles, but it is a slow, sad thing. "I told you before: you are very idealistic."

"This is about justice."

"Justice for the poor?" He laughs, sitting back. "There is justice for the rich here, lady, and justice for the powerful. But for the rest of us there is very little of anything."

"Laurel told me that there are two laws here: the King's Law and the thieves' law. If the King's Law only serves the rich, what of the thieves' law?"

His gaze sharpens, and I know he understand me, but he says only. "It is what we make of it."

"Which is what, exactly?"

"It is primarily only for thieves. It is somewhat less harsh than the King's Law, and then again somewhat harsher."

"I don't understand."

Red Hawk gestures with his hand, as if he held something weighty in his palm. "Here is an example: if one thief steals from his brother, the first question asked is why."

"Isn't stealing what thieves do?"

"Aye, but between thieves there is a code of honor. We do not encroach on each other's territory, nor steal from each other. If a man steals out of need, because his family was going hungry or the like, he is forgiven. But if he steals only to enrich himself, then the first time he is flogged. The second time, his hand is cut off so that he cannot steal again. By the King's Law, the common thief is flogged, regardless of why he steals or how often."

"By the King's Law, then, you are not a common thief."

"No," he says, amusement warming his voice. "The uncommon thief is subject to special treatment."

"And what of men who do—what was done to Violet?"

"By the King's Law, those found guilty of rape and murder are hung."

I have to hold myself still, breathe deeply once, for it is the first time I have heard anyone name what was done to Violet. My voice cracks as I ask, "And under your thieves' law?"

"These are crimes that cannot be excused to necessity, so we are in agreement with the King's Law: a public hanging. But before that the men would be flogged that their punishment not go too easily with them."

"It is very similar."

"Yes. Am I to guess that you wish Violet's attackers brought to justice?"

I meet his gaze. "I do. But I don't know what I will owe you, for you have already repaid your debt many times over."

"The accounting is not quite clear," he observes with a mock frown.

"I helped you one night, your men helped me another. You helped us find Violet. Now I am asking something in addition."

"When a thief tries to grant you a favor, don't protest it, lady. It is far too rare an occurrence to be disregarded."

I rub my cheeks and then pause, holding my head still, as if I might hold in the terror of the last few days, might somehow keep myself from breaking apart at the kindness of his words.

"You are not well," Red Hawk says.

I shake my head, dropping my hands to my lap. "I am fine."

"You have not seen a death like this before."

"No," I agree. "And I would not have believed that the only help to be had would be from those who evade the law, not swear to uphold it."

"I am sworn to my own law."

"You are. For that I am grateful."

"We can find Violet's killers and bring them to justice. It is hardly an impossible task."

"What will I owe you?"

He taps his fingers against the armrest. "Tell me, lady, what is the price of justice in your land?"

I watch his fingers, thinking of Valka, of that day long ago and the sapphire brooch. "Justice in my land is very similar to the King's Law here— it is to be had for the rich and held against the poor. True justice," I glance up to meet his eyes, "that would be priceless, I expect." His lips twitch, and I wonder if he has held back a smile, and what that smile would mean.

"Priceless," he echoes. "Can you offer me something equally priceless in return?"

"I have very little to offer—what I brought with me in my trunks from home; that is all," I say humbly.

"But there is more to you than just your belongings; what else can you offer?"

My mouth goes suddenly dry; I cannot look away from him. I am aware in an awful, sickening way that we are in a bedroom. "I—I can't," I stumble.

"Lady," he reaches out and touches my sleeve lightly. I flinch away. "Do not look at me so. Have I ever given you true reason to fear me?"

"I am sorry," I whisper, looking down to hide my relief, my shame.

"You feel for Violet because you too have been hurt before."

"I—no, not like Violet. I wasn't hurt like her. I was just—it was nothing."

"Nothing?"

I close my eyes. "My brother used to beat me. He would threaten me." The words sound strange to me, hanging in the air. Smaller than I expected. I have never voiced them before, have never admitted to anyone what my brother did. It did not matter if others knew or not, there was a safety in not speaking it aloud, admitting it to myself.

"It is nothing—when you consider what was done to Violet, to others here," I gasp into the silence. "A few bruises, that's all." I open my mouth and find that I cannot go on, that the words have robbed me of my breath. I cover my face with my hands, bending down, my back hunched. Hidden, my breath rasps back into me in a broken, strangled sob. I do not want Red Hawk to hear me, so I hold my breath, shaking, refusing to breathe again until I must.

"Thorn," he says, his voice the same soothing tone that hostlers use with a frightened colt. I hear him move away. He will leave now; he will look down on me for my weakness when so many others have carried burdens heavier than mine.

"Here," he says, walking back to me. "Drink this." He holds out a tin cup. I take it from him in surprise. He does not speak again until I lower the cup, stare down into the water left at the bottom. "I knew the night you first helped me that you were a strong woman at heart. I did not realize the depth of your courage until now."

I laugh, an ugly, harsh sound. "Courage? I am worse than the lowest coward. I've allowed—you don't know the things I haven't done, because I was afraid of what would happen to me." I press my hand to my mouth as if I might take back the truth of my words.

"As a thief," Red Hawk says, "I've found that acting when you are afraid is the greatest sign of courage there is."

"But I haven't acted. I've just let things go on because I was afraid."

"Ah," he says. "So, that night when you helped me through the depths of this city and delivered me to a safety that threatened you, you who are afraid of the brutality of men, that night is an example of when you let things go on from fear of what might happen to you?"

"Falada was there," I whisper.

"Your horse could have protected you from the soldiers?"

"No," I admit. "There were too many—but he stayed with us, and carried me home."

"It is easier to be strong when you have a friend supporting you," Red Hawk agrees. "But that does not change the fact that you chose to act, and in acting you saved my life."

"That was an exception," I tell him bitterly. "All these months here, I have been hiding from the one thing I have to do."

"I expect, when you are called upon to do it, you will rise to the occasion very well. You are made of stronger stuff than most." I don't believe him. He must see it in my eyes, because he grins and says, "I did not get this far by making mistakes. As for the question of justice, I will see to it that the attackers are found and punished. In return," he pauses, watching me. "I want something from you that, I fear, can't be traded. It makes for a difficult bargain."

"What is it?"

"I should like your friendship and trust."

I stare at him, my mind flicking to Kestrin and his apple-cakes, but the tenor of this is different; there is more truth between Red Hawk and I.

"Don't feel the need to answer at once," he says dryly.

"Why would that matter to you?"

He raises an eyebrow. "Perhaps you underestimate yourself." I do not answer. "I know," he continues, "that such things cannot be bought. So I want from you only an offer of friendship, an attempt at trust."

"That is all?" I ask. He nods. I sit back, thinking. The friendship and trust of a goose girl is one thing, but that of a princess may be an entirely different thing. And then I wonder if Red Hawk might not be one of the best friends I could have as a princess, and if I, in turn, might be able to help him as well. Except that a princess cannot uphold a thief. I bite my lip. I am not there yet, I think.

"I will try," I tell him. "And I will not betray the trust you have given me, now or in the future."

"Of course," he says. "Friends do not betray each other."

29

Laurel sits at the common room table, her back hunched, her face in her hands. I retreat into the hall and then stop. How can I leave her alone when I know the choking emptiness I feel over Violet's death? How much deeper must her grief be? I enter, moving quietly to the counter. Laurel lifts her head, watching me with dull eyes as I fill a cup of water and bring it to her. She takes it without a word, setting it on the table untouched. My hand hovers over her hair. It is matted, locks stuck together, the braid hardly there anymore. Nothing, nothing like the Laurel I know.

I fetch a comb from the cabinet and stand behind her, working through her hair, picking out the knots lock by lock. She rests her chin on her hands and lets me work, and I watch the tension slowly go out of her shoulders. When I am done, her hair resting in a braid down her back once more, I kiss the top of her head and turn away. She catches my hand and brings it to her cheek; for a long moment we stay like that, her cheek, the palm of my hand, the damp of tears in between.

After I finish in the goose barn, I return to the stables looking for her. Laurel straightens and turns towards me at my call, leaning on her pitchfork, the stall only half-mucked. There are circles under her eyes, and I know from the sound of her shifting at night on the pallet next to mine that she has not slept well.

"I wanted to tell you something—you and the boys."

"What's that?" Oak asks, stepping out of a stall two doors down. Like Laurel, Oak is exhausted, his eyes sunken and his face sallow.

"I spoke to a friend yesterday about finding those men," I say awkwardly. "I think he'll find them."

"Good. I hope they string them up and leave them to rot."

"Laurel," Oak says in surprise, turning towards her. She shakes her head, her eyes bright with tears, and goes back to mucking her stall. Oak presses his lips together, returning to his work in silence. He will leave for their family's farm in a few days' time, bearing the news of Violet's loss to their parents. I hope that he might also have news of the attackers' punishment to take with him.

I am grateful for the walk to the pasture, the solitude. In the field, I fill my cup with water from the stream and sit beneath the shade of a tree. The geese are spread about the pasture, snapping up grass and tasty bugs, or dipping into the stream. It is as if nothing has happened, as if the pasture exists out of time and none of the violence or illness I have seen can touch it.

In the late afternoon I doze, leaning back in the shade of a tree. I wake with a start, but when I look up I realize it is only the geese passing near me; Corbé still sits by his tree across the pasture. I can feel his gaze on me, though, and I stand up, leaning on my staff as I return to the stream for a drink.

The Wind comes to visit, a faint puff of warmth that hints of summer. I follow the wall down a few paces as I speak to it, my hand drifting over the stones. "You should go home," I say. "The dell is a better home for you than these empty fields."

Stay, the Wind argues.

"No. There's something I have to do, something I've been avoiding. I don't think it will go well. Even if, by the grace of God, it does, I won't be coming out with the geese anymore."

Wait, suggests the Wind.

"You can wait," I tell it. "Just don't wait too long."

Ash sprints up to the goose barn.

"Thorn! Come quickly!"

I drop my rake and run to him. His teeth are bared in a grin. "What's happened?"

"They said—we heard," he gasps, catching hold of my hand and pulling me after him as he begins to run again. "The men were caught—they're at Hanging Square." I can see Laurel running ahead, her boots flashing beneath her skirts, Rowan and Oak keeping pace beside her. We pound after them, people turning to watch our flight through the streets.

The Square is filled to overflowing, people jostling each other for a view of the central gallows. I skid to a stop, yank my hand from Ash's, and bend over, digging my fingers into my side. He waits next to me, panting and stretching up on his toes to look over the heads of the crowd. I stare at the cobblestones, not wanting to look up now that I am here.

"There's two of them," Ash tells me.

"That's right," says the man next to him. "We saw them go up—real fast and hard they did it, and then they were off. It was Red Hawk's men, so they wouldn't be waiting for the king's men to get here. But they made some proclamation afore they did it."

"Aye," a woman glances back at us. "I heard it meself. They said the girl was an innocent, and the men done raped and murdered her, and it was a crying shame the king couldn't do nothing for it, so Red Hawk figured he'd help him."

"I'd like to see that old dog Melkior's face when he hears that," the man says, flashing a gap-toothed smile.

"Who was the girl?" asks a man who has come up behind us.

Before Ash can answer, the woman does: "She wasn't nobody. Just some poor girl got caught out at night and the men thought they'd have their way with her. Didn't think Red Hawk'd get involved, did they?"

"Come on," Ash whispers. "I want to get closer." I follow him through the crowd, keeping my head down, but when we reach the gallows I have to look up. The bodies twist slowly in the faint breeze, ropes creaking. Their hands are tied in front of them and their shirts have been stripped off to reveal welts crisscrossing their backs. I swallow down bile, wanting to turn away, *but this is what I asked for.*

I stare at the bodies until I have memorized each detail. The first man was barely older than Ash, with long black hair that sticks to the raw skin of his back. His mouth gapes open, eyes protruding, dark and unseeing. His arms are roped with muscles, long and sinewy. The other man was shorter in life, his feet barely reaching further than his friend's knees. A dark beard covers his face, and his stomach hangs over his belt in fleshy rolls. The welts in his back have cut into the fat, leaving trails of blood that stain the back of his trousers. His hands are large and meaty; where his friend had muscle, this man had weight.

When I turn away, I think of Violet. I think of her terror as these men caught her. I think of her trying to fight them, of their bound hands binding her, cutting her, their limp, booted feet slamming into her ribs, her mouth, crushing her hands. I see her again as I first did when the healer uncovered her; see her lying broken and used in the corner of an alley. I stagger to the side and Ash reaches out to steady me.

"This is your doing," Ash says, his voice beside my ear. "You've brought them to justice. There are women and children that will go free this month because you've made such men afraid of punishment. Put your head up, Thorn." I force myself to meet his gaze.

"This is justice. Don't be afraid to look at it." He smiles, "It may not be pretty, but sometimes justice has to be hard to keep the rest of us straight and safe." I nod, but I am not sure what I have done, even if I am glad of these deaths. He turns to look at the bodies again. "It's done then." I follow his gaze, and note for the first time the arrow stuck into the support beam of the gallows. A string dangles from its shaft, three feathers threaded to the end of it: they are the long bright feathers of a red-tailed hawk.

A commotion erupts at the far end of the Square. Ash catches hold of my hand. "That'll be the king's men. They'll cut down the bodies and question everyone they can. Hurry." I follow him as he threads through the crowd, his hand tight in mine. We take the back alleys, slowing to a walk as soon as we have left the Square behind. Ash matches his steps to mine, letting me take my time; I am still off balance from what I have seen.

At the stables, Ash leads me to the common room. "You'd better sit and have a bit of water," he tells me. "You're a touch too pale." I take the water from him gratefully, sitting on the bench to drink. Ash takes a cup himself and sits down on a stool, leaning back to rest his head against the wall.

"Ash?" Oak's voice carries down the hall.

Ash leaps up and goes to the door. "In here."

Oak, Laurel and Rowan join us in the common room, each taking a turn of water. Laurel comes to sit next to me, wrapping her arm around my shoulders and squeezing.

"Our miracle-worker," she says, and though her voice is not happy, some of the weight of the last week has lifted from it.

Rowan comes up to me, drops to his knees, and catches hold of my hand. "Lady Thorn."

"Rowan, what are you doing?" I try to pull my hand back.

"Lady," he says with all the gallantry of youth and seriousness, hanging on to my hand. "I swear to protect you as if you were my sister, so long as I live."

"Amen," Ash says from his stool, Oak echoing him a moment later. When I glance at Ash, his eyes are slitted, his face still as stone. Oak smiles at me, a kind, gentle look, and then glances down at his hands.

Rowan stands up and claims the end of the bench. "That's all."

"You've done a good thing, Thorn," Laurel says. "It's been a long time since folks saw something like this; mayhap there're other Violets that will be safe because of you. I know our Violet would be glad of that."

I push myself to my feet. "I have to get back to the geese."

Ash nods. "I hear you won't be with them much longer."

"What's that?" Laurel asks.

"Joa spoke to the Master of Horses. Thorn'll be working with us as soon as they find another goose girl to take her place."

Rowan lets out his breath in a whistle.

"Who told you that?" I ask Ash.

"Heard it this morning over at the first stable. You've jumped rank, you know; there's a few others that have been waiting for the stables longer than you've been here at all."

"I don't want to upset anyone."

"Don't worry," Ash says, grinning. "No one's going to bother you while we're around."

"And we all know the best person gets the job here," Rowan says.

I look down at my hands, wondering how much of my reputation has been built on my friendship with Falada. "I'd better get back to the barn," I repeat, standing up. "I've still got to work those mares afterwards."

I set off for the goose pasture only a little later than usual; it is strange to imagine that I was gone for only a short while, less than an hour. I feel as though the day should have stopped, cut short with the lives of the criminals. How could something so momentous take so short a gasp of breath to happen?

I slow as I reach the city gates, looking up to Falada's head. It has grayed with damp and grime, his mane stiff and matted, but beyond that there is no change. I pause underneath, looking up.

"Falada," I call. "I'm going to find a way."

The head hangs still above me, the eyes sealed shut, stitches showing where his mouth has been sewn closed. I look down, take a step.

"Princess." I jerk my head up, staring at Falada. He meets my gaze, his eyes open and seeing, bright with life. "Princess," he says again, and the word is the warm embrace of a friend.

Behind me, I hear a half-swallowed cry. I spin around to see a guard standing at the mouth of the gate, staring up at Falada. As I turn, he drops his gaze to me, his face pale. For a moment, we stare at each other, then I turn my back and hurry through the gates, holding tight to my staff. I listen for the guard, for footsteps or a voice calling after me, but there is nothing. When I look back, the gate lies empty.

At the goose pasture, I drop down onto the grass, my legs tired. The geese are scattered as usual, Corbé seated at the other end of the stream. I set my staff across my crossed legs, watching him. He glances from me to the geese and does not look back again.

The Wind visits again in the late afternoon. I stroll through the grass in its company, watching the geese.

"I know what I need to do," I tell the Wind. "I just don't want to." The Wind tugs at my skirt, as if it could hurry me along on the path I have chosen.

"Tomorrow," I say, thinking of what that would mean: facing Kestrin, which would likely include questions about Red Hawk's involvement in finding Violet's attackers, and then also exposing Valka. And, in the end, it would mean leaving Laurel, Oak, Ash and Rowan.

"It would be so much easier to let Joa make me into a hostler," I say, trying to smile.

"You're no hostler," a voice growls behind me. I jump, turning to find Corbé glaring down at me. I take a quick step back. "I heard the talk this morning," he tells me, matching my step. "You're not going to be a hostler before me."

"I haven't agreed to it," I stammer, backing away further. He keeps walking towards me, his eyes glinting in the afternoon light.

"You think you can come in here with your rank and walk all over the rest of us?"

"No, I don't!" I cry, sickeningly aware that I have left my staff by the tree, that Corbé is taller and stronger, and no doubt faster, than me.

"You won't," Corbé agrees, and he smiles. It is an ugly smile, a smile of knowing and hatred and jealousy all mixed together. "You've made someone angry up at the palace, but you know that, don't you?" I shake my head, my breath rattling in my chest. "I've a promise that I can do what I like with you, and there won't be any price to pay. What do you think of that, girl?"

"It's not true!"

"But it is," he purrs.

"Kestrin would punish you. She can't protect you from Kestrin—or Melkior."

"What would they care for a servant like you?" Corbé sneers, and though he is wrong it does not matter: what matters is that he believes this, believes that the law will not stoop to protect a servant.

"Red Hawk just hung the men who attacked Violet—he'll come after you, too," I nearly shout, stumbling away from Corbé as he continues to walk towards me, swinging his staff along.

"He won't," Corbé says. "You're lying, but even if he did catch Violet's friends, he won't care anything for a foreigner."

I turn and run. I hear Corbé laugh behind me, but I do not look, concentrating only on the possibility of getting away. I hear the thud of his boots gaining on me, hear him grunt, and then there is a low whistle and his staff knocks into my ribs. I stumble, pain lancing through me, and his staff slams into my legs, knocking me to the ground. I scrabble to my knees, my hands closing on dirt, on a rock, anything to use against him. His staff comes down again, before I can rise, but this time it is the end of the staff driving into the small of my back. My hands fly out from under me, my cheek slamming into the ground. I hold still, trying to breathe through the pain in my back. With my face sideways, I can see the geese honking and moving away from us.

Corbé winds his fingers into the roots of my braid, twisting my head around, his weight still pressing the staff down into my back. My mouth arcs in a grimace of pain.

"Don't do this," I whisper. Pain leeches the color from my vision, but I can still see his face, see the way the breeze lifts a lock of his hair.

"This is only the beginning," he promises.

"Wind," I whisper, watching his hair.

"What?" Corbé looks up, scanning the pasture, confusion touching his brow. I can hear a soft whistling that grows, building into a shrieking gale that rips over the stream, lifting water and rocks with it as it approaches. The geese erupt in a flurry of feathers, tumbling towards us, honking frantically.

Corbé swears, dropping his grip on me and stumbling back, his eyes wide. I curl into a ball, folding my arms over my face. The wind passes over me so gently it merely fans my back, and then it slams into Corbé. I hear his scream and I press my hands to my ears, shaking.

RUN. The word echoes in my mind, the force of it driving me to my knees and then, staggering, to my feet. I do not turn to see where Corbé is, whether he has fallen or run away. I take one step forward, and then another, and then I am running, stumbling over the rocks of the streambed and clambering over the low stone wall, and running and running.

I do not know how long I run, or where. My eyes blur until I cannot see and I lose my balance, one foot tripping over the other, spilling me to the ground. I lay sprawled on the grass, gasping for breath, and it is a time before I realize that I am sobbing, that I cannot catch my breath because I am weeping. I see Corbé's face above me, his features twisted by the blackness of his emotion, and there is Violet laid out on the floor, pale and unmoving, her face marred by dark bruises, and Falada hangs above me, a head only, fur dank and blackened by soot. I wrap my arms around myself and cry until my fear and guilt have spent themselves and I am left shivering on the ground, cold despite the warmth of the day.

Finally, I sit up, pain shooting through my back and chest. I press my hands against my ribs. They leave red smudges on my tunic; when I look at them they are scraped raw, though I do not remember flaying them against the ground as Corbé pinned me down. I stagger to my feet, my legs weak beneath me, but at least I am standing. I have only to walk home, I think, seeing Oak and Ash and Rowan in my mind's eye. They will never let Corbé touch me again.

The wind whips past me and I follow it, turning my face to watch it turn, raising the dust of the plains into a swirling pillar. It is not my Wind, and as the dust it raises grows darker, funneling into the wind's small vortex, I step back once, and then again. Out of the darkness at its center, steps the Lady.

I stare at her, hearing the rasping of breath in my lungs, loud now that the wind has gone. Faintly, I hear something beating, and I wonder if it is my heart, the pulse of my fear. *Not like this.* It is almost a prayer. *I am not ready.*

"I had not planned on coming now," the Lady agrees, her voice the whisper of leaves in the fall. "But perhaps I will enjoy it more this way." She smiles, an empty curl of her lips that sends me back two more steps.

"Look there," she says, tilting her head. "See who your Wind is, who comes to rescue you."

I turn, not wanting to look. Kestrin pounds towards us on a horse, the court clothes he wears at odds with the way he rides, a warrior into battle, tensed and ready, his hair caught up in a tight knot, his mouth a grim slash across his face. He swings down before his horse has stumbled to a stop, and I cannot read the expression in his eyes. The horse drops its head between its legs, foam dripping from its mouth, and I am sorry for it, sorry for the way it has run, for the pain of its flight, driven by a force it did not understand.

Kestrin spares me only one quick glance, his eyes flicking over me, and then he turns to the Lady. "Release her."

"Come now, my prince, what has she to do with you? A mere goose girl…" The Lady laughs, a poisonous sound that leaves me lightheaded. "Why, who would even notice if she disappeared?" Her eyes turn to me; they are the empty sockets of a skull. She gestures once, lazily, and the chain jerks so tight around my throat I think my neck will snap. My knees give out with the force of it, and I fall, catching myself on my hands, the burn of my already raw palms barely registering. I raise a hand and claw at my throat, but I cannot reach the chain.

"Stop!" I feel Kestrin beside me now, his hands touching my throat, trying to grasp the choker.

"Does it not amuse you? You descend from a line that takes pleasure in such things. Surely you enjoy seeing a princess at your feet?"

Black dots dance before my vision. I feel myself slipping, hands no longer able to support me, but Kestrin is there, lowering me. *At least I will not die alone.*

"Alyrra," Kestrin cries, his hands at my throat, but he cannot touch the spell there.

"You haven't much time if you want to help her."

"Damn you," he whispers. "What do you want?"

"You."

Darkness closes in, dragging me down. Dimly, I hear the prince say, "Very well."

30

The horse grazes some distance away. I sit up painfully, my bruised back driving the other minor aches and pains from my mind. I breathe through my mouth, waiting for the pain to ebb. The plains have taken on the rosy hue of early evening, the grass waving gently beneath a light breeze. A bee buzzes past on its way back to its hive, pausing a moment to investigate me. Soon, the plains will turn gray, then be lost to darkness. I cannot remember if there will be a moon tonight to light my path to the city.

It takes me a long time to stand, for my legs will not answer to me as they should. They are soft, and when I finally manage to rise my knees knock against each other. I wonder if I have become an old woman, lying unconscious through the passing of the years, but my hands when I look at them are the same young, work-roughened hands of the goose girl I am, the palms black with dead blood.

I make my way slowly towards the horse. He turns his head as I near him, mildly curious.

"Harefoot," I whisper, recognizing the gelding. My throat is raw, and the single word fires pain through it, making my eyes water. He must recognize me as well, for he waits patiently as I struggle into the saddle, letting out an exaggerated sigh as I finally get my seat. Violet had always loved his mix of sweet temper and attitude.

Harefoot willingly starts off for the city, and we reach the gates without mishap. We pass under them silently; I do not raise my eyes to Falada, cannot imagine speaking to him now, when I have finally and truly betrayed Kestrin.

"That's her!" a man's voice cries.

"Halt!" Harefoot's ears flick towards the voices, but he keeps walking. Four soldiers surround us, their swords drawn. Harefoot snorts, moving to step around the man before him.

"Stop your horse," the soldier orders, reaching up to catch the bridle.

"Easy," I croak, as Harefoot swings his head up, his ears laid back. He snaps his teeth at the man, making him jump back, and then leaps into gallop, nearly throwing me. The soldiers shout, racing after us.

"Stop!" I gasp, but Harefoot is having none of it. With the bit between his teeth, he carries me to what he has always known as safety. The stable door stands closed and for a terrified moment I think we will crash into it; then he pivots and kicks through the door. I slide into his neck, clutching at the pommel, then nearly fall off as he turns again and charges into the stable.

"Stop," I plead, and he, having arrived, stops. I slide off of him, grateful when hands close around my elbows to support me.

"What's happened, Thorn?" Joa's face comes into focus. I shake my head, watching as Harefoot spins and bugles a challenge to the soldiers as they sprint through the broken doorway. They stumble to a halt. Around us, the other horses neigh and snort, and from one stall comes an answering bugle, the horse within kicking at his walls.

"Hold her," Joa orders, and another set of hands catch me. Joa stalks towards the soldiers. "Exactly what do you think you're doing chasing down my hostlers, spooking my horses and causing damage to my stables?"

"That girl's wanted by the king," the lead soldiers growls. "And she's the one that broke your door, or didn't you notice?"

"If the king wanted her, he would have sent for her through the stables, where she works. He wouldn't have sent four brutes to waylay her after she finds Lord Filadon's gelding that had run away, and manages to bring the creature back. Manages, you asses, despite the fact that *you* have clearly convinced it that you're going to attack." I blink. *He's lying,* I think muzzily. *Harefoot didn't run away; I did.*

The soldiers start towards us again and Harefoot snorts a warning. One of the hostlers approaches him warily, reaching out to grasp the loose reins as he murmurs soothing words. Harefoot's ears slowly come back up.

"We've orders to arrest the girl," the soldier repeats, his voice harsh. "She's wanted on charges of witchcraft."

I choke and cough so hard that, had it not been for the hostler holding me, I surely would have lost my balance.

"*Witchcraft?*" Joa echoes, equally shocked.

"I'd believe it if I were you. Didn't you just see her riding that horse like a demon?"

"Aye," says a second soldier. "And she speaks to that horse's head hanging in the gates, and the thing answers her." I shake my head, staring at them.

"The hell it does. She's a damn good hostler is what she is," Joa says.

"That girl's a goose girl; we see her bringing in the geese every night."

"She's been training as a hostler," Joa says slowly, as if speaking to idiots. "She starts in the stables in the morning."

195

"If she hasn't been burned alive for the witch she is," the second soldier agrees amiably.

"I'm no witch," I say, my voice so hoarse it barely reaches my own ears.

"Look here, Master Hostler," the first soldier says. "We've orders to arrest the girl and take her to the palace. You can go up there and argue it if you like. But if you keep her here, we'll be picking you up with her in the morning."

Joa holds his silence.

"I wouldn't want to be the one acting against the king's orders."

"All right," Joa turns and walks back to me. "I'm coming with you," he says, taking my arm. I lean on him as we walk up to the soldiers. I don't think I could run if I tried.

"No tricks," the first guard says tersely. I shake my head, but he is already turning to lead the way out, the rest of his quad falling in around us.

Joa waits until my legs begin to take more of my weight before he speaks, his voice low. "Corbé came back hours early today, without the flock and gibbering all sorts of nonsense. I took half the hostlers out with me, including Ash and Oak, and we found the geese spread across three pastures, feathers everywhere.

"I expect Ash and Oak would have killed Corbé if I'd let them. As it is, they're still out on the plains looking for you, along with a good number of my hostlers. This is the second time you've disappeared on the plains; last time a rider from the Hunt found you and brought you back. We weren't sure what we'd find this time."

I glance up at him; the moonlight softens the planes of his face, his eyes kind and veiled with concern. I look back to the road, to the straight back of the soldier in front of us, remembering the day Laurel asked me what had happened in the pasture. *I will tell him*, I think. *But not where these soldiers can hear.*

Joa does not speak again, and we reach the palace in silence. We follow the soldiers through a maze of hallways to a guardroom. We wait with the quad while their leader fetches a man carrying a ring of keys and a lantern.

"We'll lock her up for the night. She'll stand trial in the morning," the soldier tells Joa. The dungeon is dark and dank, sunk below the weight of the palace. The lantern lights up the cells as we pass them. There are people in them.

Many come up to the bars of their cells and hurl insults at us, their words echoing down the hall obscenely; others cry out as we pass, reaching through the bars towards me with dirty fingers, eyes glistening in the lantern light; some few remain silent, couched in darkness, unmoving. Everywhere there is the stench of death: rising from the bodies of the prisoners, collecting in corners, seeping out of the very stones themselves. It is as if I do not look upon people but upon animate corpses. This is a place that leeches the life from a body long before the execution arrives.

The soldiers unlock an empty cell and Joa guides me in, lowering me to the floor.

"Joa," I whisper, and he kneels beside me to see my face. "Today in the pasture, Corbé attacked me." Joa stiffens. "He hit me with his staff and knocked me down. He wasn't afraid of being caught, or being punished. He said—that he had been promised safety. That he could do what he wished. But I got away from him."

"Did he?" Joa asks, his voice steel-edged. "And who is his protection?"

"The princess." I stare at the darkness through the bars.

"We haven't got all night," one of the soldiers calls to Joa. "Get out so we can lock her up."

"I'll seek an audience with the king for you," Joa says. "He'll see justice done." I nod, knowing what justice is in this land. He stands up, touches my shoulder once, and then he is gone.

An unfamiliar soldier unlocks the door late the following morning. I heave myself up clumsily, half-numb from the cold of the stones. In the hall, the soldier's quad flanks me, escorting me up to a hearing room. It is a simple enough room: a table with three chairs stands at the end, two rows of benches face them with an aisle up the middle, and in the space between benches and table, to the right, a large fireplace fills the wall.

I walk to the center of the room and gingerly curtsy to the judges seated at the table. With a jolt, I recognize Lord Filadon, seated on the right. He watches me somberly, no hint of friendship, or even recognition, in his eyes. Beside him sits a man in a deep purple robe, embroidered with gold. He is of middle age, with a pot-belly and thick, hammy hands that rest on the table. The man on the left, a captain of some sort, frowns as he studies me. He is of slighter build, with heavy brows, a well-trimmed mustache and an arrogant mouth. By his hand sits a ceramic pitcher and cup. I have to force myself not to look at it.

"Goose girl Thorn," the captain says.

"Yes sir."

"You have been charged with witchcraft ungoverned by the Council of Mages," he gestures to the man beside him, a wizard it would seem.

"I would hear the charges, sir, if I may."

He nods. "You have been charged with the ability to converse with dead animals and bewitch unbroken horses, and the power to call the wind to act as your servant. How do you plead?"

I swallow hard. "I am innocent, sir."

"There are witnesses," the captain says mildly. He sits back, resting his elbows on his armrests, as if he has finished with this business already, but his eyes are reasoning eyes.

"May I hear them?"

"We heard them earlier today."

I lick my lips, tasting blood where they have cracked; I have not had anything to eat or drink since I left the goose pasture. "May I hear what the witnesses told you?"

He ticks them off on his fingers. "First, both a soldier and your fellow goose boy have heard the head of a horse hung at the West Road Gate answer you when you address it."

Poppycock. Corbé was never around when Falada spoke.

"Second, you had tamed and ridden that same horse, that would not answer to any man."

"Who is the witness there?" I ask, unable to help myself.

"The goose boy, though I expect that any of the hostlers in the king's stables would answer for it."

"And the third charge?" I ask, properly outraged by now. Never mind that I *had* ridden Falada—Corbé certainly hadn't seen me.

"That you called the wind to attack the goose boy and scatter the flocks."

"Witnessed also by the goose boy?"

"Yes. Do you charge him with lying?" he asks, and I know from the very quietness of his question that this will damn me in his eyes. I dare not tell them what Corbé had done to bring the Wind against him.

I tamp down on my anger and answer as mildly as I can. "No sir. I am sure he reported what he understood as truth."

"Was his understanding flawed?"

"It must be," I say, smiling wanly, "for I am innocent."

"What is your proof?"

I spread my hands before me. "The white horse could be saddled by our hostler from home. The trouble was that he was trained to answer to a single hostler and a single rider. Deprived of that, he had to be won over. I spent weeks with him before he began to forget his training; he allowed me to ride him but once or twice. Master Joa himself told me of horses trained this way from the South."

"A neat explanation," the wizard says, speaking for the first time. "Now explain how a dead horse speaks to you."

I shake my head. "Perhaps the sound was that of the wind whistling through the gates, sir. Or my own voice—I spoke to the head as a man might speak to the portrait of his dead father. How could it answer?"

"It answered," the captain says sharply.

"What did it say?"

The men regard me silently. I wonder if they understand that they have become witnesses to my identity. That Falada's words, if accepted, should lead them to another truth.

Filadon taps the table with his fingers. "Explain your command of the wind and we may accept these other explanations." The other two men stiffen but do not respond. So, he holds rank over them even here.

"I do not command the wind, my lord."

The young captain smiles. "The evidence stands against you. A great wind came through your goose pasture, scattering the flock, flaying the skin of your fellow goose boy, and stripping the leaves from the trees. You yourself escaped unharmed. It is damning evidence." He glances down the table to Filadon, and from his words I know that only truth will win me free.

"Sirs, before I answer, tell me this: what is the punishment for witchcraft?"

The wizard cracks his sizable knuckles. "Practiced by one trained by our own mages, and bound to the service of the king, there is no punishment. But practiced by one who has done neither," the wizard pauses, looking at me meaningfully, "the punishment is to be burnt at the stake."

"Is it visited upon all who practice witchcraft in secret—peasant or prince?"

The wizard and the captain bristle, but Filadon's lips only tighten, his eyes glinting. That should tell him who sent the wind, unless Kestrin kept him in the dark as to the use of his study. Not likely.

"Unbound witches are not tolerated here," the captain says coldly.

I nod. To explain the Wind, to even hint at its source, would be to betray Kestrin and his father even further. I doubt that the royal family could be taken to trial, but I do not doubt that such a revelation would further weaken the king's power over his land, and shift the balance of power towards the Council of Mages. I know too little about them to be sure, but the occasional common room conversation has at least told me that there is a tension between the king and the Council. I think of Falada, going to his death with the secret of his people locked within him, refusing to run for fear of endangering me.

"I have no explanation for you."

The wizard leans forward. "Then you admit to commanding the wind?"

"No. I have no control over the wind."

"Do you admit that it came at your call?"

I gaze at him silently.

"She is guilty," the captain says with a satisfied smile. He darts a look at Filadon.

"I would agree," the wizard says. He frowns as he looks at me. I feel a spark of disgust—what sort of wizard condemns a woman for witchcraft without even testing her for a talent?

"I do not command the wind," I repeat, my voice deepening with anger.

"How did it come to you then?"

"I cannot explain it."

The wizard glances to his left. "Well, my lord Filadon, we are decided. What is your verdict?"

He studies me, the corners of his mouth tipped down. "I think the lady requires some time to consider her predicament. Perhaps she will find a way to offer us an explanation. Let us take our lunch and leave her here to consider her fate. When we return, I will hear her and give my verdict."

"There is nothing I can tell you," I say quietly.

"So you say," he agrees, standing up.

The captain shakes his head as he pushes back his chair. "The girl has as good as confessed. I see no value in delaying the inevitable, but it will be as you wish, my lord."

"Indeed." Filadon follows the men, but he walks slowly and by the time they reach the door, he has only just reached me. He pauses. "Will you not speak the truth, lady?"

He stands a full head taller than me, but his bearing is kind, reminding me of Oak when he used to speak to Violet. I shake my head. He sighs, and his eyes wander from me to the small fire burning in its grate. "If you will not tell us, then let the fire consume your story—but do not go to your death without speaking the truth."

"Whose secret is it, then?"

Surely he is not as dull as that? "You know that as well as I," I tell him.

He hesitates. "Speak the truth then, to this empty room. Perhaps you will find a way to defend yourself without betraying a confidence."

"If you know, then how can you not defend me?" I snap.

"It is not for me defend," he replies. "Only to judge. Find a way to give me something to judge. Tell your story," he repeats, gesturing to the fireplace, "until you know what to tell me."

I shrug, caught between fury and despair. He leaves in silence. I wait, weighing the quiet, and when I am sure that the guards will not enter for me, I hurry to the judges' table and pour myself a cup of water. I drink it down in three gulps, then pour myself another one, sipping this more slowly. My eyes flick to the fireplace. What a strange thing to say: let the fire consume your story. When he must know the story, or some part of it, himself. *He only knows Kestrin is the Wind; he doesn't know why Kestrin protected me.* But the other judges will not hear any claims against Corbé; that much is also clear.

I watch the flicker of the flames. I cannot imagine my skin charring as the logs do, my flesh eaten away and falling to ash. What will happen to Valka when I die, I wonder? If the skin I wear is destroyed, will it return to her charred past recognition, or healed? Or not at all?

I approach the flames slowly, kneeling before the grate. "I am no witch." The flames do not answer, crackling softly to themselves. I breathe in the scent of the wood, but I do not recognize it. We used to burn birch and pine at home, but even in the mountains of Menaiya there are few birches, and the pines are short and stunted.

"Let us consider the charges." I close my eyes, leaning my face forward into the heat that will claim my life. "Falada's head speaks to me, calling me princess. He, a gift to the princess, allows only me to ride him. Which would make me something other than the Lady Valka, and him something more than a mere horse. Second, the wind protects me when I am attacked; that same wind that befriended me at home, that found me here, and that followed me out when I fled to the plains yesterday. The wind is not me," I grind out to the flickering flames, "but Kestrin. Even if he is lost now, I will not betray him. That is the only story I have to tell, and I will not tell it here."

Something scrapes against stone, the sound rising up from the fireplace itself. I jerk up, eyes wide, but there is only the grate, the logs burning steadily. I stand, my gaze running frantically over the fireplace, the intricate brickwork: there are gaps between the bricks, and over the mantle a stone carving spreads, some portions standing forth, others recessed.

"No." I step back. Tell the fire. I shake my head. "Who listens?" I spin on my heel, scanning the room before coming back to the fireplace. "*Who listens?*"

The king shoves the door open, striding into the room. I stare at him, unmoving. He comes to a stop a pace away, studying me, his face emotionless. In the darkness of his eyes I can see him sifting through the possibilities of what I told the fire.

"Finish your story."

Behind him, Filadon steps into the room, shutting the door with a click.

"Your Majesty," I say.

"What happened on the plains?"

I swallow, studying him. Whether he knows his son as the Wind or not, this he has the right to know. "The prince came to find me, riding my lord Filadon's horse. As he came, so did your enemy."

"Who is that?"

"She is—not human. She wears always a long dress and a gem stone on her finger. She comes from a fall of moonlight, or flowing water." Or a breath of dust in the air.

His face pales. "And in this meeting yesterday, what happened?"

"She offered him a choice, Your Majesty: my life or his."

The king makes no motion. I concentrate on my breathing, meeting his gaze, knowing that I cannot show doubt or fear now. He turns to Filadon abruptly. "Ride out with Sarkor and the royal quads. Comb the plains west of here. Follow Kestrin's trail."

"Your Majesty," Filadon says, bowing. He leaves without a glance.

"For your sake, let us hope you are not lying, lady. Else the fate you will suffer will be much worse than a burning."

"Your Majesty."

As he turns his back my hands begin to tremble and it takes most of my concentration to keep them still. I am alone for the space of a few breaths and then the guards swing the door open. "Lady," one of them calls. "You'll come with us." I wonder what the king ordered, where I will be taken. He must have spoken to them or they would not have called me 'lady.'

They escort me to a small guest room, locking the door behind me and remaining on guard in the hallway. I pull the curtains back from the window; the view is of the palace wall, and, three stories below, the road that runs between. I pull one of the chairs to the window and sit, grateful for the thin rectangle of sunlight that falls on the floor, lighting the room.

I rub my hands over my face, thinking of Kestrin, willing to give himself over to the Lady for me. *Why?* Was it guilt? Or did he truly care for me? I squeeze my eyes shut, thinking of all the times I have spoken to the Wind, all the secrets I have shared, the comfort I have taken from its presence. Kestrin. It hardly seems possible. And perhaps it isn't. Perhaps the king does not truly believe me now because I am wrong, because Kestrin has never been the Wind, has only ever dabbled in magic, unbeknownst to his father. I drop my face into my hands. I can only try, I tell myself. And if I fail, at least Falada will be there to greet me in the end.

31

"I'm to ready you for dinner." The serving girl regards me coolly, unimpressed with her duty. I pull open the bundle she has dropped on the bed. The skirt and tunic are well made though simple—something a lady-in-waiting might wear.

"Very well," I say, my voice strangely calm to my ears. The girl helps me dress, hustling me out of my work clothes. She starts when she sees the dark purple bruises on my leg and side from Corbé's staff, but she is well-trained enough not to speak. Still, I am glad to pull on the clothes she has brought, hiding myself from her eyes. At the bottom of the bundle lies a brush and an assortment of hair pins.

"You'll need help with your hair," the girl remarks.

I touch my braid; it is matted with dirt and straw, hair straggling out and frizzing into knots. She picks up the brush and waits silently for me to sit.

It takes over an hour to brush out the tangles. The girl, with a muttered apology, has only enough time to wind it into a bun at the back of my neck before leaving. I return to my seat, wiggling my feet out of my new slippers. They pinch my toes but I doubt that it will matter. I won't be wearing them more than a day or two. At least if I am to die I won't look a complete disgrace. Mother would be pleased.

My guards escort me to dinner barely a quarter of an hour later. The dining room is elegant, decorated with tapestries and lit by lamps set in wall sconces as well as an elaborate set of candelabra on the long central table. The guests are already seated; they turn to watch me as a page ushers me to my seat at the end of the table. At my right sits Filadon, his wife across from him, and across from me a lord I do not know. The foot of the table has no place setting, for which I am grateful. When I glance up to the top of the table, I meet first the king's eyes, and then Valka's. Her face is pale, her lips pressed together in cold fury. Across from her, I can just make out Lord Garrin, leaning forward to speak to her. She turns towards him and a smile flashes across her face as she replies.

Filadon greets me quietly. I cannot tell from his voice, from the faint smile and nod, whether he found anything in his search. I dare not ask him here. He keeps up an animated conversation with the nobles seated beside him through most of the meal, while his wife engages the man across from me. She is young with a quick smile and quicker wit. I do not attempt to join them, for I know that Filadon does not want these men to know who I am yet. I take little of the food, and eat even less.

As the last course is cleared, the king turns to Valka. "I have an interesting question for you, my dear. Would you mind my asking it?" He speaks in our language, but at his nod the interpreter standing at Valka's elbow translates his question to Menay, capturing the full attention of the table.

Valka smiles. "Of course not, Your Majesty."

"There is a story that accompanies it, and the story is simply this: a princess and her companion were traveling one day on their way to some unknown land. During the journey, the companion betrayed her mistress; furthermore, upon their arrival in that land she went to great lengths to turn all who were there against her lady. She brought false charges against the princess, and sought to undermine her authority. She even claimed to be the princess herself. My question is this: what punishment would such a woman deserve?"

He leans back in his chair, smiling amiably at Valka. I realize that I am shaking.

Valka glances down the table to me as the translator speaks, and in that look I see a terrible fate. Meeting the king's gaze, she answers slowly, savoring each word. "Such a woman deserves no more than to be placed in a barrel that has been pounded through with nails and be dragged through the streets behind a brace of horses until she is dead."

The horror of it takes a moment to sink in. "No," I whisper. Filadon turns towards me, but the rest do not hear, focused on the translator. I watch the king, willing him to refuse this sentence. My brother's words whisper through me, speaking of the death Kestrin would mete out to me. His prophecy will come to pass after all.

"That is the punishment you decree?" the king asks, as if she might rethink it.

"Yes," Valka says firmly.

"Very well. You have chosen your death. Take her away." At the king's words a pair of guards step forward from the back of the room. As alarm spreads across Valka's features, relief floods through me, leaving me lightheaded.

"Your Majesty!" she cries, as the guards raise her from her seat. "What can you mean by this? I am the Princess Alyrra!"

"On the contrary, lady, you are not." The guards drag her from the room, still protesting, leaving behind a stunned silence. The king, at its center, seems utterly unconcerned.

It is Melkior who speaks next. "Your Majesty, if that was the impostor, who is the true princess?"

The king nods down the table, meeting my gaze. "The Lady Thoreena."

The table turns to stare at me. If I look at them I will lose what little composure I have. Instead, I hold the king's gaze and say, "Your Majesty, the sentence that was chosen is far too brutal a death. I would ask that you ease it."

Even as I speak my plea, I remember the king's words to me this morning: *the fate you will suffer will be much worse than a burning.* I doubt he will hear me.

"The sentence chosen was for you. It is only just to visit it upon the traitor herself."

"Your Majesty," I say, but I cannot find the words to make my argument.

He shakes his head. This is Valka's payment for betraying Kestrin. "Let it be, lady."

One of the ladies seated at the table leans forward. "Your Majesty, how could this happen? How was it not found out?"

The king has not yet looked away from me. Now, instead of answering the lady, he says, "Lord Filadon, the Princess Alyrra has been through much today. Will you help her back to her rooms?" He stands as he speaks, forcing all those present to rise as well. Filadon's hand comes under my elbow, urging me up.

"Come," he murmurs. I let him lead me out, aware that no one makes any move to follow us.

In the hallway, I pause, bewildered. My quad is gone. "I don't remember the way."

"It's all right," Filadon says. "The king wants you closer to the royal wing. I will take you there."

I glance back as we turn down a stairwell. "The rest have not left."

"The king will have to answer a few questions; he deemed it best that you not be there."

The words rub against me like flint against steel. "Why?"

Filadon frowns. "He does not want them to question you until he has spoken with you."

"There are too many secrets to keep," I say wearily, my anger dying.

"There are, Your Highness."

I wince, the title jarring against my ears. I want to tell him to call me Thorn. Instead I ask, "My lord, did you find any sign of the prince?"

Filadon's face grows sober. "We found his tracks easily enough, and yours leading back. The prince's end where they meet yours."

"Yes." I swallow. "I know you have the Family's trust. If you know—if you are that closely in their confidence—then you will know how Kestrin can be helped."

"There is nothing to be done," Filadon says, his face bleak. "She will never let him go. He went of his own volition; he cannot fight her now."

My stomach gives a lurch. He cannot die. Not like this. Not for *me*. "But surely there must be some way," I plead.

Filadon stops before a door, releasing my hand to open it. "She has taken the whole Family, one by one. If there were a way, we would have found it. I am sorry, Your Highness."

I cannot sleep. I lie awake in the great bed, listening to the silence that hangs in the suite of rooms, and I miss the sound of horses shifting and snorting somewhere nearby, of Laurel's occasional snore and Violet's sweet laughter. They are lost to me now. Violet is gone, and though I might visit the stables again, I will never again be the goose girl, able to share an evening in the common room or sing Laurel and myself to sleep.

No, I am princess now, though what that means I have yet to decide. I wonder if Falada would be proud of me, and I think of his head hanging in the city gates. Even in death, he is a better friend to me than I have ever been to anyone. And, inevitably, I think of Kestrin, visiting me in the guise of the Wind since my childhood—his youth. Kestrin promising me a protection I did not believe he could provide, and coming to my aid in the goose pasture, knowing as he must have that the Lady would take his help as a sign of his concern for me. She must have known all along; she was only waiting for him to recognize the cost of his friendship. And, as with Falada, he had chosen death rather than betrayal. But this time there is something I can do.

I stand up and go to the window, throwing open the shutters. Moonlight streams down. I close my eyes, breathe in its cool wash, the night breeze. "Lady," I call, standing with my hands loose by my sides. "Lady."

I wait, listening to the faint sounds of the palace, voices drifting to me from far away. I step back from the window. In the moonlight that streams in something flickers and strengthens.

"Lady," I repeat. She looks as I remember her from that first night, her face white as bone, her dress shining as if it were itself woven of light. "What have you done with Kestrin?"

She holds her hands out to me, palm upturned. I study her features. In the corners of her mouth, the tilt of her face, there is a deep and dreadful weariness. I take her hand. The moonlight flashes once, bright and yet painless, and then we stand together on a gravel walk, sunlight streaming down on the garden surrounding us.

"Where are we?"

"In my gardens." Here, the Lady wears clothes as any mortal might: a simple white gown with white-embroidered bodice and flowing sleeves. Her darksheen hair has been braided back tightly.

"And the prince?"

"He is here. Come; I will show you." I follow her down the walk into a small square. At the center stands a statue of a man. "This is the first of my collection," she tells me. The man must have once been quite powerful, both physically and intellectually. But his massive shoulders had slumped in defeat by the time the likeness was made, his once strong features wasted into a haggard, desperate mask. He wears the traditional Menaiyan armor of metal and leather, and at his side hangs a sword in its scabbard.

"He was your prince's great-grandsire. What do you think?"

I study the face and my breath catches in my throat: every detail stands out exactly, each eyelash, each lock of lank hair that falls across the high brow. "This—this was truly him!"

"Of course. Do you think I would put up a statue of such a man? No, it is he, exactly as he came to me. Do you not like him? I think he cuts a fine figure."

"You've turned him to stone," I say stupidly, staring at the frozen features. "Why?"

"Come along, princess. There is more for you to see." The Lady starts forward once more, towards the next gate.

I stay where I am. "How could you do such a thing to someone— anyone?"

She turns back to me, her eyes glittering with anger. "Do you truly wish to know?"

"Yes."

"Then I will show you." The Lady reaches up and catches my face in her hands, and the world drops away.

The soldiers drag the prisoner through the brush to the clearing, throwing it at the feet of a mounted rider. He swings down from his horse, his armor glinting in the sunlight, and kicks the prone figure onto its back. The soldiers laugh at its muffled cry.

A child begins to shriek somewhere behind me, but I cannot turn my head to see who it is. The rider pulls off his helmet, tossing it to one of the soldiers. His features leap out at me—the high brow, the cheekbones, the dark skin.

He reaches down and grasps the captive's clothes in one gauntleted fist, dragging the person up. The child's wails turn to a high keening. A woman, I think, staring in shock. The woman's face is battered and scratched, but as she looks up at him her features twist and she spits. He laughs, a hearty, booming laugh that fills the clearing, and drags the woman to a tree, shoving her up against it. I look around frantically, but the soldiers all watch with lazy amusement. I cannot find my voice to scream for help. With a sickening *thunk*, he thrusts his dagger through her palm, pinning her hand above her head. She cries out, a hoarse sound, and then with a gasp she snaps her jaw shut. Tears spill from her eyes, trickling down her cheeks. She looks towards me and smiles.

I am screaming silently, mindlessly, unable to look away as the man impales her right hand beside her left. He steps back, considering his handiwork. Then, with the same genial laugh, he draws his sword and slits her belly open. If I could move, if I could breathe, I would be sick with horror. I cannot even look away.

The man sheathes his sword and returns to his horse. Mounted, he watches the writhing, jerking agony of the woman until her hands tear themselves free of the daggers, and she collapses on the ground. She twitches a few times, her body shuddering, the tattered remnants of her hands pressed against the gaping wound of her belly, and then she lies still in a spreading pool of blood.

The man turns his horse towards me. I can hear the clump of the horse's hooves in the rich earth, can hear it through the gasping keen of the child behind me. He looks down at me, his lips curling back in contempt. His booted foot lifts from the stirrup and snaps out, slamming into my face and sending me reeling back, the child's weeping abruptly stopped.

"The prisoner was my mother," the Lady says, dropping her hands from my face. I shiver uncontrollably, my teeth chattering as my stomach roils. "I woke up alone with her body—they left me to tell my people what had become of her. She was one of our leaders, a great general. But she was betrayed into the hands of our enemy. They caught me, you see, and used me as bait to catch her." I close my eyes, shaking my head. As if I might deny this, might rattle these images free. Over and over I see the daggers impaling the callused palms, the shine of the sword as it slices through the woman's stomach.

"I swore I would kill him, destroy his line, for what he did."

"He was..." I say hoarsely, and a deep shudder runs through me. Dark hair, eyes the rich brown of earth...

"Your Kestrin's great-grandsire. Now do you understand?" The Lady does not wait for my answer but walks to a wrought iron gate set between two high hedges. I stumble after her.

208

"Lady," I call, trying to regain my footing. My focus.

"Little princess."

"That was—not the prince. Why do you punish him for his ancestor's cruelty?"

"I swore to end his line."

"But if Kestrin himself has never harmed anyone, then to kill him for something he has no control over—"

"It is in his blood."

"But, Lady," I say, unable to argue and yet knowing she is wrong—surely she must be wrong.

"Enough. Here, then, is your prince."

The garden shifts, whirling soundlessly to resettle in a different pattern. I find myself in another square surrounded by high hedges, but at the center the stone figure does not stand. Instead, he kneels, leaning back on his feet to look ahead. One hand is curled into a tight fist pressed against his leg, but the other reaches out in front of him, curving around the air as if resting on it.

I cannot bear to look at his face. Instead, I turn to the Lady. "He is dead."

"No," she replies. "It takes a few days for the soul to tear itself away. But you cannot help him now; you have not the power."

"And will you kill the king? And Lord Garrin as well?"

"They are the last."

"Then you are just like him. You are just like the monster who killed your mother."

She stiffens. "You do not know of what you speak."

"I do—you showed him to me, and I've seen you as well. You take as much pleasure in their deaths as he did in your mother's." She takes a step towards me. "You are willing to kill innocents to have your way. You killed Falada. You would have killed me as well, through Valka, and now she will die because of the games you played. For what? So you can avenge yourself against the man you already destroyed years ago?"

"You go too far, princess."

"No, Lady. You do. You kill people who have never wronged you, destroying them as ruthlessly as your mother was killed. You've had your revenge on the man who did it and now you've become him."

"You don't know of what you speak," she repeats, and I can see the shimmer of power in the air around her.

"Then show me otherwise, Lady."

She laughs, a rippling of water over stones, her anger transforming to scorn. "What would you have me do, girl? Free him?"

"Give me the chance to win his freedom and your forgiveness."

"I think not. You have certainly learned to speak since we first met, but you are still naive. You have seen what is in his blood; if you do not understand, it is not my concern to teach you."

"Test him," I suggest. "If what you believe is true, he will succumb to his blood. But if he passes, then he must be innocent of the taint."

"Test him?" the Lady echoes, her voice the ringing of steel on stone. I swallow hard, gazing back into her deathless eyes. "Fair enough. There will be three tests. If he passes them, he is free."

"And if he fails?"

"Then he remains mine, and you will be dead by his hands."

I do not let myself falter. "Very well."

The gardens melt away, spinning to darkness. A massive mouth closes around me, sharp teeth slicing though the air. My breath catches in my throat and I stumble back blindly, knocking into something. I throw out my hand to push away from it and my fingers touch rock. All around me, the teeth hover, glistening in the dark.

I take a shaky breath. The teeth are those of a cave roof, hanging down around me. Smaller teeth rise up from the ground to meet them.

"Who's there?" Kestrin stands at one end of the cave. I can see his figure between the hanging teeth, behind him a fall of light.

"Who's there?" he repeats. "I have found no living thing in this land till now, but I heard you move. Show yourself." His voice echoes in the cave, raising goose bumps on my arms. He shifts, and in that movement I see a fear I am well familiar with. I take a step towards him, my clothes rustling in the quiet. Surprised, I glance down, for I had been wearing a night shift when I spoke to the Lady. Now I wear a white dress. Kestrin recognizes it even as I do.

"Sorceress," Kestrin says, his voice harsh with emotion. "I'll not be taunted by you here."

He raises his hand, his mouth moving. I throw myself to the side as his fingers flick towards me, the sickening memory of how hopelessly I had tried to avoid Corbé's staff flashing through my mind. The power of Kestrin's spell passes me by, only the edge of it touching me, but it is enough to slam me against the wall. The cave teeth crash down, splintering into pieces on the ground and raising a cloud of dust. I take two breaths, steadying myself, then put my hand up and pull out a strand of hair: it is darker than night.

"Are you still here?" he calls, stepping further in, turning to scan the cave. He cannot see me; there is too much dust in the air. If I stay still, he will not find me. But then I will have failed, for what I must do now is convince him not to touch me.

I stand up in one fluid motion. "Kestrin." He spins towards me. "Hold your spells."

"Why? Because I cannot touch you? I know that." His eyes burn in the faint light.

"No. It is because you can: I have no magic here."

He laughs, a low feral sound. "Don't you? In this place of your making? What a fool you must think me."

"I am as much a prisoner here as you; the difference is only that you still have your powers."

He walks towards me until he is only a pace away. Even in the dark, I can see the haggard set of his features, the dark stubble on his cheeks. "If you cannot use magic, then how will you defend yourself from this?"

His hand darts out and catches my wrist. Pain runs up my arm like wildfire, scorching my veins. I cry out, staggering back against the wall, and rip my hand from his grip. He stands perfectly still. I bring my hand to my chest. The edges of my vision are bleached white, but I cannot afford to give in to the pain now. Instead, I straighten and meet his gaze, holding out my hand to him. The wrist is charred and blackened where he held it, bits of skin flaking off like ash.

"I have no defense here."

"What game do you play?" he asks, and I do not trust the very softness of his voice. He does not believe me, I think, because the Lady would not speak to him so.

"Look at it, boy. Had I any power, do you think you could have touched me? This is no game."

"Then how did you come here, to this wasteland? Why would you come unarmed? You knew I would kill you for what you did to my mother."

I dare not lick my lips; I must become the Lady now to win against Kestrin. She would never fear him. I force a laugh. "We were never good at answering each other's questions, prince. As for your threat, you are not *quite* a murderer." I smile. "Yet."

"Yet," he agrees, and with one quick step he is before me, his hand reaching for my neck. I catch it with my good hand without thinking, and when he freezes I bring it down slowly, turning it palm up.

"Well done, Kestrin. Kill me and you will become me. You are a quick learner." He pulls his hand away. I think of the Lady, of the vision she shared with me. "My mother was murdered too." His head jerks to the side as if I have slapped him. "Did you not think I had a mother? It was a man with your face who killed her. I thought to avenge her death when I killed him. I sought vengeance when I slew your mother, and when I forced you to come to me. Hatred grows, Kestrin."

"My hatred will die with you."

"But it won't. If you find a way back you will kill Valka, the impostor princess."

"It will end there," he says roughly, but he is listening now, despite himself, his hands clenched at his side.

"It won't. You will kill Alyrra as well."

"No," he says, but I hear the slight tremor in his voice.

"Yes," I say, feeling the truth of it like a weight in my belly. "Doesn't she know your greatest weakness? Hasn't she betrayed you twice already? Having killed two, it is easy enough to kill a third, especially when there are no consequences." He backs away from me.

"Murder makes one cold." I do not see him anymore; instead I see the Lady's face when she came to my room, weary and empty. "It takes away your soul, piece by piece. It turns your heart to stone. Is that what you want?"

"I would not kill her," he says, his voice that of a young boy's.

"But you would, Kestrin," I say gently.

"It was I who betrayed her into your hands, not the other way around."

"Can you be sure? Didn't she know who I was by then, what would happen to you?" He shakes his head. "Once you start killing, Kestrin, everyone becomes your enemy."

"What do you want from me?" he cries.

My eyes wander to the shattered rock on the cave floor. I am still lost in my memory of the Lady. "Perhaps I want you to kill me. That would be a victory of sorts, because it would be an end."

"You will get nothing from me," he whispers.

I feel a smile touch my lips. "That is a good sort of revenge in its own way, Kestrin. At least no one will die for it."

"May you rot in hell, sorceress." He leaves me, striding away, but as he turns out of the cave he begins to run, his boots thudding against the ground.

I sag back against the wall, trembling. The earth reaches up and pulls me to its breast, sending sparks of pain shooting though my vision.

"You are more talented than I would have credited," the Lady says, the garden flowing into existence around us.

I catch my balance, feet spread apart, and squint at her through the bright light, then look down at my hand. My shift is gray with dust, as is my arm, but for the charred ring where Kestrin held me. I look up quickly, fighting a wave of dizziness. "You turned me to stone."

"Had he killed you, your body would have remained stone. As it is, you have only lost a dusting of yourself."

"Then how—how has my wrist been burned?" I ask.

"The wounds of the spirit are borne out upon the body," she says, as if stating the obvious. She turns from me. "Come. I will allow you a rest before the second test."

I follow the Lady back up the path to the wrought iron gate. When she swings it open for me, though, we enter instead a large apartment. "You will find all you need here," she tells me, closing the door behind me. I just make it to the bed before my senses slide into darkness.

The light in the garden has the gentle luminescence of early morning. I follow the Lady wordlessly back into the square where Kestrin waits. In my room, I had found a small pot of cream on the table beside by the bed. It cooled the burning of my wrist for a time, but now the pain jars through me with every step. I try not to look at it, for the skin is black and charred, my flesh showing red and raw beneath the burns. I lower myself to the ground before Kestrin so that I will be sitting when I return. If I return.

"Tell me," the Lady says. "How did you speak of murder when you know nothing of it?"

"I know something. I know that the men who killed Violet had no concern for her, and feared no punishment. They would have done it again." I trace the Lady's delicate features with my eyes, following the fine cheekbones, the line of her jaw, the beautiful, empty, pain-ridden eyes. "I tried to become you, Lady—or what I thought it must be like to be you—because Kestrin had to believe I was you."

The Lady gestures towards me, the gemstone on her finger flashing. "The second test, then."

The light shimmers and spins around me, taking the garden and setting me down in a strange, rocky valley cut into high cliff walls. As far as I can see, the valley continues in both directions, the cliffs riddled with caves carved out by wind and rock falls. Here, in the belly of the valley, rock formations rise up from the ground, uneven and rippled, as if formed by the currents of an ancient river.

I rise and begin walking, knowing that I will meet Kestrin. A shadow flickers at the edge of my vision. I pivot, but see only a pillar-like rock that rises from the ground, bulging at the top. I hesitate, watching the pillar. Kestrin will not hide from me, nor will he attack me on sight again. The Lady will have set a different kind of test this time; she will not allow me to walk up to him and tap him on shoulder. But what is the test? Nothing moves in the valley. Perhaps it was just my imagination. I start forward again. Kestrin himself said that nothing lives in this land.

I hear a faint sound behind me and whirl around. A creature streaks towards me, its mouth open to reveal wickedly sharp teeth, its head large and flat, legs hardly more than a blur. For one surreal moment I watch it coming and then I flee, sprinting through the maze of rocks. Its roar echoes through the valley, bouncing off the cliffs as it chases me. Desperately, I scan the valley, the cliffs—surely there must be a way out? My side cramps with pain as I weave between rocks. I can hear the beast behind me, closing the distance. I cannot outrun it. How can I possibly out think it? I must hide! I follow the turn of a larger rock formation, doubling back, then race towards a great, slab of boulder rising at an angle from the earth. I scrabble to the top, throwing myself down against its top, hoping against hope.

The beast passes below me, hurtling around the boulder to follow my path. Does it hunt by sight or smell? Can it tell it has lost my trail? I push myself to my knees, my breath sobbing in my lungs, scanning the land below for the beast. I do not see it. I sit back, raising my gaze, and see Kestrin instead.

He stands at the mouth of a cave, and as I look at him he meets my gaze. Of course. He must have witnessed the whole chase, seen the creature come after me. Watched.

"Kestrin," I whisper, staring at him.

Something scrapes against stone. I know with a knowing that turns me cold but I turn anyway to see the beast hurling itself up the boulder, its claws cutting into the stone. And then it is upon me. I throw my hands out, pushing at it and ducking to the side. Its teeth snap shut by my ear, and I smell its breath, the stench of rot and death. My fingers close on its shaggy coat and I push, trying to overbalance it, send it off the end of the boulder, but its claws dig into the soft stone and it twists, lunging for me again. My hands find its neck, and I am able to keep its teeth from me, but now it is above me and it claws my arm, snarling.

Desperately, I twist away and fall, bouncing off the boulder to land on the ground. Above me, the beast roars again. I push myself forward, my hands searching for something—anything. My fingers close around a rock and I turn as the beast leaps down. It snarls again, facing me, and I know this time I cannot escape. I hold the rock tightly, as if it might protect me, but it is round and dull, composed of a soft, crumbling stone. The creature leaps forward, an impossibly long jump, so that even as I stumble back its paws slam into my chest, claws piercing my flesh. I fall backwards, flailing at the creature with my rock, my hand.

Something hisses. The beast is ripped off of me, thrown back against the boulder. It roars, struggling up, eyes still intent on me. Again, I hear a faint hiss and watch as the beast is lifted up and tossed back, its legs pinwheeling through the air. This time when it rises, it flees.

I let out my breath in a soft, whimpering sigh, and lie still, hoping that the world will fade around me, that the Lady will take me back. I think perhaps she does, for the light now is too bright, and I am cold.

"Get up," a voice says from behind me. I squeeze my eyes shut but I know he will not leave. "Get up, sorceress."

I push myself up with my good hand, only it is no longer quite good. There is blood on it, and when I look down at my chest I see splotches of red through the cloth, the stain spreading as I watch. But Kestrin is behind me, waiting, and so I stagger to my feet, turning to face him.

His eyes widen slightly, his jaw snapping shut on the words he meant to speak. After a breath, he turns and starts back towards his cave.

"Kestrin," I say, knowing now that I cannot let him go. There is too much blood. "Don't leave me." He stops. I take a step towards him, then another. Pain lances through my arm, my chest.

"I should have let it kill you," he says. He turns as I reach him, his eyes hard and flat in his face.

"Why didn't you?"

"Why didn't you scream?" he counters. "You knew I was there."

"I needed my breath," I say. It is hard for me to keep my chin up, but when I let it sag I see the red on my dress.

"Now you have it." He begins to walk again, his pace too fast for me to match.

"Kestrin." A dry breeze whispers through the canyon. I feel myself swaying with it.

He swings around to glare at me. "You brought this on yourself, sorceress. You made this wasteland. Do not ask me for pity now."

"No, Kestrin," I say. "I did not make this place. It is of your own making."

"I would never dream such a place."

"It is your heart." My legs feel like stone. When I try to step towards him I find they are too heavy to lift. I fall, but the fall is long and sweet, and I hardly feel the ground come up to meet me.

I wake to darkness, a steady burning in my arm and a pain that slumbers in my chest. I breathe lightly, staring at the stone roof overhead. I cannot quite seem to remember things rightly. Who am I just now? Thorn or Alyrra? I turn my head to the side, my thoughts muddled, to see Kestrin. He sits watching me, his back against the opposite cave wall. I cannot read his expression.

"You really don't have your magic here, do you?" he says into the quiet. "I thought perhaps you were playing a game—forcing me to do things, making me hate you, hate myself, all the more for not being able to kill you. But these past hours you have lain here defenseless as a child. You would have bled to death out there, if that beast did not return to finish you first."

"Yes," I agree, remembering. I move my hand to touch my chest, and realize he has bound my arm with strips of cloth, that more cloth bandages my chest.

"That is all you can say? 'Yes'? You have no explanation?"

I sigh, my eyes resting on his dark form. "Why did you bring me here and close my wounds? Why not let me die outside?"

"I had no choice," he snarls.

"Neither did I."

He leaps to his feet, glaring down at me. "You speak in riddles. Do not toy with me."

"Riddles are all I have left, prince. I can give you nothing more."

"Give me my freedom," he says tightly, and I wonder how much those words cost him, his pride.

"You know I cannot."

He walks to the mouth of the cave, looking out. "What did you do to Alyrra?" I stare at his back. He turns to glare at me. "What did you do to her?"

"Nothing. I left her there."

"Then the impostor you put in her place is still there."

"Alyrra has her position once more. Your father learned the truth of her identity. The impostor will be executed."

"So she at least is free."

"Free?" I echo. I would have laughed but for the pain that sears my chest with each breath. Kestrin's hand goes to the curved dagger at his belt. "There are different types of freedom. She will blame herself for your loss. She was afraid to help you, to take back her position, until it was too late. She will always carry that with her."

"It is not a heavy burden," he says. "She hardly knew me. She will forget in time."

"Perhaps."

"You say this land is of my making."

"It is your heart."

"Then to escape, I must break out of myself." I watch him mutely. He crosses the ground to kneel beside me. "Tell me how to escape."

I close my eyes, not wanting to see him. His hands grasp my shoulders and I wait, dread coiling in my stomach, for him to shake me or press on my wounds.

"Tell me," he repeats.

I look up at him. "I cannot tell you what I do not know."

"You know. You have come and gone easily enough." His hands tighten on my shoulders and I gasp, pain lancing through my chest in response. He lets go, sitting back. I push myself up, pressing my palms into the ground, until I am sitting with my back against the cave wall.

"I can't explain."

"Try," he says tersely, his hand tightening on the hilt of his dagger.

"No."

"Enough." He slides his dagger free of its sheath, moving so fast I have only enough time to jerk back before the cold blade lies flat against my skin. "You killed my mother, you've slain my family for generations, and now you

217

are killing me. Do you think I can't see for myself what will happen to me in this wasteland?"

"That is your choice," I whisper.

"I have no choice!"

"There is always a choice."

The blade slides against my skin, and I feel a faint tingle where the skin parts beneath its pressure. "I will kill you for what you've done."

"All I've done is offer you a choice, Kestrin."

His hand closes on the front of my dress, scraping against the wounds there, and he hauls me to my feet, pinning my back to the wall. "Here's a choice for you then, sorceress. Admit you are a murderess."

"Is this your justice?" I catch hold of his wrist with my hands, but I cannot break his grip on the dagger. Instead, he draws his lips back from his teeth, and brings the butt of the dagger down, slamming the metal hilt into my chest. Somewhere behind me, a child cries out, keening softly, but it is not me—my teeth are clenched against the pain. My legs give out beneath me, darkness eating at the edges of my vision, but I cannot fall because he holds me up, holds me tight against the wall, with nowhere to run.

"Admit you are a murderess and I'll give you an easy death." The words float down around me like autumn leaves, or the first thistledown snowflakes of winter. I can no longer think past the pain in my chest, the keening of the child. I stare at the dark, stained cloth of Kestrin's tunic. Two men hang from a gibbet, turning in slow circles, ropes creaking. The woman tears her hands free of the daggers, pressing their ragged remains against the pain in her belly, the emptiness. Valka smirks as the soldiers catch hold of the serving girl, searching her for a brooch she never stole.

Kestrin's hand finds my braid and jerks my head back, forcing me to meet his gaze. "Say it."

"If you will say it with me." The words are thick and slow on my tongue, but they are not what Kestrin expects. His hand tightens on my braid, yanking my head back further, white pain streaking across my vision.

"Damn you." I feel him shift his grip on the dagger, feel it cutting into the skin of my neck. I know I cannot break his hold on it, and so I reach up to touch his cheek, the dark stubble there. He jerks his head away, my fingers leaving a dark trail across his skin. He steps back and pivots, throwing me to the ground. My head bounces against the stone floor, my vision blurring. I hear a dull thud, and then another. Kestrin kicks the wall again, then turns towards me, his rage shimmering in the air around him. But he will not kill me by magic; the death he will give me will be that of cold iron, a slow and brutal death. The dagger he holds is dark with blood, dripping as it did when it pinned my mother to the tree. My mother's blood ... three scarlet drops on a white napkin. *This alliance hinges on you.*

I raise my eyes from the dark blade to his face. *I am the Lady who has lost her soul.* I uncurl myself, letting the pain run through me as a tide does, flowing and ebbing. *I am the princess who has lost her self. I am the goose girl who has lost her way.* I press my hands against the ground, push myself to my feet. *I am the child who can scream no more.*

"Put away the dagger, Kestrin." He braces his feet, as if expecting me to attack. "Put it away." He holds the dagger in a death-grip. When I step towards him, he brings it up, warding me off. I reach out and cover his hand with mine, curling my fingers around the hilt with his. When he tries to pull away, I tighten my grip, matching his step back.

"Decide," I tell him. "Either kill me without attempting to torture a confession out of me, without this farce of justice, or put away your dagger."

"Justice is not a farce." He steps back again, twisting his hand out of mine.

"It is in your land, princeling. Ask the people. They go to thieves for protection and justice while your guards sit by and your courts condemn the innocent. Do not pretend to justice here, where you have neither evidence nor judge."

"I do not need more evidence. You killed my mother." I hold still, watching him. I wonder what it was that the Lady did to his mother, how she died. "You can't deny that she is dead," Kestrin says, as if my silence had questioned him. "I know what you are."

I laugh, a sweet trip of sound that leaves Kestrin stunned, staring. "You cannot guess what I am, Kestrin. You do not know the least of my story, just as you could not imagine me as a child with a mother, could not imagine me without my magic."

He raises the dagger, the tip wavering over my heart. "You twist meanings with your words. You killed my mother. That is all I need to know." He steps forward, the dagger touching my breast, and there he stops.

"Just as I have killed you," I agree quietly. I can feel him trembling through to the tip of the dagger, his breath ragged and unsteady. "If you want to kill me, Kestrin, if you want to watch me die by your blade, this is your chance. I am unarmed, I have no magical defense, and I am weak. But do not pretend to justice. What you do now will only and ever be murder."

The dagger falls to the ground with a dull clatter. I wait, swaying slightly, watching Kestrin. Is it over? He raises his hand to his face, passes it over his eyes.

"I wish that you were dead," he says, his voice hoarse and grating. "There is nothing here to allow for justice: this is a dead land."

"It is not quite dead."

He laughs harshly. "I had not considered the beast." His eyes are dark, but it is no longer anger that burns in his face; instead, despair loosens his skin, leaves his eyes red-rimmed and empty. He turns and makes his way to the mouth of the cave, one hand on the cave wall for support.

"Do not seek me out again, sorceress." His words fall like small stones into a pond, disappearing even as they are heard. As he passes from my sight, the cave closes in on me twisting around to spit me out into the gardens.

Night has fallen, the moon filling the garden square with silvery light. The Lady stands before me. "Come," she says. I push myself to my feet, staggering upright because I must, the garden whirling around me again, though this is no magic. Dust falls in sheets from my shift, from my shoulders and hair. I follow her to the room, keeping my eyes on the white of her dress so that I will not falter. My shift clings to me, growing wet and heavy as I walk.

I pitch forward onto the bed, unable to lower myself, and have to bite my lip to keep from crying aloud. And then the Lady's hand helps me onto my back. I close my eyes, waiting for her to leave, but she does not. Instead, I feel her push up my sleeve and wipe my arm with a damp cloth. Then she opens my shift, cleaning the wounds on my chest. Her touch is firm, neither gentle nor hurtful. I suck in my breath, staring at the ceiling as she presses the cuts, wipes the blood from the shallow cut on my neck.

When she moves away, I turn my head to inspect my wounds. A long gouge runs down my right arm, still seeping blood. Had Kestrin not bound it, I likely would have bled to death. The cuts on my chest are less deep, showing the print of the thing's claws: two sets of punctures, each an array of four holes, ripped slightly open as the beast landed on me; they cannot be stitched shut, dug as they are into my flesh.

The Lady returns, sitting beside me, a needle and thread in her hand. She holds my arm down and silently begins to stitch the edges of the cut together. I do not mean to complain, but I cannot help the whimpers that lodge in my throat. She winds a bandage around my arm, then bandages my chest.

"Why are you doing this?"

Her hands come to rest on the bed sheet. When she speaks her voice is thoughtful. "You interest me."

"Interest you?"

The Lady smiles faintly. "Yes." She stands up, brushing out her skirts in a gesture so common to all women that I am left stunned. But I should not be, I think. She is not just a sorceress following a bloody oath.

"Wait," I call after her. "I don't understand."

She pauses at the foot of my bed, looking down at me, "When you speak to Kestrin, I hear both your voice and mine."

She looks to me like and yet unlike my first vision of her, and I find myself speaking dreamily, "When I looked into your eyes for the first time, I thought I saw my death there. Perhaps I did. Now I only see your pain."

Something flickers in her face, but I cannot say whether it is an emotion winging past or only a weakness of my sight. She turns and leaves, taking the light with her.

The Lady returns with the morning, escorting me once more to the square. Despite the rest, I am exhausted. My wounds and burnt wrist ache when I am still and flare with pain at every move.

I sit down facing the stone prince and look up at the Lady. "When you send me this time, will my cuts remain bandaged?"

"Yes." The Lady glances towards the statue. "If you wish to return to Tarinon, you may. I will not force you to this last test; the first two have weakened you."

"Would you release the Prince?"

"No."

"Then why do you ask?"

The Lady purses her lips, watching me. A breeze wanders through the garden, touching a wisp of hair that has escaped her braid. I think she must have been beautiful when she was young: the kind of beauty that warms hearts and brings smiles to faces. "I do not like to send you to your death," she admits.

"Hasn't he proved himself yet?" I ask. "He saw his greatest enemy unarmed and let her go. He saw her attacked and defended her. Her saw her wounded and helped her. What more could you want?"

She looks away from me to Kestrin, kneeling before us. "I want him dead," she confesses.

"Then you are what you accuse him of. Let him go, Lady."

"Why do you fight for him?"

I pause, remembering that even when Kestrin had played his games with me, he had stopped short of ever hurting me. In the pity I had glimpsed in his eyes, before he found me out, there had also been regret. "I did not believe he would fail your tests."

"He has been very close often enough."

"He has."

"You did not doubt him last night?" she asks with a slight smile.

"I knew if I could make him pause long enough to think, he would not harm me. I do not doubt the power of his anger and hatred, but I believe there is that in him which is better and stronger.

"I do not know what your third test will be, Lady." I close my eyes. "I have tried to imagine it, and I think the only way he would fail is if he reached that pitch of helplessness and rage I saw in him last night, and then was called upon to save me rather than let me go. I think perhaps he would let me die, tricking himself for those few moments into believing he did no wrong. But I do not doubt he would regret it, even if he never learns who I am. That is the only test left which he might fail."

I look back at the Lady. "Which of us has not made mistakes when faced with more than we can handle?"

"Go back, child," the Lady says gently.

"I am not a child to be sent home, Lady. I will not go without the prince." Her hands flick over her skirts, then come to a rest clasped together in front of her. "Lady?"

"He is yours," she says, her voice heavy with weariness. "I will return him to the plains."

"What of the third test?" I whisper.

"You are right," she says simply. "So I will test him with his life. Let us see what he has learned these last few days. I put him in your keeping, princess."

"And then?" She raises an eyebrow in an eloquent, arched question. "What of the rest of the Family?"

"You will not give them up, will you?" She smiles wryly.

"They are as innocent as Kestrin."

"You know what your king has planned for Valka."

"I know." I look down to the gravel walk. "They say it is justice: she has been found a traitor and passed her own sentence." I swallow hard. "It is the law that a traitor must die, Lady. And it was you who made her into that traitor; made her so convincing that the king would not have suspected her. No doubt, one by one, she would have given them over to you as she could. For that, she cannot hope for forgiveness ... it is justice, but a cruel and ugly justice. I wish that it were tempered by mercy, that she might have an easy death." I think of the Lady herself, her mother's death. Perhaps, had the woman been cleanly executed, far from the eyes of her child, the Lady would not have become who she is.

"Do you argue for the lives of men who cloak cruelty in the guise of justice?"

"Lady, you condemn them without fair trial. You saw the taint in Kestrin, but when he was put to the test, he passed."

"What trial shall I set them, princess? Will you put yourself into my hands to pose them their tests?" She raises her hand quickly, "Do not offer. I am sending you home because in this case you are right, and I do not want you dead because I wish Kestrin dead."

"Lady, you will not give them up because you are afraid to."

"Afraid?" Her lips curl in amusement.

"What would you do if you had no more princes and kings to hunt down? You've been fighting for this one thing so long; what will you do when you achieve it? There's no one here with you, is there? You're alone, and without your oath you have no purpose. You're afraid of that."

"Enough."

"No, Lady. Do you think I can't see how tired you are? You are weary with the things you have done and seen. Can't you let go?"

"It has been too long," she says quietly. "I have been living this oath since I saw my mother die. I hardly remember anything else. What is there for me but this?" She gestures towards the garden, the myriad hidden squares with their stone people.

"Go back to your people, Lady."

"No, Alyrra. The time is too far past for settling down on some quiet mountaintop."

"Then what will you do?"

"I will send you back, and with you your prince."

I rise to meet her as she walks towards me. "And what of his family? And you?"

"Let us both keep watch on them."

"Lady?" She holds out her hand, and I clasp it in mine, ignoring the pain of my wounds. "What if I should need to speak with you again?"

"Call me by my name and I will come." The gardens melt away, the hedges rising up into walls, the Lady illuminated by a fall of morning light through shattered shutters.

"Your name," I echo.

"Sarait."

I let her hand go and she fades into the sunlight.

***

The king's mage-healer tends to me silently, his face still and stern, accented only by a small line running deep between his eyebrows. He asks no questions I cannot answer, and gives me only a cream for my burns and a strict admonition to watch my cuts for purulence. He promises to return in the afternoon, leaving me under the watchful eyes of a handful of women.

After the Lady returned me to my room, I had made my way out into the hallway, accosting a passing servant with a message for the king. The servant had run for all that he could not have understood it: *Look for the Wind on the plains.* It was only when I returned my room and caught my image reflected in a mirror that I realized his true reason: my shift was dark with dried blood, the front and sleeve stiff and black with the stuff. And so, the mage-healer.

I close my eyes when he is gone, lying back in the bed. I do not know who the women are, their names, their stations, why they are here with me. In a few moments, when I regain some small part of my strength, and before I succumb to the call of sleep, I will open my eyes and ask them. But first I will lie here, listening to the faint rustle of skirts as one of the women crosses the room. I will breathe slowly and lightly, so as not to wake the pain that slumbers in my chest, and I will remember all that I have lived, so as not to lose it in these first hours of wakefulness.

<hr />

The mage-healer is true to his word, returning regularly to see to my injuries. They heal well enough, the stitches closing up without his help, the burnt skin slowly peeling away, new skin growing in pink and shiny.

"You do not have to see anyone until you are ready," he assures me, and I let myself savor the solitude his offer affords me, sending away my attendants to stay in the adjoining room, coming only when I call.

But I cannot hide forever like a she-wolf licking her wounds deep within her den. So, after a handful of days, after listening to the murmured news passed among the women of the strange return of the prince, met walking back to the city by the king's quad, I leave my bed. I call in one of the attendants to help me dress. It is not until I am ready to leave my room that I realize that these are the clothes from Valka's trunks, left for so many months in my room in the stable.

My other attendants flutter around me, helping me to a low couch, spreading a light blanket over my lap. "I'm not dying," I say, flapping my hands at them. "I'm getting better. Sit down and talk to me."

They glance at each other surreptitiously. Of course. Attendants are meant to attend, not accompany. I try again, "I need to know what has happened while I have been ill—surely you can tell me the news?"

With widening smiles, they settle around me like a flock of jewel-hued songbirds and tell me the gossip of the palace. I listen until I can no longer think straight, then have them help me back to my room.

"Perhaps a change of rooms would do you good, Your Highness," one of the attendants, Mina, suggests as I sink back against the pillow. I look at her in consternation. I had thought she had more sense than that.

"Why would that help me?"

"You are always watching the window here, Your Highness. I thought perhaps you would find greater comfort elsewhere." Good sense and a keen mind; I wonder who holds her greatest loyalty.

"It can't hurt," I concede.

I am wrong. With Mina's help, I move into my new apartments; they are Valka's old ones. As with my last visit, I explore the rooms. The writing desk still holds the letters from my mother and Daerilin, though the portrait sketches and Kestrin's notes are missing. All of Valka's personal belongings have been removed, the chest of boards bare. I wonder what became of the clothes I had brought with me, the wedding dress and trousseau. In the wardrobe, folded on a shelf, I find a dark traveling cloak lined with fur; I lay my hand on it and know that I will wear it again come winter, showing my appreciation for this first gift from the king. For now I am grateful to leave it here, close the doors upon it and forget.

I sit on the bed wishing for the little room in the stable I shared with Laurel: the two small sleeping mats, side by side, and the wooden pegs on the wall to hold all we need. The sheer volume of my new belongings oppresses me: the huge, empty bed, the veritable forest of chairs and tables cluttering each room. I will change it, I think. In a few moments I will join my attendants in the sitting room and decide with them what will stay and what will go, how to arrange the furniture so that I can think again in straight lines and clean curves.

I glance around from my perch on the bed and notice a small inlaid wooden box on the bedside table. I open it, then dump the contents into my palm: a thin silver chain looped through an oval pendant. I turn the pendant over, knowing already what I will see: a delicately carved rose. I close my fingers over the pendant and chain, holding them tightly. Kestrin had watched me very closely indeed. I wonder if Joa had sent the pendant directly to him, or if he had to send someone to buy it back from the knacker afterwards.

"Your Highness?" Mina stands in the doorway.

"Yes?" I ask, watching her. Though she stands straight, she somehow still manages to fade into her surroundings. Perhaps it is the way her face tilts down, how even when she reaches to pick something up, her manner is confident yet unassuming. I am not sure if it is humility or a great cleverness.

"Will you dine in company tonight?" she asks, as one of my attendants has asked every night since I first left my room.

I glance down at my closed fist. "Yes."

34

The lords and ladies outdo themselves in their distress at Valka's betrayal, and their ambiguous comments on my disappearances and injuries, speaking in shocked tones and shaking their heads. Only Lord Garrin approaches close.

"You seemed quite well the night the impostor was exposed," he remarks. We stand in a tiled foyer, awaiting the last of the guests before proceeding to dinner.

"It was a long night," I temporize.

"And yet there were no flying daggers or hidden knives that I heard tell of." Garrin raises an eyebrow, his eyes lingering on my bandaged wrist.

"I am glad you are so sheltered," I reply blandly. "I hope you never meet with such yourself."

"We are pleased that the Princess Alyrra has recovered so quickly," the king says from behind me. I turn towards him, encountering the same hawk-like features and hooded eyes, but I also detect a slight twinkle, the faintest movement of his cheeks in the ghostly memory of a smile.

"I thank you, Your Majesty."

"How could we fail to be pleased?" Garrin asks, and with a courteous nod moves on to more fertile hunting grounds.

"Ah, there is Kestrin," the king murmurs.

The prince scans the room as he enters. I know from the way he finds me at once, the way his eyes fasten on the bandage at my wrist, that the Lady explained the whole of his ordeal to him.

He crosses the room to us with barely a nod to the other guests. The last week's rest has helped him, easing the tension and exhaustion from his features, but his face is eerily gaunt, as if his youth has been bled away, leaving a faint gray tinge to his skin. I wonder how much the Lady's spell took out of him, the effect of his inner exile on his body so long turned to stone. "My lord father," he says. "My lady."

"My lord," I say, aware of the eyes on us. I smile and curtsy prettily to his bow.

"Let us go in," the king says, gesturing for the servants to open the doors to the dining room. Kestrin offers his arm, and I find myself taking it. What a strange game we play, I think. One would think we had barely met at all, and then only at court.

At dinner I sit below the king, Kestrin across from me and Melkior at my side. When I look up, I see a wide band of wood carving where the walls meet the ceiling; Kestrin catches my speculative look and smiles guiltily, making me wonder if someone else might be observing our dinner tonight. The king asks me only a few questions, but they are questions of some substance and I take my time answering them: what have I learned of his city while living outside the palace? Was I treated well? Would I be averse to keeping the wedding for when it is set in a month's time?

The rest of the evening I maintain a friendly discussion with Melkior, asking after his daughters and revisiting the topics first mentioned at his dinner. I am careful not to mention Red Hawk or Violet. It is too soon, yet, to venture there. When we rise to leave, Kestrin offers me his arm, circling the table to escort me out after his father.

He leads me to a marble square with a fountain playing at its center. I drop my hand from his arm as we approach it, taking a seat on a stone bench. Kestrin sits next to me, watching me covertly. I do not speak, engrossed in the play of moonlight on water.

"Lady," he says softly. "Are you well?"

It is a strange question, for it has none of the court in it, though it should. "We are both here, are we not?" I ask.

"It has been a week."

"Yes." A week in which my arm healed enough to no longer require a sling, and my chest wounds closed enough so that each breath brings only a whisper of pain. I wonder how long it took for Kestrin to recover; perhaps his wounds were deeper, being cut into his soul and not his body. In the moonlight his face still has the look of stone upon it, only his hair, smooth and shining, softens his aspect. "Are you truly the Wind?"

"Yes." He runs his hands through his hair. "I used to plan how I would tell you, what I would do. Stupid." The word is laden with contempt.

"Childish," I amend tactlessly, but he only laughs. "Why did you wish to marry me?"

"Can you ask?"

I do not answer.

Kestrin bites his lip, then speaks. "When I first found you, I was a novice testing my abilities and you were a child hiding in the forest from your brother. I could not help returning to check on you, and with my father's tutelage I learned to send words on the Wind to you. I waited for your stories; I wished to get you away from your brother; and more than any of that, I wished I might see you with my own eyes." He clasps his hands together. "When it came time for me to seek a wife, I knew it would be you."

"I did not know what you were." It is a small betrayal; there are so many other greater things between us, yet this seems the deepest.

"I know. I am sorry."

I trace the embroidered design along the hem of my tunic, my finger running over the perfect stitches. "You have heard Valka's sentence?"

"I have."

I wait, but he says no more. "Is that how all traitors die?"

"Traditionally, a traitor is hung until dead. Then his body is left for the crows to pick and the rain to rot for a month before being thrown into a ditch and forgotten."

"Then why must she be tortured to death?"

Kestrin rubs his chin. "I believe that Red Hawk saw your friend's attackers executed, did he not?"

"Yes," I admit, wondering where his questions will take us.

"Was that your doing?"

I consider him carefully, weigh the risks. "It was."

"I thought as much. They were flogged before they were hung. Why did you agree to their 'torture' before their deaths?"

I try to swallow but my mouth has gone dry. "I didn't," I begin and then stop. Kestrin watches me keenly. I hear Red Hawk's voice discussing the flogging: *that their punishment not go too easily with them.* I had not paused to consider this addition to the punishment. They had caused physical harm, and I wished it all back upon them. There had been nothing of mercy in the justice I had sought. "I did not think," I whisper.

"They were made an example of to deter others from their path. This is much the same; the greater the offense, the greater the punishment."

"No," I say. "Even what the thieves did—it was their justice. Every man in this city knows the punishment the thieves exact for such a crime; it is the same for all. What you would do to Valka goes beyond the punishment for treason. It will only haunt the rest of us."

"Valka's deeds will die with her."

"Her memory will remain. Those who liked her will remember not just that she died, but that she was made to suffer. That will create hatred in their hearts where there was none before."

Kestrin sighs. "My father—"

"Is the law," I say, cutting him off. "But is his decision just?"

"I will speak to him on your behalf," Kestrin says. "Perhaps I will succeed where you have not yet." I look at him curiously. "My father said you spoke for Valka at once."

"I don't know what justice really is," I tell him. "But I am trying to get what I can right. The death she chose lies beyond all law. Her thoughts were cruel and the power that carries out such a sentence would be equally cruel."

"I will speak to him," Kestrin assures me.

I pick at the bandage around my wrist, fraying the cloth with my fingers, but he does not speak again. "It's late," I finally say.

"Your wrist—what happened—it's the same," he stumbles, his voice anguished.

"Yes."

His hands curl into fists and he crosses his arms quickly, as if to hide his fists, though his anger is directed towards himself now. He holds himself in tightly; I know the look, know the way he trains his breath, and I am sorry for him. This will remain between us the rest of our lives: a legacy of hidden identities and shadow truths and violence left to us by the Lady. I do not know what to say to comfort him, and I am not sure that I should speak comfortingly when I can still feel the burn of his magic, the iron-backed bite of his anger. Yet he had not known, had been forced into the most difficult of situations. I had failed to prevent a flogging when nothing threatened me and I stood safe in the company of a friend—a flogging that, by the King's Law, should never have happened. How much more terribly might I have failed in Kestrin's situation?

"I will not judge you." I feel him turn towards me, his eyes resting on my face. "I *cannot* judge you."

"Do you think that will make it easier for me?" His voice is hard; I have to keep myself from flinching away.

"I don't know," I say. "I don't know what will ease your way or make things harder."

He buries his face in his hands, his hair falling forward to hide his features. Then his hands slide through his hair to curl around the back of his neck. I wonder if his eyes rest on the marble tiles underfoot, or if they are turned elsewhere, deep inside himself.

"Can you be happy here?"

I feel the strangest tingling sensation in my chest; I think that I might cry. "Does it matter?"

He straightens, dropping his hands, but still he does not look at me. "You can return home if you wish. You have been through enough to warrant breaking the betrothal without endangering our kingdoms' friendship."

"I told you once before, there is nothing for me there."

"You did."

"I have come to love your land and your people very much, my lord. I would not leave by choice."

Finally, he turns to me, and there is a flicker of hope in his eye. "There is—would you walk with me, lady? I would like to show you something."

I take his arm, following him back into the maze of hallways. "It is a little ways from here," Kestrin explains, and then falls silent. We reach a part of the palace I have never seen before, moving through quiet corridors until we come to another set of wide doors leading into a square. But this square is unlike anything I have seen in Menaiya: there are no marble tiles, no mosaics, no elegant fountains. Here grows a wood.

I stand frozen on the threshold, gazing at the trees—pine and birch and a few slender aspens. They are silvered in the moonlight, their leaves rustling in a faint breeze, filling the air with the scent of the forest: leaves, and beneath that damp earth and moss. I move forward in a dream, reaching out to touch the rough bark of a pine tree. A gravel path wanders off through the grove, curving, for there are no straight lines in a forest. I want nothing more than to walk it, to lose sight of the palace even as I stand in the belly of it, surrounded once more by trees.

"Do you like it?" Kestrin asks from behind me.

I had forgotten him, dropped his arm and walked forward without a thought. Now, with an embarrassed smile, I turn back to him. "It's lovely. Who planted it?"

"I did—or rather," he says with uncharacteristic humility, "the gardeners did. But I planned it. For you."

My hand rests against the tree. "This garden has been here some time. These trees aren't newly planted."

"I was very sure of myself," he says with a mocking smile. "At least it served one purpose: when I brought the impostor here, she glanced at it once, thought it quaint, and wished to go on to a lunch party."

"You knew."

"I knew she wasn't you. But I didn't know who she was, or who you were." He crosses to me. "I knew that, as happy as you might be here, you would still like a memory of home."

How close we are, I think, gazing at him. And yet how far. He will not cross this final distance, will not or can not. So I will have to. I reach out, brushing his arm with my fingertips. "I am home, Kestrin."

His hand reaches up to touch mine, and we clasp hands, awkwardly, uncertainly.

"It's strange." I smile sadly. "I trusted you completely, you know. When I followed after the sorceress. I knew you wouldn't kill me. You might rage, you might act like a bully—"

He swallows a laugh.

"But I knew you wouldn't kill me."

"I wouldn't have been so sure."

"You protected me and helped me."

His mouth twists.

"Remember that, Kestrin. I do."

"Do you remember also that you have seen the wasteland that is my heart? Could you marry such a man?"

I hesitate, trying to find the right words, but I must take too long for he adds, "Could you ever come to love me?"

I respect him, I trust him, and I have come to think of him as more than just an ally, a friend. Perhaps love will flow from that. "I don't know," I admit. "But I know that there is more to your heart than those places the Lady allowed you to wander. Look around," I gesture to the trees around us, the myriad sleeping creatures hidden in the grove, "this too is a part of your heart. How could it not be?"

"Do you believe that?"

I take a step forward, so that I am barely a handspan away from him, and rest my other hand on his chest, feeling the rise and fall of each breath. "I have no doubt of it," I say, because I cannot yet tell him I love him, because we need more time without games and deceit between us to find such love.

He looks at me wonderingly, and then, hesitantly, brings his other arm around me, drawing me to him. We stand there a long time together, his cheek resting on the top of my head, my own against his chest. I close my eyes and listen to the steady beating of his heart and the gentle rustle of leaves overhead.

35

Laurel waits for me in the palace courtyard, her hand on a horse's bridle. The mare is a gentle creature, Solace, who could be trusted to children and idiots. I almost laugh. Laurel's eyes widen as she sees me, her legs bending in an awkward curtsy. I ignore it, wrapping my good arm around her.

"Your Highness," she stammers.

"Laurel," I whisper. "I'm still Thorn." She embraces me then, and though her hold is gentle, she makes no move to release me until I step back myself. The courtyard is filled with nobles and hostlers leading their charges, not a few of whom watch our exchange.

"How are the others?"

"Ash and Rowan are here, but I'm not sure they'll be able to get close." Laurel turns the mare and holds the stirrup for me. "Oak may decide to stay on at the farm."

I pat Solace's shoulder, my sleeve falling back to expose the bandage wrapped around my wrist. Laurel glances at me. "They say you were hurt after you came up here, when you disappeared those days."

"Just a few scratches," I say through gritted teeth, and heave myself up. My arm shrieks its dissension at that, but, thankfully, Laurel makes herself busy checking my stirrups and smoothing my skirts, and does not notice the set of my face until I have managed to rearrange it.

"Are Ash and Rowan well?"

"Well enough," she says. "You've heard Corbé's gone? He lit out of here like a dog with its tail on fire as soon as the news reached the stables." Laurel smiles humorlessly. "Mind you, that was after Ash and Rowan beat the living daylights out of him and Joa fired him."

"I hadn't heard."

"It would be foolish of him to stay after all he's done against you, wouldn't it? We were expecting you'd send someone after him."

I watch Solace's ears flick back to listen to us, the morning light catching in the soft, fuzzy fur of her inner ear. "I suppose I should."

"Aye," Laurel says. "A man as attacks a woman shouldn't be allowed off like that."

"There's many more in the city that have done much worse than him."

"Start somewhere and keep going," Laurel suggests practically. I nod, wishing it were as easy as that. And perhaps it is. She reaches up and pats my hand hesitantly, as if unsure that she has the right to anymore.

Kestrin walks his mount up next to us, dipping his chin to Laurel.

"Your Highness," she murmurs, and with a curtsy hurries away.

"She's your friend from the stables," Kestrin observes.

"Laurel," I agree.

"You miss them."

"Of course."

"You could ask them to join you here," he suggests, his voice pitched so that only I may hear. "Good friends are hard to come by."

"Perhaps," I say, wondering if Laurel would come. I remember how tired she has been, how little her heart has been in her work since Violet's death. Perhaps she would welcome the change. I feel myself beginning to smile, but I don't want to lose the thread of this conversation quite so fast. "I was wondering, my lord, how my attendants were selected."

"They are the younger daughters of some of our lesser noble households."

"I know that," I say, amused. "I meant them in particular. As you said, good friends are hard to come by. I would like an attendant who does not have prior allegiances that are stronger than what she holds for me."

Kestrin meets my gaze. "That will take some doing."

"Of course."

He grins and dips his head. He is pleased that I have asked this of him, because it means I trust him to do it well. And I do, for though it is a different thing to trust him not to kill me, I find that I have great faith in him to keep my trust now.

We ride down in procession: an honor guard, the king, then myself and Kestrin, follow by Lord Garrin and the king's closest vassals, all of us flanked by more guards. I feel faintly foolish riding with so many eyes on me, with so many men surrounding me as if I were afraid of the people. I have never seen Kestrin ride through the city without a guard; I wonder now if I will ever again roam these streets with only a horse for company. It seems unlikely.

Valka has preceded us to Hanging Square. She stands at the front of the platform, flanked by guards, and it is all the guards in the Square can do to keep control of the people. As I watch, a piece of rotten fruit flies through the air, splattering against the wood at Valka's feet. She does not flinch, does not even look, her chin high and her eyes trained on an unseen spot in the middle distance. She wears the clothes I sent her, a simple skirt and tunic set that Mina found for her. Her hands are bound before her, and her hair wisps free of its braid.

We come to a halt beside the platform. The king holds up his hand to the people. The crowd quiets in expectation, until all that can be heard is the faint shouting of a group of children.

"Lady Valka, you stand accused of high treason and attempted murder of a royal person. You have been found guilty. Have you any last words?"

Valka maintains a stony silence, her eyes finding mine. I tried, I want to tell her. Why couldn't you have helped me more? In her eyes, I see my own guilt, see the same betrayed, hateful look as that day, years ago, when I trumpeted her theft of the brooch to everyone. If only I had sought justice more kindly.

The king nods his head, and Valka is led to the gibbet, guided up onto the bench waiting below it. The executioner fits the rope around her neck, pulling her braid through it, and then steps back. She does not take her eyes from me and so I do not see the king gesture, or the executioner step forward to kick away the bench. I see only the way her head snaps back, caught by the rope, the jolt as her body's fall is broken with the breaking of her neck.

A coldness slides in past my skin, burning off my flesh. I watch her body swaying before me through a whirl of colorless cloud, her feet jerking in spasms. Solace sidles sideways, swinging her head around to watch me, the whites of her eyes showing. *The princess. Look at the princess.* The crowd backs away. I feel the change shudder through me, twisting my bones and squeezing the breath from my lungs. At my throat, the choker I have worn so many months burns to ash, as if it had never been. As I watch Valka's bent head, her hair writhes, the brown running to golden red, her clothes blown by an unknown wind, whipping around until they are no longer the tunic and skirt I sent her but the stiff, embroidered set gifted to me by the king.

I turn my head as the wind calms, looking out over the crowd. They stare back, a sea of faces. At the very back, standing casually against a wall, I find Red Hawk. He meets my gaze and then he smiles, a kind, encouraging smile that has nothing of the death I have just caused in it. He bows slightly, his fingers touching his heart, and then he steps to the side and is lost in the crowd.

"My lady, are you well?" Kestrin touches my elbow, eyes flickering over me. I would have laughed had I the heart; in his quick glance I see a growing fear: was it truly Valka who died?

"We are both still here," I remind him. His shoulders slump in relief even as he watches me, but I give him no further reply.

The king waits on his horse, observing me as well. I raise my voice over the growing murmur of the crowd, knowing that I must give him a reason to allow Valka's burial. "Your Majesty, Lady Valka was the daughter of a high vassal of my mother's realm. Though she betrayed her oath of fealty, her father has remained true. For his sake, I ask that you grant her a quick burial."

My words do not meet with the crowd's approval.

"Leave the traitor to rot," one man cries, and then they are all shouting their suggestions, their anger.

"Your Majesty," I repeat, my voice now only for our small party. "She has paid the price of her treachery. Do not make her actions cost my queen mother more than they already have." It is the only argument he will understand, and so I use it. I cannot bear the thought of Valka's body abused and left unburied.

"Is that your wish?"

"It is."

The king nods, gesturing to Captain Sarkor behind us. I turn Solace away so that I will not have to watch as Valka is cut down and carted off. I wonder where she will be buried, and before me flashes a vision of the graveyard where Violet now lies. Valka's grave will be just another grave there, just another small heap of stones in a field where all are nameless.

The ride back to the palace passes in a dream of quiet. Everywhere I look I see people I have known these last months, these years of my life; they smile and turn towards us, and in their eyes I see the lives of unborn children, the certain strength of the young, the lingering illnesses of the elderly. In the palace courtyard I dismount awkwardly, patting Solace until Laurel reaches us.

"You must be glad to have your old face back," she observes.

"I rather like not having a burnt wrist anymore," I agree, grinning. In truth, my body feels strange to me once more, like a half-remembered haunt, a childhood home. It has filled out, grown taller, grown softer, while Valka cared for it.

Laurel laughs grimly, shaking her head as she leads Solace away. As I turn my hand, though, I can feel the same raw pain beneath my new skin that I felt beneath the charred remains of my old one; and as I had dismounted, I felt my arm muscles cry out beneath the new seal of my skin. It will heal faster, I think; but the damage has not been undone, only removed from sight. In that, I suppose there is much to be grateful for: without the scars between us, perhaps Kestrin and I might truly find a way to look at each other without guilt or pain.

"My lady," Kestrin says, approaching me. "Will you come in?"

I take his arm as I am expected to, turning with him towards the great Hall with its doors thrown open. A stray breeze flits through the courtyard, wrapping around me and then lifting the loose locks of my hair up as it rushes towards the Hall. I glance sharply at Kestrin. He raises his eyebrows, the corner of his mouth quirked upward, a glimmer of mischief in his eyes. I let my breath out in a quiet laugh, squeezing his arm beneath my hand, and together we walk up the steps to the Hall.

 ACKNOWLEDGEMENTS

This book wouldn't have reached readers without the encouragement of my family and friends. Special thanks to my husband, who has always supported my writing and first suggested I self-publish. Thanks also to my beta readers, who innocently suggested sweeping revisions: my mom, writing circle cronies Hannah Kutcher and Janelle White, early reader Rima Dabdoub, and my husband, who alone read multiple drafts of *Thorn*. Extra gratitude to Hannah, Chief Technology Officer of House #3 Publishing, for her tech support and humor as I navigated the publishing process. And of course, thanks to my readers, without whom this book would be very lonely.

⚜ ABOUT THE AUTHOR ⚜

Intisar Khanani grew up a nomad and world traveler. Born in Wisconsin, she has lived in five different states as well as in Jeddah on the coast of the Red Sea. She first remembers seeing snow on a wintry street in Zurich, Switzerland, and vaguely recollects having breakfast with the orangutans at the Singapore Zoo when she was five. She currently resides in Cincinnati, Ohio, with her husband and two young daughters.

Until recently, Intisar wrote grants and developed projects to address community health with the Cincinnati Health Department, which was as close as she could get to saving the world. Now she focuses her time on her two passions: raising her family and writing fantasy. Intisar's next two projects include a companion trilogy to Thorn, following the heroine introduced in her short story The Bone Knife, and The Sunbolt Chronicles, a novella serial following a young thief with a propensity to play hero, and her nemesis, a dark mage intent on taking over the Eleven Kingdoms.

Connect with me online:

My website & blog: http://www.booksbyintisar.com

GoodReads: http://www.goodreads.com/intisar_khanani

Facebook: http://www.facebook.com/booksbyintisar

Thorn is also available as an e-book.

CPSIA information can be obtained at www.ICGtesting.com
Printed in the USA
LVOW08s0250051016

506956LV00008B/723/P